Praise for Liza Marklund's previous Annika Bengtzon thrillers, *The Bomber* and *Studio 69*

'Take the independence and determination of Peter Hoeg's Miss Smilla, stir in the sharpness and honesty of Clarice Starling in *Silence of the Lambs* . . . and you begin to sense the qualities that make up Annika Bengtzon' *Daily Express*

'The story moves along at high speed and with gratifying directness' *Independent*

'An entertaining story, but it's the portrayal of the newspaper office, with its internal bickering and its determination to stay ahead of its rival which particularly impresses' *Sunday Telegraph*

'A taut and well-paced read' *Observer*

'The pace never slackens' *Sunday Express*

'The efforts of the independent, gutsy reporter to establish the truth make for an enjoyable and fast-paced thriller' *The Times*

'This superbly written thriller exhibits a depth of characterisation, intelligence and energy that raises it above the competition' *Good Book Guide*

Liza Marklund is a print and television journalist. She lives in Stockholm with her husband and three children. She is the author of the international bestsellers *The Bomber* and *Studio 69*.

PARADISE

LIZA MARKLUND
Translated by Ingrid Eng-Rundlow

POCKET
BOOKS

LONDON • SYDNEY • NEW YORK • TORONTO

First published in Great Britain by Simon & Schuster UK Ltd, 2004
This edition first published by Pocket Books, 2004
An imprint of Simon & Schuster UK Ltd
A Viacom Company

1 3 5 7 9 10 8 6 4 2

Simon & Schuster UK Ltd
Africa House
64–78 Kingsway
London WC2B 6AH

www.simonsays.co.uk

Simon & Schuster Australia
Sydney

A CIP catalogue record for this book is available from
the British Library

ISBN 0-7434-6907-0

Typeset by SX Composing DTP, Rayleigh, Essex
Printed and bound in Great Britain by
Bookmarque Ltd, Croydon, Surrey

PARADISE

Time's up, she thought. *This is what it's like to die.*
Her head hit the tarmac, her consciousness getting a jolt. The terror vanished with the wounds. There was stillness.

Her thoughts were calm and clear. Stomach and groin pressed against the ground, ice and gravel against her hair and cheek.

Life's weird. There's so little that you can predict. Who would have guessed this was where it would happen? On a foreign coast, in the far north.

Then she saw the boy before her again, reaching out to her; she felt the terror, heard the shots, and was overwhelmed by her shortcomings.

'Forgive me,' she whispered. *Forgive my cowardice, my miserable failings.*

Suddenly she felt the wind again. It was tugging at her big bag, hurting her. The sounds returned and her foot ached. She became aware of the cold and the damp that had penetrated her jeans. She had only fallen, not been hit. Her mind went blank again. There were no thoughts.

Got to get away.

She pushed up onto all fours but the wind beat her back down; she struggled up again. The surrounding buildings made the gusts unpredictable, pounding up from the sea and along the street like relentless cudgels.

I've got to get out of here. Now.

She knew the man was somewhere behind her. He was blocking the way back into town. She was trapped.

I can't stay here in the floodlights. I've got to get out. Away from here!

A new gust knocked the breath out of her. She gasped for air, turned her back. More floodlights, yellow, making gold of the shabby surroundings – where would she go?

She grabbed her bag and ran with the wind at her back towards a building by the water. A loading platform on one side, a lot of rubbish that had been blown about, some of it down onto the ground. What was that – a staircase? A chimney; pieces of furniture; a gynaecologist's table; an old Model T Ford; the instrument panel from a fighter plane.

She threw the bag onto the platform and then pulled herself up. She weaved her way past old bathtubs and school desks, finding a hiding place behind an old desk.

He'll find me here, she thought. It's only a matter of time. He'll never give up.

She was crouching low, swaying and panting, soaked through with sweat and from the slush. Realizing she'd walked into the trap. There was no way out of here. All he had to do was walk up to her, put the gun against the back of her head and pull the trigger.

She peered out from behind the desk. Saw nothing, only ice and warehouses bathing in the gold of the floodlights.

I've go to wait, she thought. *I've got to know where he is. Then I can try to sneak away.*

The backs of her knees started aching after a couple of minutes. Her thighs and lower legs went numb, her ankles throbbed, especially the left one. She must have sprained it when she fell. Blood was dripping from the cut on her forehead and down onto the platform.

Then she saw him. He was standing by the edge of the dock, only ten feet away, his sharp profile dark against yellow light. The wind carried his whisper to her.

'Aida.'

She shrank back and shut her eyes tightly, making herself small, like an animal. Invisible.

'Aida, I know you're there.'

She breathed with her mouth open, soundlessly. Waiting. The wind was on his side, muffling his steps. The next time she looked up, he was walking along the fence on the other side of the wide street, holding his gun discreetly inside his jacket. She was breathing faster now, in ragged gasps; it made her dizzy. When he disappeared round the corner and into the blue warehouse she got up, jumped down on the ground and ran. Her feet pounding – treacherous wind. Her bag bouncing on her back, her hair in her eyes.

She didn't hear the shot but sensed the bullet whistling past her head. She began zigzagging in a sharp illogical pattern. Another whistle, another turn.

Suddenly she ran out of ground where the roaring Baltic Sea took over. Waves as big as sails, as sharp as glass. She only hesitated for a moment.

The man walked up to the edge where the woman had jumped in and looked out over the water. He screwed his eyes up, gun at the ready, trying to spot her head in between the waves. Useless.

She'd never make it. Too cold, the wind too fierce. Too late.

Too late for Aida from Bijelina. She grew too big. She was too alone.

He stood there for a while, letting the cold bite into him. He had the wind in his face; it was throwing lumps of ice straight at him.

The sound from the truck starting up behind him was swept away, never reaching him. The juggernaut rolled off in the golden light, soundlessly, without a trace.

PART ONE

OCTOBER

I'M NOT AN EVIL PERSON.

I'm the product of my circumstances. All human beings are born into the same life, their circumstances being all that differ: genetic, cultural, social.

I have killed, it's true, but that's of no consequence here. The question is whether the person who is no longer alive ever deserved to live. I know what my own position is on this, but it may not correspond to anybody else's.

I may be perceived as violent, which doesn't necessarily have anything to do with evil. Violence is power, just like money or influence. Anyone who chooses violence for a tool can do so without being evil. You will always have to pay the price, though.

Taking to violence does not come free of charge; you have to pledge your soul. That way, the stakes are raised; for me there wasn't much to give up.

The void is then filled with the prerequisites for having the strength to use violence: evil is one of them, despair another, revenge a third, fury a fourth, the desire of the sick.

And I'm not an evil person.

I'm the product of my circumstances.

SUNDAY 28 OCTOBER

The security guard was on the alert. The devastation after the previous night's hurricane was visible everywhere: trees blown down, bits of sheet metal from roofs, scattered pieces of the warehouses.

When he arrived at the free-port compound, he slammed on the brakes. On the open space facing the sea lay the interior of an airplane cockpit, miscellaneous hospital equipment, parts of a bathroom. It took the security guard a few seconds before he realized what he was looking at – detritus from the props storage of one of the major TV stations.

He didn't see the dead bodies until he had switched off the engine and removed his seat belt. Strangely enough, he felt neither fear nor terror, only genuine surprise. The black-clad bodies lay stretched out in front of a broken staircase from some old TV soap. He knew the men had been murdered before he'd even stepped out of the car. It didn't take any major powers of deduction; parts of their skulls were missing and something sticky had run out on the icy tarmac.

Without regard for his own safety, the guard left his car and walked up to the men. They were only a few yards away. His reaction was one of wonder. The bodies looked really weird, like Marty Feldman's kid brothers: eyes partly popped out of their sockets, tongues lolling. They both had a small mark high up on the head and both of them were missing an ear, as well as big chunks of the backs of their heads and necks.

The living man looked at the two dead men for a period of time that he later couldn't specify. He was interrupted by a gust of wind that threw him to the ground. He put out his hands to break the fall and placed one hand in a pool of brain tissue. The sticky, viscous substance seeping between his fingers made the living man suddenly feel violently sick. He threw up over the bumper of his car and then frantically wiped the sticky stuff off his hands on the upholstery of the driver's seat.

The police's central control room in Stockholm received the call from the Värtan Free Port at 5.31 a.m. The news reached the newspaper *Kvällspressen* three minutes later. Leif phoned in the tip-off.

'Car 1120 is on the way to Värtan, plus two ambulances.'

At this time in the morning, forty-nine minutes after deadline and twenty-six before the paper went to print, the usual focused and creative chaos reigned in the newsroom. The red-eyed sub-editors were punching in the last headlines, putting the final touches to the front-page lead and captions, and correcting errors. Jansson, the night editor, was scrutinizing the dummies and sending off pages to print via the new electronic highway.

The worker responsible for answering tip-off calls at this point was the night-shift sub-editor, Annika Bengtzon.

'Meaning?' she said, taking hurried notes on a Post-it pad.

'At least two murders,' Leif said and hung up, in order to be the first with the news to the next newspaper. Second in line with a tip-off didn't get any money.

Annika stood up and put the receiver down in one movement.

'Two stiffs in the Värtan Free Port. Possible murders but not confirmed,' she said to the back of Jansson's head. 'Do you want it in the first edition?'

'Nope,' said the back of the head.

'Shall I give it to Carl and Bertil?' she asked.

'Yep,' said the back of the head.

She walked over to the reporters' area, the yellow note stuck like a flag on her index finger.

'Jansson wants you to check this out,' she said and pointed her finger at the reporter.

Carl Wennergren pulled off the note, a look of mild distaste on his face.

'Bertil Strand is in, if you need to go there,' she said. 'He's in the photo lab.'

Annika turned round and walked off without waiting for a reply from Carl. Their relationship wasn't what you'd call 'hearty'. She sank down on her chair. She was done in. The night had been a hard one with lots of last-minute saves. The night before, a hurricane had swept in across Skåne and continued up the country. *Kvällspressen* had put a lot of resources into covering the storm, and with considerable success. They had flown down both reporters and photographers on the last flight to back up the Malmö team. The journalists in Växjö and Göteborg had been at it all night, assisted by a number of stringers supplying both copy and pictures. All their material had ended up on the night desk and it was Annika's job to organize and structure the articles. This meant rewriting every single one so that they would harmonize with each other and fit the context. Yet her name wouldn't appear anywhere in the paper except for under the fact box about hurricanes that she had prepared in advance. She was a sub-editor, one among the many anonymous, invisible journalists.

'Shit!' Jansson suddenly shouted. 'The damned yellow hasn't reproduced on the front-page picture. The goddamn . . .'

He raced over to the picture desk and yelled out for the picture editor Pelle Oscarsson. Annika smiled wanly – Brave New World. According to the futurist gurus, digital technology would make everything work faster, safer and simpler. In reality, the little gremlin that resided in the ISDN cable that ran between the newsroom and the printers intermittently gobbled up one of the colour plates, usually the yellow. If the mistake wasn't spotted, the outcome would be some very peculiar pictures in the paper. Jansson maintained that the colour-gobbler was the same little devil that lived in his washing machine and constantly ate that other sock.

'ISDN!' the night editor snorted derisively on his way back to his desk after the catastrophe had been averted and the picture retransmitted. "It Sends Damned Nothing."'

Annika tidied up on her desk.

'Still, it worked out in the end, didn't it?' she said.

Jansson dropped into his chair and put an unlit low-tar cigarette in his mouth.

'You did well tonight,' he said and nodded appreciatively. 'I saw the original copy. You really did a good job on it.'

'It'll do,' Annika said, embarrassed.

'What was that about some stiffs in the port?'

'Don't know. Do you want me to check?'

Jansson got up and walked over the *Smoking* cubicle.

'Go ahead,' he said.

She started out with the emergency services control room.

'We've sent two ambulances,' the manager confirmed.

'Not bag cars, then?' Annika asked.

'We discussed it, but as it was a security guard who called in, we sent ambulances.'

Annika took notes. The bag cars, or hearses, were only sent in if the victims were certifiably dead. According to the rules, a police officer could only order out a bag car if the victim's head was severed from the body.

She had difficulty getting through to the police central control room and had to wait for several minutes before anyone answered the phone. Then it was another five minutes before the officer on duty could come to the phone. When he eventually answered, he was clear and concise.

'We've got two bodies,' he said. 'Two males. Shot. We can't say whether it's murder or suicide. You'll have to get back to us.'

'They were found in the City Free Port,' Annika said quickly. 'Does that mean anything to you?'

The duty officer hesitated.

'I can't make any guesses at this point in time,' he said. 'But you've got a brain yourself.'

Putting the phone down, she knew the double murder would dominate the paper for several days to come. For some reason, two murders weren't just twice as big as one murder, but infinitely bigger.

She sighed and contemplated getting a plastic cup of coffee. She was thirsty and felt faint. It would do her good. But caffeine at this time of the night would keep her awake late into the morning, eyes staring at the ceiling, her body throbbing with fatigue.

Oh, what the heck, she thought and walked over to the machine.

It was hot and did her good. She went back to her chair at the night desk and sat down with her feet on the desk.

A small double murder in the Free Port, there you have it.

Annika blew at her coffee.

That the victims had been shot indicated that it wasn't the result of a drunken brawl. Winos killed each other with knives, bottles, fists, kicks, or they were pushed off a balcony. If they ever had access to a weapon, they'd sell it to buy booze.

She finished her coffee and threw the mug in the bin. She went to the toilet and drank some water.

Two men didn't point to murder and suicide, not in the City Free Port when a hurricane was blowing. Jealousy could probably be ruled out as a motive. That meant motives of bigger media interest were at play. A dispute in the underworld, meaning anything from biker gangs to various mafias and financial syndicates. Political motives. International mix-ups.

Annika went back to her desk. She was sure about one thing: she wasn't going anywhere near this murder. There were others who would cover the murder for *Kvällspressen*. She picked up her clothes.

There was no morning shift on weekends, which meant that Jansson would stay on until the morning editions had gone to print. Annika stopped work at six.

'I've had enough of this now,' she said to the night editor when he walked past. He looked dead tired and would probably have liked her to stay.

'You're not waiting for the first edition?' he asked.

The bundles arrived by courier from the printers fifteen minutes after printing began. Annika shook her head and called a cab, then got up and put on her jacket, scarf and mittens.

'Can you come in early tonight?' Jansson called out after her. 'Sweep up after the hurricane hell?'

Annika hung her bag over her shoulder and shrugged.

'Who's got a life, anyway?'

Thomas Samuelsson touched his wife's stomach lightly. The old firmness was gone; her flesh was soft and warm under his hands. Since she became branch manager at the bank, Eleonor didn't have time to work out as hard as before.

His hand moved in circles downward, over her navel and down to the groin. His finger slowly trailed down and slipped in between her thighs, felt the hair, found the moistness.

'Don't,' his wife mumbled and turned away from him.

He sighed and swallowed, then rolled over on his back; excitement throbbing like a hammer. He folded his hands behind his head and stared up at the ceiling. He listened as her breathing slowed down again. She was never interested these days.

Annoyed, Thomas threw the cover back and went out into the kitchen naked, his dick a wilting tulip. He drank water from a dirty glass, then put coffee in a filter, filled the coffee maker with water and switched it on. He went to the bathroom and peed. In the bathroom mirror his tousled hair gave him a reckless look that was more in keeping with his age. He sighed and pushed his hair back.

It's too early to have a midlife crisis, he thought. *Much too early*.

He returned to the kitchen and looked out the window at the sea. It was black and wild. Last night's storm lingered in the sprays and white horses; the neighbours' sundial lay overturned next to their terrace door.

What's the point? he thought to himself. *Why do we go on?*

He was filled with a huge dark melancholy and realized that it verged on self-pity. There was a draught of cold air from the window – *damned jerry-built house* – so he went and got his dressing gown. A present from his wife last Christmas: green, blue and burgundy, and expensive; slippers to match, which he'd never used.

The coffee maker started gurgling. He took out a mug with the bank logo and switched on the radio, hitting the *Eko* news. The news items were filtered through his weariness and coffee, entering his mind at random. Hurricane sweeping through southern Sweden causing considerable damage. Households without electricity. Insurance companies making assurances. Two men dead. Security zone in south Lebanon. Kosovo.

Thomas switched off, walked out into the hallway and pulled his boots on. He'd get the newspaper from the letter box instead. The wind tore at the bits of paper, found its way in under his dressing gown, chilling his thighs. He stopped short, closed his eyes and breathed. There was ice in the air; the sea would soon freeze over.

He looked down at their house, the beautiful house her parents had built, designed by an architect. The light was on in the kitchen on the upper floor, the lamp over the table by a designer whose name he'd forgotten. It gave a greenish and cold light – an evil eye watching over the sea. The white tiles were grey in the light of early dawn. His mother had always thought it was the most beautiful house in all of Vaxholm. She had offered to make curtains for all the rooms when they moved in. Eleonor had declined, politely but firmly.

Thomas went inside. He leafed through all the sections without being able to focus on anything. As usual, he ended up on the ads for houses and flats for sale. 'Four-bedroom flat in central Vasastan, tiled stove in every room. One-bedroom flat in the Old Town, penthouse w/raftered ceilings, view in three directions. Timber cottage near Malmköping, electricity and water. Autumn bargain!'

He could his his wife's voice: *Daydreamer! If you gave the stock market half the attention you give ads for flats, you'd be a millionaire by now.*

She already was.

He immediately felt ashamed. She meant well. Her love was as firm as a rock. He was the problem. He didn't have the energy. Maybe she was right in thinking that he couldn't deal with her success. Maybe they should see that counsellor after all.

He folded the paper along its original folds – Eleonor didn't like to read a second-hand newspaper – and put it on the side table that was reserved for post and magazines. Then he went back into the bedroom, slipped out of the dressing gown and crept back into bed. His wife wriggled in her sleep when she felt his cold body. He pulled her up against him and blew into her soft neck.

'I love you,' he whispered.

'I love you too,' she murmured.

Carl Wennergren and Bertil Strand arrived late at the Free Port. As they parked the photographer's Saab they were just in time to see the ambulances roll through the cordons. The reporter couldn't help letting out an annoyed curse. Strand was such an extremely careful driver, keeping to 30 or even 20 m.p.h., even if there wasn't a soul about. The photographer caught the unspoken criticism and was nettled.

'You sound like a woman,' he said to the reporter.

The men walked over to the police cordon, the space

between them accentuating the emotional distance. But as the flashing blue lights and the police officers' movements became clearly visible, the distrust faded away, action taking over.

The cops were working fast today. The storm probably had their adrenalin pumping already. The cordoned-off area was large, from the fence on the left side all the way over to the office building on the right. Strand sized up the situation: great place, almost right in the centre of the city and yet completely separate. Good light, clear yet warm. Magical shadows.

Carl Wennergren buttoned up his oilskin coat. Shit, it was cold.

They couldn't see much of the victims. Junk, police officers and ambulances blocked their view. The reporter stamped his feet against the cold, hunched his shoulders and stuffed his hands deep into his pockets; he hated the morning shift. The photographer hauled out a camera body and a telephoto lens from his rucksack and glided along the cordon tape. He got a few good shots at the far left end: uniformed officers in profile, black bodies, plainclothes technicians in caps.

'I'm done,' he yelled out to the reporter.

Wennergren's nose was red and a droplet of transparent snot hung suspended from the tip.

'What a lousy place to die,' he said when the photographer returned.

'We'd better get a move on if we're going to make the early editions,' Strand said.

'But I haven't finished,' Wennergren said. 'I haven't even started.'

'You'll have to make the calls from the car. Or the newsroom. Hurry up and soak up some atmosphere to spice up your copy with.'

The photographer walked towards his car, the

rucksack bobbing on his back. The reporter followed behind. They drove back to the office in silence.

Anders Schyman shut down the TT news agency cable-copy list on his computer; it was addictive. You could set the computer so that the cables were sorted into different subjects – domestic, international, sports, features – but he preferred having them all in the same file. He wanted to know about everything at one fell swoop.

He paced the floor of his cramped aquarium-like office, rolling his shoulders. He sat down on the sofa and picked up the day's paper, the hurricane special. He nodded to himself, satisfied: it had gone according to plan. The different desks had cooperated in the way he'd suggested. Jansson had told him that Annika Bengtzon had handled the practical coordination; it had worked really well.

Annika Bengtzon, he thought and sighed.

The young sub-editor had in a purely coincidental and unfortunate way become bound up with his standing at the newspaper. He and Annika Bengtzon had started at the paper within a few weeks of each other. His first battle with the rest of the senior editors had been over her – a long-term contract at the news desk for which he felt she was the obvious candidate. True, she was young, immature, impetuous and inexperienced, but he felt she had a potential that went far beyond the norm. She had a lot to learn, but she had ethics and possessed an undeniable passion for justice. She was on the ball and was a good stylist. Furthermore, she had the character-istics of a steamroller, a great asset for a tabloid reporter. If she couldn't go round an obstacle, she'd drive straight over it; she never gave up.

The rest of the management, with the exception of the night editor, Jansson, didn't share his opinion. They wanted to give the contract to Carl Wennergren, the son of one of the members of the board, a good-looking and wealthy guy with considerable gaps in his morals. He had shown disregard both for the truth and for the protection of his sources. For reasons that were beyond Schyman, this was considered honourable, or at least not controversial, by the rest of the senior editors.

The management of the newspaper *Kvällspressen* was composed exclusively of white, heterosexual middle-aged men with a car and a steady income, the kind that both society and the paper were built on and for. Anders Schyman suspected that Carl Wennergren reminded these men of themselves as young men or, rather, personified their illusions about their own youth.

Eventually, he found Annika a contract – which she accepted – covering maternity leave as a sub-editor on Jansson's night team. He'd had to twist several arms in the management before they'd agreed to it. Annika Bengtzon became the issue he'd had to push through to prove his drive. It ended in disaster.

A few days after the appointment was made public, the girl went and killed her boyfriend. She had hit him with an iron pipe so that he'd fallen into a disused furnace at the Hälleforsnäs works. The very first rumours to reach the paper had mentioned self-defence, but Schyman could still recall the feeling when he heard about it, wishing the ground could swallow him up; and then the thought: *Talk about backing the wrong horse!* She'd phoned him in the evening, reticent, still in shock, confirming that the rumours were true. She had been questioned and was suspected of manslaughter, but she hadn't been arrested. She would be staying in a cottage in the woods for a couple of weeks until the police investigation was complete. She wanted to know whether she still had a job at the paper.

Schyman had told her the truth: the contract was hers even though there were people at the paper who complained – she wasn't the flavour of the day with the union representatives. Manslaughter meant some form of accident. If she were to be convicted of causing an accident where someone lost their life, it was unfortunate, but it didn't constitute grounds for dismissal. But she had to understand that if she were to be sentenced to prison, it would make it difficult for her to get an extension of the contract.

When he'd got that far, Annika had begun to cry. He had fought the instinct to shout at her, to criticize her for being so monumentally clumsy and dragging him down with her.

'I won't be sent to prison,' she had whispered into the phone. 'It was him or me. He would have killed me if I hadn't hit him. The prosecutor knows that.'

She had begun her work on the night team as planned, paler and thinner than ever before. From time to time she'd talk to him, to Jansson, Berit, Picture Pelle and a few others, but mostly she kept to herself. According to Jansson, she did a hell of a job rewriting, adding copy, checking facts, writing captions and front-page leads, never making a great fuss. The rumours died out, sooner than Schyman would have expected. The newspaper dealt with murder and scandal every day; there were limits to how long people had the energy to gossip about a tragic and unfortunate death.

The case of the death of the abusive hockey-player Sven Matsson from Hälleforsnäs wasn't given high priority by the Eskilstuna County Court. Annika was charged with justifiable homicide or involuntary manslaughter. The sentence had been passed the week before Midsummer last year. Annika Bengtzon was acquitted of justifiable homicide but convicted of the lesser charge and given a probational sentence. A period of counselling had been part of the probation, but as far as he knew, the matter was by now settled in the eyes of the court.

The deputy editor returned to his desk and clicked on the list of cable copy again. He quickly scrolled through the last additions. The Sunday sports results were beginning to come in; there were reports of the continued after-effects of the hurricane; a series of rehashed cables from Saturday. He heaved another sigh – things rolled on, it was never-ending, and now there was going to be another reorganisation.

The editor-in-chief, Torstensson, wanted to introduce a new managerial level in order to centralize the decision-making. The model was already in place at their biggest rival tabloid, as well as at several other national media. Torstensson had decided it was time for *Kvällspressen* to follow suit and become a 'modern' enterprise. Anders Schyman was in two minds about it. All the signs of an impending disaster were in place: the poor state of the finances; the falling circulation; the grim faces of the members of the board; the newsroom that swayed in a storm, poorly guided and with a run-down radar. The truth was that *Kvällspressen* didn't know where it was headed or why. He hadn't succeeded in establishing a collective vision of their boundaries, despite numerous seminars and conferences on the aims and responsibility of the media. They had steered clear of any regular shipwrecks since his arrival at the newspaper, but the repairs to previous damage were slow.

Furthermore, and this worried Schyman slightly more than he wanted to admit, Torstensson had hinted at a new job, some fancy post in Brussels. Maybe that was the reason for this hurried reorganization. Torstensson wanted to make a mark, and God knows he hadn't had any editorial achievements.

Schyman groaned and impatiently shut down the list again.

Something had to happen soon.

Darkness lurked in the corners by the time she woke. The brief day had spent itself while she had perspired and tossed in bed; she never should have had that last cup of coffee. She took a few deep breaths and forced herself to lie still, exploring how she felt. It didn't hurt anywhere. Her head felt a bit heavy, but that was due to working nights. She glanced up at the ceiling, so spotty and grey. The previous tenant had applied latex paint on top of the old distemper, leaving the entire surface streaked with cracks in a range of hues. She traced the cracks, broken and irregular, with her gaze. Found the butterfly, the car, the skull. A single note began to peal loudly in her ear: the note of loneliness, wobbling slightly up and down the scale.

Feeling the need to pee, she sighed; what a bother. She got out of bed, the wooden floor rough under her feet and an occasional source of splinters. Pulling on her robe made her shiver, the material silky and cool against her skin. She opened the front door and listened for sounds in the stairwell. Apart from the note in her ear there was silence. She quickly padded down a half-flight of stairs to the lavatory she shared with the other occupants of the building, her feet immediately getting cold and sandy, but she lacked the energy to care.

She noticed the draught as soon as she returned to her apartment. The sheer curtains billowed against the walls even though she wasn't airing the room. The voile subsided as she closed the door behind her and wiped her feet on the rug in the hall before walking into the living room.

One of the window-panes had been smashed during

the night, either by a gust of wind or by flying debris. The outer pane appeared to have disappeared completely, while a few substantial shards of the inner one still clung to the frame. Plaster and glass were heaped on the floor beneath the window. She regarded the mess, closed her eyes and rubbed her forehead.

Isn't that typical? she thought, lacking the strength to conjure up the word 'glazier'.

A draught swept around her legs. She left the living room and went into the kitchen instead. Sank down on a chair and looked out the window at the apartment on the opposite side of the courtyard, the one on the third floor of the building facing the street. A construction company used it to put up official guests, and the bathroom windows had frosted-glass panes. The people who spent a night or two there never knew that their every visit to the bathroom was visible. As soon as they turned on the light, their wavy contours leapt into view. For the past two years or so, she had seen the construction-company guests making love, taking a dump or changing their tampons. At first it had embarrassed her – but after a while she found it amusing. Later on it irritated her, she didn't want to see people taking a leak while she had dinner. These days she was simply indifferent. There were fewer guest over time, the building was so run-down there was nothing much to show. Now the window was grey and still, empty.

A great deal of plaster from the exterior of the building had fallen down during the night and it mingled with the grimy slush out in the courtyard. Two windows on the first floor had been smashed. She got up, went over to the window and saw the black holes down below just like hers. The electric radiator in the kitchen warmed her legs and she remained standing there until she felt a burning sensation. She wasn't hungry, even though she should have been, and she drank some water straight from the tap.

I'm doing fine, she thought. *I have everything I want*.

Restless, she went back into the living room. Sat on the couch, feet up on the cushions, arms clasping her knees, gently rocking. Breathed deeply – in out, in out – it was pretty cold. There was no central heating, and the portable space heaters she had put in barely managed to keep the apartment warm even when the windows were intact. The draught swirled unchecked across the empty floor. What furnishings she had came from thrift shops and IKEA; there was nothing with a shared history.

She looked around the room, rocking, rocking, and saw the shadows chase each other. The pure light, one of the things that she'd loved so much at first about the place, was no longer white. The dull shimmering surface of the walls that used to absorb and reflect light at the same time had dried out, turned opaque. Daylight no longer made it into her rooms. Everything remained grey, regardless of the season. The air was as thick and stifling as mud.

The couch was scratchy, the rough fabric left imprints on her buttocks that she raked over lightly with her nails as she walked back to her bedroom and sank down under the sweaty bedclothes. She pulled the duvet over her head – it was damp under the covers. It soon got warm and the bedclothes gave off a slightly sour odour. The hard-rock fan on the ground floor turned on his stereo; the bass line travelled through the stone walls and made her bed quiver. The tone came back on in her ear, irritatingly high, and she forced herself to remain in bed. There were still quite a few hours left until it was time for her shift.

She turned and faced the wall, staring at the wallpaper. Through the thin layer of white primer the old pattern showed: medallions. The neighbours at the other end of her floor were home now; she heard them thudding around and laughing. A pillow over her head muffled their laughter while the ringing in her ears got louder.

I want to get some sleep, she thought. *Just let me sleep a little while longer and I might be able to go on.*

The man lit a cigarette, took a long drag and forced the chaos in his mind to back down. He wasn't sure which emotion was the strongest: rage about being betrayed, fear of the consequences, embarrassment about being tricked, or hatred of the guilty parties.

He was going to get his revenge, those bastards were going to pay.

It took him two minutes to finish his cigarette, turning it into one long pillar of ash and ember. He stubbed it out on the floor of the bar and waved to get another shot of liquor. Just one, just one more, he needed to have a clear head, needed to get around. He downed the drink, his shoulder holster rubbing up against his armpit reassuringly. Damn, he was dangerous.

An explanation, he thought. *I need to come up with a fucking good explanation of why things went so wrong.*

He was about to order another shot, but stopped in midair.

'Coffee, black.'

He couldn't figure it out. He didn't understand what the hell had happened, and he couldn't figure out how he was supposed to explain it to his superiors. They would demand total retribution. Dead bodies weren't the problem, even if liquidation had certain drawbacks. Murders attracted the attention of the police – you had to be more cautious for a while. The problem was the truck. It wouldn't be enough to locate the shipment and replace it, he personally would have to clean up all the loose ends

after the screw-up. Someone had squealed. He had to find
the shipment and he had to find the person who arranged
for it to disappear.

No matter how he twisted and turned the facts, he
realized that what happened must have something to do
with the woman. She had to be involved, or she wouldn't
have been there.

He downed his coffee like he had his drink, in a single
gulp. Scalding his throat.

'You're dead, whore.'

The elevator lighting was as cold and unflattering as ever
– she looked like a dead fish. Annika shut her eyes to blot
out her reflection. She hadn't been able to go back to sleep
and had taken a walk in the park at Rålambshov instead
in an unsuccessful attempt to find some light and air. The
ground had been soft and worn by rain and thousands of
feet until it was mushy and brown. She had walked over
to the paper.

Being a Sunday, the newsroom was deserted. She went
over to her desk. The news-desk editor Ingvar Johansson
was at the desk next to hers, talking on the phone, so she
went over to the crime desk instead. Her mind a blank,
she sank down on Berit Hamrin's chair and called her
grandmother.

The elderly lady was in her apartment in Hälleforsnäs,
taking care of the laundry and the shopping.

'How are you doing?' her grandmother asked. 'Has it
been windy?'

Annika laughed.

'That's for sure. One of my windows was blown
out.'

'I hope you weren't hurt,' the elderly lady said in a
concerned voice.

Annika laughed again.

'No, and don't be such a worrywart. How are things over at your end? Are the woods still standing?'

Her grandmother sighed.

'More or less, but quite a few trees have fallen down. There was a blackout this morning, but now the power's back on again. When are you coming down for a visit?'

Annika's grandmother had been allotted a cottage in the grounds of Harpsund after years of service as the matron of the estate used by the Prime Minister for official functions and recreation, a small cottage with no electricity or running water, where Annika had spent every school vacation she could remember.

'I'll be working tonight and tomorrow night, so I'll be coming over sometime Tuesday afternoon,' Annika replied. 'Would you like me to bring anything?'

'Nothing at all,' her grandmother replied. 'Just bring yourself, that's all I want.'

'I miss you,' Annika said.

She took a paper, leafing through it mechanically. Today's edition of *Kvällspressen* maintained fairly high standards. Already familiar with the coverage of the hurricane, she skipped it. Carl Wennergren's piece about the double homicide at the free port, on the other hand, was hardly anything to write home about. The dead men had been shot in the head, it said, and the police had eliminated the possibility of suicide. Right. This was followed by a description of the free-port compound that was actually vaguely poetic. Carl had obviously cased the area and picked up on the vibes. The place was 'beautifully weathered' and had a 'Continental atmosphere'.

'Hello, gorgeous, *que pasa*?'

Annika swallowed.

'Hello, Sjölander,' she replied.

As was his habit, the crime-desk editor plunked himself down on top of the desk next to her.

'How are you?'

Annika tried to smile.

'I'm fine, thanks. A little tired.'

Aiming a playful punch at her shoulder, the man winked.

'Rough night, huh?'

She got up, picked up her paper and collected her bag and her coat.

'Extremely rough,' she said. 'Just me and these seven guys.'

Sjölander chuckled.

'You really know how to party.'

She held the paper under the crime-desk editor's nose.

'I was working,' she said. 'What's the deal with this free-port thing?'

He gazed at her for a few seconds, then pushed the hair off his forehead.

'No ID found on the bodies,' he said. 'No keys, no money, no weapons, no gum, no condoms.'

'They were picked clean,' Annika said.

Sjölander nodded.

'The police don't have any leads, they don't even know who the victims were. Their prints aren't in any Swedish records.'

'So they don't have a clue, then? What about their clothes?'

The crime-desk editor went over to his desk and switched on his computer.

'Their coats, jeans and shoes came from Italy, France and the US, but their underwear had Cyrillic letters on the labels.'

Annika looked up.

'Imported designer clothing,' she said, 'but cheap local underwear. Sounds like the former Soviet Union, the former Yugoslav Republic or Bulgaria.'

'Kind of interested in the crime beat, aren't you?' Sjölander said with a grin.

He knew, they all knew. She shrugged.

'You know what it's like, a leopard never changes its spots.'

Annika turned around and walked over to the night desk. Heard Sjölander snort behind her back. *Why do I go along with it?* she asked herself.

She started up the computer to the right of the night desk, drew up her legs as she sat down and settled into position with her chin resting on one knee. *Might as well check and see if anything's happened.* She waited patiently for all the programs to start up. Opened one when the screen was ready. Read, checked, clicked.

'Hey, Bengtzon, what's your extension number?'

She turned and saw Sjölander waving a receiver, shouted out her number and got him on the line.

'This broad wants to talk about the Social Services, something to do with troubled women,' the crime-desk editor said. 'I'm pretty busy. Besides, it's, um, more your turf. What do you say?'

She closed her eyes, took a few breaths, swallowed.

'I haven't actually gone on duty yet,' she said. 'I was going to check out . . .'

'Are you going to take it, or shall I blow her off?'

Sigh.

'All right, put her on.'

A voice, cool and calm.

'Hello, I'd like to speak to someone, it's confidential.'

'Newspapers have a confidentiality clause,' Annika said while letting her eyes skim over the new agency reports on the screen. 'Now, what would you like to tell me?'

Click, click. The big game between the local soccer favourites had ended in a tie.

'I'm not sure I've reached the right department. This is about a new set-up, a new way to protect people whose lives are threatened.'

Annika stopped reading.

'Really?' she said. 'How does it work?'

The woman hesitated.

'I have information about a unique way of providing people under threat with a new lease on life. The method is not common knowledge, but I've been authorized to issue this information to the media. I would like to do so in a controlled and orderly fashion, which is why I'm wondering if I could contact any of your associates?'

She didn't want to hear this, didn't want to care. So she stared at the screen: Some households still had to make do without electricity and there had been new missile attacks on Grozny. She cradled her head in one hand.

'Could you send me a letter or a fax?' she asked.

The woman remained silent for quite some time.

'Hello?' Annika said, preparing to hang up with a sense of relief.

'I prefer to talk face to face, in safe surroundings,' the woman said.

She sagged over her desk.

'That's not possible,' she said. 'No one's in yet.'

'What about you?'

Swept back her hair and conjured up an excuse.

'We have to know what's it's all about before we send anyone,' she claimed.

The woman at the other end of the line grew silent again. Annika sighed and tried to wind up the call.

'If that's all . . .?'

'Are you aware that there are people living under-ground? Here and now, in Sweden?' the woman asked quietly. 'Women and children who are being abused and mistreated?'

No, Annika thought. *Not this.*

'Thank you for calling, but this isn't really a story we can cover tonight.'

The woman on the other end raised her voice.

'Are you going to hang up? Are you just going to ignore me and the work I do? Do you know how many people I've helped? Don't you care at all about abused women? You reporters, all you do is sit around in your newsrooms. You have no idea what real life is all about.'

Annika felt dizzy, smothered.

'You don't know anything about me,' she said.

'You media people are all alike. I thought *Kvällspressen* would be better than the highbrow papers, but you don't care about abused women and children, people at risk.'

The blood rushed to Annika's head.

'Don't you tell me what I do, or do not, stand for,' she said, way too loud. 'Don't make claims you know nothing about!'

'Then why don't you want to listen to me?'

The woman sounded peeved.

Annika covered her face with her hands and waited.

'These people are isolated,' the woman went on. 'Their lives are threatened, they're terrified. No matter how they try to hide, there's always someone or something that could lead people to them – social workers, courts, bank accounts, day-care centres . . .'

Annika didn't respond, just listened silently.

'As you are probably aware, most of these people are women and children,' the woman went on. 'They belong to the group most at risk in society. Other groups are witnesses, people who have left different types of sects, or who are being harassed by organized crime, and whistle-blowing journalists, but the bulk is obviously women and children whose lives are in danger.'

Hesitantly, Annika picked up a pen and began to take notes.

'This is a group effort,' the woman said. 'We have devised this special method. And I'm in charge. Are you still there?'

Annika cleared her throat.

'What makes your operation any different to a regular women's shelter?'

The caller sighed with an air of resignation.

'Everything. Women's shelters are run on insufficient public funds. They don't have the resources to go as far as we can. This is a purely private endeavour with completely different means.'

Her pen stopped working. Annika tossed it in the recycling bin and dug out a new one.

'In what way?'

'I'd prefer not to say anything more on the phone. Could we possibly meet?'

Annika hunched over, not wanting to face any more, not having the strength.

'Bengtzon!'

Ingvar Johansson loomed over her.

'Please hold,' she said into the receiver and rested it on her chest. 'What is it?'

'If you're not busy, you could enter these results.'

The news editor held out a stack of scores from the lower sporting divisions.

The question hit Annika like a punch in the gut. *What the hell!* They were going to have her do the kind of stuff she'd done back at the local paper, *Katrineholms-Kuriren*, as a fourteen-year-old, filling in tables with scores.

She turned away from Ingvar Johansson, picked up the receiver and said: 'I could meet you straight away.'

The woman was pleased. 'Tonight? That's great.'

Annika clenched her teeth, sensing the presence of the news-desk editor behind her.

'What location would suit you?' she asked.

The woman mentioned a hotel in a suburb where Annika had never been before.

'In an hour?'

Ingvar Johansson was gone by the time Annika had hung up. She quickly pulled on her jacket, slung her bag over her shoulder and checked with the attendants at the desk, but no cars were in, so she dialled a taxi service. She wasn't on the clock, so could do whatever she liked.

Fill out your own tables, dickhead!

'Are you ready, dear?'

Thomas Samuelsson's wife stood in the doorway leading to their recreation room, with her coat on, pulling on her fine leather gloves.

He heard the surprised tone in his voice as he wondered: 'Ready for what?'

In irritation, she yanked at the thin material.

'The trade association,' she replied. 'You promised you'd go with me.'

Thomas folded the evening paper and put his feet down on the heated tile floor.

'That's right,' he said. 'I'm sorry, it slipped my mind.'

'I'll go wait outside,' she said, turning away and leaving.

He sighed quietly. Good thing he'd already showered and shaved.

He went up to their bedroom, removing his jeans and T-shirt on the way. Jumped into a white shirt and a suit and draped a tie around his neck. He heard the BMW start outside, revving up imperiously.

'All right, already!' he said.

Every single lamp in the house was on, but he certainly

wasn't going to run around and switch them all off. Leaving the house with his coat over one arm, and without tying his shoelaces, he slipped on a patch of ice and almost fell.

'You *could* sand the walk and the driveway, you know,' Eleonor said.

Thomas didn't reply, simply slammed the car door and held on to the dashboard as she turned out on Östra Ekuddsgatan. He tied his tie on the way – the shoelaces would have to wait until he got there.

It was dark out. Where had the day gone? It had died before it was born. Had there even been any daylight?

He sighed.

'What's wrong, honey?' she asked, friendly again.

He stared out the window, out towards the sea. 'I feel out of it,' he said.

'Maybe you caught that bug Nisse had,' she said.

He nodded without interest.

The trade association. He knew exactly what they would talk about. Tourists. How many there had been, how to attract more of them, and how to keep the ones that had already discovered their community. They would discuss the problem with businesses that only operated during the brief summer months, taking revenue that rightfully belonged to the resident shopkeepers. The good food at the Waxholm Hotel. Preparations for the Christmas fair, longer opening hours on evenings and weekends. Everyone would be there. Everyone would be happy and committed. That's the way it always was, no matter which event they went to. Lately, they'd been heavily involved in art. Church affairs had figured prominently too. Lots of talk about the preservation of old houses and gardens, preferably at someone else's expense.

Thomas sighed again.

'Cheer up,' his wife said.

'Annika Bengtzon? I'm Rebecka Björkstig.'

The woman was young, much younger than Annika had expected. Tiny, slim, a bit like a porcelain figurine. They exchanged greetings.

'I apologize for the somewhat unusual spot,' Rebecka said 'Only we can't be too careful.'

They crossed a deserted passage leading to a combined lobby and bar. The lights were low and the atmosphere was reminiscent of the state-run hotels of the former Soviet Union. Round brown tables, chairs where the backrests merged with the armrests. Some men spoke in hushed tones in the opposite corner while the rest of the room was empty.

The surreal feeling that she was starring in an old spy thriller washed over Annika and she felt a strong impulse to get the hell out of there. What was she doing there?

'I'm so glad we could meet so soon,' Rebecka said as she sat down at a table, glancing cautiously over her shoulder at the men seated further away.

Annika mumbled an inaudible reply.

'Will this be featured in tomorrow's paper?' the woman asked with a hopeful smile.

Slightly dizzy, Annika shook her head. The air was stale.

'No, it won't. It might not be included at all. The publisher decides what material will be printed.'

Having been dishonest and evasive, she looked down at the table top.

The woman straightened her pale skirt and smoothed her slicked-back hair.

'What subject matter do you usually cover?' she asked,

in slightly lacklustre soprano tones, trying to catch Annika's eye.

Annika cleared her throat.

'Currently I've been compiling and reviewing text material,' she replied truthfully.

'What kinds of texts?'

Annika rubbed her forehead.

'All different kinds. Last night it was material about the hurricane, earlier in the week I reviewed the case of a handicapped boy that the local authorities refused to deal with responsibly . . .'

'Oh,' Rebecka Björkstig exclaimed while crossing her legs. 'Then our work will fit right in with your beat. Our main contractors are the local authorities. Could I have a cup of coffee?'

A waiter in a stained apron had materialized next to them. Annika nodded curtly when he asked if she wanted coffee too; she was feeling queasy, wanting to go home, to get away. Rebecka leaned back against the curved backrest of the chair. Her eyes were pale and round, calm and expressionless.

'We run a non-profit foundation, but we do have to charge money for our services. Generally, the Social Services agencies in different communities all over the country cover our expenditure. We don't make a bean.'

Her voice remained gentle, but the words had a harsh impact.

She's a gold-digger, Annika thought as she looked up at the woman. *She does this to make money off women and children who are in dire circumstances.*

The woman smiled.

'I know what you're thinking. I can assure you that you're wrong.'

Annika looked down and fingered a toothpick.

'Why did you call our paper, and why this particular evening?'

Rebecka sighed faintly and wiped her fingertips on a tissue she had in her purse.

'To be honest, I had only planned to call and make some enquiries,' she said. 'I read the paper, about the damage caused by the hurricane, and saw the newsroom number. We've been talking about going public with our services for some time now, and I acted on an impulse, so to speak.'

Annika swallowed.

'I've never heard of you,' she said.

The woman smiled again, a smile as fleeting as a draught in a room.

'Previously we lacked the resources to accommodate the numbers we anticipate receiving when we go public, but now we can have them. Today we have the means and the skills to expand, and we feel a certain urgency to do so. So many people need our help."

Annika fished her notepad and her pen out of her bag.

'Tell me what it's all about.'

The woman looked around the room once more and wiped the corner of her mouth.

'We pick up where the authorities fail,' she said, a bit breathlessly. 'Our sole purpose is to help the people truly at risk to start over. For the past three years we have focused on making our system work. Now we're certain that it does.'

Annika waited silently.

'Why is that?'

The waiter arrived with their coffee. It was grey and bitter. Rebecka inserted a paper napkin in between the cup and the saucer and stirred the beverage with a spoon.

'Our society is so thoroughly computerized that no one can hide,' she said in hushed tones after the waiter had sailed off again. 'No matter where these individuals turn, they have to deal with the fact that there are people who know their new addresses, their new telephone numbers, their new bank-account numbers, and know that they've leased a new place. Even if all this information is supposed to be kept confidential, it may turn up in hospital records, at Social Service agencies, in city court records, on tax rolls, in stockholder directories, anywhere.'

'Can't this be arranged in some way?' Annika wondered cautiously. 'Isn't there some way to remove addresses from all lists and directories? To obtain new personal ID numbers and things like that?'

The woman let another faint sigh escape her lips.

'Sure, there are other ways. The problem is that they don't work. Our group has designed a way to wipe people completely off the record. Did you know that there are more than sixty different public computerized directories that list practically everyone residing in Sweden?'

Annika uttered a negative response and made a face – the coffee was truly disgusting.

'For the first six months I was completely occupied with mapping out the different directories. I worked out plans and approaches to get around them. There were lots of questions, while the answers would sometimes be a long time in coming. The method we have worked out is completely unique.'

That last sentence reverberating in her mind, Annika swallowed a mouthful of the grey sludge, spilling a drop or two when she set down her cup.

'Why are you involved in this?' she asked.

The silence became oppressive.

'I've been exposed to threats myself,' the woman replied.

'Why was that?' Annika wondered.

Rebecka cleared her throat, hesitated and wiped her wrists with the tissue.

'I'm sorry, but I really don't want to talk about it. Fear is such a paralysing feeling. I've worked hard to make a new life for myself, and I want to put my experience to good use.'

Annika looked at Rebecka Björkstig, so cold and so soft at the same time.

'Tell me about the foundation,' she said.

Rebecka carefully sipped her coffee.

'Our operations are conducted in the form of a non-profit organization, a foundation that we decided to call Paradise. We don't really do anything all that remarkable, we just give our clients back a regular life. But for anyone who has ever been stalked and knows the meaning of terror and fear, for a person like that, a new lease on life *is* like paradise.'

Annika looked down at her pad, embarrassed by the hackneyed cliché.

'And how do you accomplish that?'

The woman smiled slightly, her voice confident.

'The Garden of Eden was a sheltered place,' she said. 'It was surrounded by invisible walls that kept evil out. That's how we operate too. The client comes to us, passes through our set-up and disappears behind an impenetrable wall. They simply vanish. Whenever anyone tries to trace a client of ours, no matter which route they try, they will run up against a great big wall of silence: us.'

Annika looked up.

'But aren't you afraid?'

'We're aware of the risks, but the Paradise Foundation is impossible to trace as well. We maintain several different offices that we alternate between. Our phone connections are directed through other stations in other provinces. Five of us work full time for Paradise – we've

all had our records wiped clean. The only route into
Paradise is an unlisted telephone number.'

Annika studied the tiny porcelain-figurine lady unconsciously twisting a tissue around her fingers. She was so
out of place in this environment, so pale and pure in the
shabby bar with its shady decor.

'How do you manage to get them removed from all the
different records?'

Someone switched on an overhead lamp diagonally
behind Rebecka Björkstig, shadowing her face and
turning the pale inexpressive eyes into black holes.

'I think that will be all for now,' she said. 'I hope you
don't mind, but I'd like to wait a bit until I give you the
rest of the information.'

Feeling a mixture of disappointment and relief,
Annika exhaled. Rebecka Björkstig pulled a card out of
her purse.

'Talk to your publisher and ask if your paper would
like to write about our endeavour. Then give me a call –
this is our unlisted number. I guess I don't have to tell you
that you need to be extremely careful with it.'

Annika swallowed, stammering in agreement.

'As soon as you've got the go-ahead, we can meet
again,' Rebecka said as she got up, a small pale figure
veiled in shadows.

Annika smiled sheepishly and got up. They shook
hands.

'Then maybe I'll be getting back to you,' Annika said.

'If you'll excuse me, I'm in a bit of a hurry,' Rebecka
said. 'I'm looking forward to your call.'

And then she was gone.

The waiter drifted over to the table.

'That will be fifty-five kronor for the coffee.'

Annika paid the bill.

In the taxi back to the newsroom, her mind wandered.

The suburbs flashed past through the dirty glass: industrial areas with sheet-metal siding, dreary high-rise buildings, thoroughfares with red lights.

What did she actually look like, this Rebecka Björkstig? Annika realized that she'd already forgotten, remembering only a certain intangible evasive quality.

People at risk, abused women. If ever there was a subject she ought to avoid, this was it. She was disqualified for all eternity.

And what had Rebecka said about the Garden of Eden, anyway? Annika searched her memory, the information slipping beyond her grasp. She got her notes out, leafed through them and tried to read by the flashes of yellow light produced by the street lamps.

It was surrounded by an invisible wall that evil couldn't penetrate.

She put her pad down again and saw the high-rise buildings of the neighbourhood known as 'the Blues' flash by.

Then what about the serpent? she thought. *Where did it come from?*

Berit Hamrin was sitting at her desk in the newsroom by the time she returned. Annika walked over to her and hugged her.

'The double homicide?' she asked.

Berit smiled.

'There's nothing like a mob war,' she said.

Annika took off her jacket, letting it fall in a small pile on the floor.

'Have you had anything to eat?'

They went down to the lunch room commonly referred to as 'Seven Rats' and had the special.

'What's up?' Berit asked and buttered a piece of crispbread.

Annika sighed.

'I guess there'll be more hurricane coverage tonight,' she said. 'And I just met this woman with a really strange story.'

Interested, Berit raised an eyebrow as she sampled the potatoes au gratin.

'Strange stories can be a lot of fun,' she said. 'Pass the salt, please.'

Annika leaned back and reached over to take the salt and pepper shakers from the table behind her.

'This woman claims that there is this foundation called Paradise that helps women and children whose lives have been threatened to make new lives for themselves.'

Berit nodded in approval.

'Sounds exciting. Is it on the level?'

Annika hesitated.

'I'm not sure, I didn't get the whole story. The director seemed to be on the level. Apparently they've devised some sort of process to wipe people who fear for their lives off public records.'

She took the salt from Berit and sprinkled her own food liberally.

'Do you think . . . that my checking this lead would be a problem?' she asked cautiously.

Berit chewed her food a while.

'No, I shouldn't think so,' she said. 'Because of Sven, you mean?'

Annika nodded, her voice failing her.

Her older colleague sighed.

'I can see that the thought occurred to you, but what you went through can't disqualify you from being able to perform as a journalist for all eternity. It was an accident – you've got the decree to prove it.'

There was nothing she could say; Annika looked down at her plate as she sliced a piece of lettuce into shreds.

'Just talk to the executives,' Berit said. 'It's easier to get stuff in the paper if the guys upstairs think that a story is their idea.'

Annika smiled, chewing on a mouthful of salad. They ate in comfortable silence.

'Have you been over to the free-port compound?' Annika asked as she pushed her plate away and reached for a toothpick.

Berit got up. 'Coffee?'

'Black.'

Berit went and got them both a cup.

'Nasty affair,' she said, placing a cup in front of Annika. 'The two dead guys might possibly be Serbs – the cops think it's a mob killing, that it's the Yugo Mafia. They're afraid people will start slaughtering each other.'

'Any leads?'

Berit sighed. 'Hard to tell,' she said. 'The forensics team were at the site until nightfall, sifting through every last bit of gravel in search of bullets and evidence.'

Annika blew on her coffee. 'Will we be able to trot out the grand old clichés? Slayings? Underworld liquidation? The police fear that gang wars are in the works?'

They both laughed a little.

'Probably all three,' Berit said.

Annika typed up her notes about the Paradise Foundation, then Jansson wanted her to doctor some follow-up copy about the hurricane. The long night shifts left more and more of a mark – she had to rub her eyes to keep the letters in check. Luckily, the large document about the handicapped boy had been edited beforehand and was ready to go, four pages about how the Social Services had broken municipal laws by not providing the care that he was entitled to. It would be a quiet night, maybe even too quiet.

Right before midnight, the rest of the night shift went downstairs to eat. Annika stayed behind, monitoring the phones and the news-agency bulletins, relieved not to be going with them. Once the gang had gone, she hesitated a moment, choosing between vegging out or checking a few items. Then she sat down at Jansson's desk – he was always on-line – and did a Yahoo search about the Paradise Foundation. The computer churned and deliberated, but came up with zip. The keyword 'Paradise' got a few hits: an advertising agency, a minister from Vetlanda, Sweden's Bible belt, with his own website, a Leonardo DiCaprio movie. Nothing about an organization that helped women and children at risk.

She returned to her desk and checked the news-agency bulletins. No breaking news. Using the speed dial, she called the 'morgue' on the third floor; they had a folder about foundations, provided by the Swedish IRS and titled 'Tax Liability'. She ordered it, but by the time the attendant had managed to drag himself downstairs and get it she couldn't face reading it. She took a short walk around the place and rubbed her eyes, weary, sluggish, uninterested. Sat down at her desk again and wished that the shift was over so she wouldn't have to be there. Even though she knew she would end up counting the hours until she was able to come back to work and not have to be at home. Pressure started to constrict her chest and a sense of futility crept up on her.

'Hey, Sjölander,' she shouted. 'Want me to write something? A sidebar on the history of the Yugo Mafia?'

He was on the phone, but flashed her a thumbs-up.

Annika closed her eyes, swallowed, went back to Jansson's desk and got on-line with the Data Archives, typing in 'Yugo' and 'Mafia'.

According to the press excerpts, criminal Yugoslav

groups had been established in many parts of Sweden for decades, in cities as well as in the country. Their main focus was smuggling and selling drugs, often using restaurants as a front, but in later years their operations had changed. After the Swedish government raised the taxes on tobacco products dramatically, not once, but twice, a few years back, many of these smugglers had switched from drugs to cigarettes. A carton of cigarettes could be had for thirty to fifty kronor in Eastern Europe, where brands like Prince and Blend were manufactured under licence. After they'd been obtained they were brought into Sweden either directly or via Estonia.

Annika sat silently for a moment and read the material that came up, then went over to Sjölander. He had stopped talking and was thrashing away at his computer keyboard with his index fingers.

'Are we going to establish that there's a Yugo connection in these homicides?' she wondered.

Sjölander sighed heavily. 'Well,' he said, 'that's a question of semantics. It is a gang-land killing, some kind of Mafia showdown.'

'Maybe we'd better not settle on any particular country for the time being,' Annika said. 'There are lots of criminal groups that have been in business here for years. How about a brief review of different gangs and their favourite criminal pursuits?'

Sjölander flexed his index fingers. 'All right.'

Annika went back to her desk and called her source. He picked up after one ring.

'Working late,' Annika pointed out.

'They let you out of the deep freeze?' the detective wondered.

'Nope,' Annika said. 'I'm still eating dirt. Have time for some quick questions?'

The man groaned.

'I've got these two boys,' he said, 'with their brains blown out.'

'Oh my,' Annika said. 'That sounds painful. Are you sure they're Yugoslav?'

'Go to hell,' 'Q' said.

'All right. Some general questions about different ethnic gangs. Tell me, what do . . . the South Americans do?'

'I don't have time for this.'

Annika adopted a meek approach: 'Just throw me a bone,' she wheedled.

The detective laughed. 'Cocaine,' he said. 'From Colombia. Last year, the volumes seized increased by more than one hundred per cent.'

'The Baltic States?' Annika asked, furiously taking notes.

'To a certain extent, cigarettes. A lot of stolen cars. We believe that Sweden is on its way to becoming a transit country for the stolen-car trade. Cars stolen in Italy and Spain are transported through Europe directly to Sweden and are then taken into the Baltic States and Russia on the ferries.'

'Okay, any more groups? You're more familiar with them.'

'The Turks have been into heroin, but in later years their operations have been taken over by the ethnic Albanian groups in Kosovo. The Russians launder money – so far they've invested half a billion in real estate in this country. The Yugoslavs excel at smuggling cigarettes and liquor. Some gambling and protection rackets too. At times they use restaurants as a front. Satisfied?'

'Keep going,' Annika replied.

'The biker gangs run the protection and muscle rackets. They're all Swedes or Scandinavians. The porn industry is also run by Swedes, but you know that already . . .'

'Ha, ha, ha,' Annika said dryly.

'Financial crime is mainly the province of Swedish men. They often work together in different constellations: corporate raiding, tax fraud, stuff like that. A lot of these guys use muscle. We've got a few Gambian rings that move heroin.'

'All right, that ought to fill a sidebar.'

'Always glad to lend a helping hand,' Q replied tartly and hung up.

Annika smiled. He was such a sweetheart.

'So, what's up?' asked Jansson, plastic coffee cup in hand.

'Work,' Annika replied. She finished the sidebar, added her byline and sent her article to the server.

'I'm going for a walk,' she said, but Jansson didn't react. Once again, a sense of futility made her chest constrict like a belt tightening a notch.

The woman coughed, a muffled and hollow sound. Her head was exploding with pain, the wound on her forehead throbbing. Shivering slightly, she figured that she was running a temperature, and suspected that she had a bacterial infection of the airways or lungs. She'd taken the first dose of broad-spectrum antibiotics around lunchtime. The glowing red digits on the clock told her that it was time for the next dose.

Shivering, she staggered out of bed, grabbed her first-aid kit and rummaged through the contents. The antibiotics were under the compresses and she also took an analgesic to bring down the fever. The pills were old, a remnant from her days in Sarajevo, and they'd expired years ago. There was nothing to be done about it, it wasn't like she had a choice.

She crawled back into bed – might as well try to sleep it off.

Only sleep evaded her. Her failure gnawed at her. Scenes were replayed in her mind, her imagination unleashed images, people dying, her temperature was going up. Then, finally, there he was, the little boy, his arms outstretched imploringly, always in slow motion, running, screaming, death in his eyes.

Upset and coughing, she got up and downed a half-litre of water. She had to shake this off before they found her. She didn't have time to be sick.

Then she tried to clear her head. Compared to what might have happened, a cold was nothing. The sea closing in over her head, icy and harsh, dark and painful. She had suppressed the waves of panic threatening to engulf her and had forced her body into action, swimming under the surface as far away from the dock as possible, coming up for air, plunging under the surface again. The waves had tossed her the last few metres towards the dock on the other side of the harbour, her shoulder banging against the concrete as she turned to see him looking out over the water, a black silhouette standing out against the ware-houses in the golden light.

She had pulled herself up on to a quay of the oil dock. Stretched out between two yellow bollards, she had passed out for a while, fear and adrenalin keeping numbness at bay. Finding shelter from the wind, she had checked the contents of her bag. After a few attempts, her cellphone had worked and she'd ordered a taxi to come and pick her up at the Loudden oil terminal. The stupid driver had thought she was too wet and didn't want to let her in the cab, but she'd persisted and he had dropped her off at this shabby hotel.

She closed her eyes and rubbed them.

The cab driver presented a problem. He would

definitely remember her, and probably would tell tales if he was offered enough money.

She really should leave. Pack her things and leave tonight.

Suddenly she felt a sense of urgency. She got up, slightly more steady on her feet now that the medication had started to kick in and bring down her temperature, and pulled on her rumpled clothes. The pockets of her coat were still a bit damp.

Just as she put the first-aid kit back in her bag, there was a knock on the door. Her heart leapt to the base of her throat, causing her to pant softly.

'Aida?' The voice was deep and silky, muffled through the door. A cat toying with a mouse.

'I know you're in there, Aida.'

She grabbed her bag and dashed into the bathroom, locked the door, perched on the rim of the bathtub and pushed the tiny window open. A chilly breeze blew in. She tossed the bag out through the window, then tore off her coat and pushed it through the opening. At that moment she registered the sound of breaking glass in the motel room.

'Aida!'

She gathered strength and hurtled herself out the window, stretching out her hands to break her fall and turning a somersault as she landed. The blows on the bathroom door ricocheted through the open window, the sound of splintering wood filling the air. She pulled on her coat, grabbed her bag and started to run towards the expressway.

Annika got off at the end of the 41 bus line. Exhaled and watched the bus disappear behind a low-rise administration building. Everything was quiet, no people were out and about. The day was fading, spent before it had emerged. She didn't miss it.

She slung her bag over her shoulder and took a few steps, studying her surroundings. A strange atmosphere prevailed around these buildings and warehouses. This was where Sweden ended. A sign indicated the location of Tallinn, Klaipeda, Riga, St Petersburg, the new economies, the young democracies.

Capitalism, Annika mused. *Personal accountability, free enterprise. Is that the answer?*

She turned her face into the wind, squinting. Everything was grey. The sea. The docks, the buildings, the cranes. Cold, lingering squalls. She closed her eyes, letting the wind whip her.

I have everything I ever wanted, she thought. *This is how I want to live my life. It was my decision. No one else is to blame.*

Annika looked directly into the wind, which caused

tears to well up in her eyes. The main office of the
Stockholm Harbour Authority was right in front of her, a
beautiful old brick building with nooks, terraces, and a
multilevel sheet-metal roof. Behind the building, a row of
gigantic grain silos pointed skywards like erect penises.
The Estonia ferry terminal was located on the left, then
came the waterfront. To the right, there was a dock with
cranes and warehouses on either side.

She turned up the collar of her jacket, tightened her
scarf and slowly headed for the office. A ferry destined for
Tallinn was in, looming behind the buildings. The Baltic
States' window to the west.

As she turned the corner of the office building, the area
cordoned off by the police came into view. The blue and
white tape fluttered in the breeze over by the silos, forlorn
there in the cold. No police officers were in sight. She
stopped and studied the tongue of land ahead of her. This
had to be the very heart of the harbour. The area was a
few hundred metres in length and it was bordered by
enormous warehouses on either side. At the far end,
beyond the cordoned-off zone, she could glimpse a
parking lot for trailers. The only people around, over by
the trailers were a few workers in bright yellow vests.

Slowly Annika approached the crime scene, glancing
up at the towering silos. Even though her feet were firmly
on the ground, their loftiness made her feel giddy. The
tips of the silos blended almost seamlessly into the sky,
grey on grey. She followed them with her gaze until she
felt the leathery crime scene tape brush against her thigh.

There was a narrow strip between the silos that
daylight couldn't reach. This was where life had drained
out of the victims. She blinked a few times to get used to
the darkness and could just make out the dark stains left
by their blood. The bodies had been found at the start of
the passage, not hidden in the shadows.

She turned her back on death and took a look around. Rows of huge floodlights were lined up along the docks. The entire harbour area would be bathed in light, apart from the spaces between the silos.

If you were going to shoot a person, why leave him in the floodlights? Why not drag him into the shadows? I guess that would depend on if you were in a hurry or not, she figured.

She lowered her gaze, stamped her feet and blew on her hands, splattering slush around her. What a God-awful winter. Beyond the cordoned-off area she noticed the warehouse where SVT, the Swedish public-service television network, stored their props and sets. *Is this where it is?* she thought.

Annika went past the crime scene. Icy Baltic winds made the drizzle frigid, leaving her shivering with cold. She looped her scarf one more time around her neck and continued down to the waterfront, following a chain link fence that constituted the border with the Baltic States. A truck that had seen better days stood spewing exhaust fumes on the other side, so she pulled her scarf up over her nose. The fence ended with a large gate right next to the parking lot for trailers. Three Customs officers were inspecting the next-to-last truck of the day, the last being the environmental hazard behind her.

'Can I help you?' The man, dressed in the uniform of a Customs officer under his yellow vest, was florid from the cold. His eyes had a bright and cheerful expression. Annika smiled.

'I was just curious. I work for a paper and I read about the murders back there,' she said, pointing over her shoulder.

'If you're planning on writing something, you'd better contact our press relations manager,' the man replied in a friendly voice.

'Oh no, I'm not a reporter, I just check the articles and

see that everything's right. That's why it's good to get out once in a while, so you'll know if the reporters are out of line.'

The Customs officer laughed. 'Well then, you've got your work cut out for you,' he said.

'So do you, I bet,' Annika countered.

They shook hands and introduced themselves.

'That about it for today?' Annika asked and pointed at the last vehicle as it puffed its way to the gate.

The man sighed lightly. 'It will be for me, at any rate,' he said. 'The past few days have been a headache, what with that crime scene and all. Not to mention the cigarettes.'

Annika raised an eyebrow. 'Anything particular happen today?'

'We caught a phoney refrigeration truck this morning. It was loaded with tobacco products; floorboards, ceiling, walls. They'd removed all the insulation and filled the space with cigarettes.'

'Wow,' Annika exclaimed. 'How did you figure that out?'

The Customs officer shrugged. 'By unscrewing a plate in the back of the vehicle and finding a thin layer of insulation. Beneath that layer there was another plate, and the cigarettes were behind that.'

'How many?'

'The floor of a trailer holds five hundred thousand, the ceiling another five hundred thousand, and the walls hold about as many more. We're looking at something like two million, and you can estimate one krona per smoke.'

'Oh man,' Annika said.

'It's nothing compared to what gets into the country. There's no end to the amounts smuggled. Gangs have quit dealing in drugs and have turned to tobacco products instead. Ever since the state raised the tax, cigarettes yield profits on a par with heroin, but it's nowhere near as risky. A drug bust worth millions will put you in jail 'til you rot, while cigarettes won't get you much prison time. They use layered covers, hinged floors, hollow steel beams . . .'

'Crafty little devils,' Annika said.

'You're dead right,' the Customs officer agreed.

Annika moved in. 'Any idea who the stiffs were?'

The man shook his head. 'Nope, never saw them before.'

Annika's eyes widened. 'You saw them?'

'Yes. They were lying out there when I got here. Shot in the head.'

'Gee, how awful!' Annika said.

The Customs officer pulled a face and revived his feet by stamping them. 'Well, it's almost time to close up shop. Any more questions?'

Annika looked around. 'One, could you tell me what's in these buildings?'

The customs officer pointed at them in turn. 'Warehouse eight,' he began. 'It's vacant at the moment. Number two over there is the Tallinn terminal and the Port Customs Authority. Every single carrier from Tallinn has to go over there and show their papers before they come to us.'

'What papers would those be?'

'Shipping documents – every crate and its contents have to be listed. Then they receive one of these, and show it to us over here.' The man showed her a bright green paper strip with stamps, signatures and the letters IN.

'And you check every single item?' Annika asked.

'Most of it, but we don't have time for everything.'

Annika flashed him an understanding smile. 'What makes you skip certain vehicles?'

The Customs officer sighed. 'When you open a trailer and there are crates and boxes wedged in from floor to ceiling, you sometimes just can't face it. If we're checking a load like that, we have to drive it to number seven over there, in the container section, unload the whole thing and pry the stuff out with a fork-lift. Some Customs officers are licensed fork-lift operators, but not all of us.'

'No, that makes sense,' Annika said.

'Then we have the sealed trucks, the ones that just drive through Sweden with sealed cargo compartments. No one is permitted to remove, add or exchange any portion of the shipment until the transport has reached its specific destination.'

'Are those the ones marked with the letters TIR?'

The man nodded. 'There are other types of seals too, but TIR is the most well-known variety.'

Annika pointed. 'What are all those trailers doing here?'

He turned and looked out over the parking lot. 'That's cargo destined for the Baltic States awaiting shipment, or stuff that's been cleared through Customs and will be shipped throughout Sweden.'

'Can you rent space here?'

'No, you just park your trailer. No one actually keeps track of what's out here. Or why. Or for how long. It could be anything.'

'Like the occasional smuggled carton of cigarettes?'

'That's highly probable.'

They smiled at each other.

'Thank you for taking the time,' Annika said.

They walked together over to the entrance of the free port. As soon as they reached the crime scene, the flood-lights went on, relentlessly blazing light throughout the area.

'It's a goddamn tragedy,' the Customs officer said.

'Young guys, barely in their twenties.'

'What did they look like?' Annika asked.

'They were clueless about winter clothing,' the Customs officer replied. 'Must have been damn cold: all they had on were fancy leather jackets and jeans. No hats or gloves. Sports shoes.'

'How were they lying?'

'Practically on top of each other – both of them had holes in their heads.' The Customs officer tapped the crown of his head.

Annika stopped walking. 'Didn't anyone hear anything? Don't guards patrol the area at night?'

'Every warehouse has watchdogs, except for number eight – that's empty. They bark like crazy if anyone tries to enter. There are far fewer break-ins and burglaries since they brought in the dogs, but they're not much good as eyewitnesses. I really don't know if anyone heard shots ring out. We were having hurricane-force gales, after all.'

They exchanged business cards and pleasantries. Annika walked quickly to the bus stop near the sign indicating Tallinn, Klaipeda, Riga and St Petersburg. She was so cold that her teeth were chattering. Loneliness engulfed her, heavy and wet. She stood there in the bus shelter, a grey shape fading into the grey background. It was too early to go to the office, too late to go home and the sense of emptiness was so vast it precluded thought.

When the 76 bus suddenly appeared behind the SVEX administration building, she acted on an impulse. Instead of taking the 41 bus back to Kungsholmen, she headed for the Old Town. Got off at Slottsbacken, near the palace, and weaved her way through the narrow streets towards Tyska Brinken. The rain had stopped, the wind had died down. Time stood still around these stone buildings: the sounds of traffic from Skeppsbron subsided and her footsteps were muffled on the icy cobblestones. Night fell quickly, colours shifting in the golden light of the cast-iron street lamps, reduced to spots in the limited pools of lamplight. Black cast iron. Red ochre. Gleaming hand-blown window-panes in tiny criss-crossed frames. Stockholm's Old Town was another world, another time, an echo from the past. And naturally Anne Snapphane had managed to get herself an attic flat near the German Church. It was only a sub-let, but still.

Anne was at home and in the process of making pasta. 'Get a bowl out, there's enough for you too,' she said after letting Annika in and locking the door behind her. 'To what do I owe this honour?'

'I was out and about – I've been to see the free port.' Annika sank down on a chair under the sloping ceiling of the tiny kitchen, inhaling the warmth and the steam from the potful of pasta. Her sense of futility faded as the void filled with the rise and fall of Anne Snapphane's chatter. Annika answered in monosyllables. They sat across from one another at the table, tossing their tagliatelle with butter, cheese and soy sauce. The cheese melted into stringy tentacles between the strips of pasta. Annika twirled her fork in the mixture and looked out the dormer window. Rooftops, chimneys and terraces created dark contours on the deep blue winter sky. Suddenly she realized how hungry she was, ate until she was breathless and drank a large beer glass full of Coke.

'Didn't someone get killed out in the free port this morning?' Anne said as she shovelled in the last of her food and filled the electric kettle.

'Two people, yesterday,' Annika replied and put her plate in the dishwasher.

'Great,' Anne exclaimed. 'When did they reinstate you as a reporter?' She poured water into the Bodum coffee maker.

'Don't jump to any conclusions. The deep-freeze

they've put me in is deeper than you'd know,' Annika said and went out to the living room with its timbered ceiling.

Anne Snapphane followed, carrying a tray with two mugs, the coffee maker and a bag of marshmallow candy bars.

'But they have let you start writing again, haven't they? For real?'

They sat down on the couch and Annika swallowed. 'No, they haven't. I just couldn't stand being at home, that's all. A double homicide is still a double homicide.'

Anne made a face, blew on her steaming beverage and took a slurp. 'I don't know how you manage,' she said. 'I'm so grateful for female relationships, fashion and eating disorders.'

Annika smiled. 'How's it going?'

'The programming supervisor sees *The Women's Sofa* as a raging success. Personally, I'm not quite as thrilled. The entire staff is working itself to death, everyone detests the show's host and the producer is having an affair with the project manager.'

'What kind of ratings do you have? A million viewers?'

Anne Snapphane gazed at Annika with mournful eyes. 'My dear,' she said. 'We're talking about the satellite universe here. Audience shares. Target group impact. Only boring public-service outfits still talk about ratings.'

'In that case, why do we always write about them?' Annika said before opening the bag of candy.

'How the hell should I know?' said Anne. 'I guess you guys don't know any better. And *The Women's Sofa* will never amount to much unless we get some real journalists on board.'

'So it's that bad, is it? Wasn't someone new supposed to join you?' Annika asked and stuffed her mouth full of candy.

Anne Snapphane groaned. 'Michelle Carlsson. Incompetent, brainless, but red-hot for the camera.'

Annika laughed. 'Isn't that the TV industry in a nutshell?'

'Hey,' Anne replied, 'watch it with the attitude. Tabloid journalists in glass houses shouldn't throw stones.'

Anne switched on her TV right in the middle of the theme song heralding a newscast on one of the public-service channels. '*Voilà*, the pretentious news hour!'

'Hush,' said Annika, 'let's see if they feature the free-port killings.'

The newscast opened with the aftermath of the hurricane that had hit the southern part of Sweden. The local news team down in Malmö had shot footage of twisted bus shelters, barn roofs that had been swept away and shattered shop windows. An old man in a Farmers' Union cap scratched his neck anxiously while he surveyed the remains of his greenhouse and, in the drawling dialect of the province of Skåne, uttered something that ought to have been subtitled to be comprehensible. Then viewers were transported inside a power company, where a hollow-eyed representative testified that every possible effort was being made after the blackout to get things up and running again by nightfall. This or that many households were still affected in Skåne, Blekinge and Småland.

Annika sighed silently. So incredibly boring.

The segment continued with an estimate of the damage, which came to millions upon millions. A woman in Denmark had been killed when her car was crushed by a falling tree.

'Denmark has forests?' Anne Snapphane remarked.

Annika gave her friend, who hailed from the far north of Sweden, a weary look. 'Haven't you ever ventured below the tree line?'

Next came the compulsory voice-over drone to feed-footage from Chechnya and Kosovo. Russian troops had blah, blah, blah and the UCK had yada, yada . . . The cameras panned over bombed-out buildings and truck-loads of grimy refugees.

'Looks like they couldn't care less about your homicide,' Anne Snapphane remarked.

'It's not mine,' Annika countered. 'It's Sjölander's.'

After a brief flash about something that the Prime Minister had said, there was a live segment about the free-port killings. The reporter went on as they aired footage showing the spot by the silos. They featured pretty much the same information as *Kvällspressen* had published twelve hours earlier.

'It's astonishing that TV reporters never go dig up anything,' Annika claimed. 'They've had all day at their disposal, and they haven't found a damn thing.'

'This stuff isn't high priority for them,' Anne countered.

'Television is stuck in the fifties,' Annika continued. 'They settle for moving pictures and sound. They don't give a damn about journalism, or maybe they just don't know how to do it. TV reporters suck.'

'Amen,' Anne concluded. 'God's gift to journalism has spoken. Christ, did you polish off all the candy? You could have saved some for me.'

'Sorry,' Annika replied sheepishly. 'I've got to go.'

She left Anne behind in her attic flat and headed down Stora Nygatan towards Norrmalm. The air didn't seem as piercing now, only fresh and crisp. Something inside came to life – she felt like singing. Waiting for the signal to cross the street by the House of the Nobility and the Supreme Court, she was humming away when a little man wheeled up alongside her to the left.

'I rode my bike all the way from Huddinge,' the man

said, and Annika jumped. He was utterly exhausted. His whole body was shaking and his nose was running copiously.

'Boy, that's quite a distance,' Annika replied. 'Don't your legs ache?'

'Not one bit,' the man said as tears started rolling down his cheeks. 'I could keep on going just as far.'

The lights turned green. When Annika started to cross the street, the man followed suit. He stumbled after her, leaning heavily on his bike. Annika waited for him. 'Where are you headed?' she asked.

'To the train,' he whispered. 'To get back home.'

She helped him across Tegelbacken over to the Central Station. He didn't have a bean, so Annika paid his ticket.

'Is there anyone to take care of you at home?' she asked.

The man shook his head, the mucus bobbing from his nose. 'I just got discharged from the hospital,' he said.

She left him on a bench at the station, his head bowed and the bicycle resting against his legs.

The picture was big, dominating the middle of the spread. The main colour was a shimmering golden yellow, the subjects were in crisp, sharp focus. The police officers in their heavy leather jackets, all black in profile; the incandescent whiteness of the ambulances; grave-looking men in grey-blue holding little tools; the rubble; the stairs; the gynaecologist's examination chair.

And the body bags: lifeless, diminished, black packages. So big they were in life, taking up all that space. So small they looked there on the ground, waste for ready disposal.

She coughed and shivered. During the course of the day, her temperature kept going up. The antibiotics didn't seem to be helping. The wound on her forehead hurt.

I've got to get some rest, she thought. *I've got to get some sleep.*

She let the newspaper dip and leaned back against the pillows. The sensation of falling that heralded sleep appeared immediately: the backwards motion, the rapid intake of breath, trying to clutch at the railing. And then, the boy, his terror and his screams, her own infinite inadequacy.

She forced her eyes open. On the other side of the wall, conference delegates were laughing. She had arrived at the hotel at the same time as the busload of delegates and had managed to disguise herself as part of the group. It had helped her temporarily, but now it wasn't enough. If her old medication didn't kick in during the night, she would have to get professional help. The thought terrified her: the exposure would make her an easy target. She drank some water, her arm stiff and heavy, and tried to concentrate on the article again.

A showdown in the underworld. The Yugoslav Mafia. No suspects, but several leads existed. She turned the page. A picture of a taxi driver.

Startled, she tried to focus on the page as she struggled to pull herself up among the pillows.

The taxi driver, the guy who didn't want to let her get into his nice cab. She recognized him. A reporter had talked to him. According to the article, he had picked up a woman at the oil dock that night. She had been soaked to the skin. The police would like to get in touch with her and see if she had any information.

See if she had any information.

She sank back against the pillows and closed her eyes, breathing rapidly.

What if there was a warrant out for her arrest? Then there would be no way she could go to a doctor.

She groaned, her breathing rough and erratic – the police were looking for her.

Don't panic, she thought. *Don't get hysterical. There might not be a warrant after all.*

Forcing herself to be calm, she consciously tried to slow down her pulse and breathing.

How was she going to find out if there was a warrant out or not? She couldn't very well call the police and ask, within fifteen minutes they'd be picking her up. She could call in and try to milk them, pretend to have information and see if she could trick them into telling what they knew.

Once more she groaned, picking up the paper to read the rest of the article. There wasn't much more, and there was nothing about any warrant.

Then she looked at the byline. The reporter. Occasionally, reporters embroidered the truth, speculated and made things up, but sometimes they knew more than they wrote.

She coughed violently. She couldn't go on like this, she needed help. She picked up the paper and read the name again: Sjölander.

Then she reached for the phone.

Annika had managed to get her jacket half off when Sjölander called out her name and waved the phone at her. 'Some dumb broad needs help. Can you take it?'

Annika closed her eyes. This was her turf. *Just go along with it, be game.*

The woman on the other end sounded ill and weak, and she spoke with a heavy accent.

'Help me,' she gasped.

Annika sat down, overcome by emptiness again, longing for a cup of coffee.

'He's out to get me,' the woman said. 'He's stalking me.'

Blotting out the newsroom by shutting her eyes, Annika leaned over her desk.

'I'm a Bosnian refugee,' the woman said. 'He's trying to kill me.'

Good Lord, was everything that went wrong in the whole damn world her responsibility?

The woman mumbled something. It sounded like she was passing out.

'Hey,' Annika said, opening her eyes. 'Are you all right?'

The woman started to cry. 'I'm sick,' she said. 'I don't dare go to the hospital. I'm so scared he'll find me. Could you please help me?'

Annika groaned silently and scanned the newsroom for someone she could transfer the call to. There was no one.

'Have you called the police?' she asked.

'If he finds me, I'm dead,' the woman whispered. 'He's tried to shoot me several times. I won't have the strength to escape next time.'

The woman's rough breathing echoed on the line. Annika felt a growing sense of futility.

'I can't help you,' she said. 'I'm a reporter, I write articles. Have you called Social Services? Or one of the women's shelters?'

'The free port,' the woman whispered. 'The dead men at the free port. I can tell you about them.'

Annika's reaction was physical. With a jerk, she sat up straight. 'How? What?'

'If you tell me what you know, I'll talk to you,' the woman replied.

Annika licked her lips and looked for Sjölander without finding him.

'You'll have to come here,' the woman gasped. 'Don't tell anyone who I am.'

Jansson was standing in front of Annika when she hung up.

'The free-port killings,' she explained.

'Why didn't Sjölander take the call?' Jansson asked.

'The call was made by a woman,' Annika replied.

'Oh,' Jansson said and answered his phone.

'I'm checking this out,' she said. 'It might take a while.'

Jansson waved her away.

Annika brought the *Yellow Pages* with her and, over at the front desk, Tore Brand's son handed her the keys to one of the paper's unmarked cars. She took the elevator down to the garage and located the car after a certain amount of confusion. Using the steering wheel to prop up the telephone book, she looked up the hotel. It was pretty far, and it was in another part of town she'd never been in before.

There wasn't much traffic and the road was slippery. She drove carefully, not wanting to die tonight.

'It will work out,' she figured. 'Things will work out.'

She looked up at the sky through the windshield.

Someone is watching me, she thought. *I can sense it*.

Thomas Samuelsson switched off the babbling newscast, got a heated debate instead, moved on and found a soap set in the southern states of the US, and ended up on MTV: 'Give it to me, baby, uh-huh . . .' He realized that he was staring at the girls' breasts, their golden stomachs and flowing manes.

'Honey . . .' Eleonor pulled the front door shut behind her and stamped off the slush.

'I'm downstairs,' he shouted in reply, quickly changing channels – more news.

'Christ, what a day,' his wife exclaimed after coming

downstairs, pulling her silk blouse free from the waist-band of her skirt, unbuttoning the pearl buttons at the wrists and ending up on the sofa next to him.

He pulled her close and kissed her on the ear. 'You work too hard,' he told her.

She unfastened the clip in her hair and shook it free.

'It's that leadership course,' she said. 'You knew I was going there tonight. I've told you that several times.'

He let got of her and reached for the remote control. 'Right,' he said.

'Any mail?'

She got up and headed back upstairs to the hall. He didn't reply. Heard her nylon-clad feet rub against the varnished wooden steps: squish, squish, squish. Heard the rustling of envelopes being torn open, the drawer where the bills were kept being opened and shut, followed by the door to the cupboard under the kitchen sink where they kept the recycling bin.

'Any calls?' she said.

He cleared his throat. 'No.'

'Not a single one?'

He sighed silently. 'Well, yes – my mother.'

'What did she want?'

'To talk about Christmas. I told her I'd talk to you and get back to her later.'

Eleonor came downstairs again – squish, squish, squish – holding a crispbread low-cal-cheese sandwich.

'We were at their house last year,' she said. 'It's my parents' turn.'

Thomas picked up the TV guide from the coffee table and leafed through the movie reviews.

'What about staying home this year?' he said. 'We could serve lunch here. Both sets of parents could come.'

She frantically chewed her sandwich, so rich in fibre. 'And who's supposed to take care of everything?'

'There's always catering,' he replied.

She stood next to the couch, looking down on him with high-fibre crumbs in the corners of her mouth. 'Catering?' she said. 'Your mother always makes her own pork brawn, my mother makes her special garlic sausage, and you talk about catering?'

He got up, suddenly irritated. 'So forget all about it,' he said as he walked past her without a glance.

'What's wrong with you?' she demanded, addressing his back. 'Nothing's ever good enough any more! What's wrong with our lives?'

Halfway up the stairs, Thomas stopped and looked at her. So beautiful. So tired. So distant.

'Of course we'll go to your parents' place,' he said.

Eleonor turned away, sat at the far end of the couch and switched channels.

His sight grew fuzzy and the hard lump in his chest got even harder.

'All right if I air out the room?' Annika asked and walked towards the window.

'No,' the woman hissed and sank back in the bed.

Annika stopped short, feeling stupid and insensitive, and drew the curtains again. The room was semi-dark, a grey and unhealthy atmosphere smelling of fever and phlegm. In one corner, she could detect a desk, a chair and a table lamp. She switched the lamp on, pulled the chair over to the bed and took her jacket off. The woman looked very ill. She needed to be taken care of.

'What's happened to you?' Annika asked.

Suddenly the woman began to laugh. She curled up into a foetal position and laughed so hard that she started to cry. Annika waited uncomfortably, keeping her hands folded in her lap, uncertain how to react.

Another one fresh from the hospital, she mused to herself.

Then the woman pulled herself together and, breathing heavily, looked at Annika. Her face gleaming with tears and sweat.

'I come from Bijelina,' she said quietly. 'Are you familiar with Bijelina?'

Annika shook her head.

'That's where the war in Bosnia began,' the woman said.

Annika waited for her to go on, expectantly. Only she didn't. The woman closed her eyes and her breathing grew heavier. She looked like she was slipping away.

Softly, Annika cleared her throat and regarded the sick woman in the bed uncertainly.

'Who are you?' she asked out loud.

The woman started. 'Aida,' she replied. 'My name is Aida Begovic.'

'What are you doing here?'

'Someone's out to get me.'

Once more her breathing was shallow and rapid – she seemed to be on the brink of consciousness. Annika's uneasiness increased.

'Isn't there someone who could take care of you?'

No reply. Sweet Jesus, maybe she should call for an ambulance?

Annika walked over to the bed and bent over the woman. 'Are you all right? Should I call someone? Where do you live, where do you come from?'

Her reply was breathless.

'Fredriksberg in Vaxholm. I can never go back there. He'll find me in no time.'

Annika went over to her bag, pulled out her pad and a pen and wrote down the words *Fredriksberg*, *Vaxholm* and *stalker*.

'Who will find you?'

'A man.'

'What man? Your husband?'

She didn't reply, only panted.

'What did you want to tell me about the free port?'

'I was there.'

Annika stared at the woman. 'What do you mean? Did you see the killings?'

Suddenly Annika recalled the article in the paper, the cab driver that Sjölander had found.

'That was you,' she exclaimed.

Aida Begovic from Bijelina struggled to prop herself up in bed, pushing the pillows against the headboard and leaning back.

'I ought to be dead too, only I got away.'

The woman's face was red and blotchy, her hair was stringy and sweaty. She sported a good-sized wound on her forehead and one cheek was bruised. She looked at Annika with eyes like deep pools, black and unfathomable. Annika sat down again, her mouth dry.

'What happened?'

'I ran and fell, tried to hide, there was a lot of junk on a long loading dock. Then I ran, he fired shots at me, I jumped into the water. It was so cold, that's why I'm sick.'

'Who shot at you?'

Hesitant, Aida Begovic closed her eyes.

'It might be dangerous for you to have that information,' she said. 'He's killed before.'

'How do you know that?' Annika asked.

Aida laughed wearily, touching her forehead. 'Let's just say I know him well.'

The same old story, Annika thought.

'Who were the dead men?'

Aida from Bijelina opened her eyes. 'They're not important,' she said.

Annika's uncertainty gave way to a rush of irritation.

'What do you mean, not important? Two young people shot in the head like that?'

The woman met her gaze. 'Do you have any idea how many people died in Bosnia during the war?'

'That's not the issue here,' Annika said. 'We're talking about the Stockholm Free Port.'

'Do you think that makes a difference?'

They stared at each other in silence. The woman's feverish eyes had seen too much. Annika was the first to avert her gaze.

'Maybe not,' she said. 'Why were they killed?'

'How much do you know?' Aida from Bijelina asked.

'Not much more than what's been in the papers. That the men were probably Serbs – they were wearing Serbian clothing. No ID, no fingerprints. Interpol has already contacted Belgrade. The police are looking for you.'

'Am I wanted?' The question shot out.

Annika studied her carefully. 'I don't know,' she said. 'I think so. Why don't you contact them and ask?'

The woman regarded her through her feverish haze. 'You don't understand,' she said. 'You are aware of my situation. I can't talk to the police, not at this time. What do you know about the killer?'

'Organized crime, according to the police.'

'And the motive?'

'Someone settling a score, just like it said in the papers. What exactly do you know?'

Aida from Bijelina closed her eyes and rested a while.

'Don't tell anyone you've talked to me.'

'No problem,' Annika said. 'You're a source, and by rights protected. The authorities aren't allowed to try and find out from me who you are – it's against Swedish law.'

'You don't get it, you might be in danger. You can't write about what I've told you – if you do, then they'll know that you know.'

Annika studied the woman, hesitated, didn't reply, didn't want to make any promises. Aida propped herself up against the pillows again.

'Have you been there? Have you seen the trucks out by the sea?'

Annika nodded.

'One of those trucks is missing,' said Aida from Bijelina. 'A truck loaded with cigarettes, not just hidden under the floor: the entire cargo, fifty million cigarettes, fifty million kronor.'

Annika gasped.

'More people will die. The man who owns that shipment isn't going to let the thieves get away.'

'Is that the guy who's after you?'

The woman nodded.

'What for?'

Aida closed her eyes. 'Because I know everything,' she said.

They sat in silence for a while, until they heard the knock on the door. Aida blanched. More knocking was heard. A silky voice spoke, deep and masculine, almost a whisper.

'Aida?'

'That's him,' the woman whispered. 'He'll shoot us both.' She looked like she was going to pass out at any minute.

Annika suddenly felt intensely dizzy. She got up and the room started spinning. She stumbled.

Another knock. 'Aida?'

'We're going to die,' the woman said in a resigned voice. Annika saw how she bowed her head in prayer.

No, Annika thought. *Not here, not now.*

'Come,' she whispered, pulling the woman out of bed and dragging her over to the bathroom. She tossed Aida's clothes in after her, took off her own top and held it to her chest as she walked over to open the door.

'Hello . . .?' she asked in a surprised voice.

The man on the other side was big and good-looking, dressed in black and holding one hand inside his jacket.

'Where's Aida?' he asked with a slight accent.

'Who?' Annika asked in puzzled tones, her mouth parched, her temples throbbing.

'Aida Begovic. I know she's in here.'

Annika swallowed, blinked up at the lamp overhead and pushed her sweater up under her chin. 'You must have the wrong room,' Annika said in a breathless voice. 'This is my room. And if you'll excuse me, I don't feel very well. I've already . . . turned in, you see.'

The man took a step forward, placing his left hand on the door in an attempt to push it open. Annika automatically put her foot against the other side of the door to block any movement. At that very moment, the door to the next room opened. Ten or so slightly tipsy delegates from the IT department of the telephone company Telia tumbled out into the hallway.

The big man in black hesitated. Annika forced air into her lungs and yelled: 'Go away! Beat it!' and desperately tried to shut the door.

A few of the delegates stopped and looked around.

'Go away!' Annika shouted. 'Help, he's trying to force his way in.'

Two of the men from Telia swaggered over to Annika. 'What's going on?' one of them asked.

'I'm sorry, honey,' the man said as he let go of the door. 'We'll talk later.'

He turned around and walked rapidly towards the lobby. Annika shut the door, her stomach churning with fear.

Oh my God, oh my God! Please let me live.

Her legs were quaking so much that she had to sit on the floor. Her hands were shaking and she felt like throwing up. The bathroom door opened.

'Is he gone?'

Annika nodded silently, Aida from Bijelina sobbed.

'You saved my life, how will I ever . . .?'

'We've got to get out of here,' Annika said. 'Both of us – and pretty darn quick, too.'

She got up, turned off the lamp on the table and started collecting up her belongings in the dark.

'Wait,' Aida said. 'It's better to wait until he's gone.'

'He'll be lying in wait for us,' Annika explained. 'Oh, damn it!'

She struggled to keep from crying. The woman staggered over to the bed and sank down.

'No,' she said. 'He thinks he's been had. He paid for information, and now he'll go and check if the source was tricking him.'

Annika took three deep breaths. *Calm down, calm down . . .*

'How did he know you were here?' she said. 'Did you tell anyone?'

'He found me yesterday too. He figured that I couldn't have got very far. He's had people out looking for me. Could you see if he's gone?'

Annika wiped her eyes and peered out from behind the curtain. In the parking lot below she could see the big guy, accompanied by two other men. They all got into the car next to hers and drove off.

'They're gone,' Annika said, letting go of the curtain. 'Let's get moving.'

She switched the table lamp back on, pulled on her jacket, shoved her pen in her bag, and picked up the pad from the floor, her back drenched in sweat, her hands cold.

'No,' Aida from Bijelina said. 'I'm staying here. He won't be back.'

Annika straightened herself up, her face growing hot.

'How can you be so sure? That guy is dangerous! I'll drive you to the airport or the train station.'

The woman closed her eyes. 'You've seen him,' she said. 'You know that he's looking for Aida Begovic. There's no way he'll kill me here, not tonight. He doesn't make a move if he might get caught. He'll get me tomorrow, or the day after.'

Annika collapsed on the chair again and rested the pad on her lap, the same pad she'd brought along to another hotel in another part of town.

'Don't you have anywhere safe to go?' she asked. Aida shook her head.

'Isn't there anyone out there who can take care of you?'

'I dare not go to a hospital.'

Annika swallowed hesitantly. 'There might be a way out,' she said. 'There might be someone who could help you.'

The Bosnian woman didn't respond.

Annika thumbed through her pad, not finding what she was looking for.

'There's this foundation that helps people like you,' Annika told Aida and started rummaging through her bag. There – the business card was at the bottom. 'Call this number tonight.'

She jotted down the unlisted number for Paradise on a scrap of paper and put it on the night-stand.

'What is this place?' Aida asked.

Annika sat down next to the ill woman, pushing back her hair and trying to appear calm and collected.

'I'm not exactly sure how it works, but it's possible that these people can help you out. They make people disappear from the system.'

The woman's eyes gleamed with disbelief. 'What do you mean, "disappear"?'

Annika tried to smile. 'Call them tonight, ask for Rebecka and tell her I sent you.' She got up.

'Wait,' Aida said. 'I want to thank you.'

With great effort she pulled out a large bag from under the bed. It was rectangular, had a handle and a shoulder strap and was equipped with a sizeable metal lock that required a key.

'I would like you to have this,' said Aida from Bijelina as she handed a chunky gold necklace with two charms on it to Annika. It was as heavy as a chain.

Annika backed away, all sweaty in her jacket, wanting to leave. 'I can't accept a gift like this,' she said.

Aida smiled for the first time, sadly.

'We'll never see each other again,' she told Annika. 'I'll feel hurt if you don't accept my gift.'

Annika gingerly took the compact heavy necklace.

'Thank you,' she said as she dropped it in her bag. 'Good luck.'

She turned around, escaping from the sick woman, leaving her sitting on the bed clasping the big bag in her arms.

The parking lot was empty. Annika hurried across the asphalt, her heels clicking, sounding too hesitant and uncertain. Glanced over her shoulder – no one had seen her get into the newspaper's car. She pulled out on the expressway, checked the rear-view mirror, took the first turn-off, parked behind a filling station, waited, looked around, then slowly headed back towards downtown Stockholm, driving in circles.

No one was following her.

As soon as Annika had parked in the garage she sat there for several minutes, leaning against the wheel, forcing her breathing back to normal.

She hadn't been so damned scared in ages.

It had been more than two years ago.

The big man dressed in black deftly broke open the door in the corridor of the conference hotel on the edge of town. He could tell by the way the room smelled that he'd come to the right place. It reeked of shit and fear. The darkness was interrupted by a street light that left wedges of whiteness on the ceiling. He shut the door behind him. It closed with a faint click. Walked into the room, aiming for the bed. Switched on the light.

Empty.

The bedclothes were in disarray and a roll of toilet paper was on the night-stand, but apart from that the room was in standard order.

Rage swept through him like a wave, making him feel weak. He sank down on the bed, placing his hand on a pile of soiled tissues. A small box was on the floor next to his foot. He picked it up and read the instructions.

An empty package of antibiotics with instructions in Serbo-Croat.

It must have been her, she must have been here.

He got up and gave the headboard three hard kicks before it fell apart.

You whore. I'm going to find you.

He went through the entire room, centimetre by centimetre, drawer by drawer; checking wastebaskets and closets, pulling out the desk and the mattresses.

Nothing.

Then he pulled out a knife and began to systematically slice up the bedclothes, the duvet, the pillows, the box spring, the cushion on the chair, and the shower curtain, nearly exploding from the pressure inside him.

He sat down on the bathtub, leaning his forehead against the cold blade of his knife.

She had been here – his source was reliable. Where the hell had she gone? Pretty soon he would be the butt of jokes, the guy who couldn't catch the cunt. He should have forced his way in, but no such luck, those damn guests in the hallway, that Swedish whore.

He sat up.

The Swedish woman – who the hell was she? He'd never seen her before. She didn't have an accent and she must have known Aida. How? And what was she doing there? In what way was she involved?

Suddenly the cellphone in his pocket starting ringing. The man yanked his jacket open and whipped out the phone, caressing his weapon in the process. Molim?

Good news, finally some good news.

He left the room, slipped out of the hotel, seen by no one.

Annika Bengtzon walked in without knocking first, and sank down on Schyman's old couch without noticing the stench.

'I've got a tip that I want to discuss with you as soon as possible,' she said. 'Do you have time right now?'

She looked tired, almost ill.

'It doesn't look like I have much choice, does it?' Anders Schyman said irritably.

She took a deep breath and exhaled slowly.

'I'm sorry, I'm kind of hyper. I was just out on a damned unpleasant—'

She struggled out of her coat.

'Last night I met a woman named Rebecka. She runs a new outfit, a foundation called Paradise. They help people whose lives are threatened to find a new life, mainly women and children. It sounds damn exciting.'

'What do you mean, help?'

'They remove every trace of a person from all public

records. She wouldn't go into detail until I get the go-ahead for the article.'

Schyman studied her. She was nervous.

'We can't guarantee publication until we know what's going on, you know that,' he said. 'An operation like that needs to be investigated in depth before we go public. That Rebecka person could be anyone: a conwoman, an extortionist, a killer – you don't know.'

She looked at him for a long while.

'Do you think I should find out? I mean, do you think I . . .?'

She stopped talking, swallowed. He realized what she wanted.

'See her again and tell her we're interested. But I don't want this business to take time and energy from your work on the night shift.'

Annika got up from the couch and sat down on one of the chairs over by Schyman's desk instead.

'You've got to get rid of this God-awful couch,' she told him. 'Why don't you have someone chuck it out for you?'

She put her pad on his desk. He hesitated momentarily, then decided to be frank. 'I know what you want. You want me to take you off the night shift and reinstate you as a reporter.'

He leaned back in his chair, finishing his train of thought: 'It's not possible right now.'

'Why not?' she shot back. 'I've been assigned to night duty for one year and three hundred and sixty-three days now. I've been a permanent member of the staff ever since the court ruling. In my opinion, I've done my bit. I want to write. For real.'

Fatigue overcame Schyman. '*I want this. I'm going to do that. Why don't I get to . . .?*' Spoiled brats, that's what they were, all two hundred-plus of them always wanting to have things their way, acting like their articles or assignments or salary issues were the only important matters on Earth. He couldn't reassign her now, not with the reorganization coming up.

'Listen to me,' he said. 'Now is not a good time. Trust me.'

Annika studied him closely for a few seconds, then nodded.

'I understand,' she said and left, scooping up her bag and coat untidily in her arms.

Anders Schyman sighed when the door closed behind her.

The freshly waxed floor shimmered, computer screens flickered in the dim room. Ice-blue faces focused exclusively on virtual reality, keyboards hummed, clickety-clack, clickety-clack. Cursors darted across the screens, one computer mouse after the other gnawed away at the words that appeared: rewriting, deleting. Jansson on the phone, smoking and hammering away at the keys, disregarding the designated smoking area. Annika dropped her things on the floor next to the night desk and went to the restroom, running hot water over her wrists, feeling chilled to the bone.

She closed her eyes and saw the man in front of her, the handsome man in black with one hand inside his jacket pocket. The killer. She couldn't recall what she had said, or what he had said, only her own awkward confusion and paralysing fear.

Why me? She thought. *Why does stuff like this always happen to me?* She dried her hands, looking at her miserable face in the mirror.

Grandma, she thought. *I'll go and see Gran tomorrow and be able to sleep, rest, live.*

A slight sensation of relief emerged, her pulse returned

to her body, her hands. The tightness in her chest uncoiled a bit.

Paradise, she thought, *maybe I should try to get moving on the Paradise Foundation story after all. I might not spend the entire weekend at Lyckebo, I might get in some writing too.*

Annika smiled to herself; that tip about the foundation might be a turning point. She would be thorough, she would really work on it. Schyman would . . .

Suddenly she went cold, her chest constricting sharply again.

Schyman! What if he was right? What if Rebecka was bogus, a fake, a crook? She raised a hand to her mouth and gasped. Good grief, Aida from Bijelina – she had already sent someone to Paradise!

The chill had her in its grip again, it spread throughout her entire body.

Oh God, how could she have done such a stupid thing? Recommend something she didn't know a thing about?

She entered a stall and sat down on a toilet, dizzy and weak. *I mean, how stupid can a person get?*

She took a breath, trying to pull herself together.

What have I done? What choice did Aida Begovic have? If I hadn't been there, Aida would have been dead.

Annika got up, went over to a washbasin and drank water straight from the tap, registering her blazing face in the mirror.

On the other hand, how could she be so sure? Aida might be a liar too, a maniac. Maybe she liked to ride a bike from Huddinge to downtown Stockholm until she collapsed, and not have money for the fare home? The handsome man in black might have been a brother wanting to bring her back home.

Annika closed her eyes, the back of her head against the tiled wall, and took a few deep breaths.

No one would ever know. No one would ever find out what she had done. Aida was right. They would never meet again.

If Paradise was on the level, she would disappear for good.

If it wasn't, she would die.

There was a way to verify that Aida knew what she was talking about.

Annika went over to her desk and dialled Q's number.

'This is not a good time for me,' her source at the police said.

'Have you found that truck?' she asked quickly.

A lengthy and stunned silence followed.

'I know you're looking for one,' she added.

'How the hell did you know about the truck?' he asked. 'We just found out that it was missing – we haven't even put out an alert yet.'

She exhaled in relief. Aida hadn't lied.

'I have my sources,' she replied.

'You get scarier every day,' said Q. 'What are you, psychic?'

She couldn't help laughing, a bit too loud.

'I'm serious,' said Q. 'This isn't a game. You'd better be careful about who you discuss this with.'

Annika's laughter got caught in her throat.

'What do you mean?'

'Everyone who knows about the missing truck is in major trouble, including your source.'

She closed her eyes and swallowed.

'I know.'

'Know what?'

'What do the police know?'

He sighed quietly.

'This is far from over,' he said.

'More murders are on the way,' Annika added quietly.

'We're trying to stop them, but they're way ahead of us,' Q said.

'What can I write?'

'The stuff about the truck or rather the trailer is all right. You can write that we know it's missing and that it contains a shipment of cigarettes, value unknown.'

'Fifty million,' Annika said.

She could hear him breathing on the other end.

'You know more than I do, but I'll take your word for it.'

'Who were the men?' she asked.

'We still don't know.'

'My source says they weren't important. What do you think she meant?'

Silence.

'So your source is a woman? You *do* know we're looking for her, don't you? She might have been intended to be the third victim – we found blood on the dock next to the site.'

Silence.

'Bengtzon, watch your back.'

Then he hung up.

Annika held the receiver, the dead line buzzing for a few seconds. She was filled with an abstract sense of discomfort.

'What was that all about?' Jansson asked.

'Just checking a lead,' she said as she headed over to the crime desk.

Sjölander was cooing into the phone and looked up in irritation. She perched on the edge of his desk, just like he usually did on hers.

'Those murders down at the free port. More instalments will follow. A truckload of contraband cigarettes are missing and the police are waiting for the next homicide.'

The head of the crime desk nodded appreciatively.

'Good stuff,' he said. 'Want to write it yourself?'

'Preferably not,' she said. 'But it's on the level, I've got two sources. One of which is the police.'

'E-mail me what you've got,' he said.

'How about a more detailed background piece about cigarette rings?'

By that time, he'd picked up the phone again, so he gave her a thumbs up.

TUESDAY 30 OCTOBER

Annika was wide awake and stared up at the ceiling, so cracked and grey. The daylight making its way through the white curtain told her that it was lunchtime and that the weather was lousy. Strangely enough she felt rested and it didn't hurt anywhere.

She rolled over on her side, her gaze stopping at the card she had put on the night-stand. Rebecka's number. The decision came from out of nowhere; she simply sat up in bed and dialled the number on an impulse, out of curiosity.

It rang. Regular tones – nothing sounded unlisted or unusual. Tense, she waited.

'Paradise.' The voice was that of an older woman.

'Umm, my name is Annika Bengtzon, and I'd like to speak to Rebecka.'

'Hang on . . .'

The telephone crackled with the ordinary sounds of silence: heels tapping along the floor, approaching, a toilet flushing. She listened attentively. So far the sounds at the Paradise Foundation appeared fully normal.

'Annika, how nice to hear from you.'

The high voice, a bit drawling and slightly cool.

Annika felt the old familiar surge of excitement; she'd almost forgotten its pull.

'I'd like to see you again,' she said. 'When would be good for you?'

'This week's a bit tricky, we've got several new clients on the way in. Next week looks pretty busy too.'

Her heart sank. *Shit . . .*

'Why did you call us if you don't have time to talk?' Annika challenged her.

More silence, crackling.

'I'd be happy to see you again when I have the time,' Rebecka said in an airy voice, cool, neutral.

'And when would that be?'

'I have a meeting in Stockholm at two p.m. We could meet right before that. It's the only time slot I can offer.'

Annika looked at her alarm clock.

'Right now? Today?'

'If that's all right with you.'

Annika lay down again, keeping the receiver to her ear.

'Sure,' she said.

After they hung up, Annika remained in bed for a while, calm. For a brief spell light filled the room again, shimmering. Then she tossed the covers aside, pulled on her jogging pants and her sweatshirt and ran down to the shower in the building across the courtyard, clutching some soap and shampoo. The water was warm and caressing; she washed her hair and dried herself languidly. The light had returned.

She dashed up the stairs, made some coffee and had some yogurt, then brushed her teeth by the kitchen sink. Wiped up some water she had splashed on the floor.

There was a cold draught from the broken living-room

windows. She swept up the shattered glass and the plaster, and found a paper bag from that crappy store ICA that she taped over the hole in the pane.

Soon, soon I'll know how Paradise works.

Soon I'll be with Gran over at Lyckebo.

Rebecka was dressed in the same clothes as last time: linen, or some cotton blend. Her hair scraped back, blonde, a slightly taut mouth.

Evita Perón helping the poor and the weak, Annika thought. *Don't cry for me, Argentina.*

'I'm in a bit of a hurry,' the woman said, 'so could we wrap this up quickly?'

She was fond of hotel lounges, Annika noted as Rebecka flagged down the waiter and ordered a bottle of mineral water for each for them.

'We got as far as the removal process last time,' Annika said, leaning back, her hair still wet and smelling of Wella. 'You make people disappear. How does it work?'

Rebecka sighed and picked up a napkin. 'I'm sorry,' she said as she wiped her hands, 'but we're fairly busy right now. We just got a case that's rather complicated.'

Annika looked at her pad and tried out her pen. *Could that be Aida from Bijelina?* she wondered to herself.

The waiter brought her water over. His apron was clean. Rebecka waited for him to leave, just like last time.

'You have to remember that these people are extremely frightened,' she said. 'Some of them are almost paralysed by fear. They can't go shopping or go to the post office, they aren't able to function like ordinary people.'

She shook her head over her poor clients.

'It's awful. We have to help them with everything – practical details like childcare, a new place to live, work, schools. And, of course, psychiatric care and welfare issues: many of them are in poor shape.'

Annika nodded and wrote notes – this was something she could relate to – and thought about Aida again.

'So what do you do?' she asked.

Rebecka wiped a spot off her glass and took a sip of water.

'Clients have around-the-clock access to their contacts. It's vital that someone is always there for them when things are rough.'

Get to the point, Annika thought.

'Where do these people live? Do you have a large house?'

'Paradise has access to a number of properties all over Sweden. We either own them outright or lease them through a figurehead that makes it impossible to trace us. Our clients stay there temporarily. At this point, any necessary treatment takes place without the physician knowing the patient's identity. No records are kept. Instead of the regular state patient ID card, they receive a card with a reference number. Paradise notifies the hospital or the clinic about which city council will be responsible for billing. Generally clients don't apply for help in the community that is footing the bill . . .'

Annika took notes. This sounded pretty good.

'How long are you able to keep . . . a client with you?'

'As long as necessary,' Rebecka replied, with determination in her breathless voice. 'There is no maximum time limit.'

'How about a normal case?'

The woman dabbed at the corner of her mouth.

'If things go according to plan, we're done in three months.'

'And when you've arranged for a new place to live and medical treatment, anything else?'

Rebecka smiled.

'Of course. There are lots of other things that need to be

taken care of when a person moves on to a new life. Salary payments and child benefits, for example. Our banking procedures work along the same lines as for housing. We have a few select partners. The client doesn't have to have an account in the community where she lives. Every time pay day rolls around, or bills need to be paid, the banks contact Paradise, and we arrange the transactions using a reference number. The same procedure applies for contacts with day care, schools, pediatric care, health insurance, the internal revenue service – the works. Many clients require legal aid, and we arrange that as well.'

Annika took notes.

'So you help them arrange new jobs, new places to live, new day-care centres, schools, doctors and lawyers within the framework of Paradise?'

Rebecka nodded.

'The victimized person disappears behind a wall. Anyone looking for someone whose record has been wiped clean will find us, and that's it.'

'What do these people live on during the removal process? They can't very well work, can they?'

'No, of course they can't,' Rebecka said. 'Several are ill and receive compensation, some are on welfare, quite a few have children and are eligible for child benefits and maintenance advances. Legal aid is often available in the case of court proceedings such as custody hearings.'

Annika mulled this over.

'But,' she said, 'what if the stalker doesn't give up, what do you do then? Can you help your clients get new social security numbers, the personal ID numbers we use here in Sweden, too?'

'We have completed sixty successful removal procedures. Not a single client has had to change her identity. It hasn't been necessary.'

Annika finished writing and relaxed her grip on her

pen. This sounded really incredible. She looked up and glanced around the bar. Round tables, brass fixtures. Thick wall-to-wall carpeting, subdued make-out lighting.

Where were the holes in the story?

Annika shook her head.

'How can you be certain that everyone who comes to you is telling the truth? They might be criminals trying to evade justice.'

Rebecka shushed her as the waiter drifted past them.

'May I have a new glass? This one was dirty. Thank you. I understand why you would ask such a thing, but Paradise doesn't accept people off the streets. We only accept referrals by the authorities. Our clients are sent by the police, the DA's office, the Foreign Office, embassies, agencies working with immigrants and schools.'

Annika scratched her head. *Okay.*

'But if you're such a secret, how do you get your clients?'

The woman received her fresh glass. The ice cubes rattled.

'So far our clients have come to us by way of contacts and recommendations. They've come from all over the country. Like I said, the reason we contacted you was that we felt ready to expand our operations.'

Her words hung in the air, Annika let them reverberate a few seconds.

'Exactly how much do you charge for your services?' she asked.

Rebecka smiled.

'Nothing. We charge the local social welfare authorities for our time and the costs we incur while we cover our tracks. We do not profit financially. We get reimbursed for our expenses, that's all. Even though we are a non-profit foundation we need to be paid for our efforts.'

That's right, she said that last time.

'How much are we talking about, in terms of money?'

The porcelain figurine bent over and pulled something out of her bag.

'Here are some leaflets about our organization. They are rather informal, not particularly elegant, but the authorities we've been in contact with have all known about us in one way or another, and they're aware of our qualifications.'

Annika took the leaflet. A post-office box number in Järfälla was listed at the top. Then there was a list of the services that Rebecka had just detailed. At the bottom Annika read: *For cost estimates, please contact us at the address and number listed in the heading.*

'How much do you charge?' Annika asked again.

Rebecka looked for something in her purse.

'3,500 kronor a day per person. That's a fairly modest rate for treatment. Here, have a look at this too,' she said as she handed over another leaflet.

It contained more or less the same information, only in more detail.

'Well,' Rebecka said, 'what do you think, is it worth writing about?'

Annika put the papers in her bag.

'I can't tell you that right now. First I have to talk to my superiors and find out if our paper wants to cover this story. Then I have to check the information you gave me with some of the authorities you've been in contact with. Could you possibly give me a name now?'

Rebecka thought for a minute while folding her napkin.

'I guess,' she said. 'I could probably do that. But you have to realize that these cases are extremely delicate, everything is kept confidential. No one will talk about us unless I tell them it's all right. That's why I'd like to get back to you with a list.'

'Sure,' Annika said. 'Once that's done, I'd like to talk to a client who's gone through your removal process.'

That smile again, the cool one.

'That might be more difficult. You won't be able to find them.'

'Maybe you could ask them to call me?'

The dainty woman nodded.

'Of course, that would be a possibility. But they know nothing about our procedures. We don't tell them anything, just so they won't be able to give themselves away.'

'I wasn't going to ask your clients about your methods. I want to meet a woman who will say: "Paradise saved my life."'

For the first time, Rebecka smiled so that Anika could see her teeth. They were small and pearly white.

'That I can do,' she said. 'There are lots of them around. Anything else?'

Annika hesitated.

'Only one thing,' she said. 'Exactly why do you do this?'

Rebecka quickly folded her arms across her chest and crossed her legs: classic defensive body language.

'I can't tell you that.'

'Why not?' Annika asked calmly. 'Your organization is very unusual, to say the least. Something must have inspired you.'

They sat in silence for a while, Rebecka's foot swinging rhythmically back and forth.

'I don't want you to put this in,' she said. 'This is private, just between you and me.'

Annika nodded.

The woman leaned forward, wide-eyed.

'Like I said,' she whispered, 'I've been threatened too.

It was a terrifying experience, terrifying! In the end I wasn't able to function, I couldn't eat or sleep.'

Rebecka looked over her shoulder, glancing at the other guests at the bar, then leaned closer.

'I made up my mind that I would survive. That's how I began to set up this method of protection. While I was working on it, I encountered lots of people in similar circumstances. I decided to do something, to shoulder the responsibility that the authorities couldn't deal with.'

'Who threatened you?' Annika asked.

Rebecka swallowed, her lower lip quivering.

'The Yugoslav Mafia,' she said. 'Have you heard of them?'

Annika blinked in surprise.

'How are you involved with them?'

'I'm not!' Rebecka shot back. 'The whole thing was a misunderstanding. It was awful, just awful!'

Suddenly she got up.

'Excuse me,' she said and ran off to the restroom. A small heap of twisted and crumpled paper napkins remained on the table.

Annika looked after her for a long time. What the heck was going on? Had she run into more cigarette thieves?

She sighed, drank her tepid water and read through her notes. Despite the considerable amounts of information there were holes in the story, she just couldn't pinpoint them yet. And what did the Yugo Mafia have to do with it all?

The porcelain figurine was taking her time. Feeling impatient, Annika checked her watch and saw that it was almost time to take the train to Flen. She paid the bill and had put her jacket on by the time Rebecka returned, looking clear-eyed and unperturbed.

'I'm sorry,' the woman said and smiled. 'The memories are so painful.'

Annika studied her; she might as well ask her question and be done with it.

'Do you have anything to do with the missing cigarettes?' she asked in a strained voice.

Rebecka smiled and blinked with a blank expression in her eyes.

'Have you lost your own cigarettes? I don't smoke.'

Annika sighed. 'I won't be able to write a thing until I have that list of authorities,' she said. 'It's important that I get it as soon as possible.'

'Of course,' Rebecka said. 'You'll be hearing from me shortly. If you don't mind, I'd like to leave first so no one sees us together. Could you wait a few minutes?'

Mission Impossible, Annika thought. *The subject has left the building*.

'Sure,' she said.

The rhythmic thumping of the train plunged Annika into a state of calm concentration before she had got as far as Årstabron. Tanto slipped past on the left, large houses with picture windows facing the waterfront. Soon the view was nothing but greenery: Stockholm wasn't all that big, after all. The blur of pines filled her vision, dark and wintergreen, swaying in time with the train; clickity-clack, clickity-clack.

Wiping all traces of someone off the record, she thought. Could that really be possible? An organization as proxy on all documents, one that maintains contacts with the authorities and signs contracts. *Is that actually legal?*

She took out her pad and pen and started making outlines.

If city councils actually buy the services of Paradise, everything must be above board, she figured.

Then there was the money; how much did the removal process cost?

She leafed through her notes.

Three thousand, five hundred kronor a day per person. The amount might be reasonable, she really couldn't tell.

Methodically, Annika outlined possible costs:

Five people working on a full-time basis: say they earned fifteen thousand kronor a month, plus social security expenses, which would amount to one hundred thousand kronor a month in total. And then there was the housing: say they had ten houses that each cost ten thousand a month in rent or interest – that would cost another hundred thousand. What else? Medical care was provided by the county councils. The city councils provided welfare payments, the state health insurance paid sick benefits, and legal aid footed the bill for lawyers.

Expenditure should come to about two hundred thousand a month.

What about revenue?

Three thousand, five hundred a day would amount to a monthly total of one hundred and five thousand kronor per person.

If they help a woman and a child each month, they make a profit of ten thousand kronor, she realized.

Disconcerted, she stared at her calculations.

Could that really be true?

She went through the numbers again.

Sixty cases at three thousand, five hundred kronor a pop per day for three months per case would come to nearly nineteen million.

For the past three years their expenditure had been somewhat more than seven million, which would mean a profit of almost twelve million.

Something must be wrong, Annika thought. *I've based my calculations on estimates and assumptions. They might have more expenses, ones that I don't know anything about. Maybe they have doctors and psychologists and lawyers on retainer,*

and lots of contacts standing by around the clock all year long.
That would certainly be expensive.

She packed her stuff back down in her bag, leaned back against the seat and let herself be rocked to sleep. Clickety-clack, clickety-clack.

The sounds were always the same, Anders Schyman thought. Chairs scraping, a talk show droning away on the radio, CNN on the TV with the volume turned down low, papers rustling, a cacophony of male voices rising and falling, short emphatic sentences. Laughter, always laughter, in hard, rapid bursts.

The smells: the ever-prevalent aroma of coffee, a whiff of sweaty feet, aftershave. A lingering trace of tobacco on someone's breath. Testosterone.

The management group met every Tuesday and Friday afternoon to run through larger projects and long-term strategies. The members were all male and over forty, they all drove company cars and wore identical dark blue flannel sports coats. He knew that they were referred to as 'the Flannel Pack'.

They always met in a fancy corner office belonging to Torstensson, the editor-in-chief, which overlooked the Russian embassy. They always had Danishes and macaroons. Jansson would be the last one to arrive, as usual. He always spilled coffee on the carpet, never apologizing and never cleaning up the mess. Schyman sighed.

'Well, perhaps we should . . .' the editor-in-chief said, not knowing where to look. No one took any notice of him. Jansson strolled in, sleepy-eyed, his hair on end and with a cigarette dangling from the corner of his mouth.

'No smoking,' the editor-in-chief said.

Jansson spilled coffee on the carpet, took a deep drag on his cigarette and sat down at the far end of the table.

Sjölander, the crime-desk editor, was talking on his cell-phone in the seat next to him. Ingvar Johansson was leafing through a sheaf of telegrams, Picture Pelle the photographer was laughing at something the entertainment-desk editor had said.

'Okay,' Schyman said. 'Sit down, so we can get this over with soon.'

The noise died down. Someone turned off the radio and Sjölander wound up his call. Jansson took a macaroon. Schyman remained on his feet.

'In retrospect we see that covering the hurricane was the right decision,' he continued while those men still standing took a seat. He held up Saturday's paper in one hand while leafing through their competitors' papers with the other.

'We were number one from the onset right up to the conclusion, and we deserve it. We displayed foresight and coordinated our resources in a new way. All the different desks and teams pulled together, giving us the heft that no one else could match.'

Schyman put the papers down. No one said a word. This was more controversial than it appeared. All these men ruled their own particular turf. Not one of them wanted to relinquish power and influence to anyone. That was why, in extreme situations, editors might hold back news in order to break a story with their own team or in their own edition. If they pulled together the power would be transferred further up in the hierarchy, to the level of deputy editors that the editor-in-chief hoped to create.

Schyman sorted through the papers and sat down.

'Our coverage of the handicapped boy seems to be yielding results as well. Apparently the city council intends to reassess its decision and provide the care he's entitled to.'

The silence was massive. Only the faints sounds of CNN and the ventilation system could be heard. Anders Schyman knew that the others disliked going through old issues of the paper, yesterday's news. They lived by the credo *Today is a fresh start, you have to move forward to get ahead*. The deputy editor didn't agree. He felt that you had to learn from yesterday's mistakes in order to avoid making new ones tomorrow, a self-evident bit of reasoning that never seemed to register.

'How are the preparations for the Social Democrat Congress coming along?' Schyman asked, turning to the editor of political and community affairs.

'We're raring to go,' said the guy in the flannel coat as he leaned forward with some papers clutched in his hand. 'Carl Wennergren got a damn hot tip about one of our female politicians. It seems that she went shopping using her government-issue credit card and bought diapers and chocolate.'

The men chuckled; the ladies were no good at managing money, that was for sure. Diapers. And chocolate!

Schyman looked expressionlessly at the other man.

'Really,' he said. 'So what's the scoop?'

The laughter died down. Mr Flannel Jacket smiled uncomprehendingly.

'In a private capacity,' he said. 'She bought personal stuff with the government card.' The rest of the group nodded in agreement. Now that *was* a scoop.

'All right,' Schyman said. 'We'll pursue it. Where did the tip come from?'

The room filled with agitated murmuring – you didn't discuss things like that. Schyman sighed.

'For the love of God,' he said. 'It's pretty obvious that someone's trying to set her up. Check out who it is. That might be the real scoop, the power struggle within the

Social Democrat camp. What they are prepared to do to hurt each other before the congress gets started. Anything else? What about members of the Riksdag?'

They continued to go through the assignments that were under way: politics, entertainment, foreign and domestic news. The manager of the editorial staff took notes and made comments, different policies were established, guidelines were drawn up.

'What about the "Doughboys"?'

The work amd finances editor suggested with great enthusiasm a new series, exploring different monetary funds: which ones were on the way up, which ones to avoid, which were ethically sound and which were safe for the long haul. Headlines like 'Be a winner' always sold papers. Everyone nodded, no one had any reservations about this. Every single member of the entire Flannel Pack owned a substantial portfolio of options.

'What about the crime beat?'

Sjölander cleared his throat and sat up straight. He had almost dozed off there on his chair.

'Right, we've got that double homicide down at the free port, and the police say it's only the beginning. As you can see in today's paper, we're the only ones that have the story about the missing cigarettes. Fifty million. They're going to be killing each other in droves over this truckload.'

Everyone nodded appreciatively. This was good stuff.

'And then there's the privatization of the public sector,' the editor-in-chief said, his voice slightly higher-pitched than the others. 'Are any reporters working on that yet?'

Schyman ignored him.

'Annika Bengtzon is on to something, I'm not sure where it will lead. She's found some shady foundation that does things Social Services no longer has the capacity to do: they hide women and children whose lives are threatened.'

The Flannel Pack squirmed uncomfortably. *What the hell is it anyway, 'some foundation'? Sounds pretty damn vague.*

'Annika Bengtzon is good at digging up stuff, but she's too damn preoccupied with women's issues,' Sjölander said.

They all nodded. Yeah, it was just a lot of ranting. Nothing newsworthy about it, no cred, it was just messy and tragic stuff.

'Then again, we've got to remember where she's coming from,' Sjölander said with a smirk. The others smirked too. *Yeah, right.*

Schyman regarded them in silence.

'Would the story be better if they were hiding *men* whose lives are threatened?' he asked.

This set off more scraping of chairs and looking at watches; *Christ, is that the time? Better get back to business. Was that it?*

Time to go, the radio was switched back on, the room was filled with hustling and bustling.

Anders Schyman returned to his room with the sense of slight frustration that these planning sessions usually produced. The way the management categorized reality, its uniformly incestuous view of the way things were, the unenlightened lack of self-criticism.

As he sat down and turned on the news bulletins his mind was filled with only one thought: *How the hell is this going to work out?*

Annika got off the bus at the stop in front of the Co-op store. The sidewalk was slick and slippery. Hunching her shoulders, she ignored the looks of the crowd. Out of the corners of her eyes she observed people in loud ski-suits walking nearby. She turned away; if they wanted to stare, then let them, she wouldn't be bothered. Gravel had been spread on the street. She stepped down on to the road and headed for the works. The industrial section of town clashed against the massive greyness of the winter sky, the smell of slush filled the air. As usual, she avoided looking at the abandoned blast-furnace, shifting her gaze to the left, resting her eyes lovingly on the beautiful old housing for workmen, thick wooden beams painted in rich brick-red hues. Her old apartment was on the right. She shot a glance in that direction – it had remained unoccupied since she moved out.

That was no longer the case.

Surprised, Annika stopped short in the middle of the street.

Curtains and flowers in the window, a shoemaker's tiny lamp.

Someone had taken over her kitchen and was sleeping in her bedroom. Someone who decorated, watered plants and cared. The vacant windows had sprung back to life.

The intensity of the relief that she felt amazed her – it was almost physical. A weight was lifted off her chest. The familiar feeling of wanting to disappear subsided. For the first time since the terrible event she felt a pang of tenderness towards the old industrial community.

I had good times here too, she thought. *We had nice moments*. Now and then there had been love between them.

Annika left the neighbourhood, reached Granheds-vägen, picked up her pace, hiked her bag up on her shoulder, looked up at the sky. The wind was murmuring in the treetops of the pines. Darkness wasn't far off.

I wonder if there are trees on other planets, she thought.

The road was icy and rough as she picked her way

along it. A few cars passed, their dipped beams hazy – no one she knew.

Silence crept closer. The crunching of her footfall, her regular breathing, the muffled roar of a plane going in for a landing at Arlanda Airport. Her body grew light, dancing, as she gazed at her surroundings.

The woods had taken a beating from the storm. In the clearing behind Tallsjön, nearly all the pine seedlings had snapped. Power and telephone poles were down. Trees had been broken in any number of places and at different levels: lying uprooted and exposed, snapped off at the height of a man, split, treetops splayed. The road was littered with branches that had been torn off. She had to step over the remains of a fallen birch tree.

We're so vulnerable, Annika thought. *There's not really much we can control.*

The drive leading up to Lyckebo hadn't been snow-ploughed. A car had been there a day or so earlier, tracks spreading to twice their width as they defrosted only to refreeze into channels of ice. Walking was difficult. Her bag banged against her hip.

The road barrier that marked the boundaries of Harpsund was open. The fir trees closed in around her. Here the darkness was more intense, the storm hadn't caused as much damage. The government could afford to take good care of its forest.

She passed the brook. There was an ice sculpture where the water welled out. Under the crust you could hear trickling. Various sizes and shapes of animal tracks criss-crossed each other: moose, deer, rabbit, wild boar. The ones that were a few days old had spread into giant prints.

Then the clearing appeared with its three brick-red buildings: the cottage, the woodshed and the barn. Everything was still. The treehouse to the left, the sloping meadow leading down to the jetty. Annika stopped and pulled off her hat and her gloves, allowing the breeze from the lake to ruffle her hair, closing her eyes and breathing deeply. The image of the clearing remained on her retina like a black-and-white negative, still, colourless, soundless. Slowly a sense of unease began to take hold: what was wrong with this picture?

She opened her eyes wide, the light hitting them, the scene crystal clear, in two seconds she knew.

There was no smoke coming out of the chimney.

Annika dropped her bag on the ground and ran, her heartbeat like a roaring pulse in her brain. As she yanked the front door open she was confronted by a chill and a darkness, an unpleasant whiff of danger.

'Gran!'

The old woman's legs were visible under the gateleg table, clad in brown support hose, one shoe missing.

'Gran!!'

Annika picked up the table, getting her left ring finger caught in the hinge of the table leaf.

'Oh, my God, oh, my God . . .'

The elderly woman was lying in a semi-prone position. Some blood had dribbled out of her mouth. Annika flung herself at her, took her hand, it was so icy, stroked her hair, the tears welling up, adrenalin surging.

'Gran, good Lord, can you hear me, Gran . . .?'

Annika felt her grandmother's wrist for a pulse, couldn't find the right spot, felt her throat, nothing there either. With hot and damp hands she rolled the old lady over on her back and bent over her, trying to detect breathing. Yes, she was breathing.

'Gran?'

A moan, followed by murmuring.

'Gran!'

The old woman's head fell to one side. The blood had

dried on her cheek. Her jaw was slack. More moans, then whimpering.

'Hurts,' she said. 'Help me.'

'Gran, it's me. Oh, God, Gran, you fell down, I'm going to help you . . .'

Basic life-saving skills, Annika thought as she stroked the old woman's head. *Check for breathing, bleeding and shock*. Her grandmother had to be kept warm.

Annika got up quickly and hurried over to the bedroom. The antique Gustavian-era bed was carefully made. With a single motion, she jerked off all the bedding, including the sheet and the thin top mattress, and rushed back to the kitchen. She spread out the mattress on the floor, lifted her grandmother's upper body and kicked the mattress in under her, then lifted her hips and legs over it, the bedding bunching up under her. Then Annika spread the blankets and sheets over her grandmother, lifting her legs up and tucking the covers in. The next step was to put her woollen cap on her grandmother's head, touching the wiry grey hair with her shaking hands.

An ambulance, Annika thought.

'Wait here, Gran,' she said. 'I'm going to go get help. I'll be right back.'

The old woman whimpered in reply.

Annika rushed outdoors, through the woods, past the brook, past the road barrier, across the road, ducked under a fallen power line, jumped from tuft to tuft across the marsh and ran up the hill to Lillsjötorp.

'Dear God, please let old man Gustav be in!'

The old man was chopping wood. Hard of hearing, he didn't hear Annika coming. She didn't bother saying hello to him, just entered the house.

The Slut was there, Gustav's home help and the woman Sven had once had on the side. Her name was

Ingela. She was washing the dishes and looked at Annika in consternation.

'What on Earth . . .?'

Annika rushed over to the telephone and dialled Emergency Services.

'You could at least have closed the front door,' the Slut said irritably as she wiped her hands on a towel and headed for the door.

'Emergency Services, how may we help you, please?' a lady's voice said on the phone.

Annika started bawling.

'It's my grandmother!' she howled.

'Why don't we start from the beginning? Tell me what happened.'

Annika closed her eyes and rubbed her forehead.

'Something's happened to my grandmother,' she explained. 'I thought she was dead. She's at a cottage outside Granhed, you have to come and pick her up.'

'What did you do to your hand?' the Slut asked, alarmed.

'Which Granhed would that be?' the lady asked.

Annika stammered out a description: 'Turn off at Valla in the direction of Hälleforsnäs, then take Stöttastensvägen, past Granhed, and then it's the first right after Hosjön.'

'Has something happened to Sofia?' the Slut asked with an incredulous stare.

Annika put the receiver down and left the house, running back the same way she had come. It had grown dark and she fell several times. The small cottage had begun to blend into the background, the black forest.

The woman hadn't moved; she was completely still, breathing calmly. Annika sat down beside her, put her grandmother's head in her lap and cried.

'Don't you die, you hear? Don't you die and leave me!'

Slowly Annika calmed down. It would take at least

half an hour for the ambulance to arrive. She wiped her runny nose and her tears with the back of her hand, then she noticed the blood. The skin and flesh on her left ring finger had been severely pinched when she'd moved the gateleg table. Blood had dried to a crust under her finger-nails and was still dripping down her wrist. The pain hit her at that very moment. She moaned and felt the room spin. What a baby she was! She wrapped the wound with a dishrag and tied it.

It would probably be a good idea to try to heat the kitchen.

Annika went over to the stove to start a fire, placing her hand on the iron surface. It was cool but not cold – it hadn't been used since early morning. She crumpled up a few pieces of newspaper and put in a stick of firewood and some birch-bark kindling. Her hand was shaking as she lit the match, her finger throbbing painfully. She struck another match to light the kerosene lamp that she set in the window facing the waterfront.

She got a pillow and placed it under her grand-mother's head, carefully studying the old face. Sofia Katarina. The same name as the youngest foster child in the Kulla-Gulla girls' books of the 1940s. Annika remem-bered how beautiful she'd thought the name was. When she'd been a child, she'd liked to pretend that Martha Sandwall-Bergström's books were about her grand-mother. Sofia Katarina, 'Sossatina'.

Where was that damn ambulance?

Annika looked around the kitchen. There was no trace of anyone making coffee, sandwiches, porridge or lunch. Her grandmother must have collapsed early this morning, right after she had got up, made a fire in the stove and made her bed. That would make it eight hours ago, Annika concluded. Eight hours. *Is that too long?* Would she be able to make it?

The fire was burning nicely and she added a few more pieces of firewood. The heat swirled out around the room, causing the chill to give up without a fight. This house was used to warmth and light, love and harmony. Now the conditions had changed.

Her grandmother moved her head and moaned. Annika's sense of powerlessness increased to the point of rage.

That fucking ambulance – where was it?

The woods were dense, poorly managed, thick with underbrush, practically impenetrable. The road was muddy and battered by cars. Ratko cursed when the rear left tyre slid around in the muck. He stopped, changed to a lower gear and pressed down slowly on the accelerator again. The large diesel engine growled softly, the tyre came unstuck and the vehicle continued to lurch ahead. He ought to have been there by now.

Another small tree had fallen across the road. Ratko's uncontrollable temper instantly got the better of him. He pounded the steering wheel, hard; goddamn it, he'd had enough hassles already. With a lunge he put the gearstick in 'park' and went out to clear away the birch tree. He tossed the trunk into the ditch and jumped on the tiny tree, then realized that he had reached his destination. The gap in the surrounding landscape where the trailer was parked was a few dozen metres away – the yellow cab showed through the denuded straggly deciduous trees. If the tree hadn't blocked the road he might not have found his way back here. Fate caressed him like a feather tickling his neck. He brushed it away.

He remained where he was for a while, his breath coming out like puffs of smoke around him.

There was no such thing as luck. You created your own

success, that was what he firmly believed in. The fact that they'd found the truck and the losers who'd stolen it wasn't luck, it was the result of a network that he'd painstakingly built over decades.

No one could escape – he always found them. Those bastards thought they could trick him.

Ratko's euphoria at finding the truck again had been transformed into impotent rage when they'd opened the trailer. The smokes were gone. Someone had hidden them away; the guys insisted that they had no idea who it was or where they were.

Ratko clenched his teeth until his jaws hurt.

There was only one reason why the guys hadn't talked: they really didn't have the faintest idea where the shipment was.

He took his gloves off and lit a cigarette. Smoked it slowly, all the way down to the filter. Stubbed it out on the sole of his shoe and put the butt in his pocket. Nowadays they could process the filters for DNA from traces of saliva. He had to remember to throw away these shoes too. He was in enough trouble already, he didn't need the Swedish police force on his back too.

Ratko stood there for a while and pulled his gloves back on. He had to admit that he was still a long way from reaching his objective. There'd been many times in his life when he'd had reason to be angry, but this time things were different. He wasn't sure if he was the hunter or the prey. He could smell danger coming from several different directions. His superiors said they trusted him, that they knew he would put things right again, but he knew their patience was limited. His efforts during the night hadn't brought him closer to the shipment, but it hadn't been a total waste of time either. He had displayed initiative and resourcefulness. But still he wasn't sure. The woman had vanished and he couldn't understand where she had gone. He still didn't know what part she played in this.

He got into his car and checked the rear-view mirror. Nothing. Only the packages that slightly obstructed his view. He drove about thirty metres and turned in to the right among the trees. The car heaved and rocked, then he reached the spot. He put the gearstick in park, switched off the ignition and left the key in place. Pulled out the cans and got moving. Carefully and methodically he doused the trailer and the cab with gasoline; it splashed and splattered, his hair and his clothes absorbing the pinkish fluid. When he was done he put the cans back. He'd better hurry up, night was falling fast. Fire would be more visible at night.

Finally, only the 'packages' remained. Ratko carried the first one over his shoulder, almost glad of the gasoline fumes. This was one smelly bastard. When he was about to stuff the corpse into the cab, he dropped it and lost his temper again. Steel-reinforced boots kicked flesh and bone, making the body jerk and roll over and over again until he was spent. He had to rest for a moment – the gasoline fumes from his clothes made him woozy. With a determined grip he heaved the package up into the passenger seat and went to get the other one. Suddenly he heard the sounds of an engine at a distance. He froze in mid-movement, the other corpse halfway out of the car. Overcome by fear he hurled the package on the ground and jumped into the bushes. Stretched out in the damp moss, he was soaked through in seconds.

Slowly, the sound retreated and disappeared. Ratko got up on his hands and knees, panting, nose running, and brushed some twigs from his hair. Damn lucky that no one saw him.

Shamefaced, he got up, saw the crumpled corpse lying there – and his anger returned. He pulled at the package and kicked and beat it, then resolutely hauled it over to the driver's seat of the cab and shoved it on to the floor. His efforts were quick and determined as he went for the last two cans and brought them over, one in each hand. The gasoline splashed over the bodies, drenching the corpses. The last drops went to the fuse, a line of droplets on the ground leading into the woods. Ratko exhaled, suddenly realizing how exhausted he was. Rested for a few minutes, took off his clothes, including his underwear, pulled out a sports bag with fresh gear. Shivering in the brutal cold air he quickly got dressed, then slapped his arms against his sides to get warmer.

Better, much better. Now only the fireworks remained.

He briefly regarded the scene in front of him – the truck, the bodies and the woods – and felt fairly satisfied.

Then he flicked his lighter, put it to the ground, turned around and ran.

The emergency room looked like a garage. The ambulance parked and a swarm of medical personnel in flapping coats with breast pockets full of ballpoint pens descended upon them. They spoke to each other calmly and worked efficiently. All the women had freshly washed hair and all the men were clean-shaven. Annika's grandmother was wheeled away by a standard-issue polyester herd.

Annika got out of the car and saw the troop sail over to the clinic. A lady behind a glass window directed her to the waiting room. It was brimming over with droopy kids, restless parents, hollow-eyed senior citizens and a noisy family of immigrants. Annika rummaged through her bag and found a prepaid telephone card. She went over to the phone booth, apologizing when she had to squeeze past the noisy family, picked up the receiver with her left hand, rested her forehead against the phone and took a deep breath. She had to do this.

Her mother picked up after four rings, slightly irritated.

'It's Gran,' Annika told her. 'She's in real bad shape. I found her at the cottage, she was almost dead.'

'What?' her mother replied, then told someone else in the room: 'No, not those, use the red glasses instead . . .'

'Gran is really ill!' Annika yelled. 'Aren't you listening to me?!'

Once again focusing on the call, her mother echoed: 'Ill?' in a voice that was surprised, not frightened or shocked. Merely quizzical.

'She was alive in the ambulance, but then they took off and I don't know what's going on now . . .'

Soundlessly, Annika began to cry.

'Mom, could you please come over?'

Her mother was quiet, the line buzzing softly.

'We were going to have a dinner party. Where are you?'

'The Kullberg Hospital.'

Finally someone ushered the noisy family into another room. The thud of the receiver being hung up reverberated in the new-found silence.

An intern approached Annika, coat fluttering.

'Are you related to Sofia Katarina? Please follow me.'

The man's snowy back disappeared behind the glass door. Annika swallowed and followed suit. *Oh, Lord, she's dead, now he's going to tell me she's dead. He'll say you found her too late. Why don't you take better care of your elderly relatives?*

The examination room was tiny, dismal and windowless. The doctor introduced himself, a quick mumble and a brief handshake. Then he clicked a ballpoint pen and bent over his papers. Annika swallowed.

'Is she dead?'

The doctor put down the pen and rubbed his eyes.

'We're going to perform a neurological examination to find out what went wrong. Right now we're running some tests, like sucrose levels, blood screens and blood pressure.'

'And?' Annika asked.

'The situation appears to be stable,' he said, looking her in the eye. 'She isn't getting worse, she's a bit more alert. We've ruled out diabetic complications at this point, but her reflexes are weak and one side is limp. Perhaps you noticed that her mouth drooped on one side.'

The last words were expressed as a statement, not a question.

'What about the blood?' Annika wondered. 'Why was there blood in her mouth?'

The doctor got up.

'She bit herself when she fell. What's that on your hand?'

'A dishrag. I got caught in something. Will she be all right?'

Annika got up too. The doctor hooked his pen on the edge of his breast pocket.

'When we're finished here, we'll take a CAT scan. It will take a while before we can assess the effects of what happened.'

'A brain scan? What's wrong? Is she going to die?'

Sweat had made Annika's palms slick.

'It's too early to—'

'*Is she going to die?*'

Her voice was too shrill and cracked. The doctor backed away.

'Something happened to the left side of her brain, some kind of vascular trauma. It was either a blood clot, cerebral thrombosis, or there was some bleeding, a cerebral haemorrhage. It's too early to tell for sure what it might have been.'

'What's the difference?'

The man placed his hand on the doorknob.

'Haemorrhages strike quickly and generally cause unconsciousness. Usually the patient has a history of high blood pressure. I'll see that your hand is taken care of – you'll need a tetanus shot too.'

He left the room with a crackle of static electricity as his coat brushed against the plastic door post. Annika sat back down again, paralysed, mouth half-open, not getting any air.

This can't be happening to me, not now.

She remained where she was until a nurse came in and gave her finger three stitches, gave her a shot in the behind and applied a white gauze fingerstall that tied at the wrist. Then she returned to the waiting room, running one hand along the painted fibreglass wall for support as she walked down the corridor. The sounds of the hospital seemed far away while panic lurked just under the surface of her mind.

Her mother showed up in the waiting room wearing an unbuttoned mink coat in an out-of-fashion cut, tight at the shoulder, and talked to the receptionist in a loud voice. Then she sank down in the chair next to Annika's without taking her coat off.

'Have they told you anything?'

Annika sighed emphatically, fought back the tears, held out her arms and embraced her mother.

'It's something to do with her brain. Oh, Mom, what if she dies?' she murmured into her shoulder, getting snot all over the fur.

'Where is she now?'

'Having a scan.'

Her mother disengaged herself, patted Annika on the cheek, coughed and wiped her brow with her glove.

'Take off your coat or you'll be too hot,' Annika said.

'I know what you're thinking, that it's all my fault.'

Annika looked at her mother, noticing how the anticipated criticism had carved a dismissive expression on her face. Rage struck her like a bolt of white lightning.

'Oh, no, you don't,' she said. 'Don't blame me for your own guilty feelings.'

Her mother fanned herself with one hand.

'I don't feel guilty, but you think I ought to.'

Annika was unable to stay seated. She got up and went over to the reception window.

'When will you let us know about Sofia Katarina's condition?'

'Please take a seat and wait,' the lady replied.

The fur coat had slipped down her mother's shoulders.

'Do you know where you can go to smoke?' she asked, fingering her handbag.

'Now that you mention it,' Annika said, 'I do think it's strange that I'm the one who finds her when I live 120 kilometres away. You live within three kilometres of her.'

She sat down two chairs further along, her back to a heater.

'So you're throwing that in my face too,' her mother said.

Annika turned away, closed her eyes and let the heat radiate through her sweater. She leaned back, a metal ridge cutting into her neck. Tears burning in her eyes.

'Not now, Mom,' she whispered.

'Annika Bengtzon?'

The female doctor had a ponytail and was holding a folder filled with papers. Annika sat up, quickly blotted her eyes and lowered her gaze to the floor. The doctor sat down facing her and leaned in.

'The CAT scan confirmed our suspicions,' she said. 'There's been a haemorrhage in the left hemisphere of the brain, right in the middle of the centre for the nervous system. This is consistent with the symptoms displayed on the right side and with the fact that the eye appears to be unaffected.'

'A stroke?' her mother said breathlessly.

'That's right, a stroke.'

'Oh, my God,' her mother said faintly. 'Will she be able to recuperate?'

'Some of the symptoms usually recede. However, at this age, and when there's been such a sudden onset, we will probably have to allow for relatively severe residual symptoms, unfortunately.'

'Will she be a vegetable?' Annika asked.

The doctor gave her a friendly look.

'We don't know if the haemorrhage has affected her intellect. That might not be the case. Things will depend a great deal on rehabilitation, which is very important in cases like this.'

Annika swallowed again and caught her lower lip between her teeth.

'Will she be able to live at home again?'

'We'll have to wait and see before we can tell. Generally, patients who live at home usually recuperate better, as long as they are provided with substantial at-home care. The alternative is an institution or a geriatric ward at a hospital.'

'An institution?' Annika said. 'Not Lövåsen, I hope?'

The doctor smiled.

'There's nothing wrong with Lövåsen. Don't believe everything you read in the papers.'

'I wrote the articles,' Annika said.

'I have nothing against Lövåsen,' her mother said.

The doctor got up.

'She's back from the scan now. Once her temperature has stabilized you can go in to see her. It will take a while.'

Annika and her mother nodded in unison.

*

Thomas Samuelsson crumpled the wrappers from his hamburger meal and tossed them into the waste-paper basket. He'd have to remember to empty it on his way out, or else his office would smell like a fast-food joint all week.

Heaving a sigh, he leaned back in his chair and stared out the window. The darkness outdoors produced a reflection of his office, another civil servant in charge of finances in some other world that was identical, only inverted. City Hall was quiet – nearly all the employees had gone home. Soon, the members of the social welfare board would gather in the conference room next door, but at this point it was quiet. Thomas felt strangely content, free and at peace. He had used work as an excuse when Eleonor had discussed dinner, which wasn't really a lie, but it wasn't the truth either. His workload was always heavy this time of year, but it wasn't any heavier than usual. It never used to stop him from going home for dinner. Dinner was their couple time. An appetizer and a main course; Eleonor never had dessert. Always with candles during the dark winter months, always with crisp cloth napkins. He had enjoyed it, Eleonor had adored it and often told their friends about it. So romantic. So fantastic. What a perfect couple, a match made in heaven.

No, not in heaven, he thought. *In Perugia.*

Thomas couldn't say when boredom had started to set in. The feeling of being grown-up had faded and something else took hold, something more honest. They weren't grown-ups, they only played at being grown-up. They went sailing, had dinner parties, were involved in clubs and societies. Vaxholm was their world, the development and growth of their community was their greatest interest and the focus of their ambition. They had both been born and raised there; neither of them had ever lived anywhere else. No one could say that they weren't responsible, both socially and at work.

But when it came to their own relationship the commitment had worn thin. They still acted like two teenagers who had just moved away from home, playing romantic games and always having to defer to their parents.

Thomas sighed. There it was again.

Parenthood.

Eleonor didn't want to have children. She loved their life, their time together, the dinners, the trips, her career, her stock portfolio, the neighbours, the clubs, the boat.

'I don't need to prove that I'm a woman by having kids,' she told him the last time they had quarrelled about the subject. 'It's my life. I can do what I like with it. I want to have fun, meet people, go places at work, put top priority on our relationship, and the house.'

'We're ready to begin.'

The administration manager was standing in his doorway. Thomas blinked in surprise.

'Sure, I'm on my way.'

Slightly embarrassed, he swiftly gathered his papers. He knew he had grown absent-minded and wondered how obvious it was.

The eleven members of the board were seated at the table. Thomas sat down opposite the secretary of the board who was sitting at the far end to one side. The supervisors flanked one side of the table. A few civil servants were present. The agenda covered some twenty items, most of which did not concern him. The budget was going to be presented at a special two-day meeting at the hotel and today he was only supposed to account for a few particular items, then be available if any critical issues came up.

While the chairman opened the meeting Thomas

glanced at the agenda: the usual stuff – the day-care plan, personnel issues, the care of the disabled, the home-help service. Half of the items had been disputed time and time again, and would hardly be resolved this evening either. His item about out-of-control costs for the transportation of the elderly and the disabled was number eight on the list. With a faint sigh he scanned the rest of the list and drank some ice water. Item number seven was new: the Paradise Foundation.

What kind of revolutionary set-up was this? Did they actually believe that they could take on new contracts now, when their finances were so strained? Thomas sighed as quietly as he could and turned his attention to the members of the board.

The party demagogues, the Social Democrat and the Conservative, sat at either end of the table, ready to argue their case and make reservations. 'Individual freedom', the Conservative would say, while the Social Democrat would counter this with the word 'solidarity'. Soon the politicians' desire for something *real* would surface, they would demand a *follow-up,* and Thomas would make a reference to numbers and tables that wouldn't satisfy anyone.

Perugia, he thought. That was where he was at this very minute, on the crest of a mountain in Umbria, king of the hill.

He smiled at the thought.

Oddly enough, I think of that city as a man.

'Thomas?'

The chairman was looking at him in a friendly fashion. Thomas cleared his throat and fished out the right paper.

'We have to do something about transportation costs,' he said. 'Costs have escalated to a sum three times as high as this year's budget allows for. I can't see how we are going to avoid this increase, the laws pertaining to these matters don't give us any answers. Should we allow free access, the need for these services will be insatiable.'

He reeled off numbers and tables, consequences and alternatives. The chairman produced a circular with new guidelines from the Association of Local Authorities: they were not the only ones with this problem. The Association had taken notice and their standardized directives were as pompous and vague as ever. Soon they were bogged down in a discussion about how to keep social workers abreast of the situation; would it be better to send them off for a course or to hire a contractor?

Paradise Foundation, he thought. *Nice name.*

The meeting plodded along. They got bogged down again in another detail, a playground that needed repairs, and Thomas could feel himself getting annoyed. By the time they reached item number seven he leaned forward. One of the civil servants, a female social worker who had worked for the city for many years, presented the matter.

'The idea is to resolve in principle whether we should purchase the services of a new organization or not,' she said. 'We have an urgent case pending that has already been treated by the board for special issues, but we wanted to present the contract to you before we said yes.'

'What is this foundation all about?' the Social Democrat asked suspiciously, and Thomas knew where they were heading: if the Social Democrat was against an issue, the Conservative would automatically champion it.

The social worker hesitated. She couldn't go into detail since the minutes of the meeting were made public.

'Broadly speaking, the organization protects people whose lives are threatened,' she said. 'The director has just run through their procedures for us, and in this particular case they offer services that we need, in our opinion . . .'

Everyone studied the contract carefully, even though

there wasn't much to read. The local authorities of Vaxholm committed themselves to pay for safe housing for three thousand, five hundred kronor a day until a satisfactory solution could be arranged for this particular client.

'What exactly is this?' the Social Democrat continued. 'We have several treatment facilities on contract already – do we really need another one?'

The social worker looked ill at ease.

'This is a totally new and unique service,' she said. 'The Paradise Foundation focuses entirely on protecting and helping people whose lives are in danger, mostly women and children. These individuals are wiped off all public records so that their persecutors won't be able to trace them. All efforts at finding them will lead to a blank wall, this foundation.'

Everyone present stared at the social worker.

'Is that really legal?' the newly elected delegate from the Greens, a young woman, asked. As usual, she was ignored.

'Why can't we take care of this ourselves with our own resources?' the Conservative asked.

The supervisor in charge of welfare issues and child protection services, who was obviously familiar with the case at hand, took the floor.

'There's nothing strange about this,' he said. 'You might say that it's all about an approach, a capacity that only a fully private organization can supply. They have a flexibility that government authorities like ourselves lack. I believe in this.'

'It's awfully expensive,' the Social Democrat said.

'Care costs. When are you ever going to realize that?' the Conservative countered, and then they were off.

Thomas leaned back and studied the contract. It was very bare-bones. No specific services were detailed, there

was no information about the location of the organization, there wasn't even a corporate identity number. A
reference to a post office box number in Järfälla was all
there was.

As usual he wished he had the power to speak out, that
he could present pertinent and specific objections.

Obviously, they had to request references from this
organization and check with the legal staff at Social
Services that these measures were legitimate. And how
could they justify such an expenditure at this time? And
why the hell hadn't anyone asked him if this was
financially feasible? He was the only person around here
who knew all the angles of their budget, why else was he
on the board? Was he some kind of goddamn decoration?

'Do we have to reach a decision tonight?' the chairman
asked.

Both the social worker and the supervisor nodded.

The chairman sighed.

Something snapped inside Thomas. For the first time
in the seven years he'd worked for the local authorities, he
raised his voice at a board meeting.

'This is insane!' he said in an agitated tone. 'How can
you even consider buying services without considering
the consequences? What kind of organization is this,
anyway? And it's a foundation, to boot. Jesus! And what
about that cheesy contract? They don't even submit a
corporate identity number. This stinks, if you ask me, and
I damn well think you should!'

Everyone stared at Thomas as if he was a ghost.
Suddenly he was aware that he was on his feet, that he
had been leaning over the table, gripping the contract in
his fist and waving it overhead like a flag. His face
burned, he felt sweaty. He dropped the contract on the
table, raked his hair back with his fingers and
straightened his tie.

'Please excuse me,' he said. 'I apologize . . .'

In confusion Thomas sat down and started leafing through his papers. The board members averted their eyes and looked uncomfortably down at the table top instead. He wanted to die, to sink through the floor and disappear.

The chairman took a resounding breath.

'Well then, perhaps we should conclude this matter . . .'

The contract was approved, the vote coming to seven ayes and four nays.

'I've got one heck of a lead.'

Sjölander and Ingvar Johansson looked up at the reporter interrupting them in irritation. The displeasure on their faces was transformed into indulgence as soon as they saw it was Carl Wennergren.

'Go ahead, shoot,' Sjölander said.

The reporter perched on the crime-desk editor's desk.

'The free-port killings,' he said. 'I've got a damn hot tip.'

Both Sjölander and the news editor planted their feet on the floor and sat up straight.

'What is it?' Ingvar Johansson asked.

Lowering his voice, Carl Wennergren said: 'I just talked to a cop. They think Ratko is involved.'

The older pair regarded the younger man.

'Why?' Sjölander asked.

'You know,' Carl Wennergren said. 'Organized crime mobs, Yugoslavs, missing cigarettes – it certainly has Ratko written all over it.'

'Who did you talk to?'

'A police detective.'

'Did you call him, or did he call you?'

The reporter cocked an eyebrow at him.

'He called me. Why?'

Sjölander and Ingvar Johansson exchanged a quick glance.

'Okay,' the editor said. 'So what did the police want?'

'To tip us off that Ratko is involved – they're looking all over the place for him. The police want us to run his name and his picture.'

'Is there a warrant out for him?'

The reporter knitted his brows.

'The detective didn't mention that, only that they were looking for him.'

'This is good stuff,' Ingvar Johansson said as he scribbled on a pad. 'We'll do it like this: Sjölander will compile a background piece on Ratko, you'll go out to the Yugo-controlled restaurants and clubs and interview people tonight. This could be headline material.'

'Right on!' Carl Wennerholm exclaimed and bounded off to the photo desk.

The two supervisors followed him with their gazes until he disappeared from view.

'Did you know about this?' Ingvar Johansson asked.

Sjölander sighed and put his feet back up on the desk.

'The police don't have a single good lead. The guys who were killed were rookies fresh from Serbia. There weren't any witnesses, no one can talk. I don't know why, but the cops obviously want to smoke out Ratko.'

'Is he involved, do you think?'

The crime-desk editor laughed.

'Of course he is. Ratko controls the Yugoslav cigarette operations in Scandinavia. He might not have pulled the trigger, but he definitely has something to do with those killings.'

The men were lost in their own thoughts for a minute or so and then came to the same conclusion.

'A police plant, no doubt about it,' Ingvar Johansson said.

'A plant if ever there was one,' Sjölander seconded.

'But why?' the news-desk editor wondered.

The crime-desk editor shrugged.

'The cops don't have diddly, they want to stir things up. Either they want to undermine Ratko's position or cement it, it doesn't matter to us. If a police detective goes public with the information that they're looking for Ratko, we're talking headlines here.'

They nodded to each other.

'Will you notify Jansson?' Sjölander asked.

Ingvar Johansson got up and went over to the night desk.

In one corner, a low-wattage bulb emitted a yellowish glow. An EKG beeped rhythmically and monotonously. Sofia Katarina was hooked up to drips and machines. Her body appeared diminished and dry, so still and small, under the flimsy blanket, Annika went up to her, stroked her head and was struck by how old she seemed. How odd. She had never thought of her grandmother as old.

'Just look at her,' her mother said. 'Look at her mouth.'

The right-hand corner of Gran's mouth drooped. Some drool ran down her neck. Annika grabbed a paper towel and wiped it away.

'She's asleep right now,' the doctor told them. 'You can stay here for a while if you like.'

Then she left the room, the door swishing shut.

They sat on either side of the bed, Annika's mother still wearing her fur. The room was filled with hospital sounds: the whoosh of the ventilation system, the electronic song of the machines, the clicking of clogs in the hallway. Despite all this, the silence was oppressive.

'Who would've thought it could happen?' Annika's mother said. 'And today of all days . . .'

She started to sob.

'Of course you couldn't have known,' Annika said softly. 'No one's blaming you.'

'She was out shopping yesterday. I was working at the checkout counter and she seemed so cheerful and fit.'

They fell silent again. Annika's mother was crying soundlessly.

'We need to find a place for her to live,' Annika said. 'Lövåsen is out of the question.'

'Well, *I* can't do it,' her mother said in a determined voice and looked up.

'Patients getting the wrong medication, neglect . . . I wrote a whole series of articles about the shoddy conditions at Lövåsen. Gran is *not* going there.'

'That was a long time ago – I'm sure things are better now.'

Her mother blotted her face with a tissue as Annika got up.

'Maybe we could find a private solution,' Annika said.

'Well, she's not staying with me!'

Her mother was sitting up straight and had stopped using the tissue. Annika saw her sitting there: asthmatic from smoking, sweating from the combined heat of fur and hot flushes, her hair getting thin, extra weight creeping up on her, distant and self-centred. Before Annika realized it she had seized her mother by the shoulders.

'Don't be so goddamned immature,' Annika hissed. 'I mean private-care options. This isn't about you, understand? For once in your life you're not the centre of attention.'

The woman gaped, a red splotchy rash breaking out on her neck.

'You . . .!' she started to say as she pushed Annika away and stood up.

The younger woman looked at the older woman and sensed the outburst that was imminent.

'Spit it out,' Annika said tersely. 'Tell me what's on your mind.'

Her mother pulled her fur coat tight across her chest and swooped over to Annika.

'If you only knew how much crap I've had to take on account of you!' she whispered heatedly. 'Have you ever considered what it's been like for me all these years? The way people exchange looks behind my back? The gossip? No wonder your sister moved – she always looked up to you before. It's amazing that Leif has been able to stand it; he's been on the verge of leaving me several times. You'd like that, wouldn't you? You've always begrudged me love, you've never been able to stand Leif . . .'

Annika blanched as her mother circled her, backing towards the exit, pointing an accusing finger at her.

'And not to mention Sofia!' the older woman went on, louder now. 'She was such a respected person. The matron of Harpsund. And now she has to end her days as the grandmother of the girl who murdered—'

Annika couldn't breathe.

'Go to hell!' she managed to sputter.

Her mother moved in closer, spittle flying from her mouth.

'A fine journalist like you should be able face the truth!'

Suddenly Annika was transported back to the foundry, to the coke room next to the blast furnace. She saw her dead cat, saw the iron pipe lying nearby. She clasped her hands to her head and doubled over.

'Go,' she whispered. 'Go away, Mother.'

Her mother pulled out a leather cigarette case and a green plastic lighter.

'Sit here and think about what you put us through.'

Silence: the room grew darker, it was difficult to get any air. Shock had lodged like a stone at the base of Annika's throat, making it hard to breathe.

She hates me, she thought. *My own mother hates me. I've ruined her life.*

A wave of self-pity enveloped her, crushing her down to the ground.

What have I done to the people I love? Dear God, what have I done?

Sofia Katarina's left hand fluttered on the yellow hospital blanket.

'Barbro?' she murmured.

Annika looked up. *Gran, oh, Gran!* Flew to her side, took her cold immobile right hand, pulled herself together and tried to smile.

'Hello, Gran, it's me, Annika.'

'Barbro?' her grandmother slurred, gazing at her with unfocused eyes.

Tears welled up, obscuring her vision.

'No, it's me, Annika. Barbro's daughter.'

The old lady gazed around the room, her left hand fidgeting and fluttering.

'Am I at Lyckebo?'

Unable to hold back the tears any longer, Annika let them fall as she breathed with her mouth open.

'No, Gran, you're ill. You're in the hospital.'

The old lady's gaze returned to Annika.

'Who are you?'

'Annika,' she whispered. 'It's me.'

A flicker came through the haze.

'Of course,' Sofia Katarina said. 'My favourite girl.'

Annika sobbed, resting her head in the old woman's lap as she held her hand. After a while she got up to blow her nose.

'You've been in pretty bad shape, Gran,' she said as she walked around the bed. 'We've got to patch you up as soon as possible.'

But her grandmother had gone back to sleep.

WEDNESDAY 31 OCTOBER

Aida steeled herself. The hill ahead of her seemed endless. The road seemed to waver before her as she staggered on, sweat pouring down behind her ears and down her neck. Wasn't she ever going to get there?

She sat down on the pavement, her legs in the gutter, and rested her head on her knees. Oblivious to the cold and the damp, she sat there, needing to rest before she continued.

A car came over the crest and slowed down as it passed. Aida could sense the occupants looking at her. This was no place to sit. In a well-tended neighbourhood like this someone was sure to call the police before long.

She got up, and for a split second she blacked out.

I've got to find that house. Now.

She walked straight ahead and saw the number she'd been searching for at the next drive. How silly: she'd almost given up with only twenty metres left to go. She tried to laugh. Instead she tripped on a rock, almost fell and had to fight back the tears.

'Help me,' she murmured.

She made it to the stairs, pulled herself up along the railing and rang the bell. A solid front door equipped with two extra bolts. A bell clanged somewhere on the inside. Nothing happened. She rang again. And again. And again. Tried to peek in through the dark glass insets in the door – saw only darkness, emptiness, not even any furniture.

Aida sank down on the stairs and rested her forehead against the wall of the house. Her strength had run out. He could come. It didn't matter. Call the police. Things couldn't get any worse.

'Aida?'

She could barely manage to look up.

'Oh dear, how are you?'

She was losing consciousness and clutched at the wall.

'Christ, she's ill. Anders, come and give me a hand.'

Someone took hold of her and pulled her to her feet. An agitated woman's voice, a calmer man's voice, it was warm and dark, she was indoors.

'Put her down on the couch.'

The room was spinning, she was being moved, then she was resting on something. She found herself looking into a couch; it was brown and scratchy. A blanket was smoothed over her, but she was still cold.

'She's terribly ill,' the woman remarked, 'and she's running a very high temperature. We've got to get her to a doctor.'

'We can't bring a doctor here, you know that,' the man said.

Aida wanted to say something, to protest. *No, no doctor, no hospital.*

The people went into another room. She could hear them murmuring. Perhaps she drifted off to sleep, because the next thing she knew was that the man and the woman were standing over her with a cup of steaming hot tea.

'You must be Aida, right?' the woman said. 'I'm Mia, Mia Eriksson. This is my husband, Anders. When did you get this ill?'

Aida tried to reply.

'No doctors,' she whispered.

The woman called Mia nodded.

'All right,' she said. 'No doctors. We understand. But you need medical care and we have a suggestion.'

Aida shook her head.

'They're looking for me.'

Mia stroked her head.

'We know. There are ways of helping you without anyone finding out.'

Aida closed her eyes and exhaled.

'Is this Paradise?' she whispered.

The answer came from far away – she was drifting off again.

'Yes,' the woman replied. 'We're going to take care of you.'

Interludes of sleep and consciousness had alternated all night. Sofia Katarina had been confused, frightened and sentimental in turn.

After performing a brief examination, the physiotherapist submitted a disheartening report

'Her functional capacity on the right-hand side is very poor,' the physiotherapist said. 'This is going to require a lot of effort.'

'What do you have to do to regain mobility?' Annika asked.

The woman gave her a faint smile.

'The problem is not in the limbs, it's in the head. There isn't any treatment that can revive dead nerve cells. That's why we need to focus on the ones that are left. Nerve cells that remain intact, but happen to be inactive, need to be activated. You can do this with several different types of physiotherapy.'

'But will she get well?'

'It might take six months before you can see any results. The most important thing right now is to get started soon and to keep up treatment.'

Annika swallowed.

'What can I do?'

The physiotherapist took her hand and smiled.

'Do what you've been doing. Care. Talk to her, get her involved, sing old songs with her. You'll notice that she'll like to talk about the past. Let her do so.'

'But when will she be herself again?'

'Your grandmother will never be her old self again.'

Annika blinked. A bottomless pit opened up and she felt panic creeping up on her.

'How am I supposed to deal with this? She's always been the strong one.'

Her voice was too shrill, desperate.

'Well, now you'll have to be strong for her sake.'

The physiotherapist patted her hand, Annika didn't notice her leaving.

'Gran,' she whispered, stroking the woman's hand.

But the old lady slept. The sounds of the day crept in through the crack in the door and spread throughout the cramped little room. Even though Annika had woken up often and hadn't got much sleep, she felt all geared up, restless to the point of being hyperactive.

She had to arrange for a place that could rehabilitate her grandmother in the best way. Lövåsen wasn't the right place, she was absolutely convinced of that. All edgy, she got up and paced around the room over and over again. Her leg hurt, her finger throbbed.

There had to be other alternatives – private nursing homes, service flats, home nursing.

Annika didn't notice the door opening, she simply felt the draught around her ankles.

It was the female doctor again, followed by Annika's mink-clad mother.

'We are going to discuss Sofia's future,' the doctor said, and Annika grabbed her things and joined them.

'I can't nurse her at home,' her mother said once they had parked themselves in the doctor's office. 'I have a job.'

'Barbro, you would be entitled to care allowance if you took care of your mother, you know,' the doctor informed her.

Annika's mother fidgeted.

'I'm not ready to give up my career.'

Something snapped inside Annika. The lack of sleep, the absence of any affection on her mother's part, and the fact that nothing was making any sense any more made her brain explode. She got up and started shouting.

'You're only a substitute at the checkout stand over at the Co-op, for Christ's sake! What's stopping you from taking care of Gran?'

'Sit down,' the doctor commanded.

'Damned if I will!' Annika shouted, still standing, her voice unsteady, her legs trembling. 'None of you give a damn about Gran! You want to shut her away in that miserable excuse for a home at Lövåsen and throw away the key. I know what it's like there! I wrote about it! Neglect, understaffing, medicine mix-ups!'

The doctor got to her feet and approached Annika.

'Either you sit down,' she said calmly, 'or you leave.'

Annika rubbed her forehead, feeling weak. She sat down again. Barbro fingered her fur, looking for understanding in the doctor's eyes. *Now you know what I have to put up with*.

'Lövåsen would have been a satisfactory alternative . . .'

'The hell it would be!'

'That is, if there had been any vacancies there. But there aren't. The waiting list is long. Very soon Sofia's course of medical treatment will be concluded, but she will require around-the-clock assistance and intensive rehabilitation. That's why we have to come up with other solutions in a hurry. That's why I'm turning to you. Do you have any other suggestions?'

Annika's mother licked her lips uncertainly.

'Well,' she said, 'I have no idea – you always expect society to do right by you in a situation like this. That is why we pay taxes, after all . . .'

Annika stared down at her hands, her face burning.

'Is there anything else available, somewhere else?' she asked.

'Possibly over in Bettna,' the doctor replied.

'But that's miles from Hälleforsnäs, for goodness' sake. It's practically 200 kilometres from Stockholm,' Annika said and looked up. 'How are we supposed to be able to visit her?'

'I'm not saying it's ideal . . .'

'What about Stockholm?' Annika asked. 'Could she get admitted to a place in Stockholm? Then I could visit her every day.'

She had risen to her feet again, the doctor motioned her to sit down.

'If so, that would be the last alternative. First we have to try to find her accommodations within our own community.'

Annika's mother didn't say anything, merely fingering the hooks down the front of her fur. Annika was slumped in her chair, staring at the floor. The doctor regarded them in silence for a while: mother and daughter, the young woman in a state of shock, the older woman confused and worried.

'This has been a terrible experience,' the doctor said and turned to Annika. 'It's likely that you will be hit by a few side effects of this trauma. You might start having chills, crying spells and bouts of depression.'

Annika met the doctor's gaze.

'Great,' she said. 'So what do I do about it?'

The doctor sighed faintly.

'Drink,' she said and got up.

Annika stared at her.

'Are you serious?'

The doctor smiled a little and stretched out her hand.

'It's a tried and true course of treatment in cases like these. I'm sure we'll have reason to meet again soon. If you like, you can stay here for a while. I have to go and do my rounds.'

She left the two women in the small room andthe door closed behind her. The silence grew to monumental proportions. Annika's mother cleared her throat.

'Have you spoken to the physiotherapist?' she asked cautiously.

'Of course, I've been here all night.'

Barbro got up, went over to Annika and stroked her hair.

'I don't want us to fight,' her mother whispered. 'We've got to stick together now that Mother is unwell.'

Annika sighed, hesitated and then put her arms around her mother's ample waist and rested the side of her head against her stomach. She could detect a faint rumble.

'No, of course we shouldn't fight,' she whispered back.

'Go home and get some rest,' Barbro said and fished in her pocket for her keys. 'I'll stay with Sofia.'

Annika let go.

'Thanks,' she said, 'but I'd rather go back to Stockholm and sleep there. I can get back here in no time – the X2000 only takes fifty-eight minutes.'

She gathered her things and gave her mother a hug.

'Everything will be all right, you'll see,' Barbro said.

Annika went out into the hospital corridor, so endless and cold.

Just like the doctor had predicted, she started to shiver when she was on the train. She had bought the papers – they were spread out on the table in front of her – but she didn't feel up to reading them.

Drink, she thought. Wasn't that a great piece of advice?

She wasn't planning on drinking. Her father had done enough of that to last the whole family the rest of their lives. He boozed it up until he died, drunk as a skunk in a ditch along the road to Granhed.

Annika curled up in her seat. Wrapped her jacket around her, to no avail. The chill came from within, from her heart.

Everyone I love dies, she thought in a fit of self-pity. *Dad, Sven, maybe even Gran soon*.

No, she thought after that. *Not Gran. She'll be fine, she'll get back in pretty good shape. We're going to find her a place that will get her back on her feet again.*

Annika fingered the papers, but still couldn't conjure up the strength to read them. Instead she leaned back, closed her eyes and tried to relax. Only she couldn't, her body jerked and trembled. She sat up again and sighed. Reached for one of the papers and went straight for the spread at pages six and seven, the main news coverage pages. A man in a picture, a bit out of focus, blown up as far as it would go, stared at her from the page. After a second she recognized him. *Where is Aida? Aida Begovic. I know she's here.*

The headline was as big and dark as the man outside the hotel room had been the other night.

The leader of the cigarette ring, it said, and the caption read: *His name is Ratko and he came to Sweden in the 1970s.*

He's been convicted of bank robbery and kidnapping. Currently, he's being charged with war crimes in the former Yugoslav Republic. The Swedish police believe he is the brains behind the cigarette smuggling rings that operate in Sweden.

Annika folded up the paper, her teeth chattering, the pinched finger with its three stitches hurting. The nausea was back.

Anders Schyman slapped the paper on the table in front of Ingvar Johansson.

'Let's hear an explanation,' he said.

The fuzzy man on the pages of the newspaper glared at the two men unseeingly. The news-desk editor took his eyes off his computer screen.

'What do you mean?'

'My office, right now.'

Sjölander was there already, hovering in a dusty spot where the couch had once been. Schyman sat down heavily in his chair and it groaned under his weight. Ingvar Johansson pulled the door shut.

'Who made the decision to run Ratko's name and picture?' The deputy editor's words filled the room.

The two men, who were standing, exchanged glances.

'I go home when my shift is over and I wouldn't know . . .', Ingvar Johansson started to say, but Schyman cut him off at once.

'That's bullshit,' he said. 'I recognize a daytime contribution when I see one. And I've already talked to Jansson and Torstensson. The editor-in-chief hadn't been informed about the decision to publish this information at all, while Jansson was sincerely surprised and said that the entire spread was a contribution from the day team. Sit down.'

In unison, Sjölander and Ingvar Johansson sat down on their chairs. No one said a word.

'This is unacceptable,' Schyman said in a low voice when the silence had grown oppressive. 'Going public with the names of non-convicted criminals has legal implications. It's a decision that belongs to the publisher – something that shouldn't come as a surprise to either of you, for God's sake.'

Sjölander looked down at the floor. Ingvar Johansson squirmed.

'We've run his name before. It isn't news that he's a mobster.'

Anders Schyman sighed heavily.

'We didn't merely write that he was a mobster. We tied him to the double homicide at the free port, indirectly fingering him as the killer. I've already talked to our legal staff and if Ratko sues us we're going down, not to mention what the Press Ethics Committee will say.'

'He won't sue,' Ingvar Johansson said, dead certain. 'He'll see this as an advertisement of his services. And we did try to get hold of the guy for comments. Carl Wennergren went to the Yugo-run clubs last night, to talk—'

Anders Schyman banged his palm on his desk and both men on the opposite side jumped.

'I bet you did,' he roared. 'That's not what I'm talking about. I'm talking about this paper's cavalier high-handedness with journalistic ethics! The two of you don't have the authority to make decisions like this! That authority belongs to the publisher alone! For God's sake, how hard is that to understand?'

Sjölander flushed and Ingvar Johansson turned pale.

Anders Schyman could tell by their reactions that he finally had their attention. He reined in his temper and concentrated on regaining a normal tone of voice.

'I assume that you have more information than what was in the paper,' he said. 'What do we know?'

This triggered the discussion that should have taken place twenty-four hours earlier.

'The police have found shell casings and one bullet,' Sjölander said. 'The ammunition is out of the ordinary. It's 30.06 calibre and an American brand, Trophy Bond. The casings are nickel-plated, shiny, and they look like mushrooms. Practically all the other types of casings are made of brass.'

Schyman took notes. Sjölander relaxed slightly.

'The bullet was found lodged in the asphalt between the silos,' he went on. 'It's not possible to conclude where the shooter was standing, since the bullet slammed into all sorts of stuff in the guy's head and changed direction several times. The casings were found behind an empty warehouse.'

'What about the gun?' Schyman asked.

Sjölander sighed.

'The police might have more details, but they haven't told me,' he said. 'But they have come to a number of conclusions. For example, the killer was very particular about his choice of weapon. These guns are extremely lethal, the kind you use for big game.'

'That might not be so strange after all,' Schyman said. 'If you really want to kill somebody, you might as well do a thorough job.'

Now Sjölander was excited. He leaned across the desk.

'That's the strange thing,' he said. 'Why would he shoot the victim in the head? Anywhere in the chest or the back would have killed the guy within seconds due to the systemic shock. There's something damn fishy about this killer. He's after something beyond efficient killing – he's driven by a huge ego that needs to show off: hate, revenge. Why go for an expert shot when any shot would kill?'

'Why isn't this in today's paper?' Schyman asked.

Sjölander leaned back.

'Because it would interfere with the investigation,' he said.

'Fingering Ratko as the killer, how does that affect the investigation?' the deputy editor asked.

Silence returned.

'We've got to talk about it,' Schyman said. 'The future stability of this paper depends on it, for crying out loud. Who supplied the tip about Ratko?'

Ingvar Johansson cleared his throat.

'We have access to a police source who felt we should go public with the guy's picture. The cops are convinced that he has something to do with this; they wanted to smoke him out.'

'And you obliged the police?' Anders Schyman said in a strained voice. 'You jeopardized the credibility of this paper, you took upon yourselves the authority that rightfully belongs to the publisher, and you were errand boys for the police. Get out of here, right this minute!'

He turned away from the men sitting in front of him, switched on the news bulletins from TT. Out of the corner of his eye he saw the two men quickly and silently slink off into the newsroom.

He relaxed, not quite sure exactly how the conversation had gone. One thing was pretty damn certain, though; it was high time he put his foot down.

The spectacle he'd made of himself during the board meeting had weighed on Thomas Samuelsson's chest like a brick lodged under his breastbone all night and the sensation wouldn't go away. He smoothed the front of his suit jacket, hesitated a moment and then went over to knock on the unit supervisor's door. She was in.

'I'll get straight to the point,' he said. 'There is no

excusing my behaviour yesterday, but I would like to give you an explanation.'

'Have a seat,' his supervisor said.

He sank down in the chair and took a few quick breaths. 'I'm not feeling well,' he said. 'I'm just not myself, there's been too much going on lately.'

The supervisor silently regarded the young man. When he didn't continue she asked him quietly: 'Does this have anything to do with Eleonor?'

His supervisor was a part of their circle, though not a close friend. She had been to dinner at their house a dozen times.

'No, not at all,' Thomas replied. 'It's me. I . . . question everything. Is this all there is? Won't things get any better than this?'

The woman behind the desk gave him a slightly wistful smile.

'A mid-life crisis,' she declared. 'But aren't you running ahead of schedule? How old are you?'

'Thirty-three.'

She sighed.

'Your outburst yesterday was inexcusable, but I suggest we put it behind us. I hope it won't happen again.'

Thomas shook his head, got up and left. Outside the door he stopped, struck by a thought, and went over to the office of the social worker who had presented the proposal about the Paradise Foundation.

'I'm rather busy,' she said curtly, obviously still miffed.

He tried to smile disarmingly.

'So I see,' he said. 'I just wanted to apologize for my behaviour yesterday. I was way out of line.'

The social worker tossed her head and wrote something down.

'Apology accepted,' she said in a frosty voice.

His smile widened.

'I'm glad. You see, I had a few questions about this arrangement. Such as what their corporate registration number is.'

'I don't have it.'

Thomas regarded her for such a long time that her cheeks started to burn. Obviously she didn't know a darn thing about this foundation.

'I can find out,' she offered.

'I think you'd better do that,' he replied.

Once again there was silence. Finally he asked: 'What's this all about?'

She gave him a stern look.

'I'm not at liberty to tell you that, you know.'

He sighed.

'Come on, we're on the same team. Do you think I would tell tales?'

The woman hesitated momentarily and then pushed her papers away.

'It's an emergency situation,' she said. 'This young woman, a Bosnian refugee, is being stalked. This man has threatened to kill her. Her case came up yesterday, and it's urgent. We're talking about a life-and-death matter here.'

Thomas looked her in the eye.

'How do we know it's the truth?'

The social worker swallowed, her eyes slightly moist.

'You should have seen her, so young, so beautiful and . . . so mutilated. Her whole body was covered with scars: gunshot wounds, knife wounds, a great big wound to the head, half of her face all black and blue . . . Two of her toes had been shot off. Last Saturday the man tried to kill her again and she survived by jumping into the water and swimming away from him, and that brought on pneumonia as well. The police aren't able to protect her.'

'But this foundation, Paradise, can do it?'

The woman became animated, and discreetly dried her eyes – after all, she was only human.

'It's a fantastic set-up. They've figured out a way to help people go underground, to wipe them off public records so that they can't be traced. Paradise takes care of all contacts with the outside world. They have people on duty around the clock, they supply medical assistance, psychologists, lawyers, a place to live, they help people find schools, jobs and day care. Believe me, investing in this service will benefit the community.'

Thomas squirmed.

'Paradise itself, where is it? In Järfälla?'

The woman leaned closer.

'That's part of the deal,' she said. 'No one knows where Paradise is. Everyone who works there has had their record wiped clean. The phones are connected to military lines in other counties. The protection is truly watertight. Neither I nor the unit manager have ever come across anything quite like it – it's an incredible organization.'

Thomas looked at the floor.

'All this secrecy means that no one can check if it's for real, though, right?'

'Sometimes you just have to trust people,' the social worker replied.

The apartment was chilled through and through. The paper bag that Annika had taped over the broken window couldn't keep the heat in. Fatigue hit her the instant she dropped her bag on the floor inside the door. She let her coat and the rest of her things fall in a heap, then crawled under the covers of the unmade bed and fell asleep with her clothes on.

Suddenly the hosts of the programme *Studio 69*

appeared in front of her. Their cold, critical spite always gave her stomach cramps.

'I didn't mean this to happen!' she shouted.

The men came closer.

'How can you say it was my fault?' she screamed.

The men tried to shoot her. The sound of their guns roared in her head.

'I didn't do it, I only found her! She was on the floor when I got there! Help!'

She woke up with a jerk, out of breath. Not much more than an hour had passed. For a while she concentrated on breathing – in-out, in-out – then she started to cry, uncontrollably, convulsively. She remained in bed for quite some time until the shaking subsided.

Oh, Gran, dear Lord, what's going to happen? Who is going to take care of you?

Annika sat up and tried to pull herself together. Somebody had to take care of things – it was her turn to be supportive.

She grabbed the telephone directory, called the community-services hotline and asked if there were any vacancies at nursing homes in Stockholm. She was told that she should contact the local authorities in her neighbourhood and discuss suitable living arrangements with a social worker.

If she liked, she could download information from the Internet or pick it up at Medborgarkontoret at Hantverkargatan 87. She jotted down the address in the margins of an old newspaper, thanked them for their help and sighed. Went out to the kitchen, tried to eat some yogurt and turned on the Text TV channel to check if anything had happened. But it hadn't. She realized that she smelled of sweat, stuffed her clothes in the laundry basket, filled the kitchen sink with cold water and washed her armpits.

Why did I go home? Why didn't I stay with Gran?

Annika sat down on the couch in her living room, put her head in her hands and decided that she would be honest with herself.

She couldn't face staying at the hospital. She wanted to go back to something that she had started to regain; something she had once had, but had lost. There was something here in Stockholm, tied to her job at *Kvällspressen*, her apartment; something that was exciting and alive, not indifferent and dead.

She got up abruptly and went to get her notepad from her bag. Then she dialled the number for Paradise without further ado.

This time Rebecka Björkstig answered the phone.

'I've been thinking about a few things,' Annika told her.

'Will you be finished with that article soon?'

The other woman sounded a bit on edge.

Annika pulled up her legs and rested her head in her left hand.

'There are a few details that need filling in,' she said. 'I hope we can wrap this up as soon as possible – my grandmother has been taken ill.'

Rebecka's voice was brimming with compassion as she said: 'Oh, that's too bad. Of course I'll help you out as much as I can. What would you like to know?'

Annika swallowed, sat up a bit straighter and leafed through her pad.

'Your employees at Paradise: how many of them are there?'

'There are five of us working full time.'

'Doctors, lawyers, social workers, psychologists?'

Rebecka sounded amused: 'Not at all. Services like that are provided by the county or local authorities and Legal Aid.'

Annika swept back her hair.

'Your around-the-clock contacts: just who are they?'

'Our employees, naturally. They are highly qualified people.'

'How much do they make a month?'

Now Rebecka acted slightly insulted.

'They earn a monthly salary of fourteen thousand kronor. They don't do this to get rich, they do it to do good.'

Annika leafed through her pad, skimming her notes.

'Your property assets: how many houses are there?'

Rebecka sounded wary: 'Why do you ask?'

'To get a picture of the scope of your operations,' Annika told her.

'We hardly own any property, we usually rent what we need,' Rebecka said after a moment's hesitation.

'What about money?' Annika said. 'If and when you make a profit, what do you do with it?'

A long silence followed. Annika almost thought the woman had hung up on her.

'Any profits we make, and they don't amount to much, go right back into the foundation. They're used to build the organization. I don't quite like what you're insinuating here,' Rebecka Björkstig told her.

'One last question,' Annika said. 'That list of authorities I could talk to – have you sent it?'

'This is a protected line,' said the woman on the other end in a low voice. 'I can talk freely. All the money has gone to building a channel for the really difficult cases. We now have the capacity to help clients who cannot remain in Sweden. We have contacts who help us arrange governmental jobs and housing arrangements in other countries. We can also arrange for medical and psychological care abroad, we can get people jobs and provide language training.'

Annika put her feet back on the floor and took notes. This was getting to be a bit too much.

'But how does it work?'

The woman sounded very satisfied.

'The procedures exist and have been very successful in two cases.'

Annika was astonished.

'Two clients have been able to start over in a foreign country? Without changing their identity? Only by way of Paradise?'

'That's correct, two whole families. But neither we, nor any other organization, can issue new personal ID numbers. Only the government can do that. But, as I told you earlier, it hasn't been necessary. About that list, I've compiled it. Just let me know where I can fax it and you'll have it within fifteen minutes.'

Annika gave her the fax number of the crime desk at the paper.

'I'll call you back and let you know when I've received it,' Annika said.

'Fine. We'll be in touch.'

They hung up. The silence had returned, less ominous now. The walls were brighter. She had a purpose, a responsibility, a mission that needed her input.

The runner picked up his pace, his feet beating a tattoo against the ground. His pulse rate increased, but his breathing remained regular. It merely got deeper, harder: *good!* He was in great shape, gunning along despite the fairly rough terrain. Lots of brushwood, poor forest management, large faults in the landscape. He glanced at the map, scale 1:1,500, based on aerial photos and extensive reconnaissance on the ground. The making of this map was a process he generally took part in himself: it was printed in five colours and issued by the Swedish

Orienteering Association. This location was at the outskirts of his regular stomping grounds, but it was a good
place to practise rough terrain.

He practised picking out the direction as he ran,
holding the compass in his right hand and the map in his
left, not slowing down even though he'd decided to
identify all the various symbols on the map: cairns,
elevated ground, bends in the paths. That was why he
didn't see the tree root. He fell headlong, taking a
nosedive into the seedlings. His forehead slammed into
the ground, he saw stars for a few seconds. When he mind
cleared, he felt the pain in his foot. *Good grief! Only one
competition left this season, and now this! What a darn shame!*

The runner groaned and sat up, touching his ankle.
Maybe it wasn't too bad after all. He tried to rotate his
foot; no, nothing was broken – it could be sprained,
though. He got up carefully and put some weight on the
foot. *Ow!* He'd better shoot for getting back to his car with
the least possible effort. He studied the map to find the
best route.

A few minutes ago he'd passed a muddy road in the
woods that ran parallel to one of the larger faults. He
could tell by the map that it led to the main road and he
could hitch a ride there back to his own car. With a heavy
sigh he tucked the map and the compass inside his jacket
and limped off.

After limping a few hundred metres along the muddy
road he noticed a few singed birch trees further in. He
stopped in surprise. A forest fire? The weather had been
so wet. Then he noticed the smell, pungent and metallic.

The runner checked that his map and compass were
hanging inside his jacket like they should be, then left the
road. He moved carefully, following some tyre tracks that
ran past some trees into a small ravine. Perplexed, he
stopped short at the edge of the woods.

There in front of him was a twisted metal skeleton, the burnt-out remains of what once must have been a truck, a large trailer. How in the world had it got there? And how come it was so totally gutted by fire?

Carefully he limped over to the remains, the soot on the ground turning his shoes black. It got warmer as he approached – the fire must be fairly recent.

The ground next to the driver's seat was covered with fine splinters of glass that crunched under the soles of his shoes. What was left of the doors hung crookedly. He went over and looked inside the cab.

There was something on the floor and something in the passenger seat; shapeless, sooty and twisted. He bent over and touched the object closest to him. Something fell off. He pulled the glove from his hand and brushed away the soot. When he saw the grinning teeth, he realized what he was looking at.

The crime-desk fax was next to Eva-Britt Qvist's desk. Eva-Britt assisted the crime-desk team with different types of research, took care of their appointments, catalogued court decisions, and so on. She wasn't in, so Annika leafed quickly through the small pile of faxes that had arrived during the day. A communiqué from the Stockholm police press department, information from the Chief Public Prosecutor, a verdict in a narcotics case.

'What are you doing with my papers?'

The solid-looking woman came charging in from the cafeteria, an angry furrow between her brows. Annika backed away.

'I'm expecting a fax,' she said. 'I just wanted to see if it had arrived.'

'Why do you give people my number? This fax belongs to the crime desk.'

Eva-Britt Qvist snatched the papers out of Annika's

hands and scooped up the ones that were lying on the desk. Annika looked at her in astonishment. They had hardly spoken to each other before – Eva-Britt Qvist worked during the day and Annika worked nights.

'I'm sorry,' Annika stammered in surprise. 'I always give people this number during the night shift. I wasn't aware there was anything wrong with that.'

The researcher glared at Annika.

'And you never fill the paper tray, either.'

The other woman's animosity pierced her like a dart, generating a defensive response of anger.

'Oh, yes I do!' Annika exclaimed. 'I did it the last time I was in. What's your problem, for God's sake? It's not like it's your own private fax. Has my list of authorities connected to the Paradise Foundation arrived?'

'What's going on, girls?'

Anders Schyman had come up behind them.

'Girls?' Annika said, whirling to face him. 'Are you going to ask us what we're doing here all by ourselves too?'

The deputy editor laughed.

'I knew that would set you off. What's up?'

'Rebecka's going to send me a fax that will help me wrap up this series about the Paradise Foundation, but Eva-Britt here doesn't like me giving people her fax number.'

Annika realized that she was upset and was ashamed of her lack of self-control.

'It hasn't arrived,' the researcher said.

Schyman turned to Eva-Britt Qvist.

'Then I think you should stay on the lookout for that list,' Schyman said slowly and distinctly. 'It's the cornerstone of an important story we're covering.'

'This is the crime desk, you know,' Eva-Britt Qvist said.

'And this is a crime feature,' Schyman said. 'Stop being so territorial. Come on, Annika, I want an update on the story.'

Annika followed the deputy editor over to his office, not seeing anything except his broad back.

The couch was gone.

'I took your advice,' Schyman said. 'From now on, anyone visiting me will have to sit on the floor. Be my guest.'

He gestured towards the dusty corner, but she pulled up a chair instead.

'I think everything is about to fall in place,' she said, brushing a hand across her forehead. 'Rebecka Björkstig has promised to fax over those last bits of information, and I got an explanation for where the money goes.'

Schyman looked up.

'Money? Do they charge for their services?'

Annika flipped through the large pad she'd taken out of her bag.

'The proceeds have been used to build a route for people who can't stay in Sweden,' she rattled off from her notes. 'Paradise has the contacts to arrange government jobs and housing in other countries. So far, they've pulled this off twice, for two families. No one has had to change their identity. Issuing new personal ID numbers is not something Paradise or any other organization can do, only the government. But this hasn't been necessary for Paradise's clients.'

She looked up at the deputy editor and tried to smile.

'Good stuff, isn't it?'

Anders Schyman regarded her calmly.

'That doesn't wash,' he said.

She looked down at the desktop and didn't reply.

'Arrange government jobs in other countries?' he went

on. 'That sounds like a tall tale to me. Does this Björkstig woman have any proof?'

Annika leafed through her pad without looking up.

'Two cases,' she said. 'Two whole families.'

'Have you talked to them?'

Annika swallowed, crossed her legs and felt herself getting on the defensive.

'Rebecka knows what she's talking about.'

The deputy editor tapped a pencil on the table top as he reflected.

'Really? The government doesn't issue new personal ID numbers. That's performed by the Internal Revenue Service at the request of the Swedish National Police Board.'

Sounds in the background receded, as Annika felt the blood drain from her face.

'Is that true?'

Schyman nodded and Annika sat up straight, frantically flipping through her pad.

'But she said it was the government, I'm sure she did.'

'I believe you,' Schyman said, 'but I don't believe that Paradise lady.'

Annika slumped down in her chair again and closed her pad.

'So I went to all that trouble for nothing.'

Anders Schyman got up.

'On the contrary,' he said. 'This is when the real work begins. If such an organization actually exists, then that's sensational, regardless of whether this woman happens to be lying. Tell me, what has she told you?'

Annika gave him a summary of how Paradise worked, how they wiped people off the record; about Rebecka's strange threats in the past that were somehow connected to the Yugoslav Mafia; and finally, she told him her own thoughts about where the money went.

Schyman walked around, nodding, and then sat down again.

'You've got pretty far,' he said. 'But we have to have that list. If this is a fake we need the help of the authorities to get hold of all the information about the foundation.'

'The alternative is,' Annika said, 'to get hold of one of the women who have experienced the organization from the inside. Or find someone who has worked there.'

'If there are any such women,' Schyman said. 'Or any employees whatsoever.'

The list still hadn't arrived. There wasn't anything wrong with the fax. More than two hours had passed since Annika had spoken to Rebecka.

Annika sat down at Berit Hamrin's desk and dialled the number – the unlisted, secret number. The signals echoed into a void. She dialled the number again. No answer. No answering machine. The call wasn't forwarded.

'Could you tell me if that list turns up?' she called out to Eva-Britt Qvist.

The researcher was on the phone and pretended not to hear her.

Annika went over to the computer with the modem and got hooked up to PubReg, the state-operated register listing every individual issued with a Swedish personal ID number, pressed F8 to do a name query and typed in *Rebecka Björkstig*. The computer chugged along for a while and then spat out its answer.

One single hit:

. . . personal data is protected.

That was it. Not so much as a comma.

Annika stared at the screen. *What the hell?*

She typed in her own name: *Bengtzon, Annika, Stockholm*, the gauze condom on her finger getting in the way; chug, bingo, there she was. Her personal ID number, address, last known official change of recorded domicile two years ago. She switched commands to F7 for a historical list and found her old address at Tattarbacken in Hälleforsnäs. The technology was working just fine.

She started over again and typed *Rebecka Björkstig, female* – and the results were the same as before.

. . . personal data is protected.

Rebecka really had been wiped off the record.

Annika looked at the screen for a long time. One of her duties during the night shift was to locate photographs of people, usually their passport photos, and in order to access them she needed their personal ID numbers, and then she used the PubReg. She had looked up nearly a thousand people over the years she'd worked the night shift, but she had never come across this particular message. She got a printout and paused. Typed in *Aida Begovic* and got eight hits. One of the women lived on Fredriksbergsvägen in Vaxholm, that must be her Aida. She got another printout and went back to Berit's desk.

'Still no list?'

Eva-Britt Qvist shook her head. Annika called Paradise again – no reply. Slammed down the receiver, hard – *damn it!*

What was she going to do now? Her finger hurt. Go back to the hospital? Try to find a nursing home in Stockholm? Go home and do some cleaning?

She rummaged through her papers and found the folder about foundations issued by the Internal Revenue Service that she had ordered from the archives.

As of 1 January 1996 there was a law for foundations, she read. This law contained regulations about how to establish a foundation, about the management of a foundation, bookkeeping and auditing procedures, maintenance, registration, and so on.

Annika skimmed the paragraphs. There were different types of foundations, apparently, that were subject to different tax brackets. The ones that had a 'qualified public service objective' paid less, she read.

Fancy statutes weren't enough to get you a tax exemption, you had to follow those statutes too, it said.

Annika put the folder down – what was this? This was just a load of garbage.

Why bother? It didn't mean a thing.

Oh, yes it does, she thought suddenly, *it means that Paradise would have to have drawn up some kind of statute as well. They would have to submit their bookkeeping to a public accountant. They would be subject to taxation. It's not like they could be wiped off the face of the Earth.*

She picked up the papers Rebecka had given her and looked at the post office box number in the heading. She called the post office in Järfälla and asked who leased the box in question.

'I can't tell you that,' a harried cashier said.

'But there would be a street address connected to the box number, right?' Annika said. 'I'd like to know who leases box number 259.'

'That's classified information,' the cashier said. 'Only the authorities can access information like that.'

Annika thought hard for a second or two.

'I might be a civil servant,' she said. 'How would you know? I haven't introduced myself, and you haven't asked who I am.'

For a moment there was silence at the other end.

'I'll have to check with Disa,' the official said.

'Who?'

'The Disa system: we're hooked up to a database that supplies us with eligibility guidelines. One moment, please . . .'

It seemed to take for ever as several minutes passed.

The official's voice was even frostier when she came back on the line.

'Ever since the state postal service was converted into a company, all contracts between ourselves and our customers are confidential. Should the police suspect that a crime that would entail a prison sentence of more than two years has been committed, we are allowed to disclose information, but only in those circumstances.'

Annika thanked her and hung up, banging down the receiver. Restlessly, she roamed the newsroom; people were talking, shouting, laughing. Phones were ringing, computer screens flickered.

The authorities, she needed access to someone working for the authorities, someone who knew the ropes. Since she didn't know of any specific case, she had to go fishing. She went back to her desk, opened the telephone directory and called the Stockholm city council offices.

'Which district would you like to be connected to?'

She picked her own, Kungsholmen, and was put on hold. After twelve minutes of uninterrupted silence she hung up.

What about Järfälla?

The Family Services Department had telephone access hours between 8:30 and 9:30 a.m., as well as 5:00 to 5:30 p.m. on Thursdays.

Annika groaned. Calling at random like this was pointless. Even if she did, against all odds, find someone who knew something, they wouldn't talk. All these cases were kept confidential. She had to find an opening, someplace where she was certain that the local authorities would be involved.

She poured herself a cup of coffee, blowing on the liquid on her way back to her desk. She passed a group of laughing women belonging to God knew what department and walked past without saying hello, her gaze fixed on the floor. In her mind, their voices seemed to die down as she passed, the conversation came to a stop, and she believed that they had been talking about her.

I'm just imagining things, Annika thought, not convincing herself.

She set down the plastic cup on Berit's desk, spilling some, and tried to concentrate on work. *There's no point in contacting social workers*, she thought. *They panic before you have time to ask questions and they never give you any answers, even if the information isn't classified.*

Where would that information be available?

Suddenly it hit her, and she ended up scalding her tongue with her coffee.

The invoices. Of course!

The invoices sent by Paradise ought to contain lots of information: their corporate identity number and their address, a bank account number or a postal giro account number. Anyone in charge of finances at the local authorities would be able to obtain details about taxes, statutes and accountants.

Annika leafed through the different districts in the green pages of the telephone directory. Which one should she choose?

Putting down the directory, she picked up the PubReg printouts instead. Rebecka's district wasn't listed, but Aida was registered in Vaxholm.

Vaxholm.

Annika had never been there: all she knew about the place was that it was located to the north, by the sea.

This is a long shot, Annika thought. Aida might not even have contacted Paradise. The local authorities in her district might not be involved. It could be that not enough time had passed.

On the other hand, it could pan out. She dialled the number and waited for ever. Her thoughts drifted off – she really ought to call and find out how her grandmother was doing. By the time the operator answered, Annika had forgotten why she was calling. She asked to speak to someone in the accounts department at Social Services. The line was busy and there was one call on hold: could she possibly call back later?

She hung up, put on her coat, stuffed her pad in her bag and headed for the attendants who handled the newspaper's cars.

'No list?'

No reply from Eva-Britt Qvist.

The E18 to Roslagen was famous for its afternoon rush-hour traffic. For about fifteen minutes Annika stood still in Bergshamra, then it picked up.

It felt great to be behind the wheel. She exceeded the speed limit, overtaking vehicle after vehicle, the *Kvällspressen* car was pretty peppy. Downtown Vaxholm appeared sooner than she'd expected. Perky little flags waved along a cobblestone street lined by dainty period buildings. A bank, a flower shop. A Co-op. It occurred to Annika that she didn't have a map.

The local authorities, she pondered. *City Hall, by the main square. It can't be all that hard to find.*

Annika kept driving until she reached the waterfront, made a right turn at a small traffic circle and came to a ferry berth. A long line of cars were waiting to take the dirty-yellow ferry out to Rindö.

She made a left turn. Östra Ekuddsgatan was the name of the street. She gazed out over the row of opulent waterfront homes belonging to wealthy tradesmen.

The fancy side of town, she thought. *The hot-shit people.*

Slowly, the car made its way up a steep road paved

with asphalt and coated with grit. Every home was fenced in and gated.

'Too bad,' she said aloud and noticed that she was back where she'd started from. She headed down the street with all the perky flags and made a left turn instead of a right. This took her to the police station near a small square. Straight ahead she could see a large orange building topped by a small Russian-style bulbous dome. The double doors in front were done in painted marbling, and so were the posts that flanked them. A small mailbox bore the legend *Vaxholm City Hall.*

The weather didn't improve. The greyness had invaded Thomas's mind. He felt like crying. The narrow street below his window looked like a ditch full of mud. The piles of papers and assignments threatened to smother him and the damn phone kept ringing. He stared at the jangling device.

I won't bother answering it, he thought. *It's only another day-care centre that imagines there's money left in this year's budget.*

With a jerk he picked up the receiver.

'Hello, this is the front desk calling. There's a reporter here who wants to speak to someone in charge of finances and contracts at Social Services, and I thought you might—'

Christ, would it never end?

'I'm not a politician. Send her over to the local-government representatives.'

The receptionist put Thomas on hold and when she came back her voice was more curt.

'She doesn't want to speak to a politician, she just wants some . . . What did you say you wanted to ask?'

Thomas rested his head in one hand and groaned. *Heaven help me!*

The murmuring in the background got louder.

'Could I possibly speak to him in person?' he heard a voice say, followed by: 'Hello?'

'What is this all about?' he said curtly, exhausted.

'Well, my name is Annika Bengtzon and I'm a reporter. I was wondering if I could come up and ask you a few brief questions about how different communities procure contracts and services.'

Why my community? he thought.

'I don't have the time,' he said.

'Why is that?' she shot back. 'Are you a burn-out case?'

Thomas burst into laughter. What kind of crazy question was that?

'You haven't made an appointment,' he said, 'and I'm extremely busy at the moment.'

'It won't take more than fifteen minutes of your time,' the reporter said. 'You won't have to move an inch, I'll come up to your office.'

He sighed soundlessly.

'To be honest . . .'

'I'm down at the front desk. It won't take long. Please?'

The last word was uttered in pleading tones.

He rubbed his eyes – they felt gritty. Getting rid of her without seeing her would take longer than meeting her.

'Come on up.'

Annika Bengtzon was very thin and had tousled hair, slightly manic lines around her mouth and shadows under her eyes that were too dark for her to be regarded as beautiful.

'I apologize for barging in on you like this,' she said as she crammed her large bag under a chair. She draped her jacket and her scarf sloppily over the back of the chair. One sleeve touched the floor. She offered her hand and smiled. Thomas shook it, swallowed, and noticed that his right hand was slightly moist. He wasn't used to people from the media.

'Let me know if I get out of line,' the woman said. 'I'm aware that Social Services cases are delicate matters.'

She sank down on the chair, keeping her gaze fixed on him, utterly concentrated, her pen poised.

Thomas cleared his throat.

'What happened to your hand?'

Annika didn't avert her stare.

'I got it caught in something. Have you ever heard of a foundation called Paradise?'

His reaction was purely physical. He did a double take.

'Christ, what do you know about Paradise?'

The woman had noticed his reaction, he could tell as much from the satisfied expression on her face.

'I know a little,' she said. 'Not enough, though. I was wondering if you might know more than me.'

'Everything connected to Social Services is classified information,' Thomas said curtly.

'No, it isn't,' the reporter said, now sounding almost amused. 'The public is allowed access to lots of it. I'm not sure how much, though, so that's what I wanted to ask you.'

He felt utterly perplexed. How the hell was he going to deal with this? He couldn't mention the case, the Bosnian woman, he wasn't even supposed to know anything about her. He certainly didn't want the press to write that Vaxholm bought pricey services from strange foundations.

'I can't help you,' he said curtly and stood up.

'She's lying,' the reporter said in a low voice. 'The director of the Paradise Foundation is a liar. Did you know that?'

Thomas froze. Annika looked up at him, dark-eyed, leaning forward slightly, legs crossed. *Big breasts*, he thought.

He sat back down again and stared at his desk.

'I don't know what you're talking about. I'm sorry, but I can't help you. If you'll excuse me, I'm very busy . . .'

She flipped through a large, unwieldy pad, showing no sign of getting up.

'Do you mind if I ask a few general questions about how you procure services?'

'Like I said, I really don't have—'

'Has the outsourcing of public services affected your work with the local authorities?'

The reporter looked deep into Thomas's eyes, focusing on him, his answer. He swallowed and cleared his throat again.

'After the decentralization that followed the new Social Services acts in 1982, we ended up with lots of numbers to crunch. Every last day-care centre and nursing home, every single unit involved was required to have a budget of its own. Now, after the privatization process, there are fewer details. Each item becomes a single cost in the budget.'

Annika listened, her face impassive, her pen still.

'What's that, in plain language?'

Feeling rebuked and annoyed Thomas felt the blood rising to his face. He decided not to show it.

'In some ways things are easier now,' he said. 'The community pays a lump sum, and the contractors get to manage the money on their own.'

Now she was taking notes, he stopped talking.

'What do you do?' she asked. 'What's your job description?'

'I'm a chief accountant, I'm responsible for the finances and business plans here at Social Services, I plan and oversee the budget. I supervise the internal administration processes, manage the financial resources, deal with the needs and requirements of the employees in our various operations, manage the quarterly follow-ups and balance the books . . . You could say that I focus on three years at a time: the previous year, the current year, and the year after that . . .'

'Amazing,' the woman said. 'Do you always talk like that?'

Surprised, Thomas faltered.

'It certainly took a damned long time to learn how,' he said.

She laughed, her teeth even and white.

'How have these changes been accepted by Social Services?' she asked. 'Do people like the new arrangement?'

Annika moved, her breasts bobbing slightly under her sweater. Thomas looked down at his desk.

'There have been mixed reactions,' he said. 'The unit supervisors have less power now, and they're not too happy about that. They can't micromanage things any more, like they could when day-care centres and nursing homes were run directly by the local authorities. But on the other hand their responsibilities are reduced too.'

His candour surprised him. The reporter took notes without looking up. Beautiful strong hands.

'Everyone has the right to their own opinion,' Thomas went on. 'Naturally, individual civil servants have different political views of the changes too, different ideologies.'

'Could you tell me exactly what you do and why?' Annika said.

Thomas nodded and did just that. Certain things he had to repeat a few times, find different words and other ways of expressing things. She didn't seem to be highly educated, but at least she was quick on the uptake. He explained his part on the Social Services board, a group he belonged to that consisted of the council's administration managers and unit managers, that was, the people in charge of day care, schools, the care of the elderly, family services . . . They went through the decision-making process, how the social welfare board voted on decisions, how the administration manager was always present, and so was the chief accountant and the civil servants presenting the various issues, and sometimes the unit managers as well.

'So, who has the power?' she asked.

Out of the corner of his eye, Thomas studied her: slim thighs, tight jeans.

'That depends on the nature of the issue,' he replied. 'Many decisions are made at an executive level. Others are dealt with by the board. Certain issues go all the way to the Administrative Court of Appeal or the Supreme Administrative Court of Appeal before a decision is reached.'

Annika mulled this over for a while, tapping her forehead with her pen.

'If you get a proposal from a new organization,' she said, looking at him for a long time, 'from, shall we say, a foundation that would like to help needy people – who would decide whether to use them or not?'

Suddenly Thomas realized where her interrogation was leading. For some reason it didn't bother him.

'The initial decision to procure services of this type would probably be dealt with by the board,' he said slowly. 'But once that decision was made, subsequent related decisions could be made by individual civil servants.'

'Do you get a lot of these offers? From foundations and private contractors?'

'Not that many,' he said. 'The city council usually solicits offers when the different units need to keep costs down.'

Annika leafed briefly through her pad.

'If Vaxholm decided to use such a foundation, would you know about it?'

Thomas heaved a deep sigh.

'Yes,' he said.

'Have they?'

He sighed again.

'Yes,' he said. 'The social welfare board passed the motion to procure the services of a foundation called Paradise at last night's meeting. The minutes are probably not ready yet, but they will state that the contract was approved, under item seven, and those minutes are a matter of public record. That's why I'm telling you this,' he said.

The young woman had some colour in her face now.

'What do you know about the woman involved, Aida Begovic from Bijelina?'

He did another double take, suddenly enraged.

'What exactly do you want?' he roared. 'Distracting me with all those questions and then insinuating—'

'Take it easy,' the reporter responded sharply. 'I think we can help each other.'

Thomas stopped short, realizing that he was standing: angry, blood boiling, face flaming, his right hand bunched into a fist and raised – what the hell was the matter with him? *For Christ's sake, get a grip, man!*

He sat down hurriedly, his hair flopping across his face. Using both hands, he pushed it back.

'I'm sorry,' he said. 'Christ, I'm sorry, I didn't mean to get upset . . .'

Annika flashed him a grin.

'Great,' she said. 'I'm not the only hot-tempered person around here.'

Thomas looked at her – that hair of hers that was somehow always in motion, the eyes that saw straight through him.

He averted his gaze.

'What exactly do you want?'

She grew serious, sounding sincere at last.

'I'm stuck. I'm checking out this organization and it's not going very well. According to the information that I've received from Rebecka Björkstig, Paradise must have generated proceeds of more than eighteen million kronor over the past three years, and if my calculations are correct, the costs should be in the neighbourhood of seven million. I don't know what kind of foundation Paradise is, so I can't figure out which tax bracket applies, but it does seem a little fishy.'

'Do you know if the set-up actually works?' he asked.

Annika shook her head, appearing to be truly concerned.

'Nope. I've met Rebecka, and I've met Aida, but I don't know if the set-up works.'

'Rebecka – is she the one in charge?'

The reporter nodded.

'She claims to be, and I believe her. You haven't met her? She seems trustworthy, but we've caught her out in a lie, or maybe we should call it an error. She doesn't know as much as she likes to pretend, and when you question her, she's evasive. How much do you actually know about Paradise?'

Thomas hesitated, but only for a second.

'Next to nothing. No one seems to know anything. The board made their decision yesterday, even though the information we had was very sketchy. I don't even have a corporate identity number.'

'But could you dig one up?'

He nodded.

'Is the set-up legally sound?'

'We asked our legal advisers that very question this morning.'

Annika Bengtzon gave Thomas an intense look.

'In a general sense, what do you know about foundations? Why do you think Rebecka Björkstig chose that particular framework for her organization?'

He leaned in closer.

'A foundation doesn't have any owners or members. There are far fewer regulations than for stock corporations or partnerships.'

Annika took notes.

'Go on.'

'As far as I know, foundations can be used as a means to siphon off money after bankruptcy. You can make use of foundations to commit various types of fraud, and you can take advantage of the fact that there isn't much public access.'

The reporter looked up.

'Why is access limited?'

'When a foundation is registered, the representatives aren't obliged to submit their personal ID numbers. There have been cases where these representatives turned out to be fictitious, make-believe.'

Annika nodded, scratched her head and pondered.

'On the one hand,' she said, 'this makes it all even more fishy. Rebecka could have established the foundation with the sole intention of defrauding people. On the other hand, if the set-up actually works like she says it does, a foundation would be the ideal arrangement.'

They sat in silence for a while. Thomas noticed that the sounds of City Hall had petered out and checked the time.

'Christ,' he exclaimed. 'Is it that late already?'

Annika smiled.

'Time flies when you're having fun.'

He got up in a hurry.

'I've got to run,' he said.

She gathered her things and stuffed them in her huge

bag. Put on her jacket and scarf and shook his hand.

'Thank you for taking the time to see me.'

She looked him straight in the eye, standing tall. Not too tall, though, and that chest . . . He felt his palms getting moist again.

'I'm going to pursue this,' Annika said, shaking his hand and holding on to it. 'There's one thing I wonder,' she said. 'If I find something, would you like to know about it?'

Thomas swallowed, his throat dry, and nodded.

She smiled.

'Good. And if you find anything out, will you let me know?'

He let go of her hand.

'We'll see . . .'

'See you.'

The next minute Annika Bengtzon was gone. Thomas stared at the closed door and heard her footsteps disappear down the hall. Then he went over to the visitor's chair and sank down on it, the seat still retaining some of her body heat. From her loins.

He got up quickly, pulled out a loose-leaf binder and looked up the Social Services personnel budget; the numbers danced in front of his eyes. Irritably he closed the book and went over to the window. The picturesque signs on the shops below taunted him: At The Seashore, the Vaxholm Tea & Spices Boutique.

He should go home. Eleonor would have dinner ready.

The traffic bound for Stockholm was considerably thinner than the steady stream of cars coming from the city. Through the windshield, Annika stared at the dismal suburban sprawl that closed in around the car. As soon as she had left downtown Vaxholm, the picturesque buildings had given way to anonymous high-rise apartment blocks. *This could be anywhere, like Flen*, she thought. A sign on the left told her it was Fredriksberg, Aida's old neighbourhood. She slowed down, wondering if she should check out Aida's address and then deciding not to.

A traffic advisory announcement came on the radio: the roads would be slippery due to freezing rain.

Well, at least I'm alive, she thought. *I get to be around for a while longer.*

Annika tried to look at the sky but the clouds were extremely thick. No stars could be seen. No one could see her from outer space.

She drove back slowly, cars passing her this time instead of the other way around. Her gut calmed down but her distress over her grandmother's condition stayed like a rock in the pit of her stomach.

The surroundings along the route bound for Stockholm were uncommonly ordinary. Route 274 could have been the road between Hälleforsnäs and Katrineholm. She switched on the radio and found a station airing a Boney M marathon. *Brown girl in the ring, sha-la-la-la. Ma Baker, she taught her four sons, ma-ma-ma-ma, Ma Baker, to handle their guns. Run, run, Rasputin, lover of the Russian queen.*

It started to drizzle a little when she reached Arninge and turned out on the E18 again, but the proper rain remained in the air, suspended there. She listened to German disco music the whole way back to the newspaper building in Marieberg.

No attendants were on duty, so she left the car keys on the counter. Then she headed for Hantverkaregatan, home, by way of the park at Rålambshov and along the northern shore of Lake Mälaren. It was cold and damp, the darkness relieved at intervals by street lights and neon signs but somehow still pervasive and massive. Her thoughts went to her grandmother: what should they do?

The cramping sensation in her gut increased as dread throbbed within her.

By the time Annika got home she was chilled to the bone, her teeth chattering. The phone rang and she dashed inside with muddy shoes.

Gran! Oh, dear God, something's happened to Gran!

Shame shot through her. Her calm had been merely a front and she felt guilty about not being there.

'I'm going to that Thai place to pick up a cashew chicken wok,' her friend Anne said. 'Want some?'

Annika slumped down to the floor.

'Yes, please.'

Anne Snapphane showed up half an hour later with two foil boxes in a bag.

'Damn, it's cold,' she said when she'd wiped her feet. 'This damp air is hell on the airways. I can feel bronchitis zeroing in on me.'

Anne had a flair for hypochondria.

'Put on a pair of thick woollen socks. Keep your feet toasty and you'll be fine, that's what Gran always says,' Annika said and burst into tears.

'Oh, honey, what's wrong?'

Anne went over, sat next to Annika on the couch and waited. Annika sobbed, felt the rock in her stomach grow warm, soften and slowly disintegrate.

'It's Gran,' she said. 'She's had a stroke and she's over at Kullbergska Hospital in Katrineholm. She's not going to get better.'

'What a shame,' Anne said, full of sympathy. 'What's going to happen to her now?'

Annika took a tissue and blew her nose, wiped her face and let her breath out in a slow *whoosh*.

'No one knows. There isn't space for her anywhere, and no one has the time to take care of her, and she needs loads of support and rehabilitation. I figure I might have to stop working and have her stay with me.'

Anne cocked her head to one side.

'Three flights of stairs, no toilet and no hot water?'

Annika put words to the thoughts that had churned in her gut all day.

'I guess I'll have to move to Katrineholm. It's not the end of the world. I mean, what do I actually do? Rewrite stuff other reporters have done for a lousy rag with no cred. Is that more important than taking care of the only person you love?'

Anne didn't reply, she just let Annika cry herself out. She went to the kitchen and got glasses and utensils. Annika turned on the TV set and they watched the news, *Rapport*, and ate chicken wok straight from the package. The stock market had gone back up. There was more unrest in Mitrovica. The state of the Social Democratic Party prior to the congress was explored.

'Are you serious about quitting?' Anne Snapphane wondered as she sank back against the cushions, too stuffed to move.

Annika rubbed her forehead and sighed deeply.

'As a last resort. I don't want to stop working, but what else can you do if there aren't any other options?'

'Competing for the "Martyrs' World Cup" isn't going to make anyone happy,' Anne said. 'You have a responsibility to yourself, too – you can't make other people your world. Want some wine?'

'The doctor actually prescribed liquor,' Annika replied. 'White, please.'

'What else? Red wine brings my face out in boils. God, it's cold in here. Are any of your windows open?'

Anne got up and went into the kitchen.

'The wind totaled one of my windows,' Annika called after her.

Anne returned with the wine. Wrapped in a blanket each, they sipped Chardonnay poured from a carton.

'How are things otherwise?' Anne asked.

Annika sighed, shut her eyes and leaned back against the cushions.

'I had a fight with my mother. She doesn't like me. I've always known that was the case, but it felt pretty damn awful to hear it spelled out like that.'

Pain welled up inside her: not being loved had its own particular brand of agony.

Anne Snapphane wore a sceptical expression on her face.

'I don't know anyone who gets along with their mother.'

Annika shook her head, discovered she could manage a smile and looked down at her wineglass.

'I really don't think she likes me. To be honest, I'm not sure I like her either. Do you have to?'

Anne considered this.

'Not really. It depends on the mother. If she deserves it, you can love her if you like, but there's no obligation. On the other hand,' Anne declared, index finger in the air admonishingly, 'mothers have to love their children. It's an obligation that there's no getting out of.'

'She doesn't think I deserve love,' Annika said.

Anne Snapphane shrugged.

'She's wrong. It just proves she's a moron. Now give me some upbeat news, please. Hasn't anything fun happened to you?'

The tightness in her chest relaxed and Annika felt relieved. She smiled.

'I've got a hot story going at work. A really fishy foundation that wipes people whose lives are in danger off the record.'

Anne Snapphane took a sip of her wine and cocked an eyebrow at her, Annika went on.

'And I met this civil-servant guy today – he's doing business with this foundation. If I played my cards right I might have an in there.'

'Was he a hottie?'

Anne Snapphane downed her wine and poured herself some more.

'A desk jockey,' Annika said. 'All he did was drone on about bureaucratic junk. I tried to get him to loosen up; you know, a little small talk and all that, but no way. Must have been the first time he'd ever run into a reporter – talk about nervous . . .'

'Come on,' Anne said, swirling the wine in her glass. 'I'm positive those boobs of yours were getting him all hot under the collar.'

Annika stared at her friend.

'Are you out of your mind?' she said. 'A civil servant?'

'He's got a penis, right? And what was he doing down at the free port?'

Annika groaned, put down her glass and got up.

'You're not keeping up with me. The free-port thing was the day before yesterday. This guy's office is in Vaxholm. Want some water?'

She got a pitcher and two fresh glasses. The long-haired weather hunk, Per, wound up his forecast and a new programme began; a bunch of middle-aged women with cultural aspirations initiated a meaningless, pretentious discussion.

Annika turned the TV off.

'How's "The Women's Sofa" going?'

Now it was Anne's turn to groan.

'Michelle Carlsson, the new girl, wants to be on camera all the time. She does her stand-up schtick in every segment and won't let anyone edit them. She's suggested that we should have a panel seated on the sofa, to discuss issues like sex and stuff, and that she should be on the panel.'

'She actually said that?' Annika asked. 'That she should be on the panel?'

Anne Snapphane groaned again.

'No, but it's pretty obvious that's why she suggested it.'

'It's a good thing someone wants to be on camera,' Annika said. 'I would flat-out refuse. I'd rather die.'

'Most people feel the other way around,' Anne Snapphane said. 'Lots of people would kill to get on the air.'

The televised debate dealt with the position of the arts in society, a subject that was almost always timely.

'Let me ask the panel,' the host said. 'What does art mean to you?'

The first guest made a circle in the air with her right hand while she spoke: 'A never-ending dialogue,' she said.

'Good art has a certain urgency to it. It goes in new directions, it has substance and an ability to move many people,' the second guest said, slicing her left hand in a horizontal fashion.

'Serious artists mirror their time. Personally, I think it's good that art comes up for discussion, controversy signals that art is an urgent matter,' the third guest said, eyebrows arched.

'But is art important only when it stirs up a debate?' the host wondered.

'There are limits,' the third guest continued, 'and it's something you have to decide from case to case. If you know who the artist is, you generally know how serious they are, but you can't have preconceived ideas.

Conceptual art, where the theme of the exhibit is the point, is—'

Thomas got up from the couch.

'I'm going to get a beer – would you like one?'

Eleonor didn't reply, the furrow between her eyes showing that she didn't want to be disturbed. He went upstairs, the cultivated voices ringing in his ears.

'. . . Contemporary art has always been an affront to the society of the day. It could very well be that churchgoers clutched their collection money tightly in their cold fists when they saw how Giotto di Bondone modernized the religious art of his time . . .'

Thomas went to the fridge: no cold beers. He sighed, went over to the pantry and opened a lukewarm one. Looked for the evening papers without finding them.

'Aren't you going to watch this?' Eleonor called to him.

He sat on a kitchen chair for a few seconds, took a large swig, gas bubbles going to his nose, sighed and went downstairs again.

'Feminism has influenced the way literature is discussed as well as the conditions for describing the history of literature,' the host remarked. 'But has it affected literature itself? And if that's the case, in what way?'

Thomas sat down on the couch. The woman taking the floor bore a striking resemblance to a pear. She was the publisher of a periodical about literature and was such a gasbag that it made Thomas want to laugh.

'. . . A boon to female authors,' the pear declared, 'by singling them out in this way. The words of a Danish author come to mind . . .'

'Talk about taking yourself seriously!' he exclaimed.

'Be quiet, I'm listening to this.'

He got up abruptly and went back to the kitchen.

'Thomas, what's the matter?' Eleonor called after him.

He groaned to himself and rummaged through his briefcase in search of the evening papers.

'Nothing.'

There they were. He fished them out; they were wrinkled, soon to be obsolete and uninteresting.

'Aren't you going to watch the debate? We're going to discuss it at the Cultural Society on Saturday.'

He didn't answer and started reading *Kvällspressen*. That was where Annika Bengtzon worked. He hadn't recognized her and presumed that she didn't write any of those articles with the little picture byline.

'Thomas . . .'

'What?'

'You don't have to shout. Do we have any video cassettes that I could use? I want to record this programme.'

He lowered the paper and squeezed his eyes shut.

'Thomas?'

'I don't know. Christ, let me read in peace!'

Demonstratively, he opened the paper again. A large man in dark clothing stared at him from the pages, the leader of some cigarette ring. He heard Eleonor fiddle with the VCR downstairs, and knew what would happen next. Soon she would start yelling at the machine and banging on it. And demand that he come down to fix it.

'Thomas!'

He threw the paper aside and bounded downstairs in three strides.

'All right,' he said. 'Here I am. Tell me what the hell you want me to do so I can go back upstairs and finish reading my paper in peace!'

She looked at him as if he were a ghost.

'What's the matter with you? Your face is all red. All I need is a little help with the VCR – is that too much to ask?'

'You could learn how to push the button yourself.'

'Don't be so intense,' she said uncertainly. 'I'm missing the debate.'

'Pretentious middle-class bags jerking each other off onscreen – like that's something to miss?'

Eleonor stared at him, her mouth half-open.

'You're out of your mind,' she said. 'Sweden would be a cultural wasteland if it wasn't for those women! They represent, and define, our cultural status, our view of contemporary society.'

Thomas looked at her, so well-spoken, so much in tune with the times.

He turned, grabbed his coat and left.

As soon as Aida woke up she realized that her fever had broken. Her mind was clear and focused, all traces of pain were gone. She was thirsty.

The woman she had met that morning sat on a stool next to her.

'Would you like something to drink?'

She nodded and the woman handed her a glass of apple juice. Annika hand shook as she took the glass. She was still weak.

'How do you feel?'

Aida swallowed, nodded and gazed around the room. A hospital room, a slight sense of discomfort in her right arm, an IV line. She was naked.

'Much better, thank you.'

The other woman got up and leaned over her.

'My name is Mia,' the woman said. 'I'm going to help you. We'll be leaving this place tonight, so try and get as much rest as you can. Would you like something to eat – are you hungry?'

Aida shook her head.

'What's this?' she asked, moving her right arm.

'Intravenous antibiotics,' Mia said. 'You had severe

double pneumonia. You'll have to take a course of antibiotics for another ten days.'

Aida closed her eyes and swept her left hand across her forehead.

'Where am I?' she whispered.

'In a hospital far from Stockholm,' Mia said. 'My husband and I brought you here.'

'Am I safe here?'

'Completely. The doctors are old friends of mine. There's no record of your stay and we'll take your chart with us when you go. The guy looking for you won't find you here.'

Aida looked up.

'So you know . . .?'

'Rebecka told me,' Mia said, leaning over her. 'Aida,' she whispered. 'Don't trust Rebecka.'

PART TWO

NOVEMBER

NO ONE IS WITHOUT BLAME.

Not even I can avoid the consequences of my actions.

However, feelings of guilt are not assigned in correct proportion to culpability. There is no divine justice when the burden is distributed. The one who should feel the most is often the one who is best able to resist and allow the one equipped with the most capacity for empathy to shoulder the inhuman weight. I won't do it.

I know what I've done and I refuse to accept the role thrust upon me. On the contrary. I intend to continue to use my tools until I reach my objective. Violence has become a part of me, it's destroying me, but I have accepted my destruction.

My guilt lies deeper, it has filled the part of my soul that I still command. I can never make amends, never be reconciled with my own failing.

I can never receive absolution. My betrayal is as immense as death itself.

I've tried to learn to live with it. It isn't possible, because the paradox lies in my consciousness.

I'm alive, thus I am guilty.

There is only one way to atone for my sins.

THURSDAY 1 NOVEMBER

It was snowing. Snowflakes stuck to Annika's jacket and frosted her hair and the front of her body white. Once on the ground, they quickly dissolved into a mush of salt and water. Annika stepped into a puddle and realized that her shoes leaked.

The civic hall in her district was on her own street, at the top, near Fridhemsplan, in the brick high-rise. The display windows reflected her image – she looked like a snowman. On the other side of the glass a small exhibit notified the public that a new hotel would be built over at the park at Rålambhov, right in the middle of the turn-off to the Essinge Highway, and invited them to share their views on the subject.

Annika rang the bell at the civic hall and was admitted. There was information posted everywhere. She took all the leaflets she could find about nursing homes and the care of the elderly. As she walked away, she noted that there was a funeral parlour next door.

The air between the snowflakes was clean and crisp. Sounds were muffled as if wrapped in blankets. She took the time to listen, to breathe, to explore her feelings. She was well rested, her mind was clear and calm.

There was a way. Things could be arranged.

Slowly, she climbed the stairs to her apartment, her gaze fixed on the steps. Which was why she didn't see the woman waiting outside her door.

'Are you Annika Bengtzon?'

She gasped, put a foot down awkwardly and almost fell backwards down the stairs.

'Who are you?'

The woman held out her hand.

'My name is Maria Eriksson. I didn't mean to startle you.'

Annika had a sensation of tunnel vision. Her body went into defence mode.

'What do you want? And how did you find me?'

The woman gave her a pensive smile.

'You're listed in the telephone directory, and so is your address. There's something I'd like to talk to you about.'

'What?'

Impatience.

'I'd rather not say it out here.'

Annika swallowed. She didn't want to talk, not right now. She wanted to sit on her couch, under a blanket, drink tea and study the leaflets on nursing homes; find the solution, gain peace of mind. She was certain that no matter what this woman wanted to discuss it simply wasn't her problem.

'I don't have the time,' Annika said. 'My grandmother is ill and I've got to find a place where she can recover from her stroke.'

'It's extremely important,' the woman said gravely.

She made no effort to move away from the door.

Annika's irritation gave way to rage and then

suddenly to fear. The woman in front of her wasn't going to budge, she commanded respect.

Aida, Annika thought, backing down.

'Who sent you?'

'No one,' Maria Eriksson replied. 'I decided to come here. It concerns the Paradise Foundation.'

Suspicion gnawed at Annika. She stared at the woman who calmly returned her gaze.

'I don't know what you're talking about,' Annika said.

A desperate expression suddenly appeared in the woman's eyes.

'Don't trust Rebecka,' she said.

Bingo. Curiosity immediately got the better of Annika. She no longer wanted to escape. This was her problem, one she had chosen to involve herself in.

'Come on in,' she said, going to the door and unlocking it. She hung up her wet things on the bathroom rail, closed the door and pulled off her slacks and socks. Took fresh clothing from the closet, towelled off her hair and went to the kitchen to put the kettle on.

'Would you like some coffee, Maria? Or tea?'

'Call me Mia. No, I'm fine, thank you.'

The woman had settled herself on the living-room couch. Annika made a large pot of lemon tea and brought a tray into the living room.

Maria Eriksson was tense, but composed.

'You've met Rebecka Björkstig, right?' she asked.

Annika nodded and poured herself some tea.

'Are you sure you wouldn't like some?'

The woman didn't seem to hear her.

'Rebecka has been talking a lot about how you're going to write a long piece about the foundation in *Kvällspressen*, about what a great set-up it is. Is that true?'

Annika stirred her tea, unable to shake off the sense of apprehension lurking behind her curiosity.

'I can't divulge anything about what will or won't be in the papers.'

Suddenly the stranger sitting on Annika's couch burst into tears. Not sure what to do, Annika put her cup down on the saucer.

'Please don't write anything until you know what's going on,' Maria Eriksson begged her. 'Wait until you have all the facts.'

'That goes without saying,' Annika replied. 'But it's extremely difficult to gain insight into a foundation. Everything's so confidential that every last bit of information has to pass through Rebecka.'

'Her name isn't Rebecka.'

Annika dropped her spoon in the cup, suddenly speechless.

'She went by some other name until quite recently, I know that much,' Maria Eriksson continued, picking up a tissue and wiping her eyes. 'I'm not sure exactly what her name was – Agneta something, I think.'

'How do you know that?' Annika asked.

Maria blew her nose.

'Rebecka claims I've been wiped off the record,' she said.

Annika stared at the young woman on her couch, so real and so tangible. *Wiped clean!*

'So it works?' she asked.

The woman put the tissue in her handbag.

'No,' she said. 'I don't think it works at all. That's the problem.'

'But your record's been wiped clean?'

Maria emitted a short burst of laughter.

'I was taken off the record years ago,' she said. 'I haven't been listed anywhere for ages, but that has nothing to do with Rebecka or Paradise. I arranged for protection myself, for me and my family. The problem is that it's not enough, that's why I went to Paradise.'

'So you're on the inside right now?'

'My case hasn't been settled, my district hasn't endorsed the contract yet,' Maria Eriksson replied. 'Which means that I'm not really in, but being on the outskirts like this has provided me with much greater insight into the set-up than if I were mixed up in this business for real.'

Annika reached for her teacup, blew on the beverage and tried to sort out her impressions: fear, doubt, excitement, astonishment. The woman was so real, so blonde and serious, her eyes saw right through things. But was she telling the truth?

Confusion started to take hold of Annika.

'How long have you been in contact with Paradise?'

'For five weeks now.'

'And you haven't been accepted yet?'

Maria Eriksson sighed.

'That's due to Social Services. They're investigating whether they should pay for our relocation abroad.'

'Courtesy of Paradise?'

The woman nodded.

'Rebecka wants six million kronor to help us leave the country. Our case is very cut and dried. The Administrative Court of Appeals has ruled that we are unable to lead a normal life in Sweden – I'll let you see the court verdict.'

Annika rubbed her forehead.

'I've got to write this down. Is that all right?'

'Sure.'

She went over to the hallway. Her bag was wet and she dumped out its contents on the floor: a packet of Tenor breath mints, sanitary napkins, a torn train ticket, a pad, a pen and a heavy gold chain.

The gold chain. Annika picked it up. Aida's gift – she'd forgotten all about it.

Quickly she stuffed everything back in her bag again, except for the pad and pen.

'Why is your life in danger?' she asked as she settled back down on the couch.

Maria Eriksson gave her a wan smile.

'I'd like to have some tea after all, please. The same old story: I fell in love with the wrong guy. I thought you might ask, so I brought my files.'

She pulled out a thick folder.

'These are copies. If you like, you're welcome to keep them, but I'd appreciate it if you kept them in a safe place.'

'Tell me about it,' Annika said, taking the folder.

'Attempted strangulation,' Maria Eriksson replied and stirred sugar in her tea. 'He pulled a knife on me. Beatings. Rape. An attempt to kidnap our daughter. Damage to our house, everything you could think of. Arson. I can go on for ever, and no one could care less.'

Maria sipped her tea cautiously. Annika felt the familiar sense of rage well up in her.

'I know what it's like,' she said. 'Why didn't the police do anything?'

Maria gave her another smile.

'My parents still live in my home town,' she said. 'He would kill them if I talked.'

'How do you know he's not bluffing?'

'He's tried to run my dad down with a car.'

'I'll look through your papers later,' Annika said, laying the folder down on the floor.

She couldn't think of anything more to say. She was going to study the documents carefully, but she suspected that they would corroborate Maria's story. She believed this woman. There was something convincing about her. Maybe it was fear.

They sat in silence for a while, the cups clattering softly.

'Is the set-up for real?' Annika wondered.

Maria Eriksson nodded.

'Rebecka charges people for her services, but that's about it. As far as I can see, they don't get anyone off the record. All I've ever noticed Rebecka do is to occasionally request a security flag for certain clients.'

'What's that?' Annika asked.

Maria leaned back.

'There are several types of protection for people who have been threatened,' she said. 'The simplest variety is a security flag, where no one can access your personal ID number, your address and your family connections from government sources. All anyone gets is the phrase "protected data".'

Annika nodded. That was what it had said when she'd looked Rebecka up.

'That's fairly unusual, isn't it?'

'Less than ten thousand people in Sweden,' Maria Eriksson replied. 'The decision to introduce a security flag is made by the director of the local tax office in the community where you are a resident. Harassment must be established before a security flag may be issued.'

'Do you have a security flag?'

'No, my family is shielded by classification measures, a more extensive and more complicated method of protection. In cases like these, only one person, the director of the local tax office where you once were a resident, has access to information about your current address. So to be eligible for classification you need to fulfil more stringent criteria as well. The harassment must be serious enough to warrant a restraining order.'

'How many people are classified in Sweden?'

'Less than one hundred,' Maria replied.

She had actually been wiped off the record, for real.

'Are there other ways?'

'Well, you can change your name and be assigned a new personal ID number. The National Swedish Police Board will then request that the Internal Revenue Service creates a new personal ID number.'

Here was someone who knew the ropes, Annika thought.

'Have you changed your identity?'

Maria hesitated, then nodded.

'I've had several different names and I had a new personal ID number for a while; I went from a Virgo to an Aries!'

They both laughed.

'What else does Rebecka do?'

Maria Eriksson became serious again.

'What does she say she does?'

Annika took a sip of her tea. She had to decide: either she trusted this woman, or she would show her the door. She went for the first alternative.

'She claims to have assisted sixty cases in three years,' she said. 'Two entire families relocated abroad; a full-time staff of five with a salary of fourteen thousand kronor a month each; all contacts take place by proxy, through Paradise, using a system of reference numbers; there's an around-the-clock hotline; rerouted phone lines; safe houses all over Sweden; they claim to have the capacity to arrange government jobs in other countries; complete medical coverage; legal assistance; care from A to Z.'

Maria sighed and nodded.

'More or less the usual tale. I'm surprised that she mentioned the business about relocation abroad – she usually plays that card close to the chest.'

'She did, for the longest time.'

'All right,' Maria said. 'The staff includes herself, her

brother, her sister and her parents. I presume they're on the payroll, but they don't actually do anything. No real work takes place at Paradise at all. Her mother answers the phones at times, but that's it.'

Silence.

'What about the safe houses?'

Maria chuckled.

'They have a run-down house in Järfälla, that's where we're staying. That's where the telephone is connected. It rings periodically whenever Rebecka has a new case. Some poor desperate soul keeps calling, but no one answers . . .'

Annika shook her head.

'So it's all a pack of lies, then, every last word of it?'

Maria Eriksson blinked, tears in her eyes.

'I don't know,' she said. 'I don't know what happens to the others.'

'The others?'

The woman leaned closer and said in a whisper: 'The other people who come to Paradise – I don't know what happens to them. They come, they pass through the system and they disappear.'

'Don't they stay at the house?'

Maria Eriksson laughed mirthlessly.

'No, just us, we rent a room that we pay for under the table. She thinks she's going to make a bundle out of us since our case is so clear-cut, that's why we get to live there. But I've figured her out. If the Social Services office in our district makes that payment, she'll take the money and run. We wouldn't get a penny.'

Maria hid her face in her hands.

'And I believed her! I ended up going from the frying pan into the fire!'

Annika suddenly thought about the civil servant from Vaxholm, the guy she'd met yesterday, Thomas.

'You've got to get in touch with your district,' she said.

The woman picked up another tissue.

'I know. We've got to find somewhere else to stay, my husband is trying to arrange a cottage he's heard about. As soon as that's taken care of, we'll slip away from Paradise and then I'll contact my district. I can't do anything as long as we're staying at the foundation's house.'

'How long do you figure it will take?'

'A few more days, this weekend by the latest.'

Annika reflected on this and asked: 'The threat Rebecka has referred to, have you heard about it?'

Maria sighed.

'Rebecka claims that the Mafia is after her, though I have no idea why. It sounds kind of far-fetched to me. What could she possibly have done to them?'

Annika shrugged.

'Do you know what happens to the money?'

Maria shook her head.

'I can't get into the office. She keeps her records in one of the rooms on the ground floor, the door is always locked. But she does pay herself a high salary – I found a pay slip in the trash at the end of last week.'

Annika sat up straight. Pay slips, that would mean bank-account numbers, personal ID numbers, loads of information.

'Did you bring it?'

'Yes, I think I did . . .'

Maria rooted through her handbag and located a wrinkled slip of paper stained by coffee grounds.

'It's kind of messy,' she apologized as she handed it to Annika.

Everything was listed: a bank account, a personal ID number, an address, the tax rate – everything but a corporate ID number for Paradise. A hefty salary, too: fifty-five thousand kronor a month.

'It's a Föreningssparbanken account,' Maria said, 'the address is the same as for the Paradise Foundation, a post office box in Järfälla.'

'What's the street address?' Annika wondered.

Maria told her.

As usual, the eleven o'clock meeting was too focused on the future and not concerned enough with yesterday. The visions that the news editors had of the newspaper of tomorrow were generally reminiscent of soufflés: gonzo takes presuming that people would spill their guts, confess or deny scandals, share the tragedy, pain, rage, wrongdoing or injustice that had been visited upon them. Disasters were made out to be worse than they actually were, the lives and loves of celebrities were exaggerated out of all proportion. The consequences of new political proposals were oversimplified and the general public was invariably described as being a winner or a loser.

Anders Schyman sighed: that's what the business was like, after all. Overly enthusiastic news editors weren't exclusive to *Kvällspressen*. The same phenomenon was present at the national public-service broadcasting company where he had worked for many years, only with a slightly different twist. The starting point for whoever was in charge of planning was the necessity to make the greatest possible impact. For *Kvällspressen* this might mean concentrating on a TV celebrity who broke an ankle during a game show, while a television debate forum would hit the jackpot if an authority figure got rattled on air and made a fool of himself. At this moment Ingvar Johansson was reporting to the group his take on the follow-up of the handicapped boy who had taken his local government to court and won. A cake and flowers, no champagne, a photo spread with the whole family gathered around the kid, giving him a hug. He pictured a centre spread; the header declaring 'Kvällspressen made a difference!' had already been set up.

'Do we know if the family will do the picture?' Schyman asked.

'No,' Ingvar Johansson replied, 'but the reporter will take care of that. It's Carl Wennergren, so we're home free.'

They all nodded appreciatively.

'The free-port homicide story has developments,' Sjölander informed them. 'This man who competes in the old-boy class in orienteering found the missing truckload of cigarettes yesterday. It was completely gutted by fire and had been hidden in some kind of a ravine at the vicinity where the three provinces Östergtland, Södermanland and Närke meet.'

'Maybe someone was dying for a smoke,' Picture Pelle said, getting a few laughs.

'Two dead bodies were found in the cab,' Sjölander said unsmilingly. 'The coroner's office hasn't completed their post-mortem yet, but the police are pretty worked up. The victims appear to have been tortured. Every last joint in their bodies was smashed. The officer I spoke to had never seen anything so God-awful in his life.'

The room grew silent. The air-conditioning whooshed.

'What can the police go public with?' Schyman asked.

Sjölander flipped through his notes.

'The spot where the bodies were recovered is located in very rugged woodlands to the north of Hävla, in the greater Finnspång region. There is an extremely poor road through the woods that follows the fault line where the truck was found. Some interesting clues have been discovered. There are some tyre tracks from a vehicle other than the truck, and they're pretty distinctive. Some type of winter tyre without studs. Broad, American, used by only a few brands of cars. We're talking about a big four-wheel drive, like a Range Rover or the biggest Toyota Land Cruiser models. The police have already towed away the wreckage, which apparently wasn't an easy thing to do, and they would like us to write that anyone who's seen something should to get in touch with them.'

'How did they get the truck down the ravine?' Ingvar Johansson wondered.

Sjölander sighed.

'They drove it there, obviously; picked a day when the ground was frozen. The owner of the property isn't too pleased – they've totaled hundreds of saplings along the road.'

'Who did it?' Schyman wondered.

'The Yugo Mafia,' Sjölander replied. 'That's crystal clear. And we haven't seen the end of this, either. The guys in the car couldn't have told them anything, or they would have had one or two unbroken joints. Whoever owns the cigarettes is going to keep on killing people until they find the shipment. Anyone who knows anything about it is in deep shit.'

'What more do we know about the Yugo Mafia?' Schyman asked. 'Stuff we can't go public with, I mean.'

'They figure the Serbian government is behind it all,' Sjölander said, 'but no one has ever been able to prove it. Since the resources used in these operations are so extensive, it's a good guess that some state has indeed sanctioned them. That's why there aren't any snitches who would have a full insight into the set-up, who would know the whole picture. The people in the know are either a part of the government in Belgrade or are connected to it – like police commissioners, top military brass.'

'Would it be dangerous to dig deeper?' Schyman asked.

Sjölander hesitated.

'Not really,' he replied. 'Covering the murders would be fairly harmless. They're prepared for that. This is business, remember. It's just another day at the office for these operators. Only, don't try to trick them. Don't steal their booty and don't sit on any information about the people who did it.'

The meeting drifted on to other subjects, but Anders Schyman wasn't really paying attention. They had hardly ever had a discussion quite like this one. Relief and satisfaction flooded his entire gut. Ever since that clash yesterday he had been worried, but now he knew.

He had won.

The end of October and beginning of November was always a hectic time. The board considered the budget in October and the council had its say in November. Well, to be perfectly honest, the process usually dragged on into the first week of December. Every single solitary nursery in the city had called and asked if it was really true that they only had three thousand kronor left, and Thomas Samuelsson had to deal with the last quarterly follow-up at the same time.

But still he couldn't concentrate. He was seriously concerned about his outbursts. That journalist had asked him if he was a burn-out case, and he'd thought about her words several times. But there wasn't any real reason for him to break down because of stress. He was doing what he had been doing for seven years now: living in the same house with the same wife and going to the same job.

It was something else. He didn't want to put it into words because of the ramifications.

The truth of the matter was that Thomas wanted more out of life. That was it, there it was. He wanted to move on, he knew this job inside out by now. He wanted to move to the big city, he wanted to go to the movies and to the theatre without excessive planning, to walk home along streets lined with high-rise buildings and Indian restaurants and people he didn't know.

Yesterday he had walked around Vaxholm for hours, street after street. He knew every cobblestone by name, and then some. He had whiled away some time at a grungy restaurant, drinking beer, but he had left when a bunch of noisy high-school kids had barrelled in. It had been past midnight by the time he got home. He had hoped that Eleonor would have waited up so that they could talk, but she was fast asleep with a copy of the business magazine *Moderna Tider* next to her on the nightstand.

The telephone rang again. Thomas resisted an impulse to yank its lead out of the socket and smash the device against the wall.

'Hello,' he roared.

'Thomas Samuelsson? This is Annika Bengtzon, the reporter you met yesterday. I've uncovered certain details about the Paradise Foundation. Have you managed to find that corporate ID number?'

He groaned.

'I've been busy, you know,' he said.

'I'm glad you're doing your job,' she said. 'Then perhaps you've found out that Rebecka Björkstig used to call herself something else? That the foundation is based in a tumble-down house in Järfälla, that there's no staff, and that they don't do a thing except charge people for their services?'

He tried to think of something to say.

'Is that on the level?'

On the other end, the reporter sighed.

'Apparently. I'm not absolutely certain, but I've obtained Rebecka's personal ID number and I'm going to

check it with the debt-enforcement service over at
Sollentuna. I'm taking the commuter train that leaves in
fifteen minutes. Join me if you're interested.'

Thomas looked at his watch. He'd have to cancel three
meetings.

'I'm not sure that I can make it,' he said.

'It's your call,' the reporter said. 'If you do come, please
bring the corporate ID number for Paradise.'

Annika Bengtzon hung up. Thomas closed the
notebook on his desk and went over to see the social
worker in charge of that Bosnian woman, Aida Begovic.
She was with a client, a young man with a shaven head
who kept picking at his pimples. Thomas walked in
anyway.

'I need the number for Paradise,' he said, interrupting
her.

The woman behind the desk struggled to keep her
temper.

'I'm busy,' she said, clearly emphasizing each word.
'Would you please leave us?'

'No,' Thomas said. 'I need that number. Right now.'

The social worker's face went red.

'You really—'

'Immediately,' he roared.

Alarmed, she got up, pulled out a notebook and,
opening it, handed it to him.

'Upper right-hand corner,' she said curtly.

'Contact me as soon as you receive an invoice,' Thomas
said. 'I apologize for the interruption.'

He picked up the notebook and left. Jotted down the
number on a Post-It sticker, put it in his pocket, put on his
coat and went out. He hadn't brought his car today so he
had to go home and get it.

'I'll be out for the rest of the day,' he told the
receptionist on his way out.

When he was going uphill on Östra Ekuddsgatan it occurred to him that he had no idea where the debt-enforcement agency could be in Sollentuna. He had to go back home and look it up in the phone book. Tingsvägen 7, where the hell was that? He tore page twenty out of the map section of the *Yellow Pages* and ran over to his car.

The traffic increased as soon as Thomas reached the E18. Route 262 was at a standstill by the time he reached Edsbyn, due to some sort of accident. In frustration, he slammed the steering wheel. Finally managing to get downtown by way of Sollentunavägen, he found that the offices were right behind the Convention Centre, in a yellowish high-rise complex that the debt-enforcement people shared with the police and other legal authorities. He parked in a reserved space and took the elevator to the sixth floor.

Annika Bengtzon was already there, seated at a table in a reception room with a stack of printouts in front of her, her hair all wavy as if it had dried without being combed first. She pointed with a quick gesture at the chair beside her.

'I've got something to show you,' she said. 'If that personal ID number is correct, out friend here hasn't paid a single bill for the past five years. Probably didn't do it before that either, but debt records don't go back further than five years. They'd be on microfilm.'

Thomas stared at the piles of printouts.

'What's this?'

Annika got up.

'Rebecka Björkstig's files from the Swedish Debt Enforcement Agency,' she said. 'One hundred and seven complaints. Like some coffee?'

He nodded and removed his overcoat and his scarf.

'With milk, please.'

Thomas sat down and began to leaf aimlessly through

the printouts. He couldn't tell who had incurred the debts, all it said in the 'name' box was 'ID safeguarded'. But the debt records themselves weren't confidential, they were listed in long columns; public and private, from authorities, private companies, private citizens. Unpaid back taxes. Parking tickets. Citations for using a vehicle without lawful authority. Unpaid IKEA furniture, rental cars, vacations, bank loans, credit-card debts to Konsum, Visa, Ellos, Eurocard . . .

Jesus! He continued to wade through the pile.

. . . unpaid student loans, unpaid TV licences, a loan made by a private individual called Andersson, arrears on a rental TV from Thorn . . .

'There wasn't any milk,' Annika said, and set down a brown plastic cup on top of the printout that he was reading. She had removed the white bandage from her finger and had replaced it with a Band-Aid.

'Christ,' he remarked. 'When did you find all this out?'

She sat down next to him and sighed.

'This morning. A source of mine gave me a personal ID number that presumably belongs to Rebecka. I can't swear that it is hers, since Rebecka has a protected identity, but for the time being I assume that it is. She's only thirty years old, but she's been busy getting into debt. And this is only the beginning. The receptionist is looking into any bankruptcy proceedings that she may be involved in. Do you have that corporate ID number?'

Thomas pulled out his wallet and handed her the Post-it.

'I'll be right back,' Annika said.

He sipped his coffee. It was pretty weak and went down okay without milk. Then he made an attempt at sorting out his thoughts.

What did it all mean? The fact that this lady was lousy at paying her bills wasn't really the point. She could still be good at wiping people off public records. But the total picture, the sheer bulk of the unpaid bills, smacked of a strategy and hinted at what was in store.

He finished the coffee, tossed the cup in the trash and went on leafing through the material.

. . . Unpaid American Express bills, a Finax telephone service loan, unpaid speeding tickets, unpaid Folksam insurance premiums, unpaid utility bills, telephone bills, road taxes . . .

Most of the debts were no longer current; they had been regulated in some way, either by docking her pay or her assets, or due to bankruptcy proceedings.

Where was Annika Bengtzon?

Thomas left the room. As he rounded a corner by the front desk he walked right into her. He could feel her breasts.

'Shit,' she exclaimed, tripping and dropping a sheaf of papers on the floor. He caught hold of her and helped her to her feet again. Blushing.

'I'm so sorry,' he said. 'I didn't mean to do that.'

Annika kneeled down and picked up the papers.

'Take a look at this,' she said. 'This gal has gone bankrupt in every way imaginable: personal bankruptcy, twice in the past four years; she's put a stock corporation into receivership as well as a partnership and a limited partnership. The Paradise Foundation is deep in debt for cars, TV sets, two houses on instalment plans where not a penny has been paid . . .'

Walking ahead of him, Annika entered the room again.

'The trick is to figure out what it all means,' she said, sitting down. 'It doesn't have to mean that Rebecka Björkstig is a crook, but the vibes aren't exactly good.'

Thomas stared at her: the exact same thought had crossed his mind a few minutes ago. So he sat down next to her and picked up the printouts from the Patent and Registration Office, observing the dates when debts and bankruptcy proceedings were recorded, when new companies were registered and when they were dissolved.

'I think I detect a pattern,' he said. 'Look – she starts up a company, buys a whole lot of stuff, applies for huge loans and goes bankrupt. Over and over again. Declares personal bankruptcy, again and again. Finally, it won't work any more. No one will lend her a dime. So she creates a foundation. It can't be traced to her. The other people listed as co-founders may not even exist.'

Annika followed his index finger as it indicated item after item.

'And then it was shop till you drop again,' she said, holding up the sheet with the debts incurred by the Paradise Foundation. 'Look at this, she started to default on her loans four months ago.'

'My guess is that the foundation isn't any older than that,' Thomas said.

'So much for those three years and sixty cases,' Annika said drily.

They sat next to each other in silence, reading and leafing through the material. Then Annika got up and started stacking the printouts.

'I've got to go talk to the senior enforcement officer again before he leaves for the day,' she said. 'Do you have time to join me?'

Thomas glanced at his watch. The third missed meeting of the day was about to begin.

'Yeah, no problem.'

They went down a long departmental hallway, the dark blue carpeting absorbing dust and sound. Annika Bengtzon walked in front of Thomas and headed for the next to last door.

'Hi,' she said as she entered the office. 'It's me again.

This is Thomas Samuelsson, chief accountant with the Social Services in Vaxholm.'

The senior enforcement officer sat at his desk with a pile of loose-leaf notebooks in front of him.

'Did you find what you were looking for?' he asked.

Annika sighed. 'I found *more* than I was looking for. Have you possibly come across this woman, Rebecka Björkstig, before?'

The enforcement officer shook his head. 'I've given it some thought,' he said. 'But no, it doesn't ring a bell.'

'How about this?' she asked, handing him the printouts about the debts incurred by the Paradise Foundation.

The man put on his glasses and ran his gaze over the page.

'Here,' he said, pointing at an item further down on the page. 'This looks familiar. I spoke to the company that owns these vehicles last week, and they were very upset. They haven't been able to contact the person who had leased the cars, and they haven't received a down payment of any kind.'

'How could they let anyone take the cars without making a down payment?' Thomas asked.

The senior enforcement officer glanced at him over the rims of his glasses. 'They told me that the woman appeared to be trustworthy. Would you happen to know the whereabouts of the person in charge of the Paradise Foundation?' The last question was levelled at Annika.

'No,' she replied truthfully. 'I do have the address to one of the houses used by the foundation, but she doesn't live there. That information ought to be listed on the mortgages that she's been granted.'

Annika Bengtzon handed over the printouts.

'What do you make of all these debts?'

The officer sighed. 'Times are tougher,' he said. 'Our workload has increased while our staff has been cut back time and time again. But this lady doesn't belong to the newly impoverished classes, one of your regular Joes or Janes who has got behind with their payments. She dodges her obligations in a typically pathological way.'

'You recognize the type?' Annika asked.

The man sighed again. They thanked him for his time and went back down the corridor again.

'I'm calling it a day,' Annika said as she headed for the front desk, yawning and stretching her arms in the air. 'I've got to go home and call my grandmother.'

Thomas looked at her, the wavy hair and the smooth brow.

'So soon?'

She smiled. 'Time flies,' she said. 'Would you like to make copies of the material?'

She walked over to the front desk. He remained were he was, with a blank mind and a hard-on.

'Need a ride?' he called after her.

She glanced over her shoulder at him.

'That would be great.'

Thomas went to the lavatory, washed his face and hands and tried to relax.

Annika was waiting for him by the front desk, holding his copies in a plastic folder.

'Gee,' he said. 'You sure are efficient.'

'Not me, my new friend.'

He didn't quite catch on. 'Who?'

'The receptionist. Now, where's your car?'

It was a fairly new Toyota Corolla, green, nicely waxed, and equipped with alarm and central locking systems, blip-blip. Thomas had parked in someone else's slot and that someone had left an angry note on the windshield which he yanked out, crumpled up and tossed in a waste-paper basket three metres away, sinking it. His hair flopped into his face, and he raked it back absent-mindedly. Dark grey overcoat, expensive suit and a tie.

Out of the corner of her eye, Annika studied him. Broad shoulders, quick and agile. It hadn't struck her earlier – he had either been hidden behind a desk or had been seated, so she hadn't noticed how he moved with authority and grace.

Bet he was into sports at some point, she thought. *Lots of money. Used to being taken seriously.*

Thomas tossed his briefcase into the back seat.

'Door's open,' he said.

Glancing over at the back seat as she sat down in front, Annika didn't see any kiddy seats even though he was wearing a wedding band. She stuffed her bag down by her feet. He started the car and the fan went on.

'Where do you live?'

'Right smack in the middle of town. Hantver-karegatan.'

As he was backing out the car, he put his arm along the headrest behind her. Annika felt her mouth going dry.

'The Klarastrand thoroughfare is usually a pain in the ass at this hour,' she said. 'The best option is to drive by way of Hornsberg . . .'

They sat beside each other in silence, and she noticed that a new feeling had evolved, a different kind of silence. Thomas had slender, strong hands, shifted gears often and drove pretty fast. That hair of his wouldn't stay slicked back, the blond, shiny mass flopping into his eyes.

'Have you lived in the Kungsholmen neighbourhood for long?' he asked, glancing at Annika with a certain look that she could feel herself responding to.

'It's been two years now,' she replied, her cheeks suddenly growing hot. 'I have a two-bedroom apartment on the top floor of a building facing the courtyard.'

'Was it expensive?' he asked.

She started laughing. In his circles people bought their apartments.

'No, the place is going to be torn down, so it's a short-term lease,' she explained. 'There's no central heating, no hot water, no elevator and no toilet in the flat.'

Thomas shot her a quick glance. 'Are you serious?'

She laughed some more, all warm inside.

'What about TV reception?'

'Well, there's no cable access.'

'Did you watch the debate on Channel Two yesterday?'

Annika looked at him carefully. Why had his voice gone strident all of a sudden?

'I saw a few minutes,' she said slowly. 'To be honest, I turned it off. I know the work those women do is important, but they're so damned categorical. Anything that isn't awfully pretentious or elitist is crap. I can't stand that kind of attitude, as if they're superior beings.'

Thomas nodded enthusiastically.

'Did you see the literary-journal woman? The one with the endless stream of garbage?'

'Old pear-face? I certainly heard her.'

They laughed a little together.

'So you don't belong to any cultural societies?' he asked, glancing over at her, his hair in his eyes again.

'I go to see Djurgården play ice hockey,' Annika said, 'if you could call that culture.'

Thomas took his gaze off the road and stared at her.

'You like hockey?'

She looked down at her hands.

'I went to see bandy games on a weekly basis for years, it was fun, but it's damn cold being outdoors like that. Hockey is better, you don't get cold. It's easy to get tickets while the series is under way – only the finals at the Globe Arena are sold out.'

'Did you catch the finals last spring?' he asked.

'I was right in there with the supporters,' she said, making a fist and raising her left hand and chanting: 'Hardy Nilsson's iron men! Hardy Nilsson's iron men!'

Thomas laughed, a laugh that dwindled wistfully. Annika looked at him, surprised to see the sadness on his face.

'Are you a Djurgården fan?'

He overtook an airport shuttle.

'I played hockey until I was eighteen. Österskär was my team,' he said. 'I quit because Coach and I had a falling out, and I also wanted to concentrate on school.'

His profile stood out sharply against the car window. Annika swallowed and, turning her head, started to look in the opposite direction. Her cheeks were burning and there was a tingling sensation between her legs. The Karolinska Institute drifted past on the right, causing a twinge of panic: they would be home soon, he would be gone soon, she might never see him again.

'How long have you lived in Vaxholm?' she asked, a bit too breathlessly.

He sighed deeply, and for some reason this pleased her.

'For ever,' Thomas said.

Annika looked at his profile. Had a certain tenseness appeared around his mouth?

'Sick of it?' she asked.

Lingeringly, he looked at her.

'Why do you ask?'

She looked straight ahead.

'It's not exactly Rock-and-roll City,' she said. 'It reminds me of where I come from, Hälleforsnäs.'

'Doesn't rock there much either?'

Annika took the plunge. 'Are you married?'

'It's been twelve years.'

She looked at his profile again.

'Must have robbed the cradle,' she said.

Thomas laughed.

'Suspicions of that kind were voiced at the time. Is this where you get off?'

Annika swallowed. *Shit.*

'Yes, this will be fine.'

He pressed down hard on the brakes, his gaze on the rear-view mirror, so Annika realized that he was watching the bus behind them. She got out of the car, took her bag and leaned back in through the door again.

'Thanks for the ride.'

But Thomas wasn't looking at her any more. His thoughts were elsewhere.

'You're welcome.'

A clicking and crackling noise was heard as the nurse wheeled the phone into Annika grandmother's room.

'Hello?' Annika said.

Only static.

'Gran?'

'No, it's Barbro.'

Not Mother, Barbro.

'How's she doing?'

'Not too good. She's asleep right now.'

Silence. Distance. An intense desire to bridge the gap arose.

'I've been checking into nursing homes in Stockholm,' Annika said. 'There are several on Kungsholmen. . .'

'That won't be necessary,' her mother said firmly, with a hard voice, not wanting to accept any bridges. 'This has to be sorted out in her home district. I talked to a . . . this person today, and that's what he said.'

New feelings flooded Annika's system. Injustice. Irritation. Defeat.

'Did you talk to someone at Social Services? Oh, Mother, I told you I wanted to be there for that.'

'You spend your time in Stockholm. This needed to be taken care of right away.'

'I'll be there tomorrow. There's something I have to do in the morning, then I'll come.'

'No, you don't have to do that. Birgitta was here today. We can cope, you know.'

Annika squeezed her eyes shut, put her hand to her brow, and fought back the feelings of being unjustly left out. Rage muffled her voice.

'I'll see you tomorrow.'

FRIDAY 2 NOVEMBER

In one motion, Thomas Samuelsson tore the plastic shroud off the suit, caught his finger on the sharp hook of the hanger and swore – fucking dry-cleaners! At the same time Eleonor was sighing over a pair of tights with a run in them.

'Seventy-nine kronor down the drain,' she said, tossing them in the waste-paper basket next to her bed.

'Aren't there cheaper brands?' Thomas asked, sucking on his finger to avoid getting blood on his clothes.

'Not with a shaping feature,' his wife said as she broke open a new packet. 'You do remember that Nisse and Ulrica are coming over tonight, don't you?'

Thomas turned away and went into the bathroom to get a Band-Aid. For a few seconds he stared at his reflection in the mirror: the slicked-back hair, the shirt and tie, the cuff links. Wound a Band-Aid around his fingertip and went back into the bedroom. Eleonor was wriggling into a fresh pair of tights. They resisted being pulled up over her hips. He swallowed.

'Do we really have to have guests tonight?' he said. 'I

wish we could talk instead. We have a few things to sort out.'

'Not right now, Thomas' his wife said, pulling up the tights and forcing her stomach and her hips into their confining embrace.

He walked around the woman, embracing her from behind, cupping in each hand a breast encased in a push-up bra, and gently blew on the nape of her neck.

'We could spend some time together,' he murmured, 'just the two of us. Have some wine, see a movie, talk.'

Eleonor removed herself from his grasp, then walked over to the closet to put on a white blouse and pull out a hanger with a black skirt.

'We've planned this dinner party all week. Nisse and I are going to run through some aspects of the new project. You know we can't discuss it at the bank.'

Thomas looked at her – how well he knew her. Of course she would object.

'Eleonor,' he said, 'I'm really not in the mood for this. I'm tired and pretty fed up with things right now, and I think we need to talk.'

She continued to ignore his pleas and walked over to him without looking him in the eye.

'Could you help me with this? Thanks.'

He took the necklace and fastened it around her neck. Then he let his hands caress her shoulders and hold on to her.

'I'm serious,' he said. 'If you're going to have another dinner for your colleagues tonight, I won't be there. I'll drive into Stockholm and eat out.'

Eleonor tore herself from his embrace and paced over to the closet, yanked out a pair of black pumps and stuffed them into a bag. When she looked up at Thomas her hair was mussed and her face was flushed, two red spots on her cheekbones.

'You had better get your act together,' she snapped. 'Don't you realize that you aren't free to come and go as you please? This household consists of two people – we both have to make things work.'

'That's exactly my point,' Thomas countered heatedly. 'We're a couple, but why do you have all the power and I have all the responsibilities?'

Eleonor put on her suit jacket and went out into the hallway.

'That was a tremendously unfair thing to say,' she told him tersely.

Thomas remained in the master bedroom, their bedroom, her parents' bedroom.

Damn it all to hell. He wasn't going to give in this time.

'Stop acting like you're so fucking superior,' he yelled, running after Eleonor, catching her by the front door and grabbing her by the arm.

'Take your hands off me!' she screamed, yanking her arm away. 'What's wrong with you?'

Thomas was breathing hard and his hair was in his eyes.

'I want to move,' he said. 'I don't want to live in this house any more.'

Eleonor looked at him, more frightened than angry.

'You don't know what you want,' she said, trying to pull away.

'Yes, I do,' he said in an eager voice. 'I know exactly what I want. I want us to buy an apartment in Stockholm, or a house over at Äppelviken or Stocksund. You'd like it there.'

He went up to her, hugged her, inhaling the fragrance of her perfume through her hair.

'I want to have a new job, maybe for the county council, the Association of Local Authorities, some consultant company, or some department of state. I know you want to stay here, but I'm feeling suffocated. Eleonor, I'm dying out here . . .'

She pushed him away, hurt and close to tears.

'You look down on me for liking it here. You think I'm not ambitious, that I'm lazy.'

With both hands Thomas raked back his hair.

'No,' he protested, 'it's the other way around, I envy you. I wish I was as centred as you, I wish I was satisfied with what we have.'

Eleanor wiped the corners of her eyes, her voice muffled.

'You're so ridiculously immature and spoiled that you would throw away everything we have together, everything we've worked for all these years.'

She turned away, heading for the door. He called after her, to her black Armani-clad back.

'That's not true – I don't want to throw anything away, I want to move on. We could live in Stockholm, I could get a new job. You could commute and maybe you'd like to try a new job later on too . . .'

She pulled on her coat and he saw her hands tremble as they buttoned it up.

'My life is here. I love this town. *You* get another job and start commuting, if what you need is a change.'

Thomas was stunned. The thought hadn't occurred to him.

Of course he could get a new job somewhere else. He wouldn't have to move. He could commute, maybe get a small flat in Stockholm and stay there some nights.

The door closed behind Eleanor with a well-oiled click. Loneliness enveloped Thomas like a dusty blanket, heavy and suffocating.

What the hell was he doing?

The sound pierced Annika's consciousness. Her eyes

were sleepy and gritty. She picked up the phone without lifting her head from the pillow.

'Something terrible has happened!' a voice cried out.

Annika sat up, her heart pounding.

'Gran? Does this have something to do with my grandmother?'

'It's me – Mia, Mia Eriksson. A woman has disappeared. She said she would tell the council everything and Rebecka went berserk.'

Annika rubbed her forehead and sank back against the pillows in relief. It was all right, everything would be fine.

'What happened?'

'There was quite a ruckus here yesterday, so I wanted to call you and tell you about it. It's important.'

Annika felt irritation building up in her head.

'How does this concern me?'

'The woman said she knew you, that you had recommended Paradise. Her name is Aida Begovic, she comes from Bijelina in Bosnia.'

Annika shut her eyes, a wave of heat flooding her face. *This isn't happening, this isn't happening.*

'What's happened to Aida?' she managed to say, her face flushed and throbbing.

'She said she would tell the council where she lived that the set-up was a fraud, and then Rebecka shouted that she had better watch her step, because Rebecka knew who was after her. That was last night and now Aida's gone!'

Mia began to cry. Annika shook her head in an attempt to think straight.

'Hang on,' she said. 'Take it easy. Maybe it's not that bad. Aida might just be out shopping or something like that.'

'You don't know Rebecka,' Mia Eriksson said breathlessly. 'She told me something, in confidence. That she'll kill whoever betrays her.'

Annika felt a chill sweep over her.

'No,' she said, 'that's all talk. Rebecka is full of shit, but she's not a killer. Don't get paranoid.'

'She's got a gun,' Mia said. 'I've seen it. A handgun.'

Rage took hold of Annika, forcing her to sit up in bed again.

'Don't you realize that she's only trying to scare you? She wants to make sure that no one will tell anyone about her scam.'

Mia Eriksson wasn't at all convinced.

'We're leaving – today. I'm not going to set foot in this place again.'

'Where will you be going?'

The woman on the other end of the line hesitated.

'Away from here. We've found a cottage way out in the woods.'

Annika understood: last night she had read through Mia Eriksson's files and she knew why they never let anyone know their whereabouts.

They were silent for a while, each at their own end of the line.

'I'll continue to dig for dirt on Paradise,' Annika promised.

'Don't trust Rebecka,' Mia countered.

Annika sighed.

'Good luck.'

'Write only what you can corroborate,' Mai Eriksson said.

Silence crept up on Annika after she had hung up the phone, the curtains swayed, the shadows danced. Paradise wouldn't release its hold on her.

The mail, pushed through the slot in her front door, landed on the floor with a thud. Gratefully she got out of bed, brought the letters back with her and opened them when she reached the lavatory downstairs. A gas bill. An advertisement for a book club. An invitation to a junior high school reunion.

'I'd rather die,' Annika murmured to herself and stuffed everything but the bill into the bin for sanitary napkins.

She had to go to the office.

Eva-Britt Qvist was at her desk, sorting piles of papers.

'Did that list turn up?'

The secretary looked up at Annika.

'Those sources of yours don't seem to be all that reliable,' she said.

Annika stifled a tart retort and smiled instead.

'Could you possibly put it in my in-box if it does turn up?'

Without waiting for a reply, she turned away. *Sit on your fucking fax machine, you broody old hen.* She logged on to PubReg.

'You do know that there's a charge for every item you look up, don't you?' Eva-Britt Qvist called out from her desk.

Annika got up and went over to the secretary's desk, put her hands on the stack of papers there and leaned closer to the woman.

'Do you think that I'm here just to spite you?' she asked. 'Or could it be that I'm simply trying to do my job, just like you?'

Eva-Britt leaned back, not quite following her and blinking indignantly.

'I'm responsible for the PubReg, I was just reminding you.'

'You aren't accountable for the budget, are you? That's Sjölander's job.'

Two red spots began to burn on the woman's plump cheeks.

'I'm pretty busy,' she said. 'I have some calls to make.'

Annika returned to the computer, clenching her hands tight to make them stop shaking. Why did she always have to have the last word? Why couldn't she be more easygoing?

She sat down, her back to the secretary, picked up her notes and squeezed her eyes shut in order to concentrate. Where should she start?

She entered the command F8, tried Rebecka's name again and got back 'Protected identity'.

A deep sigh. Why did she even bother?

She decided to switch to F2 and use the personal ID number she had. She entered Rebecka's digits and the machine whirred and processed.

The message was the same: 'Protected identity'.

She moved on to F7, historical data, and entered the ID number again. Whir, process: Nordin, Ingrid Agneta.

Annika stared at the information. *What the . . .?*

She checked the ID number, tried it again.

The results were the same.

Ingrid Agneta Nordin, registered in Sollentuna, street address Kungsvägen. The latest change of address had been made six months ago. She entered the new name and pressed F2. Whir, process – *Well, what do you know!*

Annika stared.

It worked. The information was accessed, and there was another historical reference listed dating back three years.

She logged out quickly, picked up the phone and dialled the direct line to the senior enforcement officer she had met the day before.

'I was just wondering,' she said, 'if the name Ingrid Agneta Nordin rings a bell?'

While the man considered her question, Annika held her breath.

'Well, yes,' he said. 'Would that be here in Sollentuna? For a couple of years I had a great deal to do with a woman by that name.'

She exhaled. *Yes!*

'She's changed her name to Rebecka Björkstig, but there's another historical reference on the PubReg that I'm unable to access. Could you possibly check if you have that information?'

The senior enforcement officer rustled some papers.

'What kind of information do you expect to find?'

'Possibly a previous address,' Annika said. 'But there could also be a reference to other name changes.'

A brief pause while the man wrote down Rebecka's personal ID number.

'When would this have taken place?'

'Three and a half years ago.'

He went off somewhere and was gone for five minutes.

'Guess what?' he said eventually, clearing his throat. 'She did have another name previously: Eva Ingrid Charlotta Andersson, and she was registered in Märsta.'

Annika closed her eyes. *What a bull's eye.*

She thanked the officer hurriedly and hung up.

Anders Schyman closed the door behind him and surveyed his dusty cubbyhole. He sat down at his desk and looked out over the newsroom through the glass partition. An energetic Annika Bengtzon skipped past his fish tank and disappeared in the direction of the cafeteria. He would call her in when she returned, to see if she'd made any progress.

Today's board meeting had done a great deal to clear the horizons around here. Torstensson, the editor-in-chief, had decided to come clean about the offer he had received from the EU. The party wanted him to go to Brussels and deal with policy issues. He was full of understated pride as he related this news to the group and Schyman reckoned he knew why he was so pleased. Torstensson had no real ties to *Kvällspressen*. He had been appointed purely for political reasons, Schyman doubted that Torstensson had ever read the paper regularly until he had been appointed editor-in-chief.

In spite of the fancy title, Torstensson hadn't been particularly satisfied with his job. He'd never really grasped what the paper was all about. He would take part in televised debates and reveal how little he actually knew every time he opened his mouth, always using sentences brimming with politically correct clichés.

Anders Schyman wondered why this opening had come up at this particular time. As far as he knew there was no urgent need for yet another lobbyist dealing with the public access of information, not with any of the Swedish parties represented in Brussels right now. His guess was that the board was tired of being in the red, but hoped to avoid the negative media coverage that would result if the editor-in-chief was dismissed and thus publicly humiliated. It was likely that someone was putting pressure on the leading factions of the party and the result was a fancy new job in a new arena.

The question was what would happen next around here. If Torstensson actually got the appointment, if he accepted it and if he carried out his reorganization of the paper before he left, then who would his successor be? Unease sliced through Schyman's gut, a sensation he quickly suppressed.

Annika Bengtzon strolled past on the other side of the glass partition, holding a mug of coffee. Schyman got up, slid the door open and summoned her into his bunker.

'How's Paradise coming along?'

The young woman sat down on a chair meant for visitors.

'You should tell them to vacuum your office. It's coming along fine. I've received a great deal of information about our friend Evita Perón.'

The deputy editor blinked, Annika Bengtzon waved her hands imperiously.

'A.k.a. Rebecka Björkstig,' she said. 'Or Ingrid Agneta Nordin, or Eva Ingrid Charlotta Andersson, as she's also called herself. She has one hundred and seven personal debts listed at the Debt Enforcement Agency and twenty of those involve Paradise. She's gone bankrupt in every way known to man at least once. I have a source who tells me that all Paradise does is charge people for services they never render, but I haven't had that fully corroborated yet.'

Schyman took notes. He wasn't surprised.

'If this is true, it sounds like your classic white-collar criminal.'

Annika nodded enthusiastically.

'You bet. I've called the police in the different communities where Björkstig or whatever her name may be has been a resident. I spoke to a police detective who has been looking for her for the past six months. Evita is suspected of criminal intent in connection with all her bankruptcies.'

Thoughtfully, Schyman studied the young reporter. She was damn good at digging up dirt on any subject. She was enjoying herself, he could tell.

'What are we going to do about this? When can you start writing an article?'

Annika Bengtzon flipped through her pad.

'The outline's ready, I just need to flesh it out. I've been in contact with a woman who has seen the set-up from the inside, and in addition to that I know of another woman involved. I found this guy at Social Services in Vaxholm, and he's talked to me. And I'm going to go to Järfälla and check out the house there. I've got to get a better picture of what, if anything goes on. And, naturally, I've got to talk to Rebecka again and ask her why she's been lying.'

Schyman nodded: that sounded reasonable.

'We can count on a chain reaction of sorts,' Annika went on. 'Once we go public with this information, more and more monsters may start creeping out of the woodwork – people may call in and tell us more.'

'There's no way we can plan for that,' he said.

'I guess not,' Annika said. 'But we need to be prepared to receive any information that comes our way.'

'And those local authorities she's defrauded,' Schyman said, 'they might want to bring charges against her.'

'In for questioning, criminal proceedings, trial, prison,' Annika said.

Schyman smiled briefly at the young woman.

'Good,' he said. 'I'm glad you have it all lined up.'

'I'm going to type up my notes,' she said. 'Then I'll spend the weekend visiting my grandmother. She's had a stroke.'

Annika Bengtzon got up and slung her bag over her shoulder.

'You've got to get this room vacuumed or you'll get asthma.'

The slush along the sidewalk had frozen into ice, making walking difficult. The sun shone, a cold white November light that made all contours shimmer.

Annika let the rays of light fall on her face. It had taken longer than she thought to type up her notes and the sun had dipped low on the horizon already.

She sighed. She hadn't told Anders Schyman

everything. She hadn't told him that she'd been responsible for sending a woman to Paradise, and that the woman had disappeared, and that Rebecka had threatened to kill her.

If that was true.

She shook off the sense of unease, got on a 62 bus, took it to Tegelbacken and walked to the train station from there. The next train to Katrineholm would leave in thirty-five minutes, so she bought a sandwich and sat with her back facing the hall. The buzz of the crowd was like a haze behind her and her thoughts began wandering.

Rebecka Agneta Charlotta, dangerous and elusive.

Thomas Samuelsson, rich and good-looking.

Annika thought that she ought to tell him about the information she had discovered, the many identities, the suspicion of crime. She finished her sandwich, picked up her stuff and walked over to the telephone booths.

Mr Samuelsson had gone for the day – could she take a message? the receptionist asked.

Gone for the day, gone home to his wife.

'No, thank you. No message.'

Annika's grandmother had been moved to a different room. The electronic equipment wasn't as prominent here, but in other respects the room looked the same. She was awake when Annika arrived.

'I'm sorry I wasn't able to make it earlier,' Annika said, taking off her coat and scarf and tossing them into the corner behind the door before she walked over to the elderly woman.

Slightly bewildered, Sofia Katarina looked up at her.

'Barbro?'

'No, it's Annika, Barbro's daughter.'

The elderly woman tried to smile.

'The light of my life,' she said, her ravaged voice a fluttery whisper, the words slurred, her eyes cloudy.

Annika felt her chest constrict, the tears suspended like a veil inside her eyes.

'Have you and my mother figured out where you're going to live?' she asked.

Her grandmother's gaze darted around the room, unseeingly, focusing on visions from the past.

'Live? We lived over at the "Horseshoe",' she said. 'They let us have a room with a stove in the middle of the wall . . .'

Annika folded her strong hands around her grandmother's paralysed hand, gently stroking the old fingers, her heart sinking.

'Have you spoken with a social worker? Do you know if they've found a home for you?'

'One room, that was all we had,' the elderly woman gasped out. 'Mother did the cooking for fifteen men, she did all her cooking on that stove by the wall, and she did laundry too, ten öre for a handkerchief, fifty öre a piece for overalls . . .'

Annika licked her lips, unsure of how to react, of what she should say, and calmly stroked the old woman's arm. Then her grandmother stopped talking – her chest heaved up and down in rapid, shallow breaths and her restless eyes tried to recover a memory.

'The fire alarm woke us up, Mother and me,' she whispered. 'It was still dark out, the alarm wailed on and on, the whole foundry was on fire. We ran outside, it was hot and I was only wearing my nightie. The fire was so huge, the flames licked the heavens, it just kept on burning and burning.'

Annika knew what her grandmother was talking about: the great fire at the foundry that had taken place during the early hours of 21 August 1934. Sofia Katarina had been fifteen at the time.

'My mother and I pitched in, we rescued papers from the office, important business papers. My father was a part of the chain that passed buckets of water from the stream. The fire engine arrived from Flen and then it started to rain . . .'

'I know,' Annika said in a low voice. 'You helped save Hälleforsnäs.'

Her grandmother nodded.

'Once it was light, the motorized fire engine from Eskilstuna arrived. Arvid helped put out the fire too. He got a job at the foundry as soon as he had finished school. Twenty-one öre an hour, ten kronor and ten öre a week, and the first thing he bought was a bicycle.'

Sofia Katerina tried to smile, one side of her mouth not responding.

'He gave me a ride on his bicycle, the whole way past Fjellskäfte and over to the big church in Floda. 'That's where we'll be married,' he told me. But that's not what happened, we were married in the church in Mellösa . . .'

Annika inclined her head, patted her grandmother's cold hand, and allowed the tears to roll down her face. She had never met her grandfather. He had died the autumn before she'd been born, his lungs ruined. Up through the years he had been a sooty, shadowy presence in her life, always coming home from work grimy, always full of stories and mischief. She had grown up with her grandfather Arvid's tales; they lived on after his death, creating a picture of him that she could never revise. Annika gazed at her grandmother's bewildered expression, she saw her see Arvid again, a young man on his bike.

'Do you miss Arvid?' Annika whispered.

Now fully conscious, her grandmother met Annika's gaze.

'I miss the young man,' she said, 'the strong and healthy lad, not the complaining drunkard he became.'

Annika was startled: she had never heard that her grandfather had a drinking problem.

'He wasted his pay on drink, there was no stopping him, but he never got his hands on mine. My salary supported my daughter and myself, and it put food on the table for my husband . . .'

Suddenly her grandmother started to cry. The tears rolled down into her ears, and Annika took a tissue and wiped them away.

'It was rough on Barbro,' Sofia Katarina murmured. 'She spent too much time alone as a child. I couldn't bring her to work all the time, you couldn't let a little girl run around a place like that with all those statesmen, presidents and members of parliament. It wasn't good for her, though, it filled her heart with sadness that never left her.'

Her grandmother put her good hand on top of Annika's and looked her in the eye.

'Don't be too hard on Barbro,' she whispered. 'You're much stronger than she is.'

Annika blinked away the tears and tried to smile.

'I won't,' she said. 'We'll get along and you're going to get well.'

Her grandmother closed her eyes for a minute or two, resting. Then she opened them once more.

'Annika,' she murmured. 'I loved you the best. I suppose it was wrong of me to do so, to love one family member more than the others.'

'That's what made me so strong,' Annika whispered.

The silence following her remark told her that her grandmother had dozed off again.

The branches of the pine trees, heavy with snow, were

like a tunnel in the winter's night. The car carrying Mia Eriksson, her husband and her children progressed slowly along the icy roads. The north wind slapped the windshield with a hiss, hurling cascades of snow at them, over them.

'We've got to get fuel,' Anders said.

The woman in the front seat didn't respond. She stared out at the surrounding forest instead: infinite, impenetrable. She knew what awaited them. Yet another icy cold, draughty log cabin with a smoky wood-burning stove, and rats that scuttled under the floorboards. Yet another kitchen without running water, with mismatched chipped china and scorched crockery. An outhouse. Mia thought that she had left all that behind her, that Paradise would be the way out.

'I know what you're thinking,' the man said, covering her hand with his. This won't go on for ever.'

They came to a village: a lone tobacconist's shop, now closed for the day, that was an agent for Svenska Spel, lotteries and sports betting; one pizzeria; a solitary cash-operated fuel pump.

'Are you okay for cash?' Mia asked.

The man nodded and left the car. Mia hesitated momentarily, but decided to stretch her legs. They had been driving for ages and the children had fallen asleep in the back seat a long time ago. Frigid air greeted her as she got out, this certainly was the far north. She walked around the tiny service station and considered taking a leak there in the shadows behind the building, but decided not to. Stuffing her hands in her pockets, she felt cold metal and stiffened.

Mia pulled out the objects: two keys for bolt locks – an Assa-brand house key and a plastic Mickey Mouse key ring. Rebecka would be furious.

Who cared? They'd never see her again. She walked

over to the trash can next to the pump to throw them away.

'Mia, could you come here?' her husband asked. 'The children are awake.'

She stopped, why throw them away? For a few seconds she considered an option, recalling Annika Bengtzon's words: *I'm going to continue to dig for dirt on Paradise.* She turned to her husband.

'Do we have an envelope around here somewhere?'

He was just about to shut the car door and stopped in mid-motion.

'Here? Why?'

'The car-inspection certificates – aren't they in the glove compartment? Could you hand me the envelope they're in, along with the kids' chewing gum?'

The man sighed and handed over what Mia had asked for. She quickly stuffed the keys in the envelope that had been slit open, popped a piece of bubble gum into her mouth and chewed it energetically for half a minute. Then she used the gum to seal the envelope and fished out a pen from an inside pocket.

'My wallet too, please,' she said.

Mia stuck four stamps in the upper right-hand corner, then wrote down a name and an address – Hantver-karegatan 32, courtyard building, three flights up. At the bottom edge she added: *The keys to Paradise. Sincerely, Mia.*

'Are you ready?' Anders asked.

'I just need to mail this,' Mia replied and headed for the yellow mailbox.

SATURDAY 3 NOVEMBER

He heard the demonstration before he saw it: a dull roar of voices chanting something rhythmic with a steady beat. Cars came to a standstill, there was confusion and a certain amount of chaos. His senses grew more acute: it was almost time. He looked around, his gaze sweeping over the buildings – glass and sheet metal, bricks and mortar – and then landing on the pattern of triangles on the square in front of him. She would be coming. Sooner or later she would show up. It was vital to strike first, to have the upper hand. He shivered in the cold air: this was one fucking cold country.

Now he could see the procession. Six women led the way, carrying a banner and a poster of a leader who had been imprisoned. A crowd followed in their wake, mostly men, but there were some women and children as well. Thousands of people protesting against something or another. He stamped his feet, freezing in his thin jacket. Some young people set fire to a Turkish flag below him. It burned up quickly and the teenagers seemed to lose interest in the proceedings after that.

The masses invaded Sergelstorg, blotting out the triangular shapes on the ground. Now he could hear what they were chanting: *Turkish terrorism, Turkish terrorism*. Flags, banners and posters swayed in the wind. A speaker's makeshift platform was set up and loud-speakers appeared. A Swedish man, probably a politician, began to speak.

'The PKK have waged a war,' he shouted. 'This has led to violations of democracy and acts of terrorism that cannot be justified. However, they have taken place in a wartime situation during a Turkish war of aggression . . .'

This was it.

He started to move swiftly and unobtrusively through the crowd and put his hand inside his jacket to caressed his weapon, a nine-millimetre calibre Beretta 92, fifteen bullets in the magazine and one in the breech. A silencer was attached to the end of the barrel.

With slightly hunched shoulders, he kept close to the wall of the underpass.

'Hey, dude, got any speed?'

He dismissed the junkie in front of him with a wave, considered attaching the scope to the gun but changed his mind. He could keep tabs on the situation better without it.

Suddenly he saw her. Twenty metres away, her back to him. The churning crowd was pushing her slowly forward, away from him. Perfect.

He picked up his pace, darted between baby buggies and banners, saw her hesitate and look around. The adrenalin was singing in his veins, a familiar tune.

When there was only a metre left between them he pulled out his handgun, took one last step, twisted the woman's arm behind her back and put the gun's muzzle against the base of her neck, under her hair.

'Game over,' he said. 'You lose.'

Sounds faded, the crowd chanted silent slogans, time stood still. The woman was motionless, frozen, not breathing.

'I know it was you,' the man hissed, the words reverberating in his head.

He pulled her even closer against him, stared at her hair gleaming with bluish lights, and wished he could see her face. The gun's muzzle was resting perfectly at the junction of her neck and the back of her head.

'Bijelina,' he whispered, 'do you remember Bijelina?'

Suddenly the pressure on the muzzle disappeared. The woman yanked her arm free and waded quickly through the crowd. It took a second before he lunged after her, almost falling over a baby buggy, and caught up with her, the adrenalin roaring through his system, and forced her arm behind her back again. She struggled, on the ball this time, a gun in her hand now. People jostled them, they were pushed back, and he smashed her fingers with the butt of his gun. She dropped her own gun. A woman stared at them with a frightened expression and he tried to smile. Then he managed to get his gun back in place at the base of her skull, saw that her mouth was moving and leaned in closer.

'What was that?'

'You won't win,' she whispered. 'I've destroyed your life.'

He saw her from the side and met her gaze.

She smiled.

Something exploded in his mind and in his pants. He squeezed the trigger and she fell limply into his arms, her eyes wide open. He laid her on the ground, stuffed his gun back under his sweater and noticed people in the crowd giving him surprised looks. The sounds returned – *Turkish terrorism* – and he walked quickly to the subway station, tore off his jacket and his gloves as soon as he was inside, thrust them into a trash receptacle and headed for the next exit.

The car pulled up at the same instant as he reached the Åhléns department store. He got into the back seat and shut the door, his whole body shaking. The driver ran a yellow light and made a right turn on Klara Norra Kyrkogata. They had to hurry before the police cordoned off the area. Once they reached Olof Palmesgata, they made a left turn, and then a quick right on Dalagatan and speeded all the way to Vanadisvägen. There they pulled up on the courtyard, continued down into the garage and parked. There were no people in sight.

'Things go okay?' the driver wondered.

The gunman opened the door, got out, lit a cigarette and slammed the door shut.

'Get rid of the car,' he said and headed for the elevators.

He had to change before the stench killed him.

The night had been a calm one. Annika had slept on a bench next to her grandmother, slept deeply all night without waking up once. Come morning, the elderly woman was still asleep and they had to wake her up for breakfast. After her meal, Sofia Katerina dozed off again.

Annika showered and turned her underwear inside out. Then she sat for a long time by her grandmother's side, studying the peaceful face: the wrinkles like ripples, the pale down on her cheeks. Her mouth drooped open and Annika repeatedly wiped away the saliva that pooled there.

After that she anxiously paced up and down the hallway. Called her mother, no reply, her sister, no reply there either. Had some coffee. Had a plastic cup of warm rose-hip soup from a vending machine.

You have to take care of the people you love.

At lunchtime Annika tried to feed her grandmother again, but the old woman told her that she wasn't hungry.

The afternoon dragged on. Annika managed to find a few newspapers, not having the concentration to read a book. *Kvällspressen*'s main story was a piece by Carl Wennergren: he had found a receipt indicating that a female member of government had bought a chocolate bar using her official state credit card.

Christ, Annika thought, *talk about a plant!* Someone must have thought that the politician was getting too powerful, that she was too young, too good-looking, and too smart. A nice little scandal shifted the focus from the major issue of the Social Democrat congress: who would be appointed party secretary and fast-track their political career?

She put the paper aside, went to sit in the lounge and turned on the TV; a Turkish programme. *It's not like you have to live in Stockholm*, she thought. *You could live in Istanbul and work at the hotel with Nese. You could live in Katrineholm and take care of your grandmother*.

She let the thought linger and take root.

Why not? What reasons were there for not letting the most important person in her life claim that very position in her life?

Her work. Her career, everything she believed in and had fought for as a journalist. Her friends – but she would still have them even if she moved. Her home, her apartment – which honestly wasn't much to lose.

Suddenly Annika started to cry. She was filled with a sense of longing, mourning the loss of the way she had felt when she had first moved in, recalling how light had flooded the rooms, making the walls and ceilings live and breathe; the stillness, the peace, the drive to move on. She'd had it all, but where had it got her?

An elderly man, accompanied by two loud women and

leaning on a walking frame, entered the room. Annika dashed away her tears.

'Are you watching this?' one of the women asked her sceptically.

Annika shook her head, got up and left. The women took over the room.

'At five there is an afternoon concert on – you'd like to see that, wouldn't you, Father?'

The hallway was only partially lit. The fluorescent overhead lighting had been switched off and daylight slipped in through open doors, making waxed floors gleam. Slowly, Annika walked to her grandmother's room, her chest constricting again. The sense of longing lingered: memories of times when it had been easy to breathe, the hot days at Nese's hotel, the good times with Sven. She rested her forehead against the doorpost of her grandmother's room, longing for love, for a context. She swallowed, felt her back pocket, yes, she had change. Went over to the tiny telephone room next to the ward and looked up the number in the directory, a number for someone's home. Östra Ekuddsgatan. She dialled seven digits and hesitated before dialing the eighth but finally did it. It rang once, twice, three times.

'The Samuelsson residence.'

A woman. They had the same last name.

'Hello?'

Did she take his or did he take hers?

'Is there anybody there? Hello?'

Without a word, Annika hung up, her mistake like a weight in her stomach. She went in and looked at her grandmother, who was asleep, went back to the TV room and found it empty. Tried to breathe, tried to read.

Things will work out. Everything will be all right.

'Who was it?' Thomas asked.

He was standing with his back to Eleanor, when she didn't reply he looked at her over his shoulder. She had a searching and wary expression on her face.

'Nobody. Were you expecting a call?'

He turned around again and focused on the knife that he was holding.

'No, not at all. Should I be?'

'It's so eerie when people don't say anything.'

'Maybe it was just a wrong number,' Thomas said and chopped the last of the onion. 'Could you pass me the oil?'

Eleanor handed him the bottle – corn oil, better for high temperatures. Thomas poured the liquid into the pan, a thin, looping stream.

'We should have a gas range,' Eleanor said. 'They're so much better for woks. Maybe we could install one when we remodel the kitchen – what do you think?'

'This is fine,' Thomas replied, briskly stirring the chopped onion.

Eleanor went up to him and kissed him on the cheek.

'You're such a good cook,' she said.

He didn't reply, just tipped in the slivers of chicken and stirred. He added fish sauce, struck, as always, by its sexual aroma and added a dollop of chili paste, some pickled coriander and fresh basil.

'Could you open the coconut milk?'

Eleanor handed him the can she'd already opened.

'There,' Thomas said once the dish was simmering.

'The rice is done,' Eleanor said.

He turned to face her, his wife, and gazed down on her smooth face devoid of make-up. She was at her best like this. He put down the spatula, took a step forward and folded her in his arms. She responded by stroking his shoulders and kissing his neck.

'I'm sorry,' she murmured.

'No, I behaved badly.'

His reply was a whisper in her hair.

'You've been miserable for a long time now,' she said in a low voice and kissed him on the mouth.

He responded to her lips, salty and slightly dry. Desire shot through him, the familiar stiffening.

'Let's go to bed,' she said.

He followed her into the bedroom. She paused by the bathroom door.

'You go ahead,' she said.

Thomas knew what she was about to do. She was going to apply some lubricant to her genitals to ease the way. Slowly, he approached the bed, removed the bedspread and slipped out of his clothes. Eleonor came in and stood behind him, reaching for his hips and rubbing his buttocks against her lower body. He sank down to his knees next to the bed and she sat down in front of him, spreading her legs and leaning back. He stared at her vulva, gleaming with lubricant, and combed the well-tended bush of hair with his fingers, finding her clitoris. He rubbed it very gently and slowly until she started to moan. His cock as rigid as a spear, he pulled her close and pushed the tip against the opening. She gasped. He pressed on, barely moving, until the warm depths enveloped him, pulling him in, making him moan. Her loins came to life under him, around him, began to breathe and rotate. He pulled back, slowly, teasing her gateway, her clitoris, making her throw her head back and cry out. Then he plunged deep into her, hard, pounding rhythmically until he felt her spasm. Then he let go, surfing on the wake of her pleasure.

'Oh, darling,' she said, 'that was wonderful.'

He collapsed on top of her, his head resting between her breasts.

'You know, that chicken must be pretty well done by now,' Eleonor said. 'Could you hand me the tissues?'

A sensation of falling through the bed rendered Thomas unable to answer. She wriggled out from under him and he saw her take tissues from the box in her nightstand and wipe herself between her legs.

'I'll go take the pot off,' she said.

He crawled up on the bed and dozed off briefly. Woke up after a minute or so, with cold feet and tender knees. Tottering, he got up, pulled on his robe, and went into the kitchen.

'I brought everything downstairs,' Eleonor said.

He took a leak, wiped the lubricant and sperm off his penis, and went downstairs to the den. There was wine and a salad and the coffee table was set for two. He sat down and Eleonor followed with the coconut chicken and a trivet. She snuggled up to him on the couch and planted a kiss on his forehead.

'Sex always makes me hungry,' she said.

They ate in silence and drank their wine.

'I've been acting like a jerk,' Thomas said after a while.

She looked down at the contents of her goblet, a crisp Australian Chardonnay.

'You've been depressed,' she said. 'It happens to everyone.'

'I don't know what got into me,' he said. 'Nothing felt good any more.'

'Well, that can happen when you work as hard as we do. We'd better watch it, or we might get burned out.'

He blinked, hearing the reporter's voice asking, *Are you a burn-out case*? He cleared his throat, put an arm around Eleonor's back, grabbed the remote with his free hand and leaned back. The news, *Aktuellt*, had started. Their party congress was drawing near and the Social Democrats were embroiled in a heated debate; it appeared to have something to do with a member of the government using her state credit card for private purchases, as far as he could gather. A fire in the Philippines threatened an entire city. A Kurdish woman had been murdered during a demonstration at Sergelstorg.

'Would you like to listen to some music?' his wife asked and got up.

Thomas mumbled something in reply as he tried to hear what had taken place. Shot in the head, in a crowd – how could something like that happen?

'Bach or Mozart?'

He stifled the sigh he felt coming on.

'It's doesn't matter,' he said. 'You choose.'

SUNDAY 4 NOVEMBER

Annika detested Sundays. They were endless. Everybody occupying themselves with useless crap, whiling away the hours with meaningless pursuits. Society turned on pointless ideals: going on picnics, visiting museums, coddling the kids, throwing barbecues. Weekdays, the normal business that kept anxiety at bay, were far away, disconnected. The only valid excuse for not being associated with all this was to work – blaming work made you exempt. She needed to rest, to get some sleep, in order to work all night.

Thank God she had her shift tonight.

Her mother and Birgitta came over to the ward after lunch. The three of them sat together and talked to Gran, Annika was starting to recognize a pattern to the conversation: Arvid, the foundry, her parents, mainly her mother, the little sister who'd died. After an hour or so the old woman grew tired and dozed off. They went downstairs to the cafeteria, which was closed, naturally – it was Sunday, the day of rest, and all – and bought

shrink-wrapped pastries from Delicato and coffee from a
vending machine.

'This isn't a good environment for her,' Annika said.
'Gran needs serious rehabilitation, the sooner, the better.'

'So, what are we supposed to do,' Birgitta said, 'when
there aren't any vacancies anywhere? Have you thought
about that?'

Startled, Annika took in her sister's expression, so
guarded and aggressive.

She's on Mother's side, the thought flashed through her
mind. *She doesn't like me either*.

'Well,' Annika said. 'I've been thinking. Maybe I could
take care of her.'

'You?' her mother said contemptuously. 'That would
be a feat, in that awful apartment with no modern
conveniences. I don't know how you stand it.'

Suddenly Annika felt close to tears, she couldn't take
any more. She got up, put on her jacket, slung her bag
over her shoulder and looked at her mother.

'Don't make any decisions without talking to me first,'
she said.

Then she looked at her sister.

'See you.'

She turned, left the hospital and went out to the
parking lot; the sun was shining, the light was hazy, there
was snow on the ground that crunched when she walked.
It was cold. She wound her scarf around her head and
breathed with her mouth open, the tears welling up in her
eyes but not spilling over.

The train station. She had to get home. Get away.

Sjölander was perched on Jansson's desk drinking coffee
when Annika arrived at the newsroom. It was already
dark by then: reality was manageable – the newsroom
was still quiet, without tension, practically deserted. Her

shift didn't begin for another hour or two, but she couldn't stand being alone for long. The train had come to a standstill outside Södertälje due to a signal error, something Annika thought only happened to the Green Line on the subway, and she had gone straight to the office as soon as she'd arrived at the Central Station.

'So what have we got?' Jansson asked as he hammered away at his computer keyboard, writing his notes directly onto the hard drive.

'Loads,' Sjölander said and put his notes on the desk.

'How much can we print?' Jansson asked without taking his gaze off the computer screen.

'Almost everything,' Sjölander replied.

'What's this?' Annika asked, taking a seat, picking up her notepad and pen and turning on her own computer. 'The Kurdish girl at Sergelstorg?'

'Yeah,' Jansson said. 'Talk about a weird story: five thousand witnesses and nobody saw a damn thing.'

'The police have found some of the killer's clothes,' Sjölander added. 'Brown gloves and a dark green poplin jacket. The gloves were purchased at the nearby Åhléns, and they were covered with fingerprints. So far prints from eighteen different individuals. The jacket was as clean as a whistle apart from the traces of cordite on the sleeve.'

'What, did they find the guy's laundry basket, or something?' Jansson said.

'A trash bin. The items were in the bin along with the regular trash over at the central subway station.'

Annika leaned back, shifting into gear, a welcome and familiar feeling.

'And nobody saw a thing?' she asked.

'Oh, yes, they did,' Sjölander said. 'About a hundred people have described a man who may have been Swedish or Turkish, though he could have been an Arab or even a Finn. It seems that he spoke to the victim beforehand, shot her and laid her on the ground, then ran into the subway station, since his gear was found stuffed in the bin by the entrance. There are witnesses who saw him take his things off, one of those being a security guard. The guy was wearing light-coloured clothing underneath. After that there are a number of different options as to where he took off. Out in the street, according to the security guard. Down to the trains, a group of young people say. And back out to the square, according to a woman with a baby buggy. He almost ran her down. In any case, he disappeared.'

'He must have nerves of steel,' Jansson said, 'pulling off a stunt like that in front of all those people.'

'Probably helped him – the crowd worked as cover for him. What a cool bastard.'

Sjölander sounded almost impressed.

'What else do we know? Any details about the gun?'

Sjölander leafed through his notes.

'A silencer, of course. We're talking about a handgun here. I have data on the bullet, we can print that. The ammo was semi-jacketed. The girl was shot at the base of the skull: a fully jacketed bullet would have blown her face off from the inside, which would have been a mess. This one lodged in her nasal cavity after trashing her brain. She looked fine from the front – people thought she had fallen.'

Annika shivered. *Pretty damn nasty.* She yawned; the first night on duty always seemed extra long.

'Do we know her name?'

'Yes, they've released her identity. She didn't have any relatives here, she was a refugee – from Kosovo, I think. No family left over there, either. Here it is. She was from Bije— how the heck do you pronounce that, Bijelina? Her name was Aida, Aida Begovic.'

The newsroom closed in like a noose. Annika was struck by a sensation of tunnel vision; colours drained away, sounds grew hollow. She got up.

'What's the matter?' Jansson said, his voice seeming to come from far away. She saw his face. The floor tilted as voices receding into the distance called: 'Annika, what's the matter? Are you sick? Sit down, you're as white as a sheet . . .'

Someone set her down on a swivel chair, forced her head between her knees and ordered her to breathe regularly.

Annika gazed at the underside of the seat, at the height-regulation mechanism. She closed her eyes, squeezed them shut and held her breath.

Aida, Aida from Bijelina was dead and she was the one who killed her.

I've done it again, she thought. *I'm a killer twice over.*

'Damn it, Annika, are you still alive?'

She sat up, letting her hair fall forward to veil her face. The whole building pitched and rolled.

'I feel sick,' she said in a strange voice. 'I have to go home.'

'I'll call a cab,' Jansson said.

Darkness. Annika didn't have the strength to turn on the lights. She just sat on the couch and stared at the gently swaying curtains, shadows dancing.

Aida was dead. A man had killed her. The man in black had found her. How?

Rebecka, of course. Aida had threatened to expose the Paradise Foundation and Rebecka had retaliated by betraying Aida, by revealing her whereabouts.

What a monster. A fucking murderer.

And she, Annika, had set Aida up.

She was guilty of manslaughter.

The tightness in her chest increased, vicelike; soon, very soon she would be crushed to bits.

She reached for the phone, needing to call someone, needing to talk. Anne Snapphane was at home.

'What's happened?' Anne said. 'Are you sick?'

'The girl who was shot to death at Sergelstorg,' Annika said. 'I knew her. It's my fault that she's dead.'

'What are you talking about?'

Annika drew up her knees, clasped her shins and rocked back and forth on the scratchy couch, sobbing into the phone.

'I sent her to Paradise and they betrayed her. And now she's dead.'

'Hang on,' Anne Snapphane said. 'The girl was murdered, right? She was shot in the head. How could you be responsible for that?'

Annika took a few breaths, her sobs dying down.

'Paradise is a sham. The director is an impostor. Aida, the dead girl, said she was going to expose the whole dirty business. That's why she died.'

'Let's take the whole story from the top,' Anne said. 'Tell me everything.'

Annika steeled herself and told her friend everything. She told how Rebecka had called her, wanting publicity. She described their first encounter at the shabby hotel, the ingenious set-up of Paradise, her own reservations; their second encounter; how Rebecka's calculations didn't add up properly; the threats from the Yugoslav Mafia; Rebecka's incredible scheme for relocating clients abroad; how she, Annika, had found out about Rebecka's debts and her name changes, the bankruptcies, the suspicion of criminal intent. Then Annika went on to tell Anne about Aida, the danger she was in, the man who tried to force his way into her hotel room, and how Annika had given her the Paradise phone number and encouraged her to go there for help. She told Anne about Mia Eriksson showing up on her doorstep, gave her an account of her story, and described that final desperate phone call when Mia had told her that Aida had disappeared, that Rebecka had threatened her.

'And you believe this is all your fault?' Anne Snapphane said.

Annika swallowed.

'It is.'

Anne sighed.

'Please,' she said. 'You aren't accountable for everything that goes wrong here on Earth. I know you want to save the world, but there's got to be a limit. And now you've crossed the line. You're all worn out. Your grandmother isn't well – don't you realize how much energy you've spent on being concerned about her? You're so incredibly considerate when it comes to other people, it's time you were a little less hard on yourself.'

Annika didn't reply, just sat in her dark apartment and let the words sink in.

'There's no way you put that bullet in that poor girl's brain,' Anne went on. 'By the time you met her, she was already up shit creek, right? You tried to help her, but it didn't work out. So let's talk about intent. Why did you send Aida to Paradise? To help her, obviously. Come on, Annika. You're not guilty of anything here. Not in any way. Do you understand?'

Annika started crying again, sobbing softly in relief.

'But she's dead. I liked her.'

'You're entitled to grieve. You tried to help her and she died anyway. It stinks, but it's not your fault.'

'No,' Annika whispered, 'it's not my fault.'

'Are you all right?' Anne asked. 'Want me to come over? I have a kilo of chocolate I could bring along.'

Annika smiled into the receiver.

'No,' she said. 'I'm fine.'

'Whatever you say,' Anne said. 'Don't think of me or of how I'm going to look after I stuff my face with a whole bag of chocolate! By the way, I might host a TV show.'

'You? Why?'

'Don't sound so damn surprised. The host of *The Women's Sofa* just landed a contract with another TV network, which must be the worst appointment choice of the year if you ask me. That means we need a new host a.s.a.p. and it will be either me or the queen of bimbos, Michelle Carlsson. Christ, I get the heebie-jeebies just thinking about it, so I'm going to stuff my face . . .'

After Anne hung up, the darkness was friendlier, the curtains' breathing motion now abstract and irregular.

Not her fault. It stank, it was awful, but there wasn't anything she could do. Too late. Too late for Aida from Bijelina.

Annika undressed in the darkness, leaving her clothes in a heap on the couch.

She slept dreamlessly.

A lengthy buzz at the door woke Annika up. In a stupor, she got out of bed, got tangled in the duvet, wrapped it around her and went to the door.

'This won't do,' the mailman admonished.

He held out a plastic bag full of junk.

Still dazed, Annika blinked uncomprehendingly at him and scratched one eyelid.

'What?' she said.

'Tell your friends to use the appropriate materials when they mail things in the future. We can't be fixing letters that fall apart like this.'

'Is that for me?' she asked sceptically.

'Aren't you Annika Bengtzon? Then here you go.'

He handed her the bag and a stack of window envelopes, every last one a bill. *What a great morning.*

'Thanks,' Annika mumbled as she closed the door.

She let the duvet drop by the door and studied the bag: what the hell could this be? She held it up to the light to see better. A torn envelope, a wad of gum and a key ring? She tore open the plastic bag and poured its contents onto the coffee table. Poked gingerly at the envelope – yes, it was addressed to her, the handwriting was even but the words had obviously been jotted down in haste, probably while writing on an irregular surface. Something else had been written at the bottom: *The keys to Paradise.*

Mia.

Annika sat down on the couch. The keys to Paradise. She picked up the envelope; it must have been a used one, the letter had been sent in great haste. She looked at the postmark: a town in Norrland.

Of course. Mia didn't need the keys any longer. The family'd had to go to that house out in Järfälla. Annika had the address. Mia had given it to her. She went and got her bag and dumped out the contents; the same sanitary napkins and breath mints as before, a pad, a pen, a gold chain . . .

She paused. The gold chain. She sat down on the floor and picked it up. Aida's gold chain with two charms; one a lily, the other a heart. Aida's way of thanking Annika for saving her life.

And she died anyway, Annika thought. *But it wasn't my fault. I did what I could.*

She pulled the chain over her head, arranging it around her neck. The metal was cold and heavy. Apart from her notepad, the rest of the contents went back in her bag. She brought the pad with her into the living room and flipped through its pages to find the address. A corner of one page was torn off; she had written down the address on it for the benefit of that bureaucrat guy, Thomas Samuelsson. Thomas who'd once played hockey and who was married to Mrs Samuelsson.

Annika got out the yellow pages and looked up the map of Järfälla.

The phone rang, making her jump.

'How are you? Jansson tells me you weren't feeling well and had to go home last night.'

It was Anders Schyman.

She swallowed.

'I'm better,' she said with some hesitation.

'What happened, did you pass out?'

'Kind of,' she said.

'You've been looking tired lately,' the deputy editor stated. 'My guess is that you've been working too hard on that foundation story.'

'But I haven't—' she started to say.

Schyman interrupted her: 'Listen to me. Take sick leave for the next few days and we'll see how you feel after that. Forget about Paradise, baby yourself instead. Isn't your mother unwell too?'

'My grandmother.'

'Spend some time with her and I'll see you the next time you're on duty. Take care.'

A sensation of warmth spread through Annika's stomach after Schyman hung up. People cared. She sighed and settled back into the couch. The prospect of free time didn't feel ominous or threatening, it felt comfortable and pleasant.

She went into her bedroom and put on a sweatsuit. First a shower, and then she knew exactly what she was going to do.

Schyman had to be careful. It wouldn't do to let the people he trusted and counted on fall apart. They would be useless to him if they got all burned out. Annika Bengtzon had to keep her wits about her a while longer.

He took a deep breath, the scent of cleansers filling his nostrils. Getting rid of that ratty old couch and having the place thoroughly cleaned had been a stroke of genius.

Feeling on top of things and at ease, Schyman leaned

back and opened the paper. His sense of satisfaction deteriorated slightly as he read on. The front page story dealt with the spectacular murder at Sergelstorg, the young woman who had been shot in the head during a demonstration. The piece was illustrated by a large, somewhat blurry picture of the girl. She had been young and beautiful. There wasn't anything controversial about going public with her name and picture, but the grue-some facts were described in too much detail. You didn't really need to know that the semi-jacketed bullet had scrambled her brains before it got lodged in her nasal cavity. Schyman sighed. Oh well, no use in worrying about petty details like that.

The next spread featured the impending governmental crisis: the Social Democratic congress was scheduled to begin on Thursday and last a week, and the power struggle was in full swing. Carl Wennergren had con-tinued to dig into the financial affairs of the female politician – it appeared that she hadn't paid her day-care bills on time – and was rapidly approaching the point of no return with regard to ethics. The paper still hadn't pursued the core issue: *why* the politician was being scrutinized at this particular time. It was a well-known fact that she was the nominating committee's main choice for party secretary, which would mean that she was being groomed for the role of prime minister, and this made the bypassed middle-aged lard-asses want to go gunning for her. That was what Schyman wanted featured in the paper: a description of men in power and what they were willing to do to hang on to it. The names of the other nominees hadn't leaked out to the press, even though people knew that three representatives would be leaving the executive committee, the elite group in power. Schyman had a hunch that the nominees might be controversial – it promised to be an exciting congress.

Gossip had it that Christer Lundgren, the former Minister of Foreign Trade who had resigned after the Studio 69 scandal, was on his way back in from the cold. Personally, Schyman didn't think this was likely: the scandal had been too great and it had never been fully cleared up – there were potentially explosive issues submerged beneath the surface. But the Minister of Culture, Karina Björnlund, could possibly be heading for a fall of her own. She had seriously proposed that the government should have the right to appoint and dismiss editors-in-chief and executive directors at media companies throughout Sweden. Somehow she had been kept on, and he knew why. Annika Bengtzon had told him the reason some two years previously.

The rest of the paper was rather thin. New stock-market tips – 'Be a winner!' – elicited a sigh. The centre spread featured an interview with a television celebrity who was about to switch networks. This change didn't appear to be due to a conflict, just greed. Schyman sighed again. They hadn't managed to dig up anything solid during the past week, something that would secure Monday's edition while they waited for real life and a new week to get rolling.

Oh, what the hell, the printing department was in good shape, they were prepared. You shouldn't overlook anything that came your way, no matter how insignificant it might be.

The pizza rested like a cheesy brick in Thomas's stomach, making him feel slightly queasy. After lunch he shut himself in his office with the evening papers, skipping coffee.

There on his desk was the invoice from Paradise for a safe house during the months of November, December and January. Three hundred and twenty-two thousand kronor. Thomas knew that the Social Services budget couldn't accommodate this. They would have to postpone the clean-up of a day-care centre with mould problems and give the money to that deceitful debt-dodger.

The social worker had handed him the invoice as he was going out to lunch with his colleagues.

'This just arrived by fax,' she had said in an icy voice, her eyes cold. She hadn't forgotten that he had embarrassed her in front of a client.

Thomas had thanked her, more mortified than he cared to admit.

Now he stared at the invoice and mentally assessed which items he could scratch in order to make his budget.

What the hell, he thought a second later and pushed the train of thought away. *It's not my problem. The board okayed this crap, so they'll have to clean up their own mess.*

Thomas sighed, leaned back and picked up *Kvälls-pressen*. He opened it to the centre spread and found an extensive interview with a female TV show host who was going to switch networks. *So incredibly uninteresting*, he thought and returned to the front pages. There was a picture of the person who'd died at Sergelstorg last Saturday, the Kurdish woman who had been murdered in the middle of a demonstration. Boy, she was young. He let his gaze wander to the caption: *Aida Begovic from Bijelina, Bosnia.*

For a few seconds, his brain froze. Then he threw down the paper and grabbed the invoice from the Paradise Foundation. It had today's date on it, 5 November.

This can't be possible, he thought. He yanked open a desk drawer, the one at the bottom, and unearthed every last piece of information he had about the case. And leafed through them. He was right.

Aida Begovic from Bijelina, Bosnia.

Rage left him breathless. His field of vision had a reddish tinge to it, spreading from top to bottom. That bitch . . . She had the gall to charge for the protection of a woman who had been murdered!

Thomas dumped the papers on his desk. Somewhere in there was a scrap of paper with an address on it. It fluttered down on the desk when he shook the stack of printouts from the Sollentuna Debt Enforcement Agency, the scrap of paper torn from Annika Bengtzon's large notepad. He stuffed the invoice and the address into the inside breast pocket of his jacket, put on his coat and left.

Annika got off the train at Jakobsberg, clutching page eighteen from the map section of the *Yellow Pages*. The .wind was biting cold, the damp lacerating her skin. Boxy brown 1960s buildings, a school, a salon, a church. Checking the map, she saw that she should head north-west. A pedestrian underpass took her under the Viksjöleden highway and she grabbed a burger at Emil's Fast Food.

Nervousness exploded in her system as she left the fast-food joint. Her mouth felt coated with the aftermath of greasy-spoon dining, the burger resting uneasily inside her, giving her heartburn. She was about to take the law into her own hands.

She contemplated the houses, so colourless and indistinct in the haze.

I don't have to do this, Annika thought. *I'm on sick leave. Paradise can wait.*

Deliberating with herself she stared at the houses.

I could go and take a look, she figured. *Just because I'm checking the place out from the outside doesn't mean I have to go in.*

Relieved to have postponed the decision, she went to the neighbourhood evidently known as Olovslund. It

didn't appear to be a product of civic planning, the layout
had no uniformity to it. The houses were all different,
built during different periods and in different styles:
Victorian houses, an old farmhouse, plain cheaply built
boxes dating from the 1930s, sprawling modern piles of
white brick and dark brown wood. The area had
developed along the slopes of a substantial ridge and
many of the streets had names describing their location:
Höjdvägen, Hill Crest Lane; *Släntvägen*, Hillside Lane;
Brantvägen, Incline Lane. Other streets were named after
seasons and months: she passed *Höstvägen*, Autumn
Lane, and *Novembervägen*, November Lane.

*I wonder how well people know each other in an area like
this*, Annika thought. *Not all that well*, she reckoned.

Finally she came to the right street and walked slowly
up the steep gravelly asphalt road with unkempt gutters,
the keyring rattling in her pocket, feeling like it was
burning a hole through the lining.

The house was near the crest of the ridge, on its
northern face. Annika stood next to the driveway and
studied it carefully. The garden was hilly and neglected –
last summer's brown and decaying leaves lay scattered
between patches of snow. Large boulders partially
obstructed the view. The house itself was from the 1940s,
possibly the early 1950s; two storeys high and coated with
pale grey-brown stucco that might have been white
originally but was now deteriorating. No curtains, no
lamps, no lights anywhere. The windows looked like
gaps in a row of bad teeth.

Her heart started pounding, her breath steaming
clouds in the cold air. She looked around; there were no
lights on in the surrounding houses and no one in sight.

Suburban Swedish neighbourhoods on a weekday
afternoon reminded her of life after the big bomb, she
mused, weighing the keys in her hand.

Mia Eriksson was renting a room in this house. She had paid rent for the entire month. Mia had given Annika the address and the keys. It practically amounted to an invitation.

Annika took a deep breath and went into the garden. Traces of footprints and inadequate shovelling had left the path leading up to the house icy and uneven. She glanced quickly over her shoulder: no one was watching her, no one was questioning her presence there. Swiftly she climbed the steps, the keys ready in her pocket, her hand perspiring. There was no sound when she listened at the door. She rang the bell; it jangled and reverberated inside the house. If someone came to the door she would dream something up, ask for directions or say that she was selling a paper for some charity like Situation Stockholm. She rang the bell again. No response. She studied the front door – solid, from the 1940s, two bolt locks – pulled out the keys, weighed them in her hand and tried a key in the lock at the top. It didn't work. Her upper lip broke out in beads of perspiration; what if this was a trap? With shaking fingers she tried another key: *click*. She exhaled, tried another key, put it in the lower lock – *clickity-clack* – then on to the Assa lock. *Swish*. The door slid open with a squeak. She went inside, her pulse roaring in her ears, and closed the door behind her. The hall was dark. She blinked to get used to the gloom, not daring to turn on the lights.

Annika stood in the hall for a long time, waiting until the darkness lightened as her eyes adjusted and her heart stopped racing. The place smelled a bit unpleasant, damp and stale, and it was pretty cold. She wiped her feet on a threadbare little mat, not wanting to leave tracks.

The hall was barren, unfurnished. There were several doors. She opened the first one on the left, revealing a staircase leading up to the next floor. Faint daylight trickled in from an upstairs window. She closed the door silently and opened the next one. It revealed a junk-filled closet space fitted under the stairs.

A car rumbled past outside. Her whole body stiffened and her heart stopped beating.

The locks, she thought. *I've got to lock the door or they'll know at once that someone is here.*

Annika tiptoed quickly back to the door, her hands suddenly clumsy, twisted the Assa lock shut and used the keys on the other two. A relieved sigh escaped her. Her armpits were damp with perspiration. She listened for more sounds from the outside, nothing. Then she stole back to the closet. When she opened the door this time a key fell to the floor with a clatter, the noise echoing through the empty house. *Shit, shit.* Hurriedly she inserted the key back in the lock, listened: nothing. Then she moved on to the next door, the one that led straight ahead. The kitchen, which hadn't been remodelled since the house was built, had low work surfaces with a rusty counter top and sink. Two windows: one facing north, the other west. An old laminate-topped table and four chairs that didn't match. A coffee maker. She went over to the sideboard and pulled out the top drawer: a few pieces of cutlery, a carving knife. Nothing in the next drawer, and nothing in the next. She checked the cabinets: a few pots and pans, a cast-iron skillet, a colander. The pantry held a box of macaroni and two cans of chopped tomatoes. She paused and looked around. The kitchen was fairly clean, something that Mia could probably take credit for.

To the east there was another door, a sliding one, which was closed. Annika walked over to it and pulled on the shiny recessed handle. Locked. She gave it another yank, using both hands this time, but it didn't budge. She picked at the lock; this one required a tiny key and none of the ones on her chain would do. She went back into the hall and tried the last remaining door. It led to a pale room containing a couch and a small low coffee table and a fireplace in the corner. The floor was covered with brown linoleum in a parquet pattern. On the left there was another door that ought to have led to the room behind the kitchen. She went over and tried to open it. Locked. Tried her keys, but none of them worked.

The office, Annika thought. *This is the room that Mia didn't have access to.*

She was on her way back to the kitchen to see if she could find a key to the locked room when she heard the top bolt on the front door rattle.

The blood drained from her head and went straight to her feet. She couldn't move – it was as if she was nailed to the floor when the first bolt clicked open. When the next bolt was released she suddenly had wings and flew to the door leading to the staircase, opened it, slipped inside, closed the door behind her and zoomed upstairs without making a sound, came to a landing covered in the same parquet-patterned linoleum, yanked open one of four doors and flung herself under the bed furthest away. *Dear God, please help me, forgive me for all the stupid things I've done . . .*

The floor under the bed was extremely dusty, so Annika covered her nose and mouth with her hands to keep the worst out and tried not to sneeze. Someone was moving around in the room below; water was running, so it had to be the kitchen. Her breathing became heavy, rapid and deep.

No, she thought. *Not an anxiety attack, not now.*

Her breathing wouldn't obey her and she started hyperventilating. She turned over on her back, checked her pockets for something to breathe into, found her gloves and covered her nose and mouth with one. Breathed in and out over and over again until the attack subsided and she was exhausted. She stared up at the underside of a sixty-year-old bed: tan webbing supporting a dusty box-spring mattress.

Annika turned her head back towards the wall, putting her ear to the floor. Excited voices, a man and a woman. The man belligerent, the woman a touch hysterical. She recognized one of the voices: Rebecka Agneta Charlotta Evita.

'It was my case,' the woman said. 'My case! What a rat! Social Services was just about to pay up and that bitch runs away!'

She must be referring to Mia, Annika thought. Something broke downstairs; she guessed it was the coffee maker. The man mumbled something she couldn't catch and then there was a loud buzz in her ear. She jumped, banging her head on the box spring. *Oh, hell.* The buzzing stopped. She lay down again and gingerly touched her forehead: she was bleeding a little. Then the buzzer went off again – it was the doorbell. It was attached high on a wall near the kitchen ceiling.

In the silence that followed Annika heard the voices murmur, now more surprised than upset, more frightened than aggressive.

'No, I'm not expecting anyone . . .'

'. . . Might be coming back . . .'

Annika heard the sound of footsteps downstairs as some blood trickled down into her eyes. She listened even more closely.

It was a man – another man had come. There was a discussion, voices were being raised. The front door closed and they returned to the kitchen.

'If you think I'm going to pay this invoice you've got another think coming!' one of the men said and Annika gasped.

Thomas Samuelsson.

The woman's voice filtered up through the ceiling, lukewarm and contemptuous.

'We have a contract, and you have to honour it.'

'For Christ's sake, the woman is dead!'

The civil servant was incensed.

'She ran away,' Rebecka Evita said. 'She chose to leave, that doesn't exempt you from payment.'

Thomas Samuelsson lowered his voice, making it difficult for Annika to make out what he said.

She thought she heard him say: 'I'm going to go to the police, you phoney bitch! I know all about your debts and your bankruptcies, and you certainly aren't going to defraud the city of Vaxholm!'

A scuffle ensued. The other man started shouting, Thomas Samuelsson responded in kind, the woman hollered and then there was a thud and the sound of wood splintering. Shouting and screaming followed and the house rocked.

'Lock him up!' Rebecka screamed.

A thumping sound further away, muffled shouts, fists thudding rhythmically.

'What the hell do we do now?' the man said.

'Shut him up,' the woman hollered.

Fists pounding – thud, thud, thud – shouts of rage: 'Let me out, you goddamned impostors.' Then footsteps, followed by another dull thump. Then silence.

'Is he dead?' the woman asked.

Annika held her breath.

'No,' the man replied. 'He'll be fine.'

Annika closed her eyes and exhaled.

'Why did you hit him so hard? You fool, we can't have him lying here on the floor.'

'We've got to go and get the car,' the man said.

'I'm not going to carry him!'

'Stop whining, for Christ's sake. I'm telling you that—'

The front door slammed shut, cutting off their voices.

In the silence that followed, Annika remained where she was, dusty and hot. A feather floated down between the bed springs and landed under her nose. Time stood still as she took shallow quiet breaths.

They'll be back. Soon they'll be back and they have a car. Then they'll take Thomas Samuelsson away and it will be too late.

The last thought echoed in her mind: *too late, too late*. Too late for Aida from Bijelina, too late for Thomas Samuelsson from Vaxholm.

Annika blew away the feather and crawled out from under the bed. She sneezed, coated with dust from head to toe, then crawled over to the window on her hands and knees and looked out. Rebecka and a man were headed downhill; they passed a car that Annika recognized as Thomas Samuelsson's green Toyota Corolla.

She sat down on the floor, her brain at a standstill: what was she going to do? She had no idea how long it would take before Rebecka and the man returned. Maybe the best thing would be to just sit tight, wait and let them pick up the accountant. Then she could sneak out of the house after dark.

Annika looked out the window again. It was almost dusk. No Rebecka. If she was going to do anything apart from waiting, she had better do it soon.

She sat down again and closed her eyes in hesitation.

If only she wasn't such a coward. If only she wasn't so weak. If only she had more time.

What a chicken you are, Annika told herself. *You don't even know how much time you have. You might be able to get him out of here if you get moving.*

She got up, stole out to the upper landing and crept down the stairs, breathless with anxiety. She looked around and saw the skillet on the floor. Where had they put him?

A faint groan from the closet under the stairs caused Annika to spin around. The key was still in the door. She walked over and turned it in the lock.

The man tumbled out on top of her and she caught him in her arms and fell to her knees. His head rested in the crook of her elbow. He was bleeding from a substantial wound at his hairline, the pale hair now tinged brown by blood. She loosened his tie and he moaned again.

Rage brought tears to her eyes. *Goddamned murderers! First Aida, now Thomas.* Would it never end?

'Hey,' Annika said, patting the accountant's cheek firmly. 'We've got to get out of here.'

She tried to get Thomas to stand up, but she lost her hold and he slumped to the floor.

'Thomas! Thomas Samuelsson from Vaxholm, where are your car keys?'

He groaned, rolled over on his back and rested his head on the threadbare mat in the hallway.

She delved in his pockets, soft cloth, clumsy hands, there they were. She went into the room that contained the couch to check if Rebecka was on her way back to the house. There was no one in sight.

When Annika was about to leave the room, she noticed that the door to the locked room was now ajar. She hesitated for a second – she ought to be getting the hell out of there. But she ought to check out that room, too.

'Christ, what happened?'

A choked and dazed voice came from the hall. She went over to Thomas.

'They whacked you on the head with a frying pan,' she said. 'We're going to get out of here, there's just something I want to check out first.'

Thomas Samuelsson tried to get up, only to collapse again.

'Sit here for a minute, I'll be right back,' Annika told him.

Then she raced over to the now unlocked door, flung it open wide and surveyed the contents of the room.

Disappointing.

Annika didn't know what she'd expected, but it certainly wasn't this. A desk. A telephone. A fax. A bookcase full of loose-leaf binders and a stack of papers. Since she didn't hear anything, she rushed in and grabbed the notebook marked *Off the record*.

It was empty.

The next one was marked *Follow-up*.

Empty.

The next one: *Invoices, social services*. Some twenty slips: City of Österåker, your reference, Helga Axelsson, our reference, Rebecka Björkstig; City of Nacka, your reference, Martin Huselius . . . Every single invoice specified a substantial amount, at the very least one hundred thousand kronor. Then Annika swiftly checked the notebooks on the top shelf, all bearing titles such as *Client Rehab*, *Safe Houses*, *Relocation Abroad*.

All empty.

The stack of papers contained personal data, court rulings, certificates and forms from *Försäkringskassan*, the Social Insurance Office. Confidential data about the people whose lives were in danger.

Turning her back on the bookcase, Annika surveyed the rest of the room. She really had to go; had she missed anything?

The desk. She hurried over to it and yanked at the drawers. They were all locked.

Okay, forget it, that's it, she thought.

Thomas Samuelsson was sitting up, leaning against the wall with his head between his knees.

'Are you alive?' Annika asked nervously.

'Just barely,' he mumbled.

She unlocked the three front-door locks and sank to her knees in front of him.

'Thomas,' she said and swallowed. 'They'll be back any minute now. We've got to get out of here. Can you walk?'

He shook his head, his hair like a brown-spotted curtain.

'Put an arm around my shoulder and I'll drag you out. Come on.'

Thomas did as he was told. He was heavier than Annika had expected. Her knees buckled under his weight. She got him to the door and kicked it open. It was almost dark out. She set the man down on the steps. He was pretty woozy and her hands were so slick and shaking that the keys slipped from her hand onto the lawn. She almost started crying. *Damn it to hell*. Maybe she should forget about locking the door? She listened for cars: nothing. She stepped over the dazed man, picked up the keys, then stepped back over him and went up to the door. It crossed Annika's mind that it would be a good thing to lock the closet door, so she raced in and did just that before shutting the front door and securing the three locks as fast as she could. She hauled Thomas up and dragged him over to the Toyota. A cheerful *blip-blip* and the car doors were open. She dumped him in the passenger seat and ran to the other side, holding the key in both hands to keep it steady as she stuck it into the ignition. *Praise the Lord* – the engine sprang to life immediately. She revved it up, shifted to first gear and drove off over the top of the hill.

The last thing that Annika saw in the rear-view mirror was a car heading uphill behind them.

She drove straight ahead, panic welling up in her and threatening to make her hyperventilate again. The road came to an intersection and she made a sharp right. Thomas Samuelsson slumped towards her and she pushed him back into his seat again.

Christ – how was she going to make it out of here? Which direction was Stockholm?

She drove downhill, figuring she would hit a thoroughfare somewhere. Now what was the name of this street? Mälarvägen?

Annika checked her rear-view mirror, seeing only the headlights of cars that didn't seem to be pursuing her. Her gaze returned to the road again and she saw a stop light. A thoroughfare? Viksjöleden! She made another right turn, leaving the house and Rebecka behind her, but soon she realized that she was driving in circles when she passed another major road, Järfällavägen, and recognized her surroundings. The Barkarby Factory Outlet! She could hear Anne Snapphane's voice joyfully exclaiming: 'Today is Outlet Day!' They usually made a run to the place every autumn and every spring to buy leather jackets, sports shoes, and offbeat fashion items from sample collections at bargain prices. There wouldn't be a problem finding her way home from here. She took the E18 and speed towards Stockholm in the fast lane.

Suddenly her passenger started to throw up. Thomas Samuelsson vomited all over his coat and trousers and banged his head against the dashboard.

'Shit,' Annika said. 'Do you need help?'

He groaned and threw up again. Annika kept driving, desperately looking for an off-ramp and not finding one, feeling trapped and helpless.

Still resting his head against the dashboard, Thomas raised his hands to his head.

'What the hell happened?' he asked her in a weak voice.

'Rebecka and her pal,' Annika replied. 'They knocked you out.'

He looked up at her.

'Hey,' he said. 'What are *you* doing here?'

Annika kept her gaze on the road. The highway was getting more congested.

'I heard them lock you into that closet. When they left to get their car, I let you out. You have a concussion, you ought to see a doctor. I'll take you to Sankt Göran.'

'No,' Thomas protested lamely. 'I'm fine. My head hurts, that's all.'

'That's a load of crap,' Annika said. 'You might have a contusion, it might haemorrhage. You don't fool around with serious things like that.'

She got a little lost among the off-ramps to the E4, but finally managed to get on track again at Järva Tavern. Then she headed past Hornsberg, pulled up outside the emergency room and parked the car. Her hands were steady as she pulled the keys from the ignition, relieved to have escaped physical harm.

It was dark, a yellow street light tinting everything sepia.

'I can't walk in there like this,' Thomas protested, indicating his soiled coat.

'We'll stuff that in the trunk,' Annika said and went to open the passenger door.

'Let's go,' she said. 'Get up, I'll give you a hand.'

The man came to his feet. He was covered with vomit.

'Let's get this coat off,' Annika said and pulled at it. Thomas swayed slightly.

'Where did you come from?' he asked, looking at her as if she was a ghost.

'I'll fill you in later,' she replied. 'Let's go inside.'

Annika draped one of Thomas's arms across her shoulders, wound an arm around his waist and lugged him into the emergency room. The lady at the desk reminded her of the one in Katrineholm where her grandmother was: the same style, the same glass window.

'My trousers,' Thomas said. 'They've got vomit on them.'

'We'll go to the john and wash you off,' Annika said. 'Hello, Thomas here has had a blow to the head. He was unconscious for a few minutes, he's been throwing up and he has a headache. He's a bit dazed and disorientated.'

'You're in luck,' the lady said. 'We're not all that busy here right now, so you can go right in. I'll be needing your personal ID number.'

'My pants,' Thomas whispered.

'That's great,' Annika said. 'He just has to go to the bathroom first . . .'

Annika waited for Thomas. The examination took no time at all: he wasn't in bad shape, there were no clinical signs of brain damage and he was pretty lucid. The doctor accompanied him out into the waiting room.

'Am I going to need a lot of rest?' Thomas asked.

The doctor smiled. 'No, that won't be necessary. Normal physical activity is beneficial – it keeps symptoms like headaches and fatigue from lingering.'

Annika and Thomas went out to the car again, both of them exhausted and relaxed.

'I'll take you home,' Thomas said, heading for the driver's seat.

'No way,' Annika exclaimed. 'No more driving for you today. I'll take you home.'

His response popped out before he should stop it.

'I don't want to go home.'

Annika looked at him without showing any surprise on her face. She studied him with an expression that he couldn't quite figure out, assessing the situation.

'All right,' she said finally. 'We'll go to my place. You need to recover for a while longer before you get behind the wheel.'

He didn't protest, just got into the passenger seat and fastened the seat belt. Something occurred to him: he never sat on that side – Eleonor never drove his car, she drove the BMW.

They drove off towards Fridhemsplan and Thomas gazed out the window in silence. So many glittering lights, so many nameless people. There were so many different ways to live your life, so many options.

'Does your head hurt much?' Annika asked.

He looked at her and gave her a little smile. 'Yeah, a lot.'

Strangely enough there were quite a few parking spaces left near her house.

'The sweeper is scheduled for tonight,' she explained. 'Anyone parking here after midnight can look forward to a four hundred kronor fine.'

Thomas put his arm around her shoulders for support while she helped him up the stairs. For such a tiny thing, she was strong. He sensed her breasts under his hand.

Her place was done completely in white; the wooden floors were wavy with wear.

'The building was built in the 1880s,' Annika said as she hung up her things. 'The owner went bankrupt during the real-estate crash in the early 1990s, so it hasn't been remodelled for a while. Would you like some coffee?'

Thomas smoothed his hands over his damp trousers, wondering if they smelled bad.

'Yes, I would. Or some wine, if you have it.'

Annika paused to think about it, her back straight, eyes clear.

'I think I have an opened carton of white wine somewhere, only I'm not sure that it's good for you to drink anything alcoholic right now. What do you think?'

Thomas flashed her a slightly dazed smile and raked back his hair, taking note of the five stitches he'd received, straightened his tie and smoothed his jacket.

'I think it's all right,' he said. 'Normal physical activity is beneficial, you know.'

Annika disappeared into the kitchen and Thomas stood there in her living room, slightly woozy and unsure of himself, checking the place out. What a strange room. White matte walls, sheer white curtains, a couch, a table, a TV set, a telephone. Apart from that, the large room was bare. A broken window had been repaired with a paper grocery bag and the draught made the snowy curtains billow. The floor was grey, matte, soft as silk.

'Go ahead and sit down, if you like,' Annika said, bringing in a tray with glasses, coffee mugs, a brick-pac carton and a coffee press. She moved gracefully and deftly as she set the table. The thick gold chain around her neck reached down to her breasts.

Thomas sat down. The couch wasn't particularly comfortable.

'Do you like it here?'

She sat next to him, poured herself a cup of coffee, poured him some wine and sighed.

'Sort of,' she said. 'At times.'

She picked up her mug and silently studied its contents.

'I used to love it here,' Annika said in a low voice. 'When I moved in I thought it was fantastic to live here. Everything was so light it sort of floated. Then . . . things changed. Not the apartment, other circumstances, my life . . .'

She stopped talking and drank some coffee. Thomas took a sip of the wine; it was surprisingly good.

'What about you?' she said, looking up at him. 'Are you happy?'

He was about to smile but decided not to bother.

'Not really,' he said. 'I'm sick and tired of my life.'

Thomas downed a large mouthful of wine, his candour surprising him. Annika just nodded and didn't ask why.

'What were you doing out in Järfälla?' she asked.

His head throbbing, he closed his eyes and tried to recall the reason.

'The invoice from Paradise' he said. 'Did I bring it with me? I was carrying it when I went to the house. Three hundred and twenty-two thousand kronor for the protection of a client for a three-month period. It came in over the fax this morning even though the woman in question was already dead. Those damned impostors!'

'I didn't see an invoice, only heard you mention it,' Annika said. 'Then again, I didn't look closely at the closet. Have you checked your jacket pockets?'

Instantly Thomas checked the garment's outer pockets: nothing. Felt the inside pocket, found a folded sheet of paper and pulled it out.

'Here it is. Thank God for that.'

He studied the figures briefly, lowered the paper and looked at Annika.

'What actually happened?' he asked. 'Where did you come from?'

She got up and headed for the kitchen.

'I think I'll have some wine too,' she said and returned with another wineglass.

'Right,' she said. 'I was going to call you. I've uncovered a lot more dirt about our friend Rebecka

Björkstig. She's used several different names and is suspected of serious fraud in connection with all her bankruptcies.'

Annika poured some wine from the carton into her glass, then poured some more into his.

'This morning a keyring arrived in the mail. I've been in touch with a woman who has been involved with Paradise: she stayed at the house in Olovslund. She and the rest of her family moved out on Friday and she mailed me the keys from some place up in the middle of Norrland. I went straight to Järfälla.'

Amazed, Thomas looked at her.

'So you used the keys and let yourself in? Wasn't there anyone there?'

Annika shook her head.

'No, but they turned up pretty soon after I got there. I hid upstairs in the attic. Then you showed up and stirred things up. They must have hit you over the head with a frying pan. Rebecka and the guy she was with left to go and get a car, I dragged you out to your Toyota and we drove off.'

Trying to sort out his thoughts, Thomas rubbed his forehead.

'So you were already there when I arrived?'

'Yes, indeed.'

'You dragged me out of that closet and got me out of there?'

'That's right. And I locked both the closet door and the front door before we left, so you can imagine their expressions when they came to get you.'

Annika grinned and Thomas stared at her for a few seconds before he gave a belly laugh.

'You locked the closet door? And the front door too?'

'All three locks.'

They both laughed and then kept on laughing even

harder – he howled with laughter, she laughed until she cried.

'That was fucking incredible!' he exclaimed.

'I bet they figured that you had dematerialized.'

Thomas calmed down, his laugher subsiding to chuckles.

'That I had what?'

Annika smiled.

'Dematerialized, dissolved, digitized. The way we'll travel in the future. You dematerialize and transmit yourself by way of a computer from one place to another: it's quick and it's easy on the environment. Just think of the possibilities when it comes to travelling in outer space – it will be so convenient.'

Thomas stared at her: what was she talking about?

'There ought to be something like ten thousand to one hundred thousand civilizations out there that are as evolved as our own, or even more highly evolved, in the Milky Way alone,' Annika said. 'Scientists have figured out that life evolves much more easily than we previously thought. It might not be such a tricky process. If the conditions are right, new lives might be created all the time, all over the place. All you need is water in liquid form.'

Surprised, Thomas laughed.

'What an amazing bullet train of thought. How on earth did you figure all that out?'

'I wonder what they look like,' she said. 'Imagine the day when we get to meet them! It'll be great. Just think of all the new foods we'll get to try. I'm so sick of carrots and potatoes. Lots of new vegetables. Spices. There ought to be zillions of new worlds out there, and I'm fed up with this one.'

Annika grew silent, no longer laughing.

'Why is that?' Thomas asked.

Now serious, she looked him in the eye.

'Why do *you* feel that way?' She queried, picking up on his earlier complaint.

He sighed quietly and polished off the wine in his glass, feeling a bit drunker than he should have.

'I don't like my life any more,' he said.

For some reason it felt so easy to tell her everything: he knew that she would understand, that she wouldn't judge him. He looked at her; she was tired, a little too thin, and her capable hands were folded in her lap.

'I love my wife,' Thomas said. 'We have a nice house, we're well off, we have lots of friends, I work in a field of my own choosing that I enjoy, but still . . .'

He grew silent, hesitated, sighed, fingered his tie, pulled it off, folded it up and put it down on the couch.

'We want different things,' he said. 'She wants to focus on her career at the bank, a top management position. She figures she'd better hurry up, she'll be forty this spring.'

They sat in silence for a while.

'So, how did you meet?' Annika asked.

Thomas sighed, smiled, and, infuriatingly, tears came to his eyes.

'She was the sister of one of the guys on the hockey team, much older than her brother. Sometimes she would give us a ride to practice and to games. Good-looking. Cool. Had a driver's licence.'

In an attempt to hold his sentimental feelings in check, he laughed.

'Your secret fantasy woman?' Annika asked and he blushed a little.

'You could say that. I would think about her at times right before I fell asleep. Once, when I was spending the night at my friend Jerker's house, I saw her leave the bathroom in only her bra and panties. She was magnificent. I jerked off like a madman that night.'

They laughed together.

'How did you hook up?'

Thomas looked into his empty wineglass, thinking that he really shouldn't have any more while simultaneously pouring what was left in the carton into his glass.

'The summer I turned seventeen a whole bunch of us guys were going to travel on an Interrail pass through Europe. Everybody was supposed to arrange some kind of summer job and earn some money and we would leave in mid-July. I guess I should have known what would happen . . .'

Annika smiled. 'No summer jobs.'

'Except for me, of course,' Thomas said. 'My parents own the ICA grocery store in Vaxholm, so there was no escape for me – I worked in the deli section. In addition to that I worked weekends and on holidays, so I had a lot of money by July.'

'But no travelling companions,' Annika added.

'And my mother wouldn't let me go all by myself,' Thomas said. 'I was desperate, slamming doors and refusing to talk either to my parents or my friends. The world was rotten. But then this miracle occurred.'

Thomas picked up his tie and unfolded it.

'Eleonor's boyfriend, an awful upper-class twit, broke up with her right before they were going to take a trip to Greece together. Eleonor tore up the tickets and threw them in his face. She decided to see Europe by Interrail, something her ex-boyfriend would never condescend to doing, only she didn't want to go alone.'

Annika put his tie on and saluted him.

'So you became her male escort.'

He yanked on the tie, Annika pretended to be throttled by it and they laughed. They sat in silence for a while and she took the impromptu noose off.

'What happened?'

Thomas drank some wine.

'Eleonor wasn't very friendly at first. 'We can stick together as far as Greece, then we'll see' was what she told me. We got on the wrong train in Munich and ended up in Rome, and it was boiling hot, forty degrees Celsius, by the time we got there. While I went off to buy water, a gang of juvenile delinquents robbed Eleonor. By the time I got back she was incensed with me, Italy, and absolutely everything. I was ashamed that I hadn't been able to protect her. We found a filthy room, which I paid for, near the station, and got blind drunk. We staggered through the streets, each clutching one of those straw-covered bottles of Chianti. Eleonor yowled her head off and made a spectacle of herself, draping herself all over strangers, and all over me. I tried to drape myself over her as much as I could. Things were okay until we reached the Piazza Navona. Then Eleonor decided she was going to take a dip in the fountain there, just like Anita Ekberg.

'Wrong fountain, though,' Annika said.

Thomas nodded.

'And the timing was all wrong too. Seven thousand drunk soccer fans were at the piazza, and when Eleonor's T-shirt got wet, you could see right through it. They literally tried to tear her clothes off – she nearly got raped then and there in the fountain.'

Annika smiled and saluted him again.

'But you saved her.'

'I hollered like the chef in Disney's *Lady and the Tramp*: 'Sacramento idioto, I'm a-going to punch-a you on the nose!' Then I pulled her out of the fountain and dragged her back to the hotel.'

'And you went to bed?'

'Unfortunately, no,' Thomas replied. 'Eleonor threw up all night. The next day she was green at the gills. We spent the morning at the police station reporting the robbery and then we spent the afternoon at the Swedish Embassy arranging for an emergency passport. That night we went over to the A1, planning to hitch a ride north and go home. We stood there by the road for ever in the awful heat and almost died of carbon monoxide poisoning. Finally this short tubby guy in a red car picked us up. He was as hung-over as Eleonor and didn't speak a word of any familiar language. He turned in at the first Area Servizio we passed, waved at us to indicate that we should follow him and marched up to the bar. He ordered three glasses of something red and viscous, exclaimed and knocked one glass back. After he'd banged the empty glass on the counter, he looked at us commandingly, waving his hands and saying 'Prego, prego!'

'We were scared to death that he would ditch us if we didn't obey, so we downed the disgusting stuff and got back into the car. The same thing happened at every Area Servizio. Three glasses, hup, bang the counter. Soon we were singing as we rode along. It got very dark. Late at night we reached this fabulous town, at the top of a very high mountain. Perugia, the man said and arranged for us to stay with a friend of his, the town baker. They gave us this room with sloping ceilings above the shop, it had rose-patterned wallpaper. We made love. It was the first time for me.'

Thomas grew silent, the memories fluttering around the room like sighs. Annika swallowed and felt simultaneously close and distant, experiencing a sensation of loss and pain.

'Last spring we toured the wine country of Tuscany,' he said. 'One day we took off and went to Umbria. Coming back to Perugia was very strange, the place had always represented something special to us. It was where we had become a couple. We've never been apart for a single day since then.'

Once again, Thomas grew quiet.

'What happened?' Annika said.

'We didn't recognize a thing. Our Perugia was a quiet medieval town with stone buildings, like a painted backdrop on a mountain top. The real Perugia was a generous, vital and bustling city with a university. I was fascinated: Perugia was like our relationship, something that had started out as a teenage fantasy and had developed into a generous, vital and intellectual partnership. I wanted to stay on, but Eleonor was appalled. She felt hoodwinked. She didn't find a dynamic marriage in what Perugia had become – she'd lost her dream.'

They sat in silence for awhile.

'Why didn't you recognize a thing?'

Thomas sighed.

'Probably because we'd never been there before. The man in the car was so drunk that he could have been mistaken, or maybe we'd misunderstood him. We could have been in any Umbrian town: Assisi, Terni, Spoleto . . .'

Annika saw Thomas struggle with his memories, bent over, elbows resting on his knees, the wild shiny hair stiff with blood, and had to suppress an impulse to brush it to one side. What an attractive man he was.

'Are you hungry?' she asked.

He looked at her, confused for a second.

'Yes,' he said.

'I make a mean pasta with canned sauce,' she said. 'Would that be all right?'

He nodded in agreement, of course.

Annika went out to the kitchen and glanced out the window. Someone was taking a dump in the fancy guest apartment. She took out a box of tagliatelle and a can of Italian-style tomato sauce and brought a pot of water to the boil. Thomas stood in the doorway, leaning against the doorpost.

'Still a bit woozy?' she asked.

'I think it's the wine,' he said. 'What a great kitchen – you've got a gas range.'

'The 1935 model,' she said.

'Where's the bathroom?'

'Go down half a flight. Put on some shoes, the floor is filthy.'

Annika set the table, considered using napkins, stopped and analysed that notion. Napkins? When did she ever use napkins? Why should she start now? To impress someone, to put on an act?

When Thomas returned, she was in the process of draining the pasta. She heard him take his shoes off and clear his throat. As he walked into the kitchen she noticed that he now had a little colour in his cheeks.

'Interesting toilet arrangement,' he said. 'How long did you say you've lived here?'

'Two years. And then some. Would you like a napkin?'

He sat down at the table.

'Yes, please,' he said.

Annika handed him a bright yellow paper napkin, reminiscent of Easter. Thomas unfolded it and put it in his lap, it was the natural thing to do. She left hers folded beside her plate.

'Good pasta,' he said.

'You don't have to say anything,' she replied.

They finished their meal, hungry and silent. At times they glanced at each other and smiled. Their knees kept bumping up against each other under the tiny kitchen table.

'I'll do the dishes,' Thomas offered.

'There's no hot water,' Annika said. 'I'll do them later.'

They left the dishes and went back into the living

room, a new kind of silence between them, a buzzing sensation in Annika's midriff. They came to a standstill on either side of the coffee table.

'What about you?' he asked. 'Have you ever been married?'

She sank down on the couch.

'Engaged,' she replied.

He sat down next to her, the distance between them charged.

'Why did it end?' he asked in an interested and friendly voice.

Trying to smile, Annika took a deep breath. The question was so friendly, so normal. *Why did it end?* She tried to find the words.

'Because . . .'

She cleared her throat and fingered the table top. A normal question deserved a normal response.

'Was it so bad? Did he leave you?'

Thomas's voice was so friendly, so full of compassion. A dam burst inside her: tears started rolling down her face, she doubled over and flung her hands over her head, she couldn't help herself. She felt his surprise, sensed how uneasy and awkward he felt, but she couldn't do anything about it.

He's going to leave, Annika thought, *get up and go and never come back again, and that's just as well.*

'Hey, what's wrong?' he said.

'I'm sorry, I didn't mean to . . .' she sobbed.

Thomas patted her softly on the back and stroked her hair a few times.

'Listen, Annika, tell me what's wrong.'

She tried to calm down and get her breathing back to normal, mucus dripping on her knees.

'I can't tell you,' she said. 'I just can't.'

He grasped her by the shoulders and turned her to

face him. Instinctively, she turned her tear-swollen face away.

'I look awful,' she mumbled.

'What happened to your fiancé?'

Annika refused to look up.

'I can't tell you,' she said. 'You'll hate me.'

'Hate you? Why?'

She looked up at him, knowing that her nose was red and her eyelashes were clumped together. Thomas's face was concerned, worried, his eyes were a sparkling blue. He cared. He really wanted to know. She looked down again, breathing open-mouthed and rapidly, hesitating, hesitating, then taking the plunge.

'I killed him,' Annika whispered to the floor.

The silence mushroomed and grew heavy. Thomas tensed up beside her.

'Why?' he asked in a low voice.

'He beat me. Nearly strangled me. I had to leave him, or I would've died. When I broke up with him, he took a knife and gutted my cat. He was about to *kill* me. I hit him and he fell down into an old blast-furnace . . .'

She stared fixedly at the floor, feeling the distance between them.

'And he died?'

Thomas's voice was different now, muffled.

Annika nodded, tears spilling from her eyes again.

'If you only knew how horrible it's been,' she said. 'If I could change anything in my whole life, it would be that day, that blow.'

'Did you stand trial?'

Distant? Remote?

Another nod.

'I was convicted of manslaughter and was sentenced to probation. I had to see a therapist for an entire year because my parole officer thought I needed therapy.

Actually, it was pretty worthless. My therapist was a head case. I haven't felt very well since it happened.'

Annika stopped talking, closed her eyes and waited for Thomas to get up and leave. He did. She buried her face in her hands and waited for the sound of the front door. A bottomless pit opened wide, monumental despair, emptiness and loneliness, *dear God, please help me . . .*

Instead she felt his hand smooth over her hair.

'Here,' he said, handing her an Easter napkin. 'Blow your nose.' Then he sat down next to her again.

'You know, to be perfectly honest,' Thomas said, 'killing them might not be such a bad thing.'

Annika jerked her head up. He gave her a wan smile.

'I'm a social worker,' he continued. 'I've worked for Social Services for seven years now. There isn't much I haven't seen. You're not unique.'

She blinked.

'Women can end up spending their lives in hell,' he said. 'In my opinion, you shouldn't feel guilty. It was self-defence. It was too bad you met a loser like that. How old were you when you started seeing each other?'

'Seventeen,' Annika said in a whisper. 'Seventeen years, four months, and six days old.'

Thomas caressed her cheek.

'Poor Annika,' he said. 'You deserve better.'

In a flash she was in his arms, her cheek resting against his chest, hearing his heart pound as his arms circled her. She put her own arms around his waist and held him, so warm and big.

'How were you able to move on?' he whispered into her hair.

She closed her eyes and listened to his heart, pulsating with life, throbbing.

'Chaos,' she said, her face burrowed into his chest. 'At first everything was just pure chaos. I couldn't talk,

couldn't think, couldn't eat. I was numb, everything was
. . . a white-out. Then it hit me, everything came crashing
down at once, I thought I was going to go to pieces,
nothing worked. I didn't dare sleep, the nightmares
would never end. Finally I had to be admitted to a
hospital for a few days. That was when my parole officer
made me start seeing a therapist . . .'

Thomas smoothed her hair and stroked her back.

'Who took care of you?'

Ever so gently.

'My grandmother,' Annika replied. 'I stayed with my
grandmother that whole first year as soon as I had time
off. I walked in the woods a lot, talked a lot, cried an awful
lot. Gran was always there, she was incredible. The chaos
receded, but afterwards there wasn't anything left.
Everything was empty and cold. Meaningless.'

Thomas rocked her a little, breathing in the scent of her
hair.

'How do you feel now?'

She swallowed.

'Gran's ill, and that's so scary. She's had a stroke. I've
been thinking about taking a leave of absence and looking
after her. It's the least I can do.'

'But how are *you* doing?' he asked.

Squeezing her eyes shut to keep from crying, Annika
whispered: 'So-so. I have a hard time eating, but it's
getting better. Apart from this business with Gran, I'm
doing all right. I'm glad I met you.'

The words words popped out. Thomas's caresses
ceased.

'You are?' he said.

Annika nodded into his chest. He let go of her and
looked at her, into her dark eyes, fathoming their depths
and seeing the sorrow there. She met his gaze, so blue,
stroked his cheek and kissed him. He hesitated

momentarily, then responded, kissing, licking, sucking on her lips . . .

Annika pulled off her sweater, her breasts bouncing into view, the gold chain dancing, no bra. Fascinated, Thomas stared at them; they were so big. He cupped one in his hand. It was very warm and soft. She took off his jacket and unbuttoned his shirt, uncovering a smooth chest, solid, not much hair, and kissed his shoulder, nipping at him until he moaned. He kissed her neck, traced her lower jaw with his tongue, found her ear lobe, nibbled, sucked and licked on it. Her hands slid up his back, raking him gently and quickly in circles with her nails. Then they stopped, looked into each other's eyes and acknowledged the emotion, the common intent there, revelled in it, let it grow until it toppled them and they tore off their clothes and became a tangle of hands, lips, tongues, breasts, bellies, genitals, arms, feet . . .

Thomas lay down on the couch, his feet dangling over the sides, and Annika eased herself on top of him, enveloping him. She felt him press home, fill her, possess the space she'd almost forgotten. He felt her warmth, the pressure, the pulse, and wanted to get moving, but she said: 'Wait.'

They looked into each other's eyes again, saw the all-encompassing excitement there and were sucked in by it. Suddenly Thomas felt dizzy, a state of complete and utter ecstasy. He closed his eyes, threw his head back and screamed. Annika began to ride him, slowly. He wanted to hurry her up but she held him in check – he gasped, moaned, cried out and thought he was going to disintegrate.

She looked at him, matching his tremendous desire, allowing his member to slide into her so slowly that their souls joined too, deep, as far as it could go, over and over, and over again, until they had release and the wave enveloped them. She felt the warmth run down her thighs. His body went rigid, every single muscle knotted, semen pumping. She collapsed on top of him, he embraced her, still inside her and stroked her hair. They were covered in sweat, all shiny and slippery. Her nose was by his clavicle, she breathed in his scent, strong and slightly sour.

'I think I love you,' Annika whispered and looked up at him. Thomas kissed her and they started moving against each other again, first gently, carefully, then faster and faster; so wet, so slick.

Thomas woke because he was cold. One foot had gone numb – Annika was lying on it, her breathing deep and regular, and he realized that she was asleep.

'Annika,' he whispered, smoothing her hair. 'Annika, I've got to get up.'

She woke, startled, gave him a dazed look and smiled.

'Hello,' she whispered.

'Hello,' he said, planting a kiss on her forehead. 'I've got to get up,' he repeated

She lay still for a second.

'Right,' she said, and got up stiffly, pulling him from the couch.

They stood facing each other, naked and sweaty, she half a head shorter than him, and kissed. Standing on tiptoe, she wound her arms around his neck. He felt her breasts, so remarkably soft press against his ribs.

'I've got to go home,' Thomas whispered.

'Yes, but not yet. Let's sleep for a while.'

Annika led him by the hand to her bedroom. The bed, a box-spring one without a headboard, was unmade. She sank down on it and pulled him close.

They made love again.

*

The building was a colossus, dark and forbidding. Ratko stared up at its brick façade and saw the street lights reflected in the windows. His mouth was dry.

Why had they summoned him in the middle of the night? Something bad was afoot.

Cars whizzed past behind Ratko as he slowly approached the main entrance, went around the corner and saw the fleet of official vehicles: a spot for the consul, a spot for the ambassador. He went up to the door and knocked swiftly.

The fat man opened the door.

'You're late,' he said, then turned his back on Ratko and waddled back inside.

Ratko followed the fat man up the few stairs leading to the large room, the waiting room, and was immediately transported back to Belgrade: Eastern Bloc green walls, grey plastic chairs. The counter straight ahead, the glass wall to the left, he could detect the light in the consul's room.

'Why was I summoned here?' Ratko asked.

The fat man pointed to the door next to the glass wall.

'Sit down and wait,' he said.

Ratko walked through the room, navigating past the table and chairs, and went down the narrow corridor where the fat man had his desk. He entered the reception area that looked the same as always: chairs lined up against the wall, a couch, bookcases, a map of Yugoslavia before its partition. He considered taking a seat, but remained standing. Whenever he had been here before the circumstances had been pleasant, or at least friendly. Now things were different. He couldn't sit down: that would put him at a disadvantage when his superiors walked in.

The table bore marks from bottles of slivovitz, and suddenly Ratko became aware of how damn thirsty he was. Vodka, straight up, cold, no ice. He swallowed and ran his tongue over his lips.

Where the hell were they? What were they up to? They really had him by the balls and he didn't like the feeling.

Ratko took a few steps and glanced out towards the corridor. Several men, some he'd never seen before, all wearing identical poorly fitting brown suits – what the hell was going on? He stole back into the room quickly without a sound. Beads of sweat broke out on his forehead: he knew who these men were – RDB officials from Belgrade. What were they doing here? Were they here because of him?

'You can go in and see the consul now.'

Ratko went back out into the hall, passed the fat man and entered the next room. The unfamiliar men took no notice of him.

'Ratko,' the consul said. 'There's a flight to Skopje with a change at Vienna tomorrow at seven a.m. Our people will pick you up at the airport. You will leave at once.'

Ratko stared at the bald little man who was fingering some documents on his desk. What the hell was going on here?

'Why?'

'We've had some bad news from the Hague.'

The threat took hold. *Damn it all to hell – the war tribunal*.

'Tomorrow at twelve noon they will be issuing a warrant charging you with war crimes.'

The sweat stinging on his body, Ratko swallowed. All these men, how were they involved?

The consul tapped the papers into a tidy little stack against the desktop, got up and went around to the other side of the desk.

'We've arranged new papers for you,' he said. 'Our visitors have been drawing them up all night. You need to sign them and have your picture taken, then they're done.'

Slowly, Ratko's mind shifted into gear.

'But isn't that kind of information confidential until it's officially released?' he said. 'How did you find out about this?'

The consul came up to him. He was a full head shorter than Ratko and his eyes were expressionless. He wasn't happy to be doing this.

'We just know,' he said. Once you've received your new passport, you have to leave the country – tonight. You'll be leaving by way of Gardemoen in Oslo.'

Ratko wanted to relax, have some vodka, make sense of things. He wouldn't be safe by lunchtime, he'd be in the air somewhere between Vienna and Macedonia, and it would take several more hours to get from Skopje to Belgrade.

'If you make it in time, you won't be able to leave Serbia for the foreseeable future,' the consul added. 'I presume you don't have any unfinished business here?'

Ratko swallowed and stared at the consul.

'Your new passport will be a Norwegian one. Your name is Runar Aakre. We hope your papers will stand the test until you've crossed the border.'

It appeared to be the sign for the unknown men in the room to approach him. Everyone had their task and time was of the essence.

TUESDAY 6 NOVEMBER

The house was dark, an ominous presence by the sea. Thomas swallowed, knowing that Eleonor was awake. Somewhere in that darkness, she was waiting. Never before had he been gone like this, not once in sixteen years.

He closed the car door carefully, the blipping sound of the lock ricocheting off the surrounding houses. He took three deep breaths, closed his eyes and tried to sort out his feelings.

The young woman he had just left asleep in bed remained with him like a huge warm presence. Christ, he had never felt like this before. This was for real. She was incredible, so real, so alive.

Annika.

Her name had reverberated inside Thomas the whole way from downtown Stockholm to Vaxholm. The course he would take had materialized during this dark ride; it was the obvious thing to do.

He would be honest. He would tell Eleonor every-thing, come clean. Their marriage was dead, she would have to realize that. He wanted to live with her, the other woman, lead a new life, have a different existence. He didn't want a divorce because of Annika, she was simply the one who had triggered this step.

Thomas walked up to the house, relieved to be able to act on his decision. The frozen lawn crackled under his shoes.

It would be tough, but Eleonor would get over it. She could keep the house. He didn't want it. On the other hand, she would have to buy him out: the profit they had made when real-estate prices went up wasn't hers alone.

She stood in the hall, in a pink robe, her face pale with rage.

'Where have you been?'

Thomas dropped his briefcase on the floor, hung up his coat and turned the light on. Eleonor screamed.

'What happened? What's happened to you?'

She rushed over to him and traced the stitches on his forehead with her fingers. He backed away and caught her hand.

'That hurts,' he explained.

She folded him in her arms, pressed up against him and started to cry, then looked up at him and stroked his hair.

'Oh, I've been so worried. What happened, what have you done?'

Thomas avoided making eye contact with her and pushed her away, not wanting to feel her body, the hard bra cups beneath her robe.

'I've got to go to bed,' he said. 'I'm exhausted.'

He walked around her and headed for the bedroom. She grabbed his arm, pulling him back.

'Well, tell me!' Eleonor cried, tears coursing down her cheeks. 'What happened? Have you been in an accident?'

Thomas saw her, so close to falling apart: her hair all

mussed, her face tracked with tears. She searched for words, couldn't find them and stood there, paralysed.

She took a step closer, her lips colourless.

'Don't you understand how frightened I've been?' she whispered. 'What if I had lost you, what would I do?'

Eleonor closed her eyes and continued to cry, the tears still streaming from her eyes. Thomas stared at her: he'd never seen her as upset as this, his wife, the woman he had promised to love and cherish until death did them part.

'If something had happened to you, I would have died,' she said, opening her eyes and gazing into his.

Guilt hit him full force, threatening to suffocate him. Christ, what had he done, Lord, what was the matter with him?

He folded her in his arms, held her tight, stroked her hair and she cried all over his shirt, cried like the other woman had cried . . .

'I'm sorry,' he whispered. 'I . . . spent the night in the emergency room.'

Eleonor pulled free and looked at him.

'Why didn't you call?'

He pulled her close again, not wanting to meet her gaze.

'I couldn't,' he said. 'I was in the examination room all night. You know, X-rays and all that . . .'

'But what happened to you?'

Suddenly Thomas got a whiff of sex, a scent emanating from his own body that shouldn't have been there. He swallowed and patted Eleonor on the back, the plush of her robe feeling slightly rough to his touch.

'Put on some coffee,' he said. 'I need to take a shower. Then I'll tell you about it. It's a long story.'

They released each other and looked into each other's eyes. He steadied his gaze and forced himself to smile.

'It's all right,' he said and planted a kiss on his wife's forehead. 'I love you.'

Eleonor kissed him on the chin, let him go and went into the kitchen. Thomas went into the bathroom, crammed every last item of clothing into the hamper, got in the shower and let the hot water gush over him. Annika was all over his body, in every pore, her scent was everywhere – it rose in the steam and filled the entire bathroom. He could feel her firm body under him: the soft breasts, the tangled wild hair. He closed his eyes and saw her bottomless dark eyes and felt his penis stiffen again. He turned on the cold water and scrubbed his groin with Wella's volume-enhancing shampoo.

His desperation increased and indecision took over.

Another meeting. Damn it, that was all he did all day, go to meetings. How the hell was anyone supposed to get a paper out when everyone just sat around yacking all the time?

Anders Schyman put a lid on his bad mood. Always having to be the responsible, tender and compassionate leader was nerve-racking.

On the other hand, he was used to the day-care factor. That and the never-ending discussions on press ethics. The real drain was something else, a new element.

The power struggle.

Schyman wasn't used to that. Every single job he had held, every last position he'd ever been offered had been his because someone wanted him there. He had been offered influence without fighting for it, he had dined at the tables of power without having to make a kill to get there.

He surveyed the newsroom. The tasks of the day were in full swing. Reporters were on the phone and editors were hammering away at keyboards; they looked, assessed, clicked a mouse and made changes. Soon he would walk the forty-five metres that would take him to the editor-in-chief's spacious corner office; a powerful man, when Schyman passed conversations would come to a halt, eyes would grow attentive, people would sit up straight.

What were powerful men prepared to do to keep that power? Out of the corner of his eye he could see that the men had gathered, their flannel-covered backs receding in the direction of the management zone: the cosy corridor, the rooms with views and lots of space. He followed them, and when he entered the room, the others took a seat, waited, grew silent.

'Let's get down to business immediately,' Schyman said and looked at Sjölander. The crime desk. 'Where is this Yugo Mafia thing going? Did the murdered woman at Sergelstorg have anything to do with that business?'

All gazes shifted to Sjölander, who sat up straighter.

'Could be,' the crime desk editor said. 'The two bodies found in the torched trailer have been identified. They were two young guys staying at a refugee camp in Upplands Väsby, to the north of Stockholm, nineteen and twenty years old respectively. They've been missing for a while – the police and the camp supervisors figured that they'd run away to avoid being deported. That wasn't the case. One of the boys could be identified by his dental records, he'd been to see a dentist since he had arrived in Sweden. The other boy's identity hasn't been entirely confirmed, but all the details indicate that he is the missing friend of the identified boy. There might be a connection between the murdered woman and the boys, according to the police.'

'What would that be?' Schyman asked. 'Were they from Bosnia too?'

'No,' Sjölander replied, 'they were ethnic Albanians

from Kosovo. But Aida, the woman, stayed at the same refugee camp. True, that was long before the boys lived there, but the staff claims that she came by now and then to say hello. She could have met the two young men.'

The deputy editor leaned back.

'What does this tell us?' he said. 'What is this story really all about?'

They all looked at him in silent anticipation, not sure what to say. Letting his gaze sweep the room he took them in, the Flannel Pack, the heads of the different departments: op-ed, show business, civic affairs, sports, Torstensson was there and the picture editor.

'There have been five murders in a little over a week,' Schyman said. 'Every last one has been extremely spectacular. First the two young men at the free port, shot in the head from a distance with a powerful hunting rifle. Then those poor bastards in the trailer, tortured to death. And the latest victim, the woman at Sergelstorg, taken out at close range in the middle of a crowd of five thousand witnesses. What do these facts tell us?'

They all stared at him.

'Power,' he explained. 'This is a power struggle. It could be over money, or maybe someone wants to have a say in things – be it politics or crime, to have the power over life and death matters. I don't think we've seen the end of this business yet. Sjölander, I want us to stay on top of this.'

They all nodded, they all agreed with him – this he duly noted.

Power. Schyman was about to make his play.

The ceiling floated above her, shimmering in the semi-darkness. For a second she lay there, wondering where she was, exhilaration filling her, a sensation of total bliss. And then it dawned on her that something was wrong.

Annika sat up in bed abruptly, putting her hand on the pillow next to her to make sure that he wasn't there. Emptiness struck, a cold, stabbing pain.

Thomas had gone. Gone home to his wife named Eleonor, Eleonor Samuelsson.

Annika jumped out of bed to see if he had left a note, a few words about their encounter or a promise to call. Searched the kitchen, the hall and the living room. Then she yanked off the bedclothes to check if there was a note on the pillow, a note that had fallen down somewhere. Then she pulled out the bed and looked under it.

Nothing.

Annika tried to sort out her feelings: joy, betrayal, emptiness, assurance, jubilant intoxication.

There, among the covers, she lay down and stared up at the ceiling again.

Bliss. She had never felt bliss before, not like this. With Sven there had always been that dark undercurrent, the performance anxiety, the insistence on happiness.

This was different. Warm, easy, peculiar, fantastic.

She turned over on her side and pulled up her legs, Thomas's sperm still sticky on her thighs. She spread the duvet over herself and inhaled his scent.

Thomas Samuelsson, the bureaucrat.

Laughing out loud, she let the bubbly emotion shimmer.

Thomas Samuelsson, with shiny hair and a broad chest, a mouth that could kiss and caress and suck and bite.

Annika curled up into a ball, rocking and humming.

She knew it. She was certain. She wanted him. *Thomas Samuelsson, the bureaucrat.*

She sat up and picked up the phone.

'I'm sorry, Thomas Samuelsson isn't in,' the receptionist at the Vaxholm city council building informed her.

'He was assaulted, you see, and we're all very upset here.'

Annika smiled to herself, knowing that the accountant was actually in fairly good shape. She thanked the receptionist and hung up. For several seconds she held the receiver uncertainly. Then she dialled the number, Thomas's home number, the eight-digit number. Her heart racing, she waited while the phone rang; soon he would be with her again. *Soon, soon, soon.* She smiled, got warmer.

'The Samuelsson residence.'

Eleonor was at home. She wasn't at the bank, she was there with him.

'Hello? Who is this? What do you want?'

Slowly, Annika replaced the receiver, her mouth dry. *Shit, shit, shit.* The shimmering desire subsided and loneliness banged on the door.

She pictured them together, the man she knew and the shadowy figure of a woman, the dream woman of his youth. She swallowed, the disturbing episode gnawing at her. Then she pulled on her jogging clothes, walked around for a while, went to the bathroom, went into the kitchen and made coffee and then walked into the living room with all her notes and the telephone.

Thomas Samuelsson and his wife. *Shit, shit, shit.*

She called Anne Snapphane: no one was there. Her mother: no reply. The ward at Kullbergska: her grandmother was sleeping.

'I'll be coming to see her this evening,' she told the nurse.

Annika's next move was to phone Berit Hamrin, using her direct line, but there was no answer and she tried Anders Schyman instead. The phone rang. She was just about to hang up when he answered, slightly out of breath.

'You busy?' she asked.

'I just got out of a meeting,' he said. 'How are you?'

A twinge of guilt stabbed at her; she was supposed to be ill.

'So-so,' she said. 'I was out in Järfälla yesterday, over by the house that Paradise owns. It was interesting.'

She heard noise – furniture being moved around and a faint sigh.

'Didn't I tell you to ease up on that business for a while?'

'I was feeling fine,' Annika said, 'so I took a walk. The information that my source gave me seems to be accurate. I went through the office and couldn't find any evidence at all that they were doing what they claim to be doing, apart from sending out invoices, that is. They're very good at charging people for their services. Every last file was empty . . .'

'Hang on,' the deputy editor said. 'Did Rebecka let you into her office?'

She closed her eyes and briefly clenched her teeth.

'Not exactly,' she said. 'But I didn't break into the place, see. I'd been invited over and I had keys.'

'Rebecka invited you?'

'One of her tenants did. And while I was there, Rebecka showed up along with a man, who might have been her brother . . .'

'And you were on their premises?'

Annika stood up, suddenly annoyed.

'Now listen,' she said. 'I hid, and while I was hiding Thomas Samuelsson came over, that civil servant from Vaxholm I've mentioned. He was royally pissed off – it seemed that Rebecka had faxed him an invoice that morning. And the client she was charging them for is dead!'

This statement was followed by silence. To Annika, it seemed as though the name 'Thomas Samuelsson' reverberated in the air, that her voice had sounded strange when she'd pronounced the words, that it had gone all warm and soft.

'Go on,' Schyman said. 'What happened?'

She cleared her throat.

'They assaulted the guy from the council, locked him in a closet and went to get their car. I let him out and drove him to an emergency room.'

'Violence, oh my God, they're dangerous! Annika, you are *not* going over there again, you hear?'

She scratched her forehead, feeling the scrape marks left by the springs under the bed and reached a conclusion: she wouldn't tell her boss about Aida.

'All right,' she said.

'We can't sit on this story,' Schyman said. 'What do you need to write it?'

Annika gave it some thought.

'Supporting statements. Interviews with legal experts, social workers, and so on. This set-up needs to be put into a context. It might take time. And Rebecka should have the opportunity to comment on these developments too.'

'This guy from the council, do you think he'll talk?'

She swallowed, her voice soft again.

'Thomas Samuelsson? He might.'

'Do you have any more official connections?'

She closed her eyes in concentration.

'It may not be legally admissible, exactly, but I did see a few invoices with references. One was Helga, Helga Axelsson, I think, from . . . Österåker. And some guy in Nacka, Martin something . . . ending with "– lius", that can't be all that common. Things were a bit hectic and I didn't have time to study the rest.'

'What you did is called trespassing,' Schyman said. Annika couldn't tell if he was pleased or concerned.

'That's right,' Annika said, 'if you get caught. I had a key and I didn't leave any traces behind.'

'Were you wearing gloves?'

She didn't answer. She hadn't been wearing gloves and she did have a police record.

'I don't think Rebecka will call the police,' she said.

The deputy editor asked her: 'Would you like some help with the research?'

As long as it's not Eva-Britt Qvist, she thought.

'I'd like to work with Berit Hamrin,' she said.

'I'll have Berit call you,' he said.

'All right.'

Silence. Annika reckoned that the man at the other end of the line was thinking hard.

'This is how we'll play it,' Anders Schyman said. 'You're relieved from your upcoming night duty. You'll take it easy for the next few days and come in on Monday, and then work days until this is wrapped up. What do you say?'

Annika closed her eyes and stopped holding her breath as a heartfelt smile spread across her face.

'Sure.'

Annika practically flew to the train station, dancing along without touching the ground, not noticing the biting cold wind. Home free at last, her heart's desire within reach. *Yes, yes, yes.* She just knew that she would be allowed back on the beat again. Interviews, articles, investigations of people in power, blowing the whistle on corruption and revealing scandals, that was what she would be doing. Sticking up for the little people, taking a stand for the disenfranchised.

Once aboard the train she could choose between a view of the luggage rack or the brownish-green pine trees flashing past. She shut her eyes, the train clattered out: *Tho-mas, Tho-mas, Tho-mas, Tho-mas* . . .

Her elation dwindled as anger stole over her, a sense of being wronged. He hadn't called. He didn't leave a note. He had left her in bed without saying a word. Had he looked at her before he left? Had he caressed her cheek? What had he been thinking? Feeling? Shame, regret? Jubilation, intoxicating bliss?

Not knowing caused her physical pain. Her chest burned and she felt shaky.

Annika clenched her teeth and gazed out the window. *Grand-ma, Grand-ma, Grand-ma, Grand-ma, Grand-ma, Grand-ma* . . .

Stability and love, where would she be without it? The elderly woman was her world, her context, her roots in an existence that shifted like quicksand. She really ought to be there for her, it was the least anyone could ask, but she didn't have the strength to do it, she didn't want to. Ashamed, she curled up on her seat, feeling cold.

Finally, she had made it. All those years at school, the endless hack work at the local paper, the dues she'd paid pulling night shifts; it was time to cash in. Was she supposed to give up everything she'd worked for and take on a responsibility that rightfully belonged to society? Or did it? *What do we really owe the people close to us?*

The train continued along the tracks as snow obscured the view. By the time Annika got off at the station in Katrineholm, the weather had turned pretty bad. The storm slapped her face like a sharp broom. Her feelings of rage, of being unjustly treated, increased. *Why here, why now?*

She staggered across the station yard and headed for Trädgårdsgatan. The headwinds were strong and it was getting more slippery by the minute. The low-pressure front made it darker, sounds were rubbed out. Cars slipped past with thin headlight beams and crunching studded tyres. Finally, the hospital, Kullbergska, appeared on the right, a blunt grey structure. She lurched into the lobby, brushed herself off, leaned against the wall and took a breather. Two young women were on their way out. Both of them were pregnant and they were dressed in colourful quilted coats.

Annika turned away, pretending not to see them.

I'd rather be dead than live in this town.

Slowly, Annika walked over to the ward, picturing the tedious hours ahead, how her grandmother would ramble on about the past, the hard bunk she would sleep on tonight.

The corridor was deserted, bathed in flickering bluish fluorescent light. Voices from the nurse's office trickled out into the corridor. She slipped past without checking in. Some of the doors were ajar and she could hear the geriatric patients wheeze and cough. Her grandmother's door was closed. When she opened it she was hit by a cool draught of air. The room was dark and the elderly woman was in her bed. Annika went up to her and switched on the small bedside lamp, spreading rays of light over the yellow government-issue blanket.

She smiled and raised her hand to caress the old woman's cheek.

'Gran?'

The elderly woman was lying on her back. Annika saw the sunken features and instantly realized what had happened. Too still, too white, too limp. Regardless of this she touched the cold, greyish skin. Awareness sank in like a knife, reaching her chest, her brain, her lungs. Then she screamed. Screamed and screamed and screamed. The nurses came running, the doctor came, she still screamed and screamed.

'Save her, you've got to do something! Heart massage,

shock treatment, a ventilator. . . Do something! Do something!'

The doctor with the ponytail appeared beside her, backlit and serious.

'Annika,' she said. 'Sofia Katarina is dead.'

'No! No!' Annika screamed, backing away, knocking something over. She was sightless. Chaos.

'Annika . . .'

'You've got to bring her back, do something, operate—'

'She passed away in her sleep, quietly. She was very ill, Annika – maybe this was for the best . . .'

Annika stared at the doctor, tunnel vision taking over.

'For the best? Are you out of your mind? You didn't take care of her, you let her lie here and die, your neglect killed her, I'm going to report you, you bastards . . .'

She had to get out, get away. She headed for the door. People were blocking the way. She turned around, bumped into a nurse and the doctor grabbed her by the shoulders.

'Annika, pull yourself together, you're hysterical. We looked in on Sofia Katarina less than an hour ago and she was sleeping peacefully.'

Annika tore herself free.

'She can't be dead, she's in a hospital, why didn't you watch over her, why did you let her die, you bastards, you bastards . . .'

Someone took hold of her and she struck out at them and screamed; they wanted to take her away from Gran, they wanted to do even more damage, they weren't going to get *her*!

'Leave me alone! Let me be with her. You let her die, let me take care of her . . .'

Faces swam by. She didn't want to see them and flung herself backwards. They yelled at her: *Annika*! She roared back at them, refusing to hear, refusing to listen.

'You damned murderers!' she howled. 'You left her to die!'

They pushed her down on a bench, held her there. So now they were going to get her too? She howled and resisted them.

'Go and get some sedatives,' a voice said. 'We've got to calm her down.'

Suddenly Annika couldn't take it any longer and collapsed on the bench, grief sucking the breath out of her. The lights went out, she no longer had the strength to cry out, she began to get cold, there was no air, she was fighting for oxygen, desperately breathing in, breathing in. Someone yelled: 'She's hyperventilating, get a bag over here.' Everything went hazy, then black.

Annika mother sat beside her. The mink had been tossed onto the adjoining chair. Annika was lying on the hard bench. She had been given pills and the room had receded, faded and floated away. She looked up at the window. It was very dark outside.

I have no idea what time it is, she thought.

Her grandmother was lying in her bed, still and white. The bed was flanked on each side by candles, their flames twin golden circlets in the darkness.

Annika sat up. Her mother was crying.

'I didn't make it in time,' Barbro sobbed. 'They called, but Mother was already dead by the time I got here. She died in her sleep – peacefully, they tell me.'

The room seemed to be rolling as if they were at sea. Annika's mouth was dry.

'How would they know?' she said. 'I was the one who found her. Get rid of those candles!'

Annika got up and started walking across the floor, reeling and lurching, wanting to get to Gran, wanting to get rid of the candles, wanting to shake life back into the body.

Her mother got up and took hold of her.

'Sit down. Don't spoil this moment. Let's say farewell to Mother in a calm and dignified way.'

She led Annika back to the bench.

'It was for the best,' her mother said, dabbing at her eyes. 'Sofia would never have regained her old lifestyle. She was such an outdoor person – just picture how awful it would have been for her to end up bedridden. She wouldn't have liked that.'

Annika sat on the bench, finding it difficult to keep her balance. Her mother appeared to roll like the waves of the sea, swinging upwards and pitching down again.

'They killed her,' Annika said.

'Rubbish,' her mother countered. 'She had another haemorrhage, the doctors told me, probably in the same part of the brain as last time. There wasn't anything they could do.'

Annika regarded her grandmother: the love, the strength, the context she offered, now reduced to this, so tiny, so white and so thin. Soon she would be gone for ever. Annika was alone now.

'How am I supposed to go on?' she whispered.

Her mother got up, walked over to the dead woman and gazed down upon the old face.

'She had her ways,' Barbro said. 'She could be unfair and judgemental, but now that she's gone we'll have to disregard all that. We should remember her good qualities.'

Annika tried to think of something to say, unable to sort out her impressions and not wanting to mouth platitudes. She didn't want to play along with her mother so she sat in silence, staring at her hands. Remembering how the cold skin and lifeless head had felt she put her hand into the warmth of her armpit.

'She had her faults,' Barbro said. 'But then, so does everyone. I always wished for a mom who would care, who would look after me. All the other girls had mothers like that when I was little.'

Annika didn't answer. She tried not to hear the words as her mother chattered on, mostly to herself.

'Then again, you always love your mother, it's such a close relationship.'

'Gran was the person I loved the most,' Annika whispered, feeling the tears spill out and roll down her cheeks. She did nothing to stop them, just let them roll, let the pain sink in.

Her mother looked at her with a faraway and dark expression in her eyes.

'Now wasn't that just a typical thing for you to say at a time like this?'

Barbro left the dead woman's side and approached Annika, her eyes red, her mouth compressed into a line.

'My mother always protected you,' Barbro said in a whisper. 'But now she's gone and can't do it any more.'

Annika closed her eyes and felt her mother close in on her.

'All these years you came first in her eyes: Birgitta was second-best, and you just hogged the spotlight. How do you think that made your sister feel?'

Annika hid her face in her hands.

'Birgitta always had you,' she said.

'And you didn't, I suppose? Have you ever figured out why? Maybe it had something to do with the kind of person you are. Look at me!'

Annika looked up and blinked. Her mother was right in front of her, towering over her. Her eyes were dark, her face was twisted with pain and contempt.

'You've always spoiled things for the rest of us,' Barbro whispered. 'You're bad luck – there's something wrong with you. Ever since the day you were born you've brought misery in your wake.'

Annika gasped and backed away.

'Mother, you don't know what you're saying.'

Her mother leaned forward.

'We would have been a happy family,' she said. 'If it hadn't been for you.'

The door opened. The doctor came in and switched on the fluorescent lighting.

'Oh, I'm sorry. Would you like us to leave?'

Her mother straightened her back and glared at Annika.

'No, that won't be necessary. I was just leaving.'

Barbro picked up her purse and her fur, shook hands with the doctor, murmured something or other and gave her dead mother one last glance before she walked out.

Annika remained where she was, her mouth open, the tears veiling her face, devastated. Had she actually heard that? Had her mother really said the words that had always remained unsaid, that had always been present as an undercurrent, the forbidden key phrases that had locked and defined her childhood?

'How are you doing?' the doctor asked and sat down beside her.

Annika bowed her head and gasped for air.

'I'm going to give you a doctor's certificate. You need to take time off for the rest of the month. I'll give you a prescription for a sedative as well: twenty-five Sobril tablets, a dosage of fifteen milligrams each. They're not strong enough to overdose on, but don't mix them with alcohol – that could be dangerous.'

Annika covered her face with her hands and tried to

stop shaking. The doctor sat next to her in silence for a while.

'Were you very close to your grandmother?' she asked.

Annika nodded.

'You've had an awful shock,' the doctor said. 'Or, rather, two shocks. You were the one who found your grandmother at her home as well, isn't that right?'

Annika nodded again.

'Everyone goes through certain stages when a loved one passes,' the doctor explained. 'The duration may vary, but the stages are the same. The first stage is shock, that's where you are now, and it's generally followed by aggression, then denial, and finally acceptance. You will have to be kind to yourself now: you could find yourself in a state of anxiety and end up with stomach trouble or sleep disturbances. This is normal and it will pass. But if things get too difficult you must go and see a professional. Take these tablets if things get tough. You're always welcome to call someone here at the hospital if you need to talk. If you like, I can arrange for you to see a counsellor.'

Annika shook her head.

'No, not a counsellor,' she said.

The doctor patted Annika on the back.

'Let us know if there's anything we can do. We are going to move Sofia Katarina now. Do you need help getting anywhere?'

'Sofia Katarina,' Annika whispered. 'I'm named after her, my name is Annika Sofia.'

'Well, Annika Sofia,' the doctor said. 'Take care of yourself.'

Annika looked up at her: so close, yet so far away.

She didn't reply.

PART THREE

DECEMBER

SHAME IS THE BIGGEST TABOO.

We can talk about anything, anything except what we are most deeply ashamed of. Other emotions, even the difficult ones, can be shared with others and brought into the open, but not shame. That's part of its nature. Shame is our deepest, darkest secret, its very secrecy a form of punishment.

When it comes to shame, there is no mercy. Everything else can be forgiven – violence, evil, injustice, guilt – but for the most heinous offence there is no absolution. It is not a privilege granted to shame.

In my case, guilt and shame are intertwined. It's a common enough occurrence, but it doesn't have to be like that. My failing was betrayal. Everything I've done for the past year or so has been an attempt to atone for my cowardice. In that sense shame is a creative force: it encourages action and invites revenge.

I am unable to deal with my shame. Along with the violence, it destroys me. It doesn't grow in size, it doesn't shrink, it's like a cancer at the very base of my consciousness.

Biding its time.

Hollowing me out.

MONDAY 3 DECEMBER

The man in black landed on the train platform without making a noise. His knees bent with the impact, muffling part of the sound, and the rubber soles of his shoes absorbed the rest. He exhaled and looked around: he was the only person to get off the train. A quick turn and he closed the door; his departure was supposed to go unnoticed.

The air was fresh and cold. A sense of triumph began to course through his veins.

Ratko was back in Sweden. Everything had gone exactly the way he had planned. All you needed was the drive, the will, the lack of compromise. They thought they had him, that he was under their thumb.

The hell he was.

The conductor opened a door further up. Ratko moved silently and fairly swiftly towards the station building – someone passing in the night at the Nässjö train station, a restless soul.

He glanced at his watch: 03:48 – the train was almost on time.

As he walked around the corner of the station, he glanced over his shoulder. The conductor had his back turned: he hadn't noticed him at all. And why should he?

He turned to face the sleeping town. The Norwegian citizen Runar Aakre was presumably slumbering in his sleeping compartment, headed for Stockholm.

He walked down the esplanade. It had been ages since he'd been here. Suddenly he was struck by a sense of uneasiness: what if something had gone wrong? It was better not to take anything for granted. Anything could have happened to the car: it could have been stolen, be iced over, or the battery might be dead.

Counting on bad luck, that's certainly the last thing I should do, Ratko thought irritably.

He cut across Stortorget, the main square, already cold. This was going to be one long chilly walk.

A bunch of bicycles were parked outside the culture centre on Rådhusgatan. Quickly, he selected an unlocked lady's bike.

This would be even chillier, but it would speed things up. Heading north towards Jönköpingsvägen, he pedalled quickly.

It was hell: headwinds, slippery roads, darkness. He was panting already.

Soon, he thought, *I'll be there soon*.

The trip had taken its toll. The phoney passport had felt like it was burning in his pocket. At every border control he'd been nervous, almost unhinged. He knew why.

Ratko no longer had the upper hand. They had taken away his power. He had been allowed to keep his night-club, but the rest of his privileges were gone. Something like that was very noticeable in a city like Belgrade. People lost respect for him. His wife asked for a divorce. Not even his reputation as a war hero was any good: to his people he was a has-been who hadn't done the right thing in Kosovo, to his superiors he was the guy whose mismanagement had cost them a shipment worth fifty million. The workers at the cigarette factory had been forced to work without pay. The entire organization lost momentum. Now everyone had to work twice as hard to make up for the loss, the loss caused by his mistake. How could ten-year-old clean-up actions compare to that?

He pedalled away. Damn, it was hilly, he'd forgotten about that – hilly and mossy and sheer hell.

They'd expected Ratko to give up, certain that the threat of the Hague tribunal would reduce him to crawling off to some suburban hell-hole and spending the rest of his life going to soccer games once a week, screwing jailbait and guzzling slivovitz. The hell it would.

He was a free agent now, his own man. He would do as he damn well pleased.

And she could sit there and rot, that deceitful whore of a wife of his, and figure out who the hell would pay for her clothes and drinks in the future.

The trip back to Belgrade a month ago had gone smoothly. No one had challenged his passport and the guys had been waiting for him in Skopje as planned. The journey by car to Belgrade had been as tedious as usual, but some slivovitz had helped him pass the time. They were all pretty sloshed by the time they arrived and no one remembered to take the bogus passport away from him.

After that, Ratko was left out in the cold. His superiors no longer contacted him. If he wanted to have body-guards, he had to pay them himself.

The bitterness ate away at him and he pedalled more furiously.

They were weaklings, he thought, they had no idea what it was like to operate out in the field. They didn't know how to survive in the enemy camp.

A downhill slope. He relaxed, once again filled with triumph as he braved the piercing winds.

He sure fooled them! Just slipped away without their knowledge. No one knew where he was: he had gone up in smoke.

Runar Aakre of the Red Cross had rented a car in Belgrade for a trip to Hungary. At the border he had explained, in English, that he needed to deal with a few things in Szeged, and that it would only take an hour or so. He had all his papers ready, the green card, the international insurance policy. The Customs officers had studied him, shining their flashlights through the car windows. A copy of *Verldens Gang*, the Norwegian evening paper, was resting on the passenger seat in front. It was twenty-five days old, but the Customs officer didn't notice; knowing that it would come in handy, Ratko had taken it with him from the airport in Oslo.

They waved him through.

Of course, he didn't go to Szeged. He continued all the way to Budapest. There he slept a few hours in the back seat of the car before abandoning it in a furniture store parking lot.

The tickets were waiting for him at a downtown post office box. He had booked them over the phone in a bar, paid for them with a clean credit card and used the post office box as an address. He had used it before.

The wind shifted direction and increased in force, whipping at him sideways. The bike's tyres skidded in the slush and Ratko groaned. Oh well, he could take the cold weather in his stride. Soon he would never have to deal with it again. His new operations would be based in locations where it never ever snowed. All he needed now was to finalize things: the financing end, the customers, his associates.

It was certainly foolish to leave Serbia when the Hague

tribunal was sniffing after him. No one had believed that he would do such a thing – they all expected him to rot away in that suburban hell-hole. But you could travel through Western Europe without being seen, as long as you took local express trains. Attempting the milk runs from the former Eastern Bloc was unthinkable, but the commuter trains for the business set destined for major cities barely slowed down as they crossed borders. It was a roundabout route, but it was necessary. He had to reach Sweden and he had to meet his eastern contact.

The train trip had been nerve-racking but uneventful: Vienna, Munich, Hamburg, Copenhagen. Ratko had gone ashore in Limhamn last night along with four hundred homeward-bound Swedes, all carting crates of beer. He had even lugged along a crate himself just to blend in. And he had sung along with a stinking-drunk man from Trelleborg as he passed through the passport-control zone.

The night train to Stockholm had pulled out exactly on schedule at 10:07 p.m. He had slept like a rock until 12:30 a.m.

He rode past Äng, pedalling swiftly and silently, not wanting to be seen. The entire town was asleep.

Then he made a right turn, disappearing into the woods, an uphill ride. The tree trunks supplied cover, making him invisible again. The road was in poor shape, making it even harder to ride a bike, and Ratko fell twice. Finally he saw the road he was looking for coming up on the left. He braked and realized how spent he was. His legs were shaking, his hands were showing the first traces of frostbite and his nose was running copiously. He rested briefly, leaning on the handlebars and panting. He hurled the bike into the woods – *Rust to pieces, you fucker* – then strode along the dry crusty snow to the garage.

There it was, the shed painted in the traditional brick-red paint developed in Falun, in Sweden's iron-mining district. His pulse rate stepped up. What if something had gone wrong, what would he do?

Fingers shaking, Ratko felt the wall at the back of the shed, thinking for a split second that it was gone, feeling panic welling up inside. Then he found what he was looking for. The key was there, exactly where he had left it.

He staggered over to the front of the shed, unlocked the doors and pushed them open, having to put his shoulder against the door to plough away a thin layer of snow. He stood there looking at the car, an unremarkable heap of junk, a two-door Fiat Uno from 1987. He pulled out the sticker that he'd peeled off the licence plate of a truck back in Malmö. The plate number didn't match, but no one would notice that unless they looked closely. He secured it in place, using the double-side tape that he had in his pocket.

This was it.

Ratko walked around the car, groped on top of the front right-hand tyre and found the car keys. He unlocked the car, got in and turned the key in the ignition.

The engine caught, sputtered, coughed and died.

He swallowed.

One more try: sputter, cough, now she was running. Relieved, he expelled his breath and noticed that his forehead was beaded with sweat despite the cold. He revved the engine a few times while the car was still in the garage, allowing the engine to get warm and the oil to flow freely.

While the car was slowly defrosting he leaned over and opened the glove compartment, trying to locate a tiny brass key. It was there as well.

He closed his eyes, resting while confidence radiated throughout his system.

The money was safe. It was in a safe-deposit box in the vault of the SE-Banken office at Gamla Stan in Stockholm. It was never his intention to use the money himself, it was meant to cover expenses that might arise in his cigarette operations, but they had only themselves to blame. They had sent him out into the cold and now they would have to pay.

Ratko didn't understand why they had left him in the lurch like this. All right, so that damned shipment was worth a great deal of money, but it still didn't explain why his superiors would cold-shoulder him. Not even the fact that he was wanted by the war tribunal should have had repercussions like this. Serbia was crawling with suspected war criminals who were still highly respected.

It was something else. He couldn't quite put his finger on it. Maybe someone, a real high-roller, wanted him out of the way, wanted to take over his power and his authority.

They can never take my place, he thought. *No one else has my experience, my contacts.*

He stepped on the gas and revved the engine again. Heat was beginning to spread throughout the car.

In addition to the money, Ratko had some other unfinished business in Stockholm. The shipment might be long gone, but he didn't like leaving any loose ends.

Slowly he let the car roll out into the night.

Advent stars hung crookedly in the window of the company apartment. Last Friday, a woman from the contracting company had been there to decorate the place and had put them up. Annika stared at them: stars fashioned out of straw, swaying in the heat rising up from the radiators. She was amazed at the way people put so much effort into meaningless pursuits, like wasting time and energy on Christmas decorations.

She went back to bed and stared at the wall, concentrating on the pattern behind the thin layer of paint, purple medallions. The courtyard building was deserted. Only the hard-rock fan on the bottom floor was in. She closed her eyes and let the bass line resonate.

This is no good, Annika thought. *I can't live like this.*

She rolled over on her back and stared at the ceiling, seeing the spider webs sway in the draught from the broken living-room window. She traced the cracks, broken and irregular, with her gaze. Found the butterfly, the car, the skull. The note of loneliness began to ring in her left ear. She tossed back over on her side again and put a pillow over her head, but she couldn't shut it out, could never, ever hide. Despair hit her, causing her body to contract into a hard ball. She threw her head back and heard the sound, her sound, the uncontrolled sobbing. She recognized it and wasn't afraid, she let it rip through her, knowing that it would end since her body couldn't take it for ever.

Afterwards she was spent and thirsty, sore from the effort. The back pain was the worst bit, it never really went away. Tension made her stomach churn. She lay there for a while, panting and heavy, and let the tears dry on her cheeks.

I wonder what my neighbours think. They might think I'm losing my mind.

Annika got up, felt dizzy and walked to the kitchen touching the walls for support. The straw stars swayed. The tap dripped. The refrigerator was empty.

She sat down at the kitchen table, sank down with her arms on the cold table top, her head in her hands, and stared at her grandmother's brass candlestick. Sofia Katarina and Arvid had received it on their wedding day and it had stood on the sideboard at Lyckebo since then.

Annika closed her eyes. Gran was gone. She could barely recall the funeral, only the despair, the tears, the sensation of helplessness. There had been quite a crowd; many staring eyes, whispers and reproachful glances.

Ashes to ashes, dust to dust . . .

She got up and went over to the couch in the living room. A cloud of dust whooshed up in the air as she sat down. She looked at the phone. Birgitta had called after the funeral and asked her why she had been so mean to their mother.

'Aren't you ever satisfied?' Annika had screamed at her. 'When will you leave me alone? How much do I have to be punished for the fact that I was loved? When will you be satisfied? When I'm dead?'

'You're nuts,' Birgitta said. 'People are right. Poor you.'

Gran hadn't owned much, but, as expected, her family squabbled over her possessions. The candlestick had been the only item that Annika wanted.

She pulled up her legs on the couch, rocking, rocking. The grocery bag from ICA covering a window rose and sank, rose and sank.

Thomas hadn't called. Not once. That night had never existed, the intoxicating feeling had been a mere recollection from a dream. She cried quietly for the love that had never got off the ground, rocking, rocking. Monday, 5 November, that was their day, their night, the one that had vanished. That had been twenty-eight days ago, she was a whole month older now, and twenty-seven days had passed since Gran had died, making her twenty-seven years lonelier. She wondered how long she would count the days following her abandonment: one year, two years, seven years?

The pain in Annika's stomach wouldn't go away and her back never stopped aching. She stopped rocking and stared at the table. Her apartment had swallowed her up; she had spent the past four weeks here, mostly alone. The doctor in Katrineholm had prescribed sick leave for the rest of the year. Anne Snapphane came by a few times a week, bringing food, a VCR and a boom-box.

'They belong to the production company,' she explained. 'I'm borrowing them for a while.'

The silence and emptiness had to compete against video rentals and the music of Jim Steinman and Andrew Lloyd Webber.

She would have liked to have him. She'd had him that one night twenty-eight days ago, a night she wouldn't be able to remember soon.

A twinge deep in her belly, a familiar sensation: it was her period. Annika groaned and went into the bedroom to find a pad.

The package was empty. She stood there holding the tattered, empty bag and tried to figure out whether she had a stash of sanitary napkins anywhere else.

She went into the hall and dug out her bag. The wrappers on the pads had come undone and now they were covered with lint from her bag. Overcome by dizziness, she sat down on the floor, feeling sick to her stomach, and checked her panties.

Nothing. No sign of her period.

Twenty-eight days ago.

She gasped, struck by an overwhelming thought, and fished out her appointment book; today's names were Oskar and Ossian, the moon was waning, and Christmas Eve would be on a Monday this year.

Counting, considering; when was the last time? Could it have been the weekend around 20 or 21 October? She couldn't remember.

What if . . .?

The thought set. Annika stared at her date book, her

hand unconsciously moving to her stomach, resting on a spot just below her navel.

It couldn't be true.

'Do you have a minute?'

Anders Schyman looked up. Söjlander and Berit Hamrin were hovering in the doorway. He indicated the chairs by his desk.

'We're ready to run the Paradise Foundation story,' the crime-desk editor said. 'Berit put the finishing touches on Annika Bengtzon's draughts. It's certainly one hell of a scam.'

Anders Schyman leaned back in his chair and Berit Hamrin placed a stack of papers on his desk.

'Here are the pieces so far,' she said. 'You can read them later. I haven't mentioned Rebecka Björkstig by name. Sjölander wants us to publish her name and photo, but let's discuss that after I've put you in the picture.'

The deputy editor waited while she arranged the papers in different stacks.

'To start off with, we have the main story,' she said. 'The information that Annika dug up appears to hold water. The authorities in Nacka and Österåker were a bit reluctant, but once the official from Vaxholm revealed what happened to him they agreed to talk.'

Berit picked up the first article and glanced through it.

'For the first day of publication,' she said. 'An exposé of the Paradise Foundation, Rebecka's version, and a review of the lies and the facts.'

'Who are we quoting on this?' Schyman asked.

'Mostly the guy from Vaxholm, a really nice accountant with Social Services there. His name is Thomas Samuelsson. You could say that he was the hero of the story. He was assaulted when he tried to discuss an invoice with Rebecka.'

'Yes,' the deputy editor responded, 'Annika told me that. Has he reported the incident to the police?'

'Yes indeed. Then there are the other bureaucrats: they want to remain anonymous but they do confirm that Paradise is a sham.'

'How much have they paid?'

'One place paid 955,500 kronor, the other 1,274,000, in instalments. Vaxholm refused to pay since their client was dead by the time the invoice arrived.'

The deputy editor whistled.

'You're already pretty familiar with the rest of the story,' Berit said. 'That's the bit that worries us.'

She picked up another article.

'Rebecka Björkstig may be guilty of plotting a murder,' Berit said.

Schyman's jaw dropped.

'What the hell . . .?' he exclaimed.

Berit handed him the article.

'The woman who was killed at Sergelstorg a month or so ago – you remember her, don't you? She was one of Paradise's clients.'

'You're kidding!' Schyman said.

The reporter sighed.

'The woman in question, Aida Begovic, threatened to blow the whistle on Björkstig. Rebecka threatened to have her killed. That's nothing remarkable, she's made statements to that effect on several occasions. All the women in contact with Paradise realized fairly quickly that they wouldn't be receiving any help. Naturally, many of them were upset and the clients from Nacka and Österåker intended to tell Social Services about the deception.'

'How did they get involved with Paradise?' Schyman asked.

'In those two particular cases the harrassed women met Rebecka while they were accompanied by a representative from Social Services. They were all served the same fantastic story and, strangely enough, they all bought into it. Once the first invoice was paid, the clients were allowed to come to the house in Järfälla owned by Paradise. Rebecka took all their documents, read through them and checked that all the pertinent information was there, and then she turned them out.'

'The clients?'

Berit nodded, her lips compressed into a straight line.

'One of the clients was a single mother of two, the other a mother of three. Rebecka threatened her, saying: 'I know who's after you, and if you breathe a single word to the authorities, I'll tell them where to find you.''

'Christ!' Schyman said.

'And Aida died,' Söjlander added. 'A witness heard Rebecka threaten her, and the next day she was dead.'

'What do the police say?'

Berit picked up the third article.

'I just talked to them. The fraud squad has been looking for Rebecka for some time now, but this new information means that there are even more charges against her, and of a more serious nature too. The police would like to arrest her straight away, so we have to run these articles as soon as possible.'

'Okay,' Schyman said. 'Day one will be dedicated to the story of the set-up, the scam and the threats. What do we have for day two?'

Berit leafed through her notes.

'The stories of the victimized women. Annika wrote the main story before she got sick: it features a woman called Maria Eriksson. I've covered the other two cases and their stories. In addition, we'll have to stand by in case people call in about any other cases after the story breaks.'

Schyman took notes.

'Good, we'll be ready. Day three?'

'Reactions,' Berit said. 'I have a few prepared: a professor specializing in Criminal Law, an associate professor specializing in Social Psychology, the chairman of the National Association of Women's Shelters. By that time I expect that the police will want to make a statement as well, and maybe even the Minister of Health and Social Affairs and the Attorney General. It's possible that other city councils will press charges as well.'

'How does the Björkstig woman justify all this?' Anders Schyman said.

'Rebecka Björkstig claims that our information is a defamation of her character, pure slander. She has no idea who would want to treat her so badly. Her organization hasn't yet been fully developed, and to maintain that she would have threatened anyone is a pack of lies.'

'Something that we can definitely disprove,' Schyman said. 'Is she threatening to sue us for libel if we publish this information?'

The reporter sighed.

'She certainly is. She mentioned the damages she had in mind, too: thirty million kronor.'

Anders Schyman smiled.

'Well, she can't sue us if we don't publish her name and picture. If she hasn't been pinpointed, they can't fault our press ethics.'

'I still think we *should* publish her name and picture,' Söjlander said. 'She ought to get a taste of how it feels to be in a tight spot.'

Schyman shot the crime-desk editor a neutral glance.

'Since when is this paper an instrument of punishment?' he asked. 'Rebecka Björkstig is not a celebrity or a public figure. Naturally, we will describe her operations and how she has changed her identity numerous times, as well as listing her shady dealings and odd threats. But revealing her name doesn't make the story any better at this point.'

'It's chicken not to use everything we've got,' Söjlander said. 'Why should we be considerate to a bitch like her?'

Anders Schyman leaned forward.

'Because we promote the truth,' he explained. 'We're not here to bash criminals. We have ethical considerations, we have been invested with the power and the authority to define reality in this society of ours. We will not use this power to destroy anyone, it doesn't matter if they happen to be politicians, criminals or celebrities. Being in the papers is not being put in a tight spot.'

Söjlander's cheeks turned a light shade of pink. Anders Schyman saw that he would be all right, though. Söjlander was good at eating crow. He'd already swallowed that particular mouthful.

'All right,' he said. 'You're the boss.'

The deputy editor leaned back in his chair again.

'No, that would be Torstensson,' he said.

The three of them looked at each other, then broke into laughter, *Torstensson, what a joke.*

'What else is up?' Schyman asked.

'It's pretty quiet,' Söjlander said, sighing. 'A little too quiet. Nothing's happened for a while. We've been considering featuring the Palme assassination again – Nils Langeby has a new lead.'

A wrinkle appeared between the deputy editor's eyes.

'Be careful, I'm not sure I entirely trust Langeby's sources. Anything come of the Yugo Mafia connection to the free-port killings?'

Söjlander sighed.

'It came to nothing. The guy they suspected, Ratko, seems to have left the country.'

'Did he do it?'

The crime-desk editor fidgeted a little, hesitated and remembered his previous accusations.

'Maybe not,' he said. 'Ratko's never been convicted of murder, but he's a nasty character. Bank robberies, threats, assault, and he's certainly been an enforcer. His speciality was scaring the crap out of people, making them talk. He'd pop the muzzle of a sub-machine gun into a person's mouth and that would generally loosen their tongues.'

'And then there's his war crimes,' Berit reminded the men.

'It must have been difficult for him to cross borders,' Anders Schyman said.

The Hague war tribunal had issued a warrant for him on Tuesday, 6 November, around noon. Ratko had been charged with war crimes committed in the early stages of the conflict in Bosnia.

'He'll probably drink himself to death in some Belgrade suburb,' Sjölander said.

Schyman sighed.

'What about the Bosnian woman who was killed downtown? Anyone know who killed her?'

Berit and Sjölander shook their heads.

'Her funeral's tomorrow,' Berit said. 'An awful business.'

'All right,' Schyman said. 'I'll run through these articles, and if you don't hear anything from me, run them verbatim.'

The crime-desk reporters got up and left the office.

Annika turned the pages of a two-year-old issue of *Vi Föräldrar*, a parenting magazine. She had already polished off three issues of *Amelia*, a ladies' magazine, two pamphlets on AIDS, and yesterday's *Metro*. She couldn't bring herself to go home, she didn't want to be alone. She told the staff that she wanted to wait until her test results were ready. The attendant midwife gave her an odd look but didn't protest.

Time had become incidental. Annika was reduced to being an onlooker. She couldn't picture what her reaction would be.

Once, back when she'd been with Sven, she'd thought that she was pregnant. It was near the end of their relationship, when she was looking for a way out. She had been extremely worried: having a baby would have been disastrous. Her test had come back negative, but she hadn't felt relieved. After all this time she still couldn't understand why she had felt disappointed and empty.

'Annika Bengtzon?'

Her pulse quickened, her heart leapt into her mouth and she swallowed. She got up and followed the white coat over to the counter inside the prenatal clinic.

'Your test was positive,' the woman said deliberately in a low voice. 'That means you are pregnant. When was your last period?'

Annika's mind began to reel. *Pregnant, expecting a baby, dear Lord, a baby . . .*

'I'm not sure, around the twentieth of October, I think.' Her mouth was dry.

The midwife turned a cardboard wheel.

'That would make you about seven weeks pregnant. You start counting from the first day of your last menstruation. That means you aren't far gone yet. Are you considering termination?'

The floor tilted. Annika grabbed hold of the counter.

'I'm . . . not sure.'

She swallowed.

'Should you opt for termination, the sooner you decide to have the procedure, the better. If you plan to have the baby, we will set up an appointment for you. The first prenatal-care check-up takes a little over an hour. You will be assigned to a midwife who will be your contact here at the centre during your entire pregnancy. Do you live on Kungsholmen?'

'Are you certain?' Annika asked. 'Am I really pregnant? It's not an error?'

The woman smiled.

'You're pregnant,' she said. 'Definitely pregnant.'

Annika turned away and headed for the door. Her back ached and smarted – what if she had a miscarriage?

'What about miscarriages?' she asked as she turned to face the counter again. 'Are miscarriages common?'

'Fairly common,' the midwife replied. 'You're most vulnerable during the first twelve weeks. We can discuss all those details at your first appointment if you choose to keep the baby. Give us a call and tell us what you plan to do.'

Annika went out into the stairwell and headed down the beautiful broad staircase at the old hospital, *Serafimerlasarettet*. This was the designated health-care centre for the residents of Kungsholmen, the offices of her family doctor, the place to go for the paediatric care of her children.

Her children.

Every step she took down the stairs resulted in a tugging sensation in her stomach.

Don't let me miscarry. Don't let anything happen to my child.

She sobbed. *Oh my God, I'm going to have a baby, Thomas and I are going to have a baby.* Joy welled up inside her and spread throughout her body. *A baby! A little baby, a reason to live!*

Annika walked up to a wall and leaned against it and cried, tears of relief, soothing and pure.

A child, her little child.

She walked out into the twilight; there hadn't been much light all day. Clouds like dark grey barrels rolled across the heavens. It would start snowing again soon. She walked home carefully: she mustn't trip and fall, she mustn't hurt her baby.

Her apartment was fairly cold. She switched on all the lamps and sat down on the couch with the phone in her lap.

She really ought to call Thomas right away, before he left work. She didn't want to get Eleonor on the line again. Her pulse pounded, what on earth was she going to say?

I'm pregnant.

We are going to have a baby.

You are going to be a father.

Annika closed her eyes, took three deep breaths, tried to calm her heart down and dialled the number.

Her voice was thick when she asked the receptionist to put her through. The buzzing sensation in her head intensified, her hands were shaking.

'Thomas Samuelsson speaking.'

She couldn't breathe, couldn't speak.

'Hello?' he said, his voice tinged with irritation.

She swallowed.

'Hi,' she said in the tiniest voice around. 'It's me.'

Her heart started racing out of control, her breathing grew ragged, there was no response at the other end.

'It's Annika Bengtzon,' she said. 'It's me, Annika.'

A muffled curt voice said: 'Don't call me here.'

She gasped.

'What do you mean?'

'Please,' he said, 'leave me alone. Don't call me.'

The click as he hung up echoed in her mind. The line went dead. Emptiness resounded instead, filling everything with its void.

Annika replaced the receiver, her hands shaking so

badly that it was difficult to put it back. Her hands were dripping with sweat. The tears came. *Oh God, he didn't want her, he didn't want their child, help me, please . . .*

The telephone jangled in her lap, the shock making her jump. *He's calling back, he's calling back.*

She grabbed the receiver.

'Annika? Hi, it's Berit, from the paper. I just wanted to tell you that we're going to start running your articles on the Paradise Foundation tomorrow . . . What's wrong?'

Annika was sobbing into the phone, tears gushing.

'Oh, honey!' Berit exclaimed in a concerned voice. 'What's wrong?'

Annika took a deep breath, forcing herself to get her emotions in check.

'Nothing,' she said, swiping at her runny nose with the back of her hand. 'I'm just sad, that's all. I'm sorry.'

She covered her nose and mouth with her hand, muffling her grief before she responded to Berit's news: 'Well, that's great. I'm glad.'

'The worst part is what happened to Aida. It's her funeral tomorrow. That poor woman. She didn't have any relatives, no one has requested to have the body released, the funeral will be a simple ceremony over at the cemetery on the north side . . .'

'I'm really sorry, Berit, but I've got to go.'

'Hey,' her colleague said, 'how are you doing? Could you use a hand in any way?'

'No,' Annika whispered, 'everything's fine.'

'Promise me you'll tell me if there's anything I can do.'

'Sure,' she said faintly.

Once more, the hot, heavy receiver was replaced.

He doesn't want me. He doesn't want our child.

There wasn't a single parking space to be found on all of the island of Kungsholmen. Thomas had been driving around for twenty minutes now without finding one. It didn't matter. He wasn't actually going to do anything here, he was just driving around around: Scheelegatan, a right on Hantverkargatan, a slow glide past number 32, up the hill, turn in on Bergsgatan, pass the police station, drive down Kungsholmsgatan and do the whole thing over again.

He had done the right thing, the only decent thing. Eleonor was his wife, he stuck to his promises, he honoured his commitments, he was a responsible person.

Still, when he'd heard Annika's voice over the phone today . . . He'd lost it. He'd reacted in a way he hadn't expected, so physically, so harshly. There was no way he could get any more work done that day. He fled the building, practically running down to the shore. It was windy, snowing, he heard her voice, remembered her body, oh God, what had he done? Why was the memory of her so relentless, so lingering?

He had stood there in the wind until his hair and his coat were drenched by the sea air and the snow, his mind filled by a tiny sad voice. After a while he had slowly made his way to his big, empty house. Eleonor had her leadership course that night, so he took his car and drove to Stockholm. He didn't reflect on what he was doing, didn't want to think, just drove.

Have some food, Thomas told himself, *stop at a restaurant, have a beer and read the papers.*

A restaurant on Kungsholmen.

He wasn't going to contact her. He would hold his ground. He just wanted to see what it could be like, what that life might have been like, what kind of people he would see, what kind of food he would eat.

What he had done to Eleonor was unforgivable. Shame had made his face burn all that first week; he had forced himself to sound normal, act normal, and make love in a normal fashion. Eleonor hadn't noticed anything amiss – or had she?

At first he had dreamed about Annika, but the memory of her had receded, until today. Thomas slapped the steering wheel with one hand: damn it, why did she have to call? Why couldn't she leave him alone? Things were hard enough as they were.

Suddenly he felt close to tears. He clenched his teeth and stepped on the gas, he had to find somewhere to eat. He turned in on Agnegatan and parked in a turning zone – who cared?

He locked the car, *blip-blip*. This was Annika's neighbourhood. He looked up at the deteriorating buildings: they should have been repaired twenty years ago.

She might be home. She might be upstairs in her third-floor apartment, those dreamlike white rooms, reading a book or watching TV.

The thought made his mouth dry and his pulse quicken.

In the passage leading to the courtyard a lamp shone wanly. The gate was open, he could walk right in, it would be so easy. Slowly he was pulled towards her apartment building, saw what she saw every day, the graffiti on the walls, the chunks of plaster falling down.

What if Annika appeared? Thomas stopped – she mustn't see him. For a long time he remained in the passage, looking up.

Two windows: the lights were on, the upper pane of the window on the right covered with a grocery bag, her apartment. She was home.

Then he saw her. She walked past the window and picked up something on the windowsill, the one on the left. For a moment he saw her dark silhouette against the bright room: her hair, her thin body, her graceful hands. Then she turned away and the lights went out.

Maybe she was on her way out.

Thomas spun around and ran back to his car, jumped in and drove off without releasing the handbrake. Became aware that his pulse was racing.

He would never see Annika again.

TUESDAY 4 DECEMBER

Annika avoided the headlines. The news-bill was yellower than ever: it howled out its message, the size of the print suggesting that a world war was imminent. 'A *Kvällspressen* exclusive: Perilous Paradise!'

She hurried past, not having the strength to take in the bill's message, pulled her jacket closer, squeezed her wallet and shivered with the cold. She jogged up the stairs to Rosetten: the guy at the checkout counter hadn't finished putting the papers on display yet and she yanked a copy from the pile.

The picture on the front page showed a photo of a woman, probably Rebecka, taken on the sly, the hair and the face checkered to hide her identity. Annika squinted, a classic trick to enhance the image, but it was still impossible to identify the woman.

Annika weighed the paper in her hand. It was so light, her efforts were of such little consequence after all. She folded it and put it in her basket; she would have to read more at home. She headed for the food department, picked up some yogurt, a loaf of sliced white bread, a slab of cheese and some hot dogs, paid for her groceries, tucked the paper under her arm and went outside. The weather was clear and cold; the sun was heading for the horizon. Hurriedly, she went back down Hantver-kargatan, slipping a little, her heart racing – she couldn't help it, Paradise was her story.

She put the bag of groceries down on the floor in the hall, brought the paper over to the couch in the living room and read the headline puff again. The story continued on pages 6, 7, 8, 9, 10 and 11. The little hairs on her arms stood on end: talk about coverage!

Quickly flipping past the editorials and the fine-arts pages, Annika reached the first piece, the one describing the set-up, Rebecka's description of how Paradise operated. There were more covert pictures of Rebecka and of some other people, probably her relatives. Annika thought that she could make out the house in Olovslund in the background, but the pictures could have been taken anywhere. She read the pieces carefully: Berit had written them, but they were based on Annika's research. The articles had a double byline, featuring both her name and Berit's.

For quite some time, Annika studied her name, trying to define what she felt. Pride, perhaps. A twinge of fear – this story would have repercussions. A certain detach-ment. She couldn't quite take it all in.

She sighed, turned the page and gasped.

Thomas Samuelsson gazed at her from a black and white picture on page eight. It had been taken at his office in Vaxholm: she recognized the bookcase in the background. The headline described him as 'The Whistleblower'. Berit's article made mincemeat out of Rebecka's statements: it revealed the lies, detailed the woman's debts and name changes. Thomas Samuelsson emerged as the hero cracking down on this shady organization. There was a wound on his forehead and the caption explained that the accountant had been assaulted when he had tried to put a stop to the scam. Several other representatives from different authorities issued anonymous statements as well, attesting to the fact that Paradise was a sham. They had paid Rebecka astronomical amounts: the grand total was over two million kronor.

It was impossible to keep on reading. Annika just wanted to look at the picture, at the man. He looked serious and resolute. His hair had fallen forward, his suit jacket was buttoned, his tie was knotted to perfection, and his hand rested on his desk – his warm, strong hand.

She felt a pang. *Dear God*, he was so very attractive, she had almost forgotten what he looked like. Tears spilled from her eyes and dripped down on the paper.

'We're going to have a baby,' she whispered to the image. 'A little boy. I know it's a boy, and you don't want us. You want your perfectly knotted tie, your bank executive and your fancy house.'

Annika traced the picture with a finger, following the line of Thomas's jaw, stroking his hair.

I can't have him if you don't want him.

She put down the paper and cried uncontrollably. When she couldn't go on any longer, when she'd run out of tears, she picked up the phone and called the hospital. They could accommodate her straight away.

Ratko had plenty of time. He had scouted the place out thoroughly yesterday, carrying a rake and pretending to tend the graves. No one had taken any notice of him in his dark, nondescript clothing. His Fiat Uno was parked on Banvaktsvägen, right next to a hole in the fence. He figured that cyclists had cut an opening in the chain link fence to be able to cut across the cemetery. In the compartment behind the back seat of the Uno there was a sports bag, the contours of a tennis racket visible among the sports clothes. The money and his weapons were concealed underneath the clothes. He was nervous, apprehensive – he even felt a little stupid. Was he losing his touch?

Ratko went over to the main entrance, by Linvävargatan. Here, the headstones were large and old, most of them dated back to the first decades of the twentieth century, well-to-do gentlemen surrounded by their families. The environment aimed at projecting a sense of peace – not an easy feat considering the roaring highway some fifty metres away. He leaned on the rake and surveyed the quiet grounds: shaped cypresses, enormous oak trees with denuded crowns, twisted pines, and black ironwork fences. Quite a contrast to the war cemetreies of Bosnia. He leaned against the fence, sighed and remembered the days back in the 1970s when he had belonged to the Yugoslav secret police: all the political opponents they had silenced, Germany, Italy, Spain, the bank robberies, the years spent in prison.

Never again, he thought. He sighed and shivered.

Slowly, Ratko headed for the chapel, *Norra Kapellet*, which was as big as a church. Recently repaired, its brown glazed roof tiles gleamed in the sun. This shrine was situated at the top of a hill at the far end of the cemetery against a backdrop of pale blue high-rise apartment complexes catering to low-income households – Hagalundsgatan, also known to as 'The Blues'. He walked around a small grove and came out on the west side, the flat corner of the cemetery, section 14 E. He stopped at the edge of the grove and contemplated the hole in the ground: Aida's final resting place. A denuded hedge stood between her grave and the street. On the other side there was a service station and a McDonald's. He turned away, picked up the rake and slowly walked over to the Jewish section.

The funeral was scheduled for two p.m. He had called to make sure of the time and he had several hours to go. Was he on the wrong track? Had he lost his mind? Was it all merely a delusion? Had his superiors truly shunned him? And why would Aida from Bijelina have anything to do with it?

Actually, he didn't give a damn. All he was interested in was his own future. He wanted to know who his opponents were, what he was up against; he needed to identify his enemies. The dead Aida would help him do this.

He lit a cigarette. Took a few deep drags, felt his lungs fill and the nicotine go to his head. *Damn* – this was one cold country.

If everything went according to plan he would never have to come back here. He would leave this God-awful country as soon as he'd cleaned up his dirty laundry and hung it out to dry.

'Thomas, you're in the papers today!'

The social worker in charge of Aida Begovic's case bounced out of her office, not quite pulling off a jogging gait. Her cheeks were red and her forehead was all shiny as she smiled sheepishly and enthusiastically waved the morning edition of *Kvällspressen*.

Thomas forced himself to smile back at her.

'I know,' he said.

'It's all there, what you did . . .'

'I know.'

He went into his office and closed the door firmly behind him, unable to face the attention. Sank down at his desk and covered his face with his hands. This morning it had been practically impossible to go to work. The budget had been approved by the city council, all the quarterly reports were done, he had pulled everything off in time.

So now it was time to start all over again, for the eighth time: each year there were fewer resources and more expenditure, staff cutbacks, media coverage of the people hurt by the system, angry, upset, sad, resigned. More people were on sick leave for extended periods and less money was allocated for rehabilitation.

He sighed and sat up straight in his chair, his gaze locking on to Annika's name in the paper. He had read the articles previously, but he hadn't known that she had written them. Some other woman had called, a more seasoned reporter, Berit Hamrin. Why hadn't Annika called?

Irritably he rejected the thought – he didn't want her to call – and smoothed out the paper in front of him. It was an awful picture, his hair in his face like that making him look untidy. He read through the piece again, Annika's piece: he recognized the facts that she had uncovered, she had told him everything, she had been honest.

There was a knock on the door. Instinctively, he folded up the paper and put it away in his top drawer.

'May I come in?'

It was his boss. He swallowed.

'Sure. Have a seat.'

The woman assessed him with her gaze as she sat down on the chair reserved for visitors, the chair that Annika had sat on. A twinge of insecurity ran up Thomas's spine even though he had discussed the publication of these articles with his boss and reviewed what he should and should not divulge. She hadn't read the articles herself, but there shouldn't be anything she could find fault with.

'I know you've had a rough time,' his boss said, 'but I want you to know that we really appreciate you here.'

She was friendly and serious and looked him in the eye. He glanced away, staring at a document on his desk.

'I'm very pleased with your work. I know you've been going through a rough patch, and I hope things will pick up now that the budget is done. If you feel like you need someone to talk to, you can always come to me.'

He looked up, unable to conceal his surprise. This time his boss averted her gaze.

'I just wanted you to know that,' she said and got up.

Thomas got up too, mumbling some words of gratitude.

When the woman had closed the door behind her, he sank back down on his chair, dumbfounded. *What was that all about?*

That very second the phone rang, making him jump.

'Thomas Samuelsson?'

It was one of the directors of the Association of Local Authorities. Christ, what did they want? Automatically, he sat up straight in his chair.

'I'm not sure if you remember me, but we met last year at the Social Services seminar on Långholmen.'

Thomas remembered the conference, all right, it had been heavy going and had lasted three days. But he couldn't recall meeting this man at all.

'Your name has come up several times since then and when we saw the article in the papers we realized that you're the right man for the job.'

Thomas cleared his throat and made enquiring noises.

'We're looking for a project manager to investigate the discrepancies between the social welfare payments made in different districts. It wouldn't have to be a full-time assignment, if you prefer to pursue these inquiries part-time it should take you about a year. Are you interested?'

Dumbstruck, Thomas closed his eyes and raked back his hair, completely overwhelmed. Work in the thick of things, investigate, manage a project, Jesus, this was exactly what he'd always dreamed of doing.

'Yes, definitely,' he managed to utter. 'It sounds like an incredibly exciting and important project.'

He stopped: he was being too enthusiastic.

'I'd be happy to discuss the baseline conditions,' he continued in a calmer voice.

'Excellent. Could you stop by on Thursday?'

After Thomas hung up, he stared at the phone for a full minute. The offer he had received caused his blood to course through his veins like a brook in the spring. *What an opportunity, what an assignment!* His smile came from a place down deep inside him. That explained why his boss had behaved so strangely – they must have called her first.

They had seen his name in the papers.

He pulled open the top drawer of his desk and took the paper out again, read her name and exhaled with a sigh.

He would forget her. Everything would get better. He just had to hang in there.

He had made the right decision.

Involuntarily, Annika gasped: the bluish gel was ice-cold when it hit her stomach. The woman in the white coat fiddled around with a probe and a cord. Wide-eyed, Annika watched her every move.

'The gel promotes better imaging during the scan,' the doctor said.

Annika lay on the green vinyl examination table. The woman sat down beside her, dipped the probe in the goo on Annika's stomach and began to move it around. Annika gasped one more time – *damn, that was cold* – and the doctor rubbed the probe far down on her stomach, practically reaching the girl's pubic hair. The edge of her panties was coated with blue goo. The doctor turned a knob on a metal box next to a small grey monitor and white streaks writhed like worms on the screen. Then she stopped.

'There,' the doctor said, pointing.

Annika hauled herself halfway up and looked at the screen. There was a tiny white ring in the upper right-hand corner.

'That is your pregnancy,' the woman said as she twisted the knob.

Annika looked at the spot suspiciously; it moved a little, writhed and swam around.

Her child. Thomas's child. She swallowed.

'I want to have an abortion,' she said.

The gynaecologist removed the implement from Annika's stomach and the image disappeared, the swimming bubble vanished. The nurse handed Annika a piece of rough green crêpe paper to wipe herself with.

'I'd like to do a pelvic exam as well,' the doctor said, handing the ultrasound implement to the nurse for cleaning. 'Would you please go over to the chair with the stirrups?'

Her voice was friendly, efficient and indifferent. Annika froze.

'Do I really have to have . . . an examination?' she asked.

'We're already behind schedule,' the nurse said in a low voice.

The doctor sighed.

'Please sit up.'

Annika removed her jeans and her underwear and obediently arranged herself in the chair, that instrument of torture. The doctor positioned herself between her patient's legs and pulled on a pair of gloves.

'Could you inch down a bit? A little bit more. More. Now relax.'

Annika took a deep breath and closed her eyes as the doctor probed her insides with her fingers.

'Relax, or the procedure will be painful.'

She squeezed her eyes shut while the doctor pressed

on her stomach, one hand up her vagina – pain, nausea.

'Your uterus is tilted,' the gynaecologist said. 'It's unusual, but it shouldn't cause you any trouble.'

As the doctor removed her hand, Annika heard a sucking sound and felt embarrassed.

'There you go. You may get dressed now. Come to my office when you're ready.'

The doctor tossed the gloves into a bucket and went quickly into the next room. In a state of confusion, Annika tried to get her knees back down from their position over her ears, feeling vulnerable and disgusting.

There was something gooey between her legs, but she didn't dare ask for a tissue to wipe herself off with. She quickly pulled on her underwear and her jeans, the whole lower half of her belly feeling sticky, and then she followed the nurse into the next room.

'You are seven weeks pregnant,' the doctor said. 'And you would like to have an abortion, you say?'

Annika nodded, swallowed, cleared her throat and sat down.

'You are entitled to see a counsellor if you like. Would you like to see one?'

She shook her head; her hands felt too big and she hid them between her thighs.

'Okay, I can give you an appointment for Friday, 7 December. Will that be all right?'

No, she thought, *do it now. Now! Friday is three days away, it's impossible, I can't stand it. I can't have this baby inside me three more days, I don't want to feel its weight, the nausea, the swollen breasts, the life beating within me.*

'So, will the seventh do?' the doctor asked again, peering over the rims of her glasses.

Annika nodded.

'Be here by seven a.m. Don't eat or drink after midnight the night before because we shall be administering a mild anaesthetic. The first step is to place a suppository by your cervix which will open the portio, and then we shall put you under. We shall perform what is known as a vacuum extraction, which involves dilating the cervical canal and suctioning out the contents of the womb. The procedure takes fifteen minutes and you can go home in the afternoon. We recommend that you abstain from sexual intercourse for two weeks after the procedure to avoid infection. Do you have any questions?'

Fifteen minutes, the contents are suctioned out.

'No, no questions.'

'Fine, then we'll see you on Friday.'

Then Annika was back out in the long grey hallway again. She bumped into a young woman on her way to the examination room; they avoided each other's gazes. She heard the doctor say hello. The seasickness returned, the nausea, the back pain – she had to get out of there.

The 48 bus swayed and swerved, and Annika almost threw up on the floor. She staggered off the bus at Kungsholmstorg and quickly made her way to her building. Standing in the courtyard, it took her a while to fight off the nausea before she could drag herself upstairs.

Her groceries were still in a bag by the door. She couldn't muster up the strength to care and sank down on the couch and stared straight ahead.

A tiny bubble, a little white dot.

She knew it was a boy, a little blond boy, like Thomas. She closed her eyes, cried, tore out the cartoon section of the paper and used it to blow her nose. Once again, she opened the paper to the pages featuring the Paradise story and skimmed the last piece. According to the police, Rebecka was suspected of conspiracy to murder. She had threatened a client, Aida Begovic, who had been murdered at Sergelstorg the following day. The woman's funeral would be at two p.m. today.

She let go of the paper, a sense of failure burning inside her, bent over, her stomach aching, the dot swimming, her heart racing faster and faster; everything was swirling, swirling. Berit's voice echoed in her mind: 'She didn't have any relatives, no one has claimed the body, the funeral will be a simple ceremony over at Norra Begravningsplatsen . . .'

No one should have to be so utterly abandoned, Annika thought. *Everyone deserves a final farewell.*

She closed her eyes and sank back into the couch.

Three more days with the baby in her belly.

She looked at her watch.

If she left now she would make it to Aida's funeral.

There were people inside the chapel.

Annika stopped in the doorway, suddenly insecure, and looked around. A few women and a young boy turned and looked at her.

At the other end of the chapel a small coffin was on display, shiny and white, topped with three red roses.

She swallowed, nauseated and shaky, took a few steps forward, took off her jacket and sat down on an empty pew at the back. Suddenly she became aware of her empty hands: she had forgotten to bring flowers.

The silence was massive, the light was spare. Ribbons of light came in through the stained-glass windows beneath the dome, painting colourful patches on the walls and floors. The sun lit up the walls, making the yellow paint glow.

A faint hum was heard. Discreetly, Annika tried to observe the other people attending the funeral. Most of them were women; half of them looked Swedish, and the other half looked like they came from Yugoslavia. In all, there were twelve to fourteen people there and all of them had flowers.

The surprise that Annika felt at first turned into annoyance.

Where were all of you when Aida needed help?

It's damn easy being available once it's too late.

The church bell began to toll above her. The sound trickled down into the nearly empty pews, sombre and ominous, and she felt each peal like a physical blow. Tears obscured her vision.

The tolling ceased, the subsequent silence reverberated. Then sobs and the clearing of throats were heard, along with the rustling of hymnals. Someone turned on a CD and Annika recognized the first movement of Mozart's Requiem. Crying now in earnest, the music filled her, the slow stanzas created by the dying Wolfgang Amadeus.

The strains died out. A man in a dark grey suit, the officiating clergyman, went over and stood in front of the coffin. He spoke about life and death: platitudes. After a few minutes Annika closed her eyes, hearing his words fall and letting them wash over her like the music: 'Twilight is the most beautiful hour', 'All the love that heaven affords', the lyrics promised. When the pop song 'I'm most at home where I'm free to roam' began, she felt annoyed again.

'Free to roam': what in God's name was this? Aida had been free to roam Sergelstorg – had she felt at home there? What fool had picked the music?

Angrily, Annika dashed the tears from her eyes. Everyone seemed to be crying. She looked at the clergyman, bowing his head in a routine show of respect as he sat in the front row. *What did you know about Aida?* He didn't have a single solitary personal thing to say about her, he had never met her.

Annika closed her eyes, tried to conjure up Aida and saw her in her mind's eye: ill, frightened, hunted.

Who were you? Annika wondered. *Why did you die?*

The man in the suit started talking again, rhythmically, reading a poem by Edith Södergran. One of the women in the first pew went up to the altar and sang *a cappella*, in a beautiful soaring voice. The words were Serbo-Croat, so Annika couldn't understand them. The notes soared upwards, swirling under the chapel dome, expanding vibrantly, and suddenly the grief rising in the chapel was genuine, piercing, *why, why, why?*

Annika sobbed into her hands, grief like a heavy lump in her chest, tangible, loaded with guilt.

We're all doing this for our own sakes, she thought, *not for Aida. It makes no difference to her.*

Another hymn, a familiar one, one that had been played at Gran's funeral. Annika mouthed the words: 'What glory there is on Earth, what glory there is in Heaven, singing praises we will enter Paradise'.

She bowed her head and pursed her lips.

A silence filled the air. She couldn't breathe. The bells began to toll again and it was over, Aida was on her way to oblivion, she would vanish for ever. She wanted to protest, to stop the men who lifted up Aida's coffin and carried it down the aisle, past her, a mere metre away, *I'm not ready to let her go, I need to know why!* Feeling nauseated, Annika got to her feet and waited until the rest of the funeral party filed past her, noticing how they looked at her. She was the last person to leave.

The cold air hit her. It was crisp and pure and the snow sparkled in the sun. The men put the casket down on a bier. She saw the rest of the funeral party gather on the steps and along the paths. They blew their noses and murmured to each other.

They all knew Aida. They all had some kind of relationship to her. Every last one of them knew her better than I did.

Annika slowly walked up to a woman who was standing a few steps below her.

'Excuse me if I'm intruding,' Annika said and introduced herself. 'I don't know many people here. How did you come to know Aida?'

The woman gave her a friendly smile and dabbed at her eyes with a tissue.

'I'm the superintendent at the refugee camp that Aida was sent to when she came to Sweden.'

They shook hands. Both women took a deep breath and smiled in embarrassment.

'I'm a journalist,' Annika said. 'I came because I thought Aida was all alone in the world.'

The woman nodded.

'She *was* all alone. Many people tried to approach her, but it was very hard to reach her. I believe she chose to be alone.'

Annika swallowed. It was certainly damned convenient to blame Aida herself, even in death.

'What about the others?' Annika asked. 'If she didn't have any friends, then who are they?'

The woman shot her a startled look.

'They're refugees too – they met Aida at the camp. She used to come and visit. I also see a neighbour of hers from Vaxholm and then there are the representatives from the Bosnian Cultural Association. One of them was the woman who sang, wasn't it beautiful?'

'Wasn't there anyone who could help Aida?' Annika asked. 'Didn't she have anyone to turn to?'

The camp supervisor looked sadly at Annika.

'You didn't know her very well, did you?'

The men had placed Aida's coffin on a wheeled bier and now the slow journey to the grave began. The woman

Annika had been talking to joined the others and she followed suit.

'It's true,' Annika said in a low voice, 'I didn't know her very well. I met her a few times before she died, that's all. When did she come to Sweden?'

The camp supervisor looked over Annika's shoulder and hesitated before answering.

'In the final days of the war,' she finally whispered. 'She had several gunshot wounds, shrapnel all over her body – it was a terrible sight. Flashbacks, the shakes, breaking into sweats, a poor perception of reality. She drank a great deal. We really did everything we could to help her: doctors, counsellors, psychologists. I don't think it made much of a difference. Aida had devastating demons.'

Annika opened her eyes wide.

'What do you mean?'

Another woman came up to the supervisor and whispered something to her and they went over to one of the refugees who was crying so hard she was about to break down. Annika looked around in confusion, slipped on a patch of ice and almost fell. She felt sick and the bier creaked in the cold. The coffin moved along the path and was obscured from view by the trees, the shadows, and then it was out of reach. She fought the impulse to run after it, to bang on the lid.

Tell me about your demons! What did they do to you? .

The grave inspired dread, a study in darkness and cold. *Why do they have to be so deep?* Carefully, Annika bent over it, looked down, saw her own shadow vanish in its depths and quickly backed away.

The coffin was resting next to the grave, propped up on a few beams. The mourners gathered around the plot. Everyone's eyes were red. The officiating clergyman said a few more words. Annika was shivering with cold and wanted to leave. Aida wasn't in that coffin, Aida wasn't there at all, Aida had already slipped away along with her demons and her secrets.

Out of the corner of her eye Annika could see someone approaching: two large black cars with dark-toned windows and blue licence plates. They braked, came to a standstill and their engines were switched off. Annika regarded them with surprise.

Suddenly all the car doors flew open at once: five, six, seven men got out. The clergyman stopped talking and the members of the funeral party looked at each other in confusion. The men in the cars were wearing grey coats. They looked around, watching the funeral party with grim expressions on their faces.

An old man stepped forward. Her mouth half-open, Annika stared at him: he was a military man who walked stiffly and his expression was stern – he had no eyes for anything but the coffin. His uniform was richly decorated, he held a small paper bag in his hand and everyone backed away as he approached the grave. Annika was standing on the other side of the hole in the ground and, to her amazement, saw the old man fall to his knees, doff his hat and start to murmur a stream of unintelligible words. His hair was sparse and grey, the pate shining through it. He was on his knees praying for quite some time, breathing heavily.

Annika couldn't help staring at him and listening intently to his ravaged voice.

Then he got up again, with a lot of effort, picked up the bag and pulled out a handful of something that he sprinkled on the coffin: soil. A handful of soil!

His murmuring increased in volume. Transfixed, Annika listened as another handful of soil rained on the casket. More words: sad, heavy, pregnant with meaning.

A third handful and then the murmuring died away. The man put the bag back in his pocket and brushed off his hands.

You know all about Aida, she thought. *You're familiar with her demons.*

Annika rushed around the grave. The man was leaving, going back to the cars and the other men. She grabbed him by the sleeve.

'Please, sir!'

Surprised, he stopped and looked over his shoulder at her.

'Who are you?' she asked in English. 'How do you know Aida?'

The man stared at her and tried to shake off her hand.

'I'm a journalist,' Annika said. 'I met Aida a few days before she died. Who are you?'

Suddenly, the men in grey coats were everywhere. They placed themselves between the man and herself; they appeared to be upset and asked the man something, repeating the same word several times. The old man dismissed them with a wave, then turned his back on her while the group began to move towards their cars, a grey mass. They got in, started the cars' engines and rode off among the trees.

Sweaty and pale, Annika stared at them.

She had been able to catch one of the words that the man had uttered by the graveside, one single word. He had repeated it several times, she was sure of it.

Bijelina.

One by one the women stepped up to the graveside, said a few words and put flowers on the coffin. Annika felt panicky: she hadn't brought any flowers, she didn't have anything to say, only that she was sorry, sorry to have let Aida down, sorry to have brought about her death.

She turned away, tripped, had to get out of there, couldn't stay.

Aida and the old man must have been close – he might even be her father.

The thought struck Annika: *What if he knows what I've done?*

I was only trying to help, she protested silently. *I didn't mean any harm.*

She started walking in the direction of the bus stop, shame and guilt making her unsteady on her feet. She felt sick and wanted to throw up.

Once she had got through the hole in the fence and had walked a few metres, someone put a hand over her mouth.

Her first thought was that the men in the grey coats had come back for her. That the old man wanted to settle the score.

'I've got a gun pointed at your spine,' the man hissed. 'Keep moving.'

Annika couldn't move. She was frozen to the sidewalk, Ratko towering behind her.

He grabbed a fistful of her hair and yanked her head back.

'Get moving!'

I'm going to die, she thought. *I'm going to die.*

'Move it, bitch!'

Breathless with fear, she closed her eyes and slowly started to stumble down the street. The man was breathing down her neck. He smelled bad. After some ten metres or so, he stopped.

'Get in the car,' he said.

Annika looked around, her neck stiff, her scalp burning. *Which car?*

He struck her in the face. She felt something warm trickle from her lip and was suddenly fully alert. Violence was familiar, she was used to beatings, she could deal with this.

'And if I don't?' she said, her lip already beginning to puff up.

The man hit her again.

'Then I'll kill you here and now,' he said.

She looked at his face, florid from the cold, shadowed by fatigue. She felt her own breathing rate increase and turn shallow. Her field of vision began to flicker – she didn't have the strength for this, didn't want this.

'Go ahead,' she said.

The words set the man off; he grabbed a rope, pushed Annika up against the car next to them, a blue compact, twisted her arms behind her back and tied her up. Then he pressed a cold gun muzzle against her neck.

'You know what happened to Aida.'

She closed her eyes and her defence mechanisms came into play. She didn't feel a thing, turning inward, tuning out.

Must do as he says.

'Get in, damn you!'

Ratko yanked the door of the blue car open. Petrified, Annika tumbled into the back seat and saw the man walk around to the other side, get in, start the car and drive off. She stared at his neck: it was chapped and red and there was dandruff on his dark collar. She felt cut off from reality, as though there was a sheet of plexiglass separating her from the rest of the world. A blur of buildings rushed past, but there were no people in sight, no one who cared.

'My gun's in my lap,' Ratko said. 'Try anything, and I'll shoot you.'

The sun was setting, the day was red and cold. The Blues whirled past, Solnavägen, cars, people, no one she could shout to, no one who could help her. She was stuck in the back seat of a dirty little car, sitting on her bound hands, and they hurt. She tried to ease the pressure on them by shifting position.

The man behind the wheel swerved and threw a quick glance at her over his shoulder.

'Sit still, damn it!'

Annika froze in mid-motion.

'This is extremely uncomfortable.'

'Shut up!'

The northbound route to Norrtull, Sveaplan and Cedersdalsgatan. Surrounded by traffic, thousands of people on the move, but still she was so alone, always alone.

She closed her eyes and pictured Aida's coffin, the man's bowed head and the words he murmured.

Maybe it's my turn now.

They got caught in traffic right before they reached Roslagstull and she could see straight into another small car, this one carrying a mother and her small child. She stared at the woman, trying to attract her attention. Finally the other woman sensed her stare and their gazes met. Annika opened her eyes very wide and mouthed a message in an exaggerated fashion.

'Help,' she said soundlessly. 'Help me!'

The woman quickly turned away.

No, Annika thought. *Look at me! Help me!*

'Help,' she yelled, banging her head against the window. 'Help me! Help me!'

The blows echoed in her head and she got all dizzy. The glass was hard and cold.

Ratko stiffened but didn't move, just kept on driving slowly towards Roslagsvägen.

Annika screamed with all her might.

'He's kidnapped me!' she screamed. 'Help me! Help!'

The cars slipped past her one by one, only a metre away from her, yet somehow thousands of years distant, isolated. She yelled, screamed, arched up at the ceiling, got all sweaty, dizzy and hoarse. She flung herself at the window, howling, banging her head against the window. A man in a new Volvo looked her in the eye and looked concerned, Ratko turned to face the man, shrugged his shoulders and smiled. The man smiled back at Ratko.

Annika stopped, panting, humiliation thumbing its nose at her.

There was no point in trying. People were too self-absorbed. Why would they want to deal with a screaming madwoman in the next lane?

She quietened down, her head aching from all the blows, and started to cry. Ratko didn't say a thing. Traffic lightened up at Roslagstull, they passed the Museum of Natural History and turned off on Albano. Annika let the tears stream down her face unchecked. *It's all over now, who would have thought that it would end like this?*

The car continued along several smaller roads. She noted a few signs – Björknäsvägen, Fiskartorpsvägen – then woods, trees.

Finally the car came to a stop, Annika stared straight ahead and through the windshield she could see an old shed. Ratko walked around the car and got something out of the trunk, opened the passenger door and yanked down the front seat.

'Get out,' he said.

She obeyed, her throat aching.

'What do you want from me?' she asked him hoarsely.

'Get in the shed,' the man said.

He shoved her and she staggered off, feeling nauseated and faint.

It was dark inside the wooden shed. The dying day couldn't quite force its way through the cracks in the wall and left the firewood and the spider webs in the shadows.

Ratko pushed her down on a chopping block over in a

corner. Annika felt terror ooze down her back as the walls tilted and rolled. He wound a rope around the block and hurriedly tied her feet up. Then he moved in closer and hissed in her ear, his voice harsh and low.

'I get to ask all the questions,' he said, 'and you get to answer them. Putting on a tough act is pointless – everyone talks sooner or later. You'll save yourself a lot of grief if you go for sooner.'

She started breathing rapidly, feeling panic well up inside. Ratko grabbed his sports bag, rummaged through it and pulled out a sub-machine gun. He stood in front of her, towering over her, and pointed the gun in her face.

'The shipment,' he said. 'Where is it?'

Annika swallowed, breathed, breathed, swallowed.

'The shipment!' he barked. 'Where the hell is it?'

She started shaking uncontrollably all over. She closed her eyes, no longer able to talk.

'Where is it?!'

She felt the muzzle of the gun poking her forehead and, panic-stricken, began to cry.

'I don't know!' she managed to get out. 'I only met Aida once.'

He removed the gun and slapped her face.

'Cut the crap,' he said, grabbing her necklace. 'You're wearing Aida's gold necklace.'

She shivered and tears streamed down her face and neck.

'She gave it to me,' she whispered.

Annika sat still, unable to think, paralysed by fear. The man let go of the necklace and remained silent for a while. She could feel him studying her.

'Who are you?' he asked in a low voice.

She gasped for breath.

'I'm a . . . reporter. Aida called the paper I work for. She needed help. I met her at a hotel. That's when you turned up and I . . . tricked you. Then I gave Aida a phone number to call, somewhere she could go for help . . .'

'Why did you trick me?'

His cry tore into her breathless explanation.

'I wanted to save Aida,' she said in a whisper.

Annika could sense that the man was moving. She saw his face appear in front of her.

'Who was the man at the funeral?' he asked, his eyes gleaming.

She stared at him in incomprehension

'Who?'

'The military man,' he screamed, his words spraying spittle on her face. 'You stupid fucking whore, who was that officer?'

Annika squeezed her eyes shut. 'I don't know,' she whispered, keeping her eyes closed.

'What the hell did you say to him?'

She panted a few times.

'That's . . . exactly what I asked him, who he was . . . How he knew Aida.'

'What did he say?'

She was shaking and didn't reply.

'What did he say?'

'I don't know,' Annika sobbed. 'He said Bijelina at the graveside, Bijelina, Bijelina, I'm certain of that . . .'

It took a few seconds before she realized that Ratko had quietened down.

'Bijelina?' he asked sceptically. 'Her home town?'

Annika swallowed and nodded.

'I think so.'

'What else?'

'I don't speak Serbo-Croat.'

'What did the watchdogs say?'

She looked at him in confusion.

'What dogs?'

He waved the gun in front of her face.

'The guards, the guys from the embassy in the grey coats! What did they say?'

She searched her memory.

'I don't know! Nothing I could understand.'

'I don't give a damn what you understood! What did they say?'

Once more, he poked her in the forehead with the gun; she collapsed, closed her eyes again and lay there panting, her mouth half-open.

'If you don't talk,' Ratko told her, 'there's no point in having a mouth, now is there?'

He moved the muzzle to her mouth, banging it against her teeth in the process. She could taste the metal, the cold. Her brain shorted out briefly and she shook.

'What did the watchdogs say? Tell me.'

Darkness, cold – were her eyes shut or had the day come to an end?

'For the last time, what did the guards say to the military man? Tell me.'

Annika nodded, slowly. The muzzle moved, banging against her teeth again. She could breathe, she wanted to throw up.

'They said something several times,' she whispered. 'Porut . . . something. Porutsch . . . Porutschn—?'

'Porutschnick?' Ratko asked, his voice tense.

'Could be,' she whispered.

'What else? What else did they say?'

'I don't know . . .'

Once more, the gun was pressed up against her lips.

'Mich . . .' she said. 'Mich . . . Michich.'

'Michich?'

The gun went away as she nodded.

'That was it, they said Michich.'

*

Ratko stared at the pathetic broad in front of him and felt triumph surge between his legs. What a lucky strike! A bull's eye! He knew, he understood; there in that dark shed, the pattern started to make sense.

Porutschnick Michich.

He hurriedly packed his things, stuffing the gun in the bag. He left the rope, it was the kind that anyone could pick up at hardware stores all over Sweden and it wouldn't retain any prints.

'I know where to find you.' He reeled off the standard phrase that he used on informants once they had squealed. 'If you so much as breathe a word of this, I'll rub you out, understand?'

She was slumped down with her head between her legs and appeared not to hear him.

'Do you understand?' he screamed in her ear. 'I'm going to kill you if you talk – is that clear?'

Her whole body was shaking and suddenly he had had enough. He looked at his watch: it was time to go.

'One fucking peep out of you, and you're dead. I'll shove this gun in your mouth and blow your brains clear across Stockholm, get the picture?'

Ratko opened the door and glanced at the girl one last time. She wouldn't talk. Even if she did, so what? If they ever caught him, they could charge him with worse crimes that this.

He went out into the winter's night, let go of the door as he passed through and exhaled triumphantly.

Porutschnick Michich, or rather Porucnik Misic.

There it was, he could hardly believe his luck.

He opened the trunk, yanked the guns out of his sports bag and tossed them under a filthy blanket.

Luck, my ass, he thought. It was skill! Start the interrogation with something you don't give a damn about and then move in for the kill.

He got behind the wheel, tossed the bag in the passenger seat beside him and started the car. It ran smoothly and he headed for the free port.

Colonel Misic, a legendary figure of the KOS, the counter-intelligence group of the Yugoslav army. The man who had survived all the purges – and who had Milosevic's ear.

Ratko turned on the heater, soon he would no longer be out in the cold in any way.

He didn't know why, but Aida and the man had been close. The details, the exact nature of their relationship didn't interest him in the least, but now he had the facts. He knew what had gone haywire, why they had taken his power away.

Aida must have had a protector, and she must have sent him a message before she died.

He shrugged his shoulders, shook them loose; the muscles were hard and tense. He no longer gave a damn about Aida from Bijelina, she could rot in her fucking grave over by that service station in Solna.

He turned off Tegeluddsvägen and cruised over to the harbour area, catching sight of the signpost: Tallinn, Klaipeda, Riga, St Petersburg. Found a vacant parking space and parked the car. The space was marked reserved, but who gave a flying fuck? He grabbed the sports bag full of cash and clothing and, turning his face to the bracing salt air, breathed deeply.

Floodlights bathed the area between the warehouses in shades of gold. He saw the trailer zone at the far end of the lot, on the waterfront.

This was where it all began, he thought.

Or rather, this was where it all would end.

He glanced at his watch.

It was time.

*

Annika heard a car start and drive off, far away, the taste of metal still lingering in her mouth. It got quiet and dark as she sat there, slumped over.

She was cold. Her body was numb, her mind was paralysed. As she slumped there on the chopping block she nearly dozed off and almost toppled over. The chill grew more intense and so did her drowsiness.

So easy it would be. So wonderful to just slip away.

The ropes around her ankles weren't tight. She shuffled out of them, freeing her feet and then lying down on the dirt floor. Uncomfortable. Her cheek to the earth, she lay still, feeling her hands go cold and numb. The familiar note of loneliness started wobbling up and down the scale in her left ear.

Soon, she thought. *Soon it will be all over. Soon it will be quiet.*

The thought banished the buzzing.

It would be the end.

The realization brought Annika to her senses. The dirt under her face was crumbly and frozen, smelly. She was lying on one arm, and it had gone numb from the elbow on down.

She groaned.

If she remained here in the cold, everything would be mighty quiet in a very short time.

She struggled to get up, leaning on the block. The chill had penetrated her jeans and numbness had set in.

What if he came back?

The thought made her breathe first faster, then slower.

Exhausted, she began to cry again.

I want to go home, she thought. *I bought hot dogs today, I want to go home.*

She cried for a while, the tears and the cold making her shake.

I've got to get out of here.

Annika got up, the rope rubbing against her wrists. It wasn't very tight, so she twisted her hands around in various circular motions for a minute or so, freeing her left hand, and the rope fell to the ground. She remained there, standing in the confining darkness, and looked for chinks of light that would show her where the door was, without seeing any.

What if he had locked the door?

She staggered over to the wall and felt her way along the wooden boards, getting splinters in her fingers, until the wall gave way and the door opened. The wind caught the door, a fiercely cold blast from the coast. She thought she could make out a small road and trees.

Dear God, where am I?

She leaned against the door post, closed her eyes and rubbed her forehead.

They had taken Roslagsvägen and had turned off not far from the University. She was somewhere in the northern part of Djurgården, behind the Stora Skuggan woodland area. She rubbed her dry, red eyes.

The 56 bus, she thought. It ran from Stora Skuggan to Kungsholmen.

She walked unsteadily out of the shed: there *was* some kind of a road down there. She stopped and looked up at the sky. To the right she could see some light: yellow and pink hues tinged the horizon.

It's not the sun, she figured. *It's the city lights.*

Annika started walking.

WEDNESDAY 5 DECEMBER

The eleven o'clock meeting started ten minutes late, as usual. Anders Schyman felt irritation well up inside him. A thought that had lately kept popping up in his mind took hold once more.

When I'm in power, I will establish routines that will be adhered to.

He had just taken a seat, a signal to the Flannel Pack – the community and political affairs editor, the picture editor, the sports editor, the crime editor, the entertainment editor, and the op-ed editor – to pipe down and listen, when Torstensson knocked on the door.

Schyman's eyebrows went up. The editor-in-chief was hardly ever present at daily planning sessions.

'Welcome,' the deputy editor said a shade too sarcastically. 'The meeting's already in session.'

Dismayed, Torstensson looked around for a chair.

'There's one over in the corner,' Schyman said and pointed to the far end of the table.

The editor-in-chief cleared his throat and remained standing.

'I have something important to tell you,' he said, his voice slightly shrill.

Anders Schyman made no effort to stand up and offer the editor-in-chief his seat at the head of the table.

'Please take a seat,' he said, once again indicating the chair at the far end of the table.

Torstensson slunk away, pulled out the chair, causing it to scrape along the floor, and sat down. The silence was deafening. They all stared at the little man. He cleared his throat again.

'My assignment in Brussels has been postponed indefinitely,' he said. 'The party secretary just informed me that the lobby dealing with public access to information was no longer a priority issue. As things stand, I shall not be leaving the paper at this point in time.'

He grew quiet. A cloud of bitterness hung in the air. The op-ed editor made commiserating noises and the rest of the group studied the deputy editor surreptitiously.

Anders Schyman didn't move a muscle: he was floored, couldn't think. This was something he hadn't considered. The possibility that the party would cancel the editor-in-chief's line of retreat had never occurred to him.

'Well, then,' he said in a neutral voice. 'Shall we run through today's paper?'

Everyone started rustling papers, leafing through newspapers and photographs, murmuring words of satisfaction or discontent. Empty-handed, Torstensson remained in his chair.

'Pelle,' Schyman said, 'hold up the pictures of the impostor.'

The picture editor showed some prints that had been taken in Järfälla that very morning. They showed Rebecka Björkstig, in handcuffs, being accompanied by three policemen to a police car.

'Torstensson,' Anders Schyman said, 'what is your opinion about going public with her name and picture at this juncture?'

The editor-in-chief blinked.

'I'm sorry . . .'

'Going public with her name and picture,' the deputy editor said. 'We could get sued for libel, do you think it's a risk worth taking in Rebecka Björkstig's case?'

'Who?'

The words 'I'm a bad person' flashed through Anders Schyman's mind. *I know how little the editor-in-chief knows and I'm exposing him to ridicule.*

'We can't run it on the front page tomorrow, anyway,' Schyman added in a friendly voice. 'So what do you think, Torstensson?'

'Why can't we run it on the front page?' the editor-in-chief asked.

Schyman let the silence speak for itself, letting the Flannel Pack digest the impact of this statement. They all knew why you couldn't run the same story as front-page news three days running: sales always went down on the third day, no matter how good the story was. Changing the top story on day three was Newspaper 101, basic stuff. Everyone knew that, everyone except for the editor-in-chief.

'It's a damn fine picture,' Schyman said. 'I suggest we go for a sky box, a tight cut, and keep the pixels. To preserve her identity. That is, unless you want to take a different route?'

He looked at the editor-in-chief who shook his head.

'All right,' he said. 'So what's on the front page?'

The entire Flannel Pack started rustling energetically, excited that a contribution from their own department might be the top story.

'How to make the most on Telia shares,' the finance editor suggested.

The room exploded with dissenting opinions.

'I don't see anyone doing cartwheels of joy,' Schyman said with a smile. 'What else do we have?'

'We've found another politician who's been using his official credit card for private purchases,' Ingvar Johansson said.

Everyone groaned. Every politician in existence was doing it: find one who didn't, and that *would* be news.

'There's this council that's decided to stop funds for a special assistant for a mentally retarded kid in Motala,' the news-desk editor went on. 'The boy lives with his mother, a single mother on welfare. The mother called the paper in tears, saying she couldn't go on. The question is whether we can run their story, since we did something similar not too long ago.'

'The story is a lot like what we've featured in our series on Paradise,' Schyman said. 'Why don't we wait until we've finished running it first? Anything else?'

'They're doing a test run of the JAS fighter plane,' the community and political affairs editor said. 'You never know when a plane will come crashing down on top of us.'

This aroused the interest of the group: the JAS fighter – when, where?

'They'll be getting started around noon today,' declared Mr Flannel-of-community-and-political-affairs. 'A whole bunch of foreign potentates have been invited to check out the fighters and do some shopping, and that means an even larger bunch of spies who *aren't* invited will be there too.'

'We should check it out,' Schyman said. 'But coverage will depend on what we find. No recycling. Anything else?'

'We're going to feature the new host of *The Women's Sofa*,' the entertainment editor said. 'A girl called Michelle Carlsson, a real hottie.'

Enthusiastic comments were heard.

'Big boobs?'

'Would she go for a photo shoot covered in body paint?'

'Do we know what the hottest Christmas gift item is this year?' Schyman asked. 'Or do we know if the classic Disney Christmas Special will be aired as usual on Christmas Eve?'

Eyebrows were raised: everyone remembered the public outrage when the segment on Ferdinand the Bull had been going to be canned. Voices blurred into each other and Schyman let them chatter on. He studied the editor-in-chief over in the corner. Torstensson looked bewildered and his forehead was beaded with perspiration.

Once again it struck Schyman: *I'm a bad person.*

On the other hand, he thought, *at least I know what I'm doing. In all honesty, how nice is it to let an incompetent person be a leader? Am I supposed to let a fool like Torstensson destroy this paper, putting hundreds of people out of work and killing a media voice in the process?*

'What do you think, Torstensson?' he asked quietly. 'Which story should we go for?'

The editor-in-chief got up.

'I have a meeting to prepare,' he said, then pushed back his chair with another scrape and left.

Once the door had closed with an angry snap, Anders Schyman shrugged his shoulders knowingly.

'All right,' he said again. 'Now where were we?'

Annika got out of bed, cold and unable to think. She went into the kitchen, her mouth still filled with the bitter, scorched taste of metal and brushed her teeth, scrubbing and scrubbing away. She poured some yogurt into a bowl, ate a mouthful and felt queasy. Then she sat quietly at the table for a while, staring at Gran's candlestick, breathing, breathing, the straw stars dancing.

She only had fuzzy, indistinct memories of how she had got home the night before. She had walked from the shed to the road, she had no idea how far, not very. Then she had come to a 4-H farm and saw a bus stop. She had almost fallen asleep there on the bench while she waited. The 56 bus appeared; the passengers had been totally normal, no one had noticed her, no one had seen that she was doomed, marked for death.

Sleep had been shattered by nightmares and her own screams had woken her up. The men from Studio 69 had tried to smother her, she had a hard time breathing and had to get up. The walls were closing in on her so she went into the living room, her legs buckled and she fell to the floor. She clasped her legs, assuming the foetal position, and her breathing became more and more shallow, rigid, convulsive. Exhausted, she remained where she was, hurting all over, unable to get up. She fell asleep and woke when the phone rang. But she didn't answer.

She sat on the couch and closed her eyes. The white coffin danced in front of her, the officer droned on, the taste of metal filled her mouth.

The walls heaved and shuddered and she took a few deep breaths. *It will pass, it will pass.* She went into the kitchen where Gran's candlestick gleamed, drank some water, lots of water, tried to get rid of the metallic taste and started crying. Opened the cabinets and stared once more at the package of pills – twenty-five tablets each containing fifteen milligrams of the sedative Sobril in a bubble-pack wrapper – and heard the doctor's voice intone: 'They're not strong enough to overdose on, but don't mix them with alcohol, that could be dangerous.'

Annika pulled the flat packets out of the box and squeezed one gently. The tablets clicked and rustled in their plastic bubbles. Placing the first pill in the first packet over a coffee mug, she pressed down; the pill tinkled as it hit the bottom of the china container. She moved the packet, pushed out the next pill, and the next, and the next: the entire package.

There was now a small heap of pills at the bottom of the mug. She sniffed, no smell. She tasted one, it was bitter. She swirled them around in the mug and closed her eyes. The pressure on her chest increased and she forced air into her lungs, gasping, panting. The tears began rolling from her eyes down her throat.

'Don't mix them with alcohol.'

She put the cup down on the counter, went into the hall, put on her shoes, wiped her eyes, clung to the railing on her way downstairs, supported herself against the buildings as she walked down Agnegatan and Garvargatan and headed for the *Systembolaget*, the state-owned liquor store, at Kungsholmstorg. It was almost empty, only a few old ladies and a gang of derelicts. She turned her back on the other patrons, found a used copy of that day's *Kvällspressen* on a bench and stared unseeingly at the black headlines. She was shaky and stammering by the time it was her turn and the cashier threw her a suspicious look. She bought vodka, a big bottle. Took the same route home, unsteady on her feet as she walked along the narrow sidewalk, the bag containing the vodka bottle swinging back and forth, the newspaper clamped under one arm. Finally, she made it home, cold and exhausted. She went into the kitchen, put the mug, the paper and the bottle next to Gran's candlestick and sat down and cried.

No more, she couldn't take any more. *The victims of Paradise tell their stories, see pages 8, 9, 10 and 11.*

She rested her head on her arms, closed her eyes and listened to herself breathe. It was all over for Aida, she didn't have to go on fighting.

Annika got up, reached for the vodka and broke the seal.

There was no point in putting it off any longer. She might as well get it over with.

Holding the bottle in one hand and the pills in the other, she closed her eyes. The glass was colder than the china.

There isn't anything left, she thought.

She opened her eyes.

Out of the frying pan into the fire: Mia Eriksson, one of the women tricked and used by Paradise, describes the reign of terror in a Kvällspressen *exclusive. Today the veil of secrecy is lifted.*

Annika put down the cup and the bottle, hesitated briefly, and went to sit on the couch in the living room, bringing the pills, the bottle and the paper along with her.

Page eight featured her article on Mia, page nine had Berit's interviews with the cases from Nacka and Österåker. Pages ten and eleven had accounts from other cases, apparently from people who had called in the day before.

She let the paper fall as she sank back in the couch. Aida's death had been her fault: Rebecka had sold Aida out, revealed her hiding place, but Annika had given Rebecka the opportunity. Annika covered her eyes with her hands, more flashbacks from the funeral: the light under the dome, 'I'm most at home where I'm free to roam', *porutschnick michich, porutschnick michich, porutschnick michich . . .*

The telephone rang again. She let it ring and waited until the jangling ceased. Afterwards, the silence was dense and oppressive. She sat up straight on the couch, took the cap off the bottle of liquor, felt her stomach churn – the baby – and swirled the pills around in the cup, throbbing with self-pity.

It doesn't make any fucking sense, she thought. *Everyone has a rotten deal. Poor Aida, poor Mia.* She picked up the paper and smoothed the pages to read her own words.

The father of Mia's first child had beaten her, threatened her, stalked her and raped her. When Mia married another man and had a child with him, the abuse escalated.

He broke all the windows of their home. Assaulted Mia's husband in the dark. Tried to run over Mia and her children with a car. Tried to slit his own daughter's throat, an encounter that had left the child unable to talk.

The authorities were at a loss. They did what they could, but it wasn't enough. They put up bars on the windows. And every time Mia had to go out she would be accompanied by social workers. Finally, Social Services decided that the family had to go underground.

For two years the family stayed at a succession of shabby motels. They couldn't let anyone know their whereabouts and had orders not to go out. Not even Mia's parents knew whether they were dead or alive. The Administrative Court of Appeal decreed that the family was unable to lead a normal life in Sweden for the time being. They had to leave the country; the problem was, where should they go? Rebecka claimed to have the solution to their woes, but the family had ended up going from the frying pan into the fire.

Annika put the paper in her lap and began to weep.

The human condition was so terrible, the price was so atrociously high. Why did young girls in Europe have to be hurt in wars and end up on the run? Why didn't we face up to our responsibilities? Why did we allow loved ones to die? Why couldn't Mia have a good life? Why wasn't she entitled to a normal life, like everyone else, with a husband and kids and a job and daily runs to the day-care centre?

She got up and got a glass of water, then returned to the couch with the article in her lap.

People's problems, she thought, shouldn't be more dramatic than having to choose which Christmas decorations to put up; or whether to visit your grandmother on Friday or Saturday; or whether you should go for a promotion at work; or live in an apartment or buy a house. Mia wished she had problems like that, but she hadn't been granted the privilege.

Annika stared at the article, at her wording, her conclusions.

The right to have a husband and kids and a job and a normal life.

Not only for Mia and Aida, but for herself as well.

Annika gasped as the realization hit home. Stared at the pills in the cup and the bottle of booze and sat motionless while the insight spread throughout her body.

The force depriving her of life was her own. She was going to bow out, give up, get off the carousel before the ride was over, let the world continue without finding out what it had in store.

She heard her mother's voice in her head: 'You never finish anything! You always screw up! You're lazy and cowardly and plenty of trouble!'

Annika put her hand to her cheek, still feeling the sting of her mother's slap twenty years previously.

No, Mother, she thought, *you were wrong, that wasn't true. I intended to finish things, but I always got ahead of myself and figured out so many different approaches, and that made you angry, you thought I was being careless. Birgitta was never careless.*

She hadn't thought of her childhood for years, so why now?

When you told us to draw a bird, Birgitta would draw a bird while I drew a forest with lots of birds and animals, making you angry; I did the wrong thing, I didn't obey you.

More memories came back to her: her mother's anger when they went skiing or swimming, or when they did the weekly cleaning on Saturdays. Her mother always found some reason to yell at her: if she was quick, she had done a sloppy job cleaning; if she was thorough, she had been dawdling; if her skis slipped during a cross-country run with the family, she was intentionally trying to spoil the day for everyone else; if she got up some speed, she was going too fast; if she tried to adapt her pace to the others, she was in the way.

I could never get it right, Annika thought, amazed by the conclusion, not knowing where it came from.

It wasn't my fault.

The words had a physical impact on her, making her fingertips tingle.

Those outbursts had nothing to do with her, her mother was the one who had a problem. Her mother couldn't stand her own life and she had made Annika pay for her problems.

Her mouth half-open, Annika stared into space. A curtain had gone up, revealing a virgin landscape; she could see the causes and effects, the consequences and the context.

Her mother didn't have the strength to love her. It was sad and painful, but it wasn't anything she could change. Her mother had done her best, but she hadn't done a very good job. The real issue was how long Annika was going to punish herself. The real issue was when she would take charge of her own life, break the vicious cycle and become an adult.

She could let Barbro boss her around and Annika could accept her role as the hopeless one, the one who spoiled things for everyone else, the one who was in the way, who never succeeded.

Her life was her own, she was entitled to have everything. Who, apart from herself, was stopping her?

Once more she began to cry. It was not a violent fit of weeping; the tears were warm and full of sorrow.

Security was a thing of the past. No one could tell that this society had been efficient a mere decade ago.

Ratko walked purposefully and quickly, his hands in his pockets. In those days this city had been known as Leningrad, and there certainly hadn't been any of these hoodlums hanging around; whores could move freely through the streets in the middle of the night without having to worry. These days everyone, himself included, had to have eyes in the backs of their heads. The gangs were unchecked: any fucking redneck could make a career out of murder and mayhem.

Capitalism, he thought with disgust. *This just proves it doesn't work.*

He tried to relax. Nevsky Prospekt was fairly safe. Main streets usually were. Two more blocks to go after he turned the corner at Mayakovskaya, and he would be there.

The side street was darker. He saw shapes lurking in the shadows and jogged to the other side of the street to avoid them, felt ashamed and realized that he was starting to get paranoid.

The door to the building was locked, so he gave the intercom a buzz. The lock clicked without anyone saying a word – all he did was glance up at the security camera mounted over the doorway.

The stairwell stank. On every landing there were trash

cans full of garbage and junk. Strips of paint were peeling off the walls and there were heaps of plaster in the corners.

Some things never change, he thought. *Why can't these people keep things clean and tidy?*

The top floor, no elevator. The doorbell didn't work, so he knocked on the wooden door: it was bare, most of the paint had been worn off. It slipped open soundlessly. The inside of the door was reinforced with steel.

'Ratko, you old bastard! I heard they were looking for you!'

His old friend from the east was fatter than ever. They embraced and kissed each other on the cheeks.

'This calls for a celebration – break out the booze.'

Some young men scurried like rats, bringing liquor, glasses and cigarettes. Ratko accompanied his friend down the hallway with its worn velvet wallpaper, the wooden flooring under the linoleum creaking, and they went into the room at the far end and took a seat. Once the liquor had materialized, his friend told the rats to leave them.

The door closed, his friend filled the glasses, they drank and then they got down to business.

'I need money,' Ratko said. 'I've got a big investment in the works.'

He told his friend about his plans, about how the new operation was set up, describing his customers, his contacts and his associates.

His friend listened without interrupting him, sitting on his chair with his legs wide apart and his head bowed, holding a glass in his hand.

'I've got seven million Swedish kronor in cash,' Ratko said. 'But, as you know, I'll need more than that to get this show on the road. I need to find the right people.'

His friend drained his glass and nodded.

'What's in it for us?'

Ratko smiled.

'This industry is in its infancy. It's going to grow like crazy. Just be in on it from the get-go.'

'The usual terms?'

'Of course,' Ratko replied.

His friend wheezed asthmatically.

'How will you get there?'

'A direct flight to Cape Town. My Norwegian passport is red-hot; it was expensive as hell to get into the country and it will be even more expensive to get out. I have to leave tonight.'

His friend didn't reply, didn't move a muscle. They drank some more.

'How much do you need?'

Once again, Ratko smiled.

THURSDAY 6 DECEMBER

The offices of the Swedish Association of Local Authorities had an unostentatious location a few blocks from Slussen. Thomas stared at the clean lines of the golden stucco building; this was the stronghold of power, this was where decisions were made. Making it here was his goal in life, or rather, one of his goals. He took a deep breath; his palms were damp.

Christ – he really wanted this assignment.

The lobby was airy and light, a woman wearing a headset sat behind a window at the counter, looking busy. Thomas left his name and sat down on a sofa near the entrance, holding his briefcase. Tried to read *Metro*, but it was impossible to concentrate.

'Thomas Samuelsson, it's good to see you!'

He got up and tried to smile. Coming from the direction of the elevators, the director walked over to him, shook his hand and patted him firmly on the shoulder with his left hand.

'So glad you could make it on such short notice. Ever been here before?'

The man didn't wait for an answer. He propelled Thomas up a flight of stairs, down a hallway, out into a courtyard, and into an elevator taking them up several floors.

I'll never find my way out of this labyrinth, Thomas thought.

Doors slipped past, closed, open, people everywhere, talking, discussing and reading.

Bewildered, he wondered: *What do all these people do?*

The two men reached the director's office, a beautiful room on the seventh floor boasting a view of the rooftops of Hornsgatan. They sat down, facing each other, on comfortable chairs arranged around a table. A woman appeared with coffee, Danish pastries and macaroons and discreetly left the room.

Thomas swallowed and concentrated on appearing relaxed.

'The local authorities spend more than twelve billion kronor a year on welfare payments,' the director said as he poured coffee into two cups bearing the emblem of the association. 'These costs increase every year, while the politicians are intent on cutting back.'

The man leaned back and blew on his coffee. Thomas met his gaze: it was intelligent and astute.

'People who are on welfare comprise a group in society that has rock-bottom priority in the minds of local government representatives. To be totally crass, people on welfare are regarded as being tedious parasites. More than two-thirds of all politicians believe that it's too easy to get welfare. The consequences of this have been devastating. Please help yourself, they're nice and fresh.'

Dutifully, Thomas took a bite of a Danish. It was unbearably sweet.

'Last year, county councils throughout the country monitored the performance of Social Services on a local basis,' the director continued. 'The results were depressing, and I believe we need to deal with the criticism in a constructive manner.'

The director handed Thomas a report. He opened it and began to skim through its contents.

'To a great extent you could say that the general public perceives Social Services in a negative way: the employees are cold-hearted and lack empathy,' the director said. 'It's difficult even to make an appointment. Many applicants are shut out on the doorstep or, when they call in, they're told they don't qualify for welfare. Since there hasn't been a formal decree, there's no way that they can appeal. This leads to justice being compromised in an unacceptable fashion.'

Thomas leafed through the report.

'More and more people are humiliated by the attitude of Social Services,' the director went on, 'but it's not the staff's fault. I'm sure that most of the social workers do what they can but their workload has increased, which makes them susceptible to overextending thmselves and making mistakes. This is unacceptable.'

Thomas closed the report.

'To be honest,' the director said, 'I'm pretty damn worried. We can't seem to control stratification and segregation. On a local level we really ought to have the opportunity to turn around negative and adverse trends, but we don't have the appropriate tools, the facts and the resources. This morning a desperate woman from Motala called me. She has taken care of her mentally retarded son full-time for ten years now, living on welfare. In October, the local authorities decided to withdraw the services of the personal assistant who helped her son, and since then she's taken care of the boy on her own, around the clock. She couldn't stop crying. I feel so goddamn inadequate in situations like this.'

The director passed a hand over his eyes. Thomas noted that the man's reaction was heartfelt and genuine, and felt slightly surprised.

'That's got to be against the law,' Thomas said. 'A decision like that is subject to appeal.'

'I tried to tell her that,' the director said, 'but the poor woman didn't even have the strength to put on her clothes in the morning. Spouting the law and explaining the appeals procedure would have been like a slap in the face for her. I called the Social Emergency Service in Motala and told them about her situation. They are going to do something.'

Thomas stared at the report in his lap. Some people went through hell.

'We'll have to coordinate our facts and our resources,' the director said. 'That's where your assignment comes in. The people who apply for welfare are treated very differently depending on where they live, the procedures a particular agency may have, and the social worker they encounter. What we need are clear-cut guidelines, a common strategy. We need to review cases on a regular basis and explore the possibilities of personal visits. In addition to all this, we need the development of team-working skills within each agency and between agencies, and we certainly need to maintain thorough documentation.'

The director sighed and smiled a little.

'Are you our man?'

Thomas smiled back at him.

'Absolutely.'

Annika got out of the shower, her body sore from jogging. She had forgotten how much she enjoyed running, what a kick it was to cover ground and fly. She padded across the courtyard in her robe and rubber boots and headed upstairs, her pulse surging pleasantly.

She had a hearty breakfast, made some coffee and sat down in the living room with the papers.

When she saw the front page of *Kvällspressen*, her head began to buzz. *Christ, Rebecka's been arrested, they've busted her!*

The Paradise story wasn't featured on the front page today, but there was a teaser in a skybox above the header. With shaky hands Annika turned to the spread on pages six and seven. There she was: Rebecka, her face still blocked out, being taken away by three police officers. *Yes!*

Annika scrutinized the picture, focusing on the details, Rebecka's pale outfit, her dainty boots, the unkempt trees in the background, it must have been taken at the house in Olovslund. She went and got more coffee and sat down with the phone in her lap, hesitating momentarily, then dialling a direct number at police headquarters.

'Well, what do you know?' Q said. 'Long time, no see.'

On her end, Annika smiled.

'Have you had the opportunity to meet my friend Rebecka Björkstig?'

'She loves you,' the policeman said. 'You really have a flair for making friends.'

Annika stopped smiling.

'What do you mean?'

'If what you wrote in the paper is true, maybe you'd better watch your step,' he said. 'You're the only one who actually ratted on Rebecka, you know.'

'I figured she was busy right now,' Annika said. 'Busy talking to you, for example.'

'Could be,' Q said. 'What do you want?'

'Is she guilty?'

'Of what? Bad debts, changing her name, being

careless with the facts when dealing with the local councils? Definitely, though it's hard to say if any of it constitutes a crime so far. Murder conspiracy? I'm not as sure as you are.'

'Do you know if her set-up worked at all?'

'It did in one case: her own. She managed to get herself off the record. She's no fool. The issue is whether she did it in good faith or if she had criminal intent.'

'But all those different identities – doesn't that seem fishy?'

'Does it? First, she took her mother's maiden name and changed her first name, then she made up a new last name. People do it every day.'

Silence.

'Anything else?' he asked.

'The free-port murders,' Annika said. 'Are you any closer to solving them?'

A deep sigh came over the wire.

'The answer is no,' Q said. 'We're not sure. Apparently the Yugoslav Mafia and the hijacked shipment of cigarettes are involved in some way, but we're not sure how. It goes beyond the regular smuggling business – there's something else going on that we can't quite figure out.'

Annika inhaled sharply.

'Does it have anything to do with Aida Begovic?'

Q was silent.

'Probably,' he replied curtly.

'Is Rebecka Björkstig involved?'

'We're checking into that.'

'She told me that she had been threatened by the Yugoslav Mafia. Could there be any truth to that?'

The policeman sighed.

'This is the way it is,' he said. 'The Yugo Mafia is up to all kinds of mischief that no one knows about, but they also get the blame for a bunch of stuff they haven't done. Björkstig ran that threat past us, too: it seems that one of her creditors, a guy named Andersson, threatened to set his Mafia contacts on her.'

'So there doesn't seem to be a connection between Rebecka and the Serbs?'

'*Nyet.*'

Annika closed her eyes, pausing for a moment.

'What about Ratko?' she said. 'The leader of the cigarette ring – do you know where he is right now?'

'Serbia, most probably; it's the only country in Europe where he's safe at all. There's no way he would be able to move freely anywhere else.'

'Could he be in Sweden?'

'It would have to be one hell of a short and sweet visit, in that case. Why do you ask?'

Annika swallowed hard and the taste of metal came back to her.

'By the way,' she said. 'What does *porutsch . . . porutschnick michich* mean?'

'What?' the detective said.

'*Porutschnick michich* – it's Serbo-Croat, I think.'

'Hang on,' Q said, 'I'm not fluent in every stray tongue spoken on the face of the Earth.'

'It's important,' Annika said. 'Do you know anybody who speaks the language?'

He groaned.

'We do have a staff of interpreters on hand,' he said. 'How important is it?'

'*Mucho.*'

There was a thud as the phone landed on the detective's desk. She heard him leave the room and then a voice in the distance called out 'Nikola', followed by 'What the hell does *porutschnick michich* mean?'

The footsteps returned.

'It's a rank and a name,' Q said. '*Porucnik* means colonel and Misic is a fairly common surname.'

'Oh shit!' Annika said.

'What? You're arousing my curiosity.'

'A man came to Aida's funeral yesterday: his uniform was plastered with medals and insignia.'

'I see,' the policeman said. 'So he was a relative of hers, what of it?'

'He arrived in an official embassy vehicle, with an escorting fleet of cars. Isn't that peculiar?'

'I guess he's in the country to check out the JAS fighter planes, along with all the other shady customers. Describe his insignia.'

Annika thought hard.

'Leaves,' she said.

'Leaves?'

'Right, leaves, and gobs of medals.'

'Did you see what was on them?'

She closed her eyes and sighed.

'One of them said Santa something, I think.'

Q whistled.

'Are you sure?'

'Of course not, do you think I'm a fucking computer or something?'

'He could be from the KOS,' Q said. 'But they're practically wiped out.'

Annika stretched out on the couch and looked up at the ceiling.

'What's the KOS? What are you talking about?'

'I bet it made you think of the Greek island, didn't it? The KOS is the counter-espionage division of the Yugoslav army. Milosevic has practically dismantled the entire organization. Over the past fifteen years there's been one hell of a power struggle going on between the KOS and the RDB, one that the KOS has lost. This has caused a lot of bitterness among the old guard.'

Confused, Annika exclaimed: 'The RDB?'

'Slobodan's boys, the secret police, the elite of the elite. They control crime *and* the police in Serbia – they're real tough customers.'

Annika digested this information for a few seconds.

'Excuse me,' she said, 'but where the hell did you work before you ended up as a detective?'

'That's classified,' Q said and she could actually hear him grinning.

'Where would a colonel of the KOS stay in Stockholm if he was here to see the JAS fighters?'

'If he gets along with the RDB boys at the embassy, he'd stay there. If not, he'd check into one of the major hotels in Stockholm.'

'Such as . . .?'

'I'd try the Royal Viking first.'

'I love you for ever,' Annika said.

'Spare me,' Q said and hung up.

Colonel Misic was staying at the Sergel Plaza Hotel. Annika stood in front of his door for several minutes with her hand poised to knock, the blood surging through her veins at a gallop, before she could bring herself to apply her knuckles to the wooden surface. She heard a questioning '*Da*?' and knocked again.

The door opened a crack.

'*Da*?'

Annika caught sight of an unshaven face, a hairy shoulder, an undershirt.

'Colonel Misic? My name is Annika Bengtzon. I would like to have a word with you.'

The smile that she tried to flash him was a bit uncertain.

The man peered at her, his face in the shadows. She couldn't make out the expression on his face.

'Why?' he asked in a throaty voice.

'I knew Aida,' she replied, her voice too high-pitched and nervous.

He didn't respond, but he didn't close the door either.

'I saw you at the funeral,' Annika said. 'I spoke to you.'

The man hesitated.

'What do you want?'

'To talk, that's all,' she said quickly. 'I want to talk about Aida, talk to someone who knew her in the old days.'

The elderly colonel stepped back and opened the door wide. He was barefoot and he'd pulled on a pair of trousers, the braces were hanging down to his knees.

'Come in and have a seat,' he said. 'I'll go and put on a shirt.'

Annika entered a small double room with two narrow beds, a TV set, a mini-bar, a desk and a chair with chrome legs. The door closed behind her and she heard herself swallow. The man disappeared into the bathroom and for a moment she panicked.

What if he came out armed with a sub-machine gun?

Or a knife?

He might have murdered Aida!

Her pulse rate leapt into overdrive. She was just about to make a run for it when the man came out of the bathroom wearing an unbuttoned white shirt and holding a pair of socks in his hand.

'How well did you know Aida?' he asked in broken English.

Annika gazed at the floor.

'Not very well,' she admitted, looking up into the elderly man's cloudy eyes. 'I wish I had been given the opportunity to know her better.'

'You're wearing her necklace,' the man said. 'The Bosnian lily and the heart to signify love. I bought it for Aida. She took off the charm with the Serbian eagles.'

Annika's hand flew to finger the necklace and she felt herself blush.

The elderly man sat down on one of the beds, crossed his legs, rested one foot on his lap and pulled on a sock.

'Sit down,' he said.

Weak at the knees, she sank down on the bed facing the officer and dropped her bag on the floor by the bed.

'Why are you doing this?' he asked.

Annika looked at the elderly man: the salt-and-pepper stubble on his cheeks, the sagging shoulders, the heavy-set body, the roomy shirt that would accommodate his stomach, the thinning hair.

Grief had left him a broken man, she realized. The kind of grief that made you ill.

Would anyone ever mourn her passing like that?

Suddenly the tears spilled from her eyes. She hid her face in her hands.

The man remained where he was, not uttering a word, not moving.

'I'm sorry,' she whispered after a while, dashing away the tears with the backs of her hands. 'You see, my grandmother died recently and I haven't been myself lately.'

The officer got up, went to the bathroom, and returned with a roll of toilet paper.

'Thank you,' Annika said, accepting the roll and blowing her nose.

The man studied her carefully, but not in an unfriendly way.

'Why are you wearing Aida's necklace?'

Annika blotted the area under her eyes with some paper.

'I met her a few days before she died,' Annika said.
'She was ill and very frightened. I'm a journalist – Aida
called the paper I work for and asked for help. I tried to
help her . . .'

'How?'

Annika took a deep breath and released it soundlessly.

'She was so alone in the world. There wasn't anyone to
help her. She feared for her life – this man was stalking
her. I agreed to meet her because she had information
about a couple of murders that were committed here in
Stockholm. But I couldn't leave her the way she was, she
was ill, so I gave her the number of an organization
named Paradise . . . where I thought they could help her.'

She glanced at the man. He was listening intently, but
he didn't react when she mentioned the name of the
foundation.

'The woman in charge of Paradise turned out to be a
fraud,' Annika continued. 'I feel so guilty for sending
Aida to a place like that.'

She bowed her head, felt the tears well up again and
waited for the colonel's wrath.

There was none.

'It is good,' he said, 'to help a friend. Aida must have
appreciated what you did since she gave you her
necklace.'

'I'm so sorry,' Annika whispered.

The elderly officer got up, went over to the window
and looked out over Sergelstorg.

'This is where she died,' he murmured. 'This is where
Aida died.'

The silence grew oppressive; Annika felt the man's
despair, saw his shoulders shake. She remained seated on
the bed, feeling uncertain, her hands cold and clumsy.
Finally, she tore off a piece of paper, got up and
approached the old officer cautiously. Tears were

streaming down his cheeks, stopped in their course by the stubble on his face. He made no effort to take the paper.

'Forgive me,' Annika said in a low voice. 'I thought I was helping her.'

The man shot a glance her way, then went back to staring at the plaza.

'Why do you feel guilty?' he asked.

'The woman in charge of Paradise, I'm afraid she was . . .'

All of a sudden, the colonel turned around, went to the refrigerator, took out a bottle of slivovitz and poured some into a glass.

'Aida chose to die,' he said, offering Annika a drink. She shook her head. He put the cap back on the bottle and placed it back in the refrigerator. He waddled back to the bed and sank down on it heavily, causing the mattress to creak.

'Who was Aida?' Annika asked. 'How did you come to know her?'

'I was born in Bijelina,' the elderly man said, 'just like Aida.'

Annika sat down on the opposite bed.

'Are you familiar with Bijelina?'

She attempted a smile.

'No, but I have seen photos from Bosnia. It's very beautiful, what with the mountains and the palm trees—'

'That's not what Bijelina is like,' the officer said. 'It's located on the plains, slightly to the north-east of Tuzla. The winters are harsh and spring is one long rainstorm.'

His gaze locked on to a spot somewhere above her head.

'Not even the river is very pretty.'

He sighed and looked at Annika.

'You've probably seen pictures of the river, the Drina,

that follows the Serbian border, but the most famous pictures were taken outside Gorazde.'

She shook her head.

'Piles of dead bodies,' he said. 'Corpses that were tossed into the Drina and that piled up near Gorazde. A Danish photographer crossed over our lines and photographed them – the pictures were published all over the world.'

Annika swallowed, yes, she remembered the pictures, she had read a book about the incident and *Kvällspressen* had bought the Swedish rights to the pictures.

Colonel Misic grew silent, once again focusing on things outside the room. Annika waited.

'So, are you a Serb?'

The elderly officer gave her a weary look.

'In those days you grew up without thinking about your background,' he said. 'I was an only child, and my closest childhood friend was like a brother to me. He was Aida's father. Jovan was a highly intelligent man, but since he was a Muslim there were no routes into public life open to him. He became a baker, and a very good one at that.'

The man stopped talking and passed his hand over his eyes, a hairy hand with hairy fingers.

'But you didn't become a baker,' Annika said in a low voice.

'I had a military career,' the old colonel said, 'just like my father and my grandfather before me. I never married, while Jovan had a wonderful family; a beautiful wife and three talented children. I visited them every year, in the summer and at Christmas. His daughter was my favourite: Aida. She was as lovely as an angel, her singing voice as clear as a silvery bell . . .'

The old man knocked back his liquor and wiped his mouth with the back of his hand.

'Why do you care about Aida?' he asked.

'I'm a journalist,' she said, 'I write about things that are important and true, like describing the conditions—'

'Ha!' the man exclaimed. 'Journalists are flunkies, just like soldiers. You fight with lies instead of weapons.'

Unprepared for his outburst, Annika blinked.

'That's not true,' she said softly. 'My only duty is to the truth.'

The officer looked down into his empty glass.

'Oh, really? So you're one of the good guys. You aren't paid for your work?'

She flung out her hands.

'Of course I get paid, but I work for an uncensored paper, with no restrictions . . .'

'A commercial paper, sold for money? How can a paper like that be free of restrictions? Its voice has been bought, it's corrupt and deceitful.'

The man got up again and filled his glass, not bothering to offer Annika any this time. When he sat down again, facing her, she saw a certain spark in his eyes: this was a man who had loved to discuss things, a man who had possessed power and a gift for words.

'Capital is true to itself,' he said. 'Its only aim is to accumulate more, regardless of the cost.'

'That's not true,' she said, surprised at her own vehemence. 'The press must be a free and independent agent in order to guarantee democracy . . .'

'Democracy, ha! All it does is create competition and instability, politicians who offer their services like whores, capitalists who use and exploit their fellow man. I don't have much faith in your democracy.'

'So what's the alternative?' Annika asked. 'A totalitarian state where the press is censored?'

The man leaned closer to her, almost smiling.

'Only the government can take responsibility for its citizens,' he said. 'The state shouldn't have any other obligations than to do the best for its people. The duty of the press is to inform and teach without financial gain. Your press and your media is not the voice of freedom, it is the voice of capitalism.'

Annika shook her head.

'You're wrong,' she said. 'How much fun are you having over in Serbia, with Slobodan Milosevic running the show?'

The colonel's face darkened and Annika could have bitten her tongue off. Why the hell did she have to go shooting her mouth off like that?

'I'm sorry,' she said in a whisper. 'I didn't mean to offend you . . .'

'Milosevic is a peasant,' the man said in a controlled voice. 'Just look at what he's done to my country! He destroyed the KOS, the only organization that had the capacity to maintain law and order, cut our budget until there was nothing left and gave the money to the RDB.'

He banged his fist on the night-stand so hard that Annika bounced on the bed.

'Those bastards at the RDB, just look at what they've done to my country! Criminal peasants are wasting the resources of Serbia. If the KOS was in power, Yugoslavia would still be a force to contend with, a unified Serbian nation. We never would have allowed the country to be divided.'

Colonel Misic sat there, his head hanging down, his elbows propped on his knees. Annika didn't dare move.

'Up to the late 1980s, certain ethics existed in the Balkans,' he said in a low voice. 'There were norms and values, but then barbarism took hold. Men like Ratko were given power, mere clean-up men, criminal idiots.'

Annika licked her lips, refusing to allow the taste of metal to intrude on her.

'Who is Ratko?'

The elderly man sighed and sat up straight.

'He comes from a wealthy family who lost everything during the Communist takeover, when wealth was supposed to be distributed to the people. His father had to work in a foundry, an honest job in a factory, but it was a blow to the family pride. Ratko decided to make a name for himself. He came to Sweden, to seek his luck here, but ended up in a truck factory, working on the production floor. He saw his countrymen wear themselves out working, so he picked a different career: crime.'

Misic took a mouthful of his drink.

'Ratko and his father felt that the new law didn't apply to them. In their view, communism had robbed them, taken their history and their superior status. The law was Ratko's enemy: obeying it would be to lose everything. The only driving forces in human beings are greed and the lust for material gain.'

'That's not true,' Annika said.

'Only the state can take responsibility for its citizens,' the man said.

'But the state, that's us,' Annika said. 'A government can never be better than the people it represents.'

The colonel looked at her.

'Society is always greater than the people. Seeing ourselves as isolated individuals means that egoism will prevail.'

'It doesn't have to be like that,' Annika said. 'The state is made up of its citizens: we can't dump the responsibility on anyone else. We shape our own destinies; the state is us. We are responsible for each other and it's a responsibility that we have to take. Every individual can make a difference!'

'And that's when it goes straight to hell!' Colonel Misic exclaimed and banged on the night-stand again. 'Just look at Serbia! When Milosevic put himself above the state, everything went to hell! The RDB doesn't have the necessary knowledge and experience, even though they have all the resources at their disposal. They use them in the wrong way, for their own gain, they abuse their power, they support crime . . .'

Slightly out of breath, he stopped talking.

Annika stared at him. The sweat gleamed on his bald pate.

'How much do you know?' she asked him in a low voice.

'I know everything.'

'Everything?'

'Everything.'

'About the Mafia too?'

The man looked at her intensely; studied her face, her hair, her hands.

'The shining knight of the freedom of expression,' he said. 'Can you handle all kinds of truth?'

Annika blinked.

'As long as I can verify them, and they're of interest to the general public.'

'Ah,' Misic said. 'And who makes that decision?'

'First I do, then my editors.'

'The censors,' the old man declared.

'Not at all,' Annika countered. 'We don't bow down to anyone, we answer only to the truth.'

'You wouldn't dare write *my* truth,' the man said. 'No one could publish what I know.'

'There's no way I can judge that without knowing what you know.'

Colonel Misic looked at Annika for a long time. Her skin started crawling – she felt naked.

'Did you bring a pen? Something to write on? Well then, write down my story. We'll see if you dare print it.'

Annika bent over, grabbed her bag and fished out a pad and a pen.

'Shoot,' she said.

'The Mafia is the state,' the old man said, 'and the state is the Mafia. Everything is controlled by Belgrade. The RDB, the secret police, is in charge of the operations. Gun-running is their largest and most important source of income. Three-quarters of the money they make comes from selling arms. They have appropriated and stock-piled all the weapons of the former Federal Republic of Yugoslavia, and they can fight on until kingdom come, or even start a war. They have a lot of dealings with the Middle East and Iraq. North Korea is very interested in chemical weapons, and Belgrade can help them out. They keep numerous conflicts going in Africa, supplying weapons to several African nations. These munitions are transported using Polish submarines out of Gdansk: shipments are loaded in Serbia and they pass through Suez, where the Customs officers are on the payroll.'

Annika stared at the Colonel; she hadn't managed to write a word.

'What do you mean?' she said. 'Is this true?'

'Cigarette smuggling is another major operation,' Misic continued, 'and, of course, liquor and drugs and prostitution. The cigarettes are manufactured in secret factories, provided with fake labels – Marlboro, for example – loaded on to sealed trucks, and then they are transported through Europe to Finland. Once they reach Sweden, the seals are broken, the shipment is unloaded and then they head for the Yugoslav Embassy for a fresh seal. Since the state is the official administrator, this is possible. Then they head back to Finland and unload a few cardboard boxes.'

Annika bowed her head.

'Wait a second,' she said, 'could you repeat the first bit? The weapons, Africa, North Korea?'

Patiently, the old man repeated the details.

'When it comes to prostitution,' he continued, 'most of the women come from the Ukraine and Belarus, and they're exported to Central European brothels, mainly in Germany, Hungary, the Czech Republic and Poland. The bulk of the drugs come from Afghanistan. The opposition, not the Taliban, is responsible for their production. The route passes through Turkey, and nowadays the ethnic Albanians of Kosovo are generally in charge of that end. Once the ethnic Albanians have the raw materials, they sell them to the Serbs. The Serbs refine the raw materials into narcotic compounds. Entire hospitals are involved in these operations and so is a sizeable sections of the agricultural industry.'

Annika swallowed. Her head was spinning and now she was writing so fast that her arm hurt. Could all this really be possible?

'Huge factories manufacture liquor that is bottled with fake labels: twelve-year-old Scotch, for example, or Finnish vodka. If these operations came to a halt, the country would collapse in a matter of days. The workers wouldn't be paid and the system would fall apart.'

Colonel Misic sighed. ·

'The RDB is able to forge all types of passports: Scandinavian, French, American. They have an efficient network throughout Europe consisting of bars, discos, Serbian Associations and chess clubs.'

He laughed mirthlessly.

'The Serbian secret service has this peculiar habit,' he said. 'They only make arrests on Wednesdays. If you manage to squeak by on a Wednesday, you're safe for a week. The clean-up patrols consist of three or five members. When they operate in foreign countries, they escape by way of the embassy or the consulate. Here in Sweden, the consulate offices in Trelleborg are very actively involved.'

Misic's voice tailed off. Annika finished up her notes and paused, her pen still resting on the page.

'How am I supposed to verify all this?' she asked.

The man got up, went into the small hall, opened the closet and started to turn the combination lock of a small safe. When he returned, he was carrying a few documents, some printed on blue paper.

'I stole these from the embassy,' he said. 'Two TIR seals. Soon they will be missed.'

He put them on the bed next to Annika. She stared at them and looked up at the colonel, feeling more and more bewildered.

'How is this possible?'

Misic sat down heavily.

'There are caches of weapons secreted throughout Sweden,' he said. 'Stockpiles of drugs, liquor, cigarettes, entire apartment buildings filled with Serbs who don't have residence permits, trailers, cars, boats . . .'

Annika swallowed.

'Do you know where they are?'

Nodding, he looked at her.

And started to talk again.

When Colonel Misic was done, Annika felt adrenalin surge through her body. This was incredible stuff!

'One thing,' she said. 'What will happen if I put my byline on this? Won't the Mafia come looking for me?'

The old man gave her a weary look.

'Worried about saving your own skin? Are you more important than the truth? Can't your nation of free citizens take care of you, protect you?'

She looked down and blushed.

'This is business, you see,' the man said. 'It's not personal. Ratko doesn't have any friends left – no one will rub you out to settle a personal score. If you shatter their framework of crime there won't be anyone left to hurt you, there would be no point in doing it.'

Annika looked up.

'What about the embassy? If what you say is true, the embassy is behind everything.'

'The Yugoslav Embassy will be your finest life insurance. It will be in their best interests that nothing happens to you. On the other hand, I wouldn't recommend a visit to the Balkan states for a while. You might run into the wrong kind of people.'

She looked down at her notes and cleared her throat.

'What will happen to Ratko?'

Misic hesitated.

'Ratko has disappeared, no one knows where to. As soon as he shows his face in Europe, he'll be a dead man. My guess is that he's gone to Africa, to one of his arms connections.'

'What will happen to *you*?'

The colonel regarded her for quite a while.

'I've done my bit,' he said eventually. 'Everyone who ever meant anything to me is dead. Aida was the last one.'

'What happened?' Annika asked in a whisper.

The old man got up again, walked over to the window and looked out over the square, now grey in the twilight.

'Ratko murdered the entire family, except for Aida. It was the prelude to the violence in Bosnia. It was in March 1992.'

Annika gasped. 'Oh my God, the whole family?'

'Jovan, his wife, his pregnant daughter-in-law and Jovan's youngest son, who was only nine years old. The older son was in the army and died at the front six months later.'

'Ratko killed them?'

Keeping his eyes fixed on the pattern of triangles on Sergelstorg, Misic continued.

'Ratko and his Panthers. For quite some time there had been considerable political tension, and there had been fighting in Croatia, but the massacre in Bijelina was the first of its kind in Bosnia.'

'And it wiped out Aida's family.'

'I don't know how she managed to survive. She never told me.'

Annika felt the tears well up again: what an unspeakable experience.

'What happened to her? How did she get to Sweden?'

The colonel stared out over the square. Snowflakes had begun to fall.

'She was seventeen at the time and, as far as I know, she walked all the way to Tuzla after the massacre. She hitched a ride to Sarajevo and joined the *Armija BiH*. Her uncle, Jovan's younger brother, lived in Sarajevo, and he accepted her into his *speciale diversansky* group.'

Breathlessly, Annika waited for the rest of the story, tears hanging on her lips.

'And?' she said.

'The *speciale diversansky* group,' Misic said, emphasizing each word carefully. 'She became a sniper. When I found out, I washed my hands of her, broke off all contact.'

Not following him, Annika blinked.

With extreme weariness the old man said: 'A sniper, she learned how to be a sniper, to lie on a rooftop and shoot people in the streets: men, women, children – it made no difference.'

Annika couldn't breathe.

'No . . . !'

Misic turned around and looked at her.

'And I can assure you,' he said, 'that she became very accomplished. Only God knows how many people Aida killed.'

He sat down across from her again.

'You didn't know?'

Annika shook her head.

'How—?' She swallowed and said, 'How did she end up here? In Stockholm?'

The colonel rubbed his eyes.

'She was injured, and she was carried out through the tunnel in Sarajevo and taken up Mount Igman. There she arranged to accompany a group of women and children that the Red Cross had rounded up. They encountered problems leaving Bosnia. At some point the transport was stopped and some of the younger women were dragged from the bus by drunken soldiers, barbarians. We don't know what happened, but after the bus had moved on, two soldiers were found dead in their guard posts, shot in the mouth with their own guns. It could only have been Aida.'

Misic hung his head. Annika felt nauseated.

'Why did she want to go to Sweden?' she asked in a whisper.

'She had heard that Ratko was here. She had sworn to get revenge. It was the only thing that mattered to her. He had taken her family, her life. I didn't hear from her for years. It is a cause of constant pain to me. I was wrong. I should have kept in touch. You cannot make it alone. Aida would have needed me.'

Suddenly, the chain around Annika neck felt red-hot and heavy, a display of gratitude from a murderer.

'This is what she wrote,' the man said in a muffled voice, 'on 3 November this year. Her mission was nearly complete, she wrote. She had contacted Ratko and arranged a meeting; one of them would die.'

'She contacted Ratko?' Annika asked. 'Are you certain that she contacted Ratko? That she took the initiative? That no one betrayed her?'

The colonel bowed his head.

'She wanted to have a showdown with Ratko,' he said softly. 'She asked me to finish the job if she failed. I have survived every purge: Milosevic still has confidence in me so I had the power to destroy Ratko's life.'

His shoulders shook again and he covered his eyes with his hands.

'Go now,' he commanded.

Annika swallowed again. 'But . . .'

'Go.'

She bent down and put away her pad and her pen. After a moment's hesitation she stuffed the TIR seals from the Yugoslav Embassy into her bag as well.

'Thank you, for everything,' she whispered.

Misic didn't reply.

Annika left him, headed for the hall in silence, opened the door and stepped out into the hotel corridor.

The elderly officer remained seated on the bed while darkness fell. His shoulders ached, his back, his hands. His feet went cold and numb. *The young journalist took the seals with her. Good.* They would never be able to prove that Misic had stolen them, even if they guessed that it was his doing.

He decided to take a bath. Went into the bathroom, turned on the light, put in the plug and turned on the water, very hot water. While the tub was filling, he sat on the toilet seat, letting the chill of the tiled floor work its way into his legs. He welcomed the pain. When the water ran over the side of the bath and reached his toes, he turned off the taps. He went into the bedroom, into the dark, undressed and placed his carefully folded clothes on a chair.

Then the colonel sank down into the hot water up to his neck, closed his eyes for a long time, and let his body dissolve.

When the water had cooled, he got up, dried himself carefully, shaved, combed his hair, and got out his dress uniform with all its decorations and the medals for services beyond the call of duty. He put on his clothes slowly and painstakingly, smoothing his hands over the lapels of his uniform and adjusting his cap. Then he went over to the safe and got out his service pistol.

He saw his reflection in the window. His hotel room floated on top of the cement triangles of Sergelstorg. A calm, determined gaze met his. He shifted the blurred focus of his vision to the plaza down below, fixing his stare on the site where Aida had died.

We'll be together, Colonel Misic thought. Then he placed the gun in his mouth and pulled the trigger.

Eleonor swiped at her forehead with the back of her hand.

'The roast is done,' she said. 'How are the potatoes au gratin doing?'

Thomas opened the oven door and tested the centre of the dish.

'They need a little more time.'

'Should we cover the dish with foil so the potatoes don't get burnt?'

'I think they'll be okay,' Thomas said.

Eleonor rinsed her hands under the kitchen tap, wiped them on her apron, and exhaled slowly.

'Are my cheeks all flushed from cooking?' she asked with a smile.

He swallowed and smiled back.

'It makes you look sweet,' he said.

She untied her apron, hung it on its peg and went to the bedroom to switch into a different pair of shoes. Thomas went into the dining room with the salad bowl and placed it on the table set with crystal, English bone china and fine silverware. He quickly assessed the table: the cold antipasto for starters, the napkins, the mineral water, the salad – apart from the wine, everything was in place.

He sighed; he was tired and would rather have spent the evening watching TV and thinking about his assignment. All afternoon he had gone through the statements made by people on welfare: how always living on the brink wore them down, how uncomfortable it was to have to justify why your kid needed new sneakers, how the social workers always seemed rushed and how claimants were left feeling humiliated and on the receiving end of charity. How they had to choose between having their teeth fixed or buying the prescription medicine they needed. Never being able to afford to put meat on the table. Their children's pleas for skates or a bicycle.

The despair these people felt had burrowed into his consciousness. It wouldn't let go, remaining as ever-present as a wound.

If I had the power to change things . . . he thought, closing his eyes, just breathing for a while.

Then he heard car doors closing in the drive and waited for the crunching and creaking of feet on gravel and ice.

'Here they come,' he called to the bedroom.

The doorbell chimed its cheerful melody. Thomas dried his hands and went into the hall to open the door.

'Welcome, please come in, may I take your fur . . .?'

Nisse from the local bank, the managers of the bank offices in Täby and Djursholm, and the regional manager from Stockholm: three men, one woman.

Eleonor, cool, smiling and beautiful, walked towards them as he was serving the drinks.

'How nice to see you,' she exclaimed. 'Welcome.'

'We have a great deal to celebrate,' the regional manager said. 'What a lovely house you have.'

He kissed her soundly on both cheeks. Thomas noticed that Eleonor blushed and he felt irritated.

'How nice of you to say so. We certainly like it here.'

She glanced at Thomas and he managed a forced smile.

They sipped their drinks and Eleonor said: 'How about a grand tour of the house?'

Enthusiastically they trooped off, leaving Thomas on his own in the living room. The bell-like tones of his wife's voice reached him.

'We've been thinking of remodelling the kitchen,' she chirped, 'and putting in a gas range, since we're so fond of cooking, and you can't beat an open flame . . . We're going to install heated floors: marble, preferably green, it's such a relaxing colour . . . And this is our den, we've been thinking about putting in a wine cellar, we really should take better care of our collection . . .'

Thomas put down his drink and saw that his hand was shaking. *What damn wine collection would that be?* Eleonor's parents had a nice wine cellar out in the country, filled with high-quality vintages, but he and Eleonor hadn't started collecting anything, they hadn't had the time.

Suddenly he felt panic creeping up on him and went cold.

No, he begged, *not now, let me keep it together for the evening, this is so important to Eleonor.*

Thomas went into the kitchen, uncorked a bottle of red wine to allow it to breathe and popped open a bottle of sparkling wine. He filled the champagne flutes.

'What a lovely home!' the regional manager said as they came upstairs again. 'Split-level houses are so nice.'

Thomas tried to smile without quite pulling it off.

'Shall we have dinner?' he said.

Eleonor smiled nervously.

'A simple meal,' she said. 'Thomas and I are both so

very busy – Thomas is the financial manager for the city of Vaxholm.'

'I work for Social Services.'

Eleonor went into the dining room and pointed out her seating arrangement.

'Nisse, you're over there; Leopold, you're next to me; Gunvor . . .'

The guests appreciated the food and the wine and the atmosphere quickly became animated. Thomas heard portions of different conversations about profits, results, and markets. He tried to eat, but the food wouldn't go down. He felt limp and dizzy. The regional manager called everyone to attention by tapping his glass.

'I would like to propose a toast to Eleonor,' he said solemnly, 'our lovely hostess, in honour of her fantastic achievements this year. I want you to know, Eleonor, that management has taken note of your achievements, your drive and your enthusiasm. Cheers!'

Thomas looked at his wife. The praise had left Eleonor's cheeks pink.

'And to top it off, I plan to reveal just how our management intends to express their gratitude.'

The four bank managers sat up straighter. Thomas realized that this was the high point of the evening – it was time to throw the doggies their bones.

'You represent the branch offices with the top results in the province of Svealand,' the regional manager said. 'The capital returns are up this year as well and our polls show that both our private and our corporate customers are very pleased.'

He paused for effect. 'I am also at liberty to inform you that the evaluation of the office managers by their staff has been concluded, and that you have done excellently in that respect as well. Therefore, it gives me great pleasure,' he said with satisfaction, 'to inform you that the bank has decided to raise your bonuses and your share in the profits.'

Eleonor gasped, her eyes shining with rapture.

'And,' the regional manager said, leaning over the table, 'you will have the opportunity to join the management option programme next year!'

At this point, the four bank managers could no longer remain silent; squeals of joy escaped their lips.

'In addition to all this,' the regional manager said, 'the bank will provide you with a very advantageous package of health-care benefits. This will allow you, and your spouse, to bypass any waiting lists within the public health-care system.'

Wildly exhilarated, Eleonor looked at Thomas.

'Did you hear that, darling? Isn't it fantastic?'

Then she turned to the regional manager again.

'Oh, Leopold, how are we ever going to live up to an acknowledgement like this? What a responsibility.'

The regional manager got to his feet.

'To a successful collaboration!'

The others chimed in: 'A successful collaboration!'

Suddenly, Thomas felt like throwing up. He ran out of the dining room, down the hallway and into the bathroom, then locked the door and flung himself over the toilet bowl, breathing heavily. Sweat was pouring down his forehead and he thought he might pass out.

Concerned, Eleonor knocked on the door.

'Are you all right, honey? What's wrong?'

He couldn't reply; all he wanted to do was cry.

'Thomas!'

'I feel sick,' he said. 'Go back in, I'll go lie down.'

'But I wanted you to make coffee.'

Thomas closed his eyes, his throat burning with suppressed acid.

'I can't,' he whispered. 'I can't go on.'

Annika woke up at three minutes to six, thirsty and starving. Outside her window, the winter night was still impenetrable, black and cold. She lay on her side and looked at the illuminated face of the alarm clock: it would go off in eighteen minutes.

She was expected at the hospital at seven o'clock. Due to the anaesthesia, she wasn't supposed to eat or drink. A suppository would be inserted into her vagina to open her cervix so that they could extract the contents of her womb.

A boy, she thought. *With fair hair, just like his daddy.*

Annika rolled over on her back and looked up at the ceiling, unable to detect any patterns in the dark.

There's no hurry. I'll make it.

She closed her eyes and listened to the newborn day as it began to draw breath. At six a.m. the fan at the back of the building started up, the brakes on the 48 bus squealed, and she heard the theme song of the radio news programme *Morgonekot* waft up through the walls from a neighbour's flat down below. Familiar sounds, comforting and friendly. She stretched, raising her arms, then put them behind her head and stared out into the darkness.

The image of the elderly Serbian officer flashed before her eyes: so burdened, bitter and alone. He had no faith in mankind, only in the state – he chose that outlook. *You always have a choice.*

Aida had been a sniper, a killer: she had chosen to become one. *Circumstances shape us, but the choice remains our own.*

Annika suddenly felt oppressed by the heavy gold chain around her neck and sat up, found the clasp, undid it and placed the necklace on the night-stand in front of the alarm clock. Green flashes from the illuminated hands of the clock glinted on the yellow metal surface.

She didn't want a murderer's gratitude.

She switched off the bell of the alarm clock, flung the covers to one side, put on her robe and her boots, grabbed the bag containing her toiletries and raced downstairs to the bathroom on the other side of the courtyard. She washed her hair and brushed her teeth, taking care to not ingest any water before the procedure.

As she walked upstairs again she considered getting a subscription to a morning paper: it might be nice to read one every day at breakfast time. A glance in the fridge revealed juice, yogurt, eggs, bacon, fresh garlic cheese, Parma-style Italian ham – she had shopped at the crummy ICA store the night before. She stared at the contents of her fridge, keeping one hand on the door handle while the other drifted down to rest on her stomach.

The choice is always our own.

Annika drew a surprised breath. It was as simple as that. Laughed. It wasn't difficult at all.

She took out the carton of juice and poured herself a

big glass, turned on the burner and put the frying pan on it.

Drank. Drank.

Broke eggs and dropped them in the pan and topped them with snipped pieces of bacon. She toasted some bread and spread it with garlic cheese. While she stirred the omelette, she munched away.

Ate. Ate.

The food landed in her stomach, followed by hot coffee, its warmth radiating inside her, the caffeine kicking in. She lit the candle on the table – Gran's wedding present, the brass candlestick from Lyckebo – and the flame danced and flickered. She smiled at the woman reflected in the window, the woman in the robe with wet hair, the candlelit woman who was going to have a child.

She went into her bedroom, turned on the overhead lamp and saw the gold glinting there on her night-stand. Got dressed, picked up the chain and weighed it in her hand.

It was heavy. Damn heavy.

For the first time in over a month Annika went into the tiny room behind the kitchen, the maid's room, almost bare apart from a table in a corner and a chair with a broken backrest. She never used the room that she still thought of as Patricia's.

Here, she thought. You could sit here and write.

She looked at her watch; it was almost seven. The goldsmith on the other side of the street opened at seven. Once, by mistake, she had gone in there to look for a pair of earrings for Anne Snapphane's birthday. A large, bald man in a heavy leather apron brandishing a pair of tongs in one hand had materialized in front of her. He had towered over her, causing her to ask with a gulp if she had come to the right place. She had, the smith really did sell gold earrings, and she had somehow ended up buying a pair of fussy-looking drop ones.

Annika blew out the candle, towel-dried her hair, pulled on a cap, put on her jacket and her shoes and went downstairs.

It had snowed during the night and a soft white blanket still covered the sidewalks. Her feet left a trail from the door of her building, across the street and over to the man's shop.

It was open. The goldsmith was wearing the same apron and the same happy expression.

'You're up early,' he said cheerfully. 'Christmas shopping?'

She smiled, shook her head and handed him Aida's necklace.

'That's one hell of a cable you've got there,' the goldsmith said, weighing the chain in his hands.

Annika saw the metal glint in his huge hands. He could probably turn the murderer's gratitude into something beautiful.

'It it real gold?' she asked.

The man scraped the surface by the clasp, then turned around and fiddled with something.

'At least eighteen-carat gold,' he said. 'Want to unload it?'

Annika nodded and the smith placed the necklace on a scale.

'That was one heavy mother,' he remarked. 'One hundred and ninety grams – a gram is worth forty-eight kronor.'

He turned on a calculator.

'Nine thousand, one hundred and twenty kronor – that all right with you?'

Another nod. The goldsmith went into the next room and came back with the money and a receipt.

'Here you go,' he said. 'Don't spend it all in one place.'
Annika smiled a little.
'Actually, that's exactly what I had in mind.'

The computer guys around the corner didn't officially open until nine, but Annika saw that one of them was there already, hammering away at a keyboard in a room behind the shop. She knocked on the window, the guy looked up, she smiled and waved and he went through the shop and unlocked the door.

'I know I'm early,' Annika said, 'but I'd like to buy a computer.'

He opened the door and laughed.

'And you can't wait until we open?'

She smiled.

'Do you have anything for nine thousand, one hundred and twenty kronor?'

'Mac or PC?'

'Doesn't matter,' she said, 'as long as it doesn't crash all the time.'

The guy looked around the untidy store. According to the sign in the window they sold computers, used ones and new ones, did repair work, programming, supplied service and support and constructed websites. Annika passed the place eight times a day or so, and as far as she could tell they mainly seemed to spend their time playing computer games.

'This one,' the guy said, lifting a big grey box up on a table. 'It's used, but the processor is new and it's got a lot of memory capacity. What do you need it for?'

'Writing,' Annika said. 'And to surf the Internet a little.'

The guy patted the box.

'Then this one's perfect. Everything's on it already, all the programs you need – Word, Excel, Explorer . . .'

'I'll take it,' she said, interrupting him. 'Along with a monitor and stuff like that.'

The computer guy hesitated.

'You mean you want the works for nine thousand kronor?'

'Nine thousand, one hundred and twenty. After all, the hard drive is used.'

He sighed.

'Okay, but only because it's so God-awful early in the morning.'

The guy left her standing in the store, went into the back room and brought out a small computer monitor.

'It's not very big, but it's a certified screen,' he said. 'It doesn't emit a lot of radiation – you've got to be careful with that kind of thing. Old screens make you dizzy, they fry your brains. Anything else? Disks and stuff?'

'All I have is nine thousand, one hundred and twenty kronor.'

He sighed again and produced a paper bag that he stuffed with a pair of speakers, a mouse, a mouse pad, a few packs of disks, cables and a keyboard.

'And a printer,' Annika said.

'Have a heart,' the guy exclaimed. 'For nine thousand, one hundred and twenty kronor?'

'I'll take a used one,' Annika said.

He went back to the storeroom again and brought out a big box with the words *Hewlett Packard* on it.

'Now I've given that hard drive away,' he said. 'Any more freebies while you're at it?'

She laughed. 'No, this will be fine, but how do I get this stuff home?'

'Now that's where I draw the line,' the guy said. 'You'll have to carry it home yourself. I know you live in the neighbourhood, I've seen you around.'

Annika's cheeks got hot.

'You have?'

He flashed her a slightly embarrassed smile. He was kind of cute, and had dark curly hair.

'You pass by the shop all the time,' he said. 'And you're always in a hurry. You must lead an interesting life.'

She took a deep breath.

'You know,' she said, 'you're right in that department. But I'm not all that strong. I'll be needing a hand.'

He groaned and rolled his eyes, got a better grip on the printer and headed for the door.

'I hope you live nearby,' he said.

'It's a top-floor flat, and there's no elevator,' Annika informed him , smiling.

The sky was beginning to get light by the time Annika could sit down at the table in the tiny maid's room, her notepad next to her. Looking out over the courtyard she saw the Christmas decorations, the straw stars, sway.

This is a great room, she thought. *Why haven't I used it before?*

She ran through the entire story, over and over again, writing, deleting, making changes. So absorbed by her task that time and space no longer mattered; the words flowing, the letters dancing.

All of a sudden she became aware that she was hungry again and ran down to pick up a pizza at the joint around the corner and ate it while she sat at the computer.

By the time the printout was done – an ink-jet printer, excruciatingly slow – it was dusk. Annika stuffed the papers in a plastic pocket, saved the document on a disk and went over to the police station.

'You can't just barge in here whenever you feel like it,' Q said in an annoyed voice when he came down to the front desk. 'What do you want?'

'I've written an article and I'd like to hear what you think of it.'

He moaned.

'And I guess this can't wait, as usual?'

'Right.'

'Let's go to the cafeteria.'

They went to the coffee shop around the corner and ordered coffee and sandwiches. Annika pulled out the plastic folder.

'I don't know if this will be published,' she said. 'I'll be going to the office after I've seen you and I'll give them the material then.'

The detective gave her a searching look and took the printout.

He read it silently, leafing through the pages and rereading certain passages.

'This,' he said, 'is a complete description of the operations conducted by the Yugoslav Mafia, in Sweden and all over the world. Every last stockpile, vehicle, headquarters, contact, procedure . . .'

She nodded and he stared at her.

'You are fucking incredible,' he said. 'Where the hell did you get this information?'

'I have two TIR seals in my purse,' she said.

He quickly leaned back in his chair, letting an arm hang down over the backrest.

'I get it,' he said. 'You have this talent for killing people.'

Annika froze, her chest hurting as if she'd been stabbed.

'What are you talking about?'

For several seconds Q stared at her, contemplating the report on his desk about last night's suicide at the Plaza, the Yugoslav colonel with a diplomatic passport.

'Nothing,' he said, leaning forward and taking a sip of his coffee. 'Nothing. It was a stupid thing to say. Sorry.'

'What do you think?' she asked. 'Is it on the level?'

He considered this for quite some time.

'I'll have to check everything out before I can make a statement of any kind. Like this pizzeria in Göteborg might not have any ties to the Yugoslav Mafia.'

A silent sigh escaped Annika.

'When can you check it out?' she asked him softly.

'Hopefully,' he said, 'before you go public with this. Afterwards won't be much use.'

'I need confirmation before I can go to press,' she said. 'I only have one source.'

He looked at her for quite a while.

'And if I don't want to?'

'All I want is for you to check around and see if there's anything to this.'

'I'd have to check out the prisons to be able to find anything,' he said. 'And as soon as I knock on the first door, the alarm will go off. Then it will be too late.'

Annika nodded.

'All right,' she said. 'That had occurred to me. Let's keep it like this: I have detailed information about the Mafia's haunts, the whereabouts of their headquarters and stockpiles, but since I can't get them verified, I can't go public with them. This means I can deal with them in general terms only. The addresses aren't the most important aspect. Once you check things out, we'll know the answer, won't we?'

Q hesitated, then nodded.

She gave him a nervous smile.

'Am I correct in supposing that the police will be conducting a coordinated early-morning sweep sometime soon? Possibly on the day the first article will be printed?'

'And when will that be?'

'I can't tell you the exact date, but the country editions start rolling right after six o'clock.'

'Prior to that, how many people will have seen the articles?'

She thought for a minute.

'Less than twenty people: the night team and the typesetters in the printing department.'

'So there's no risk of any leaks? Okay, then I can say that the check we're talking about will take place during one of the next few days at six a.m.'

Annika packed up her things.

'Then I can tell you that we will have quite a few photographers in the field that morning, around the time we get ready to go to press.'

Q pushed away his coffee cup and got up.

'We do our job,' he said, 'for the citizens of this nation. Not for anyone else.'

Annika put on her jacket and got up.

'So do we,' she said.

Anders Schyman turned the pages of that day's paper and gazed at the picture on the front page. Anneli from Motala and her retarded son Alexander, let down by the local authorities, desperate and vulnerable. Carl Wennergren's inventory of the transgressions committed by Social Services and the lame excuses made by the local government representatives.

Life is the pits for some people, Schyman thought. He longed for some Scotch. Longed for his wife, their dog, the easy chair at his house in Saltsjöbaden. It had been a tough week. Torstensson's sudden reinstatement as the editor-in-chief had aggravated him more than he cared to admit. Torstensson had to go. There were no other alternatives if the paper was to survive.

Schyman scratched his head and sighed. As far as he could tell, they had three years to turn the sales figures around, and that was it. If this paper was going to make the transition to new technology and new methods, he would have to lead the way. He was going to fight for this and he needed some Scotch. A large Scotch. Right this minute.

There was a knock on the door. *Damn it.* He couldn't take any more – what the hell could this be?

Annika Bengtzon put her head round the door.

'Could you spare a moment?'

He closed his eyes.

'I'm about to leave. What is it?'

Annika closed the door behind her, stood in front of his desk, dropped her bag on the floor and let her jacket follow.

'I've written an article,' she announced.

Well, hallelujah, Schyman thought.

'And?' he said.

'I think you'd better read it. You could say it's controversial stuff.'

'I see,' he murmured and took the disk that she was holding.

He swivelled his chair, inserted the disk, and waited until the file popped up as an icon on his desktop. A double click – he would polish this off in no time.

His heart sank.

'There are three articles here,' he said.

'Start with number one,' Annika said, sitting down on one of the uncomfortable chairs that he kept for visitors.

It was a long piece, a complete description of the Yugoslav Mafia in Belgrade, their sphere of operations, the responsibilities of the different groups.

The second piece was an inventory of how the Yugo Mafia operated in Sweden, detailing the addresses of bases for rings that smuggled drugs, cigarettes and illegal liquor, and then there was illegal immigration and prostitution as well . . .

The third piece was similar, only it omitted the addresses.

'Aren't you on sick leave?' Schyman asked.

'I happened to come across a good story,' she said.

He read the articles again and sighed.

'We can't publish this,' he said.

'What part?' Annika asked.

Another sigh.

'This bit about the TIR seals,' he said. 'Claiming that the embassy has access to something like that – it's absurd, how on earth are we going to verify it?'

She bent down, rummaged through her bag and set down a stack of documents on his desk.

'Two TIR seals,' she said. 'Stolen from the Yugoslav Embassy.'

He felt his jaw drop as she continued to dig in her bag.

'When it comes to the Swedish end of their operations,' she said, 'I know that the police are in the process of arranging a massive coordinated sweep of all these different addresses throughout the country. It will take place one day soon at six a.m.'

'How do you know that?' Schyman asked.

Annika looked him in the eye.

'Because I handed a copy of the list over to the police,' she said. 'We'll have to coordinate our publication with their sweep.'

He shook his head.

'What are you doing? What have you got involved in?'

'A dependable source gave me the information, but it's only one person. I know we can't run the articles verbatim right now, because I need to verify the facts beforehand. Only the police can give me the confirmation I need, so in order to get it I had to go to them, right?'

Schyman shook his head in disbelief again.

'On day one we can run articles one and three,' she

said, 'the general description of the Mafia set-up abroad and the one about Sweden that doesn't go into detail. While we go to press that day, we will cover the police clean-up. That will give us our stuff for day two: 'Hot on the heels of the *Kvällspressen* exposé, blah, blah, blah' – you know the drill. Day three is for reactions and comments, both from Serbia and here at home. The official embassy response will be to welcome the purge. Any suggestion of embassy involvement in criminal activities will be dismissed as malicious propaganda. They'll claim that the seals are forgeries.'

Schyman stared at her.

'How on Earth did you hatch all that?'

The young woman shrugged.

'It's your call. I wrote this on my own time and I don't expect to be paid for these articles. The police will do their clean-up whether we have our photographers there or not. You decide if the paper is going to be where the action is or not. I'm on sick leave.'

Annika got up.

'You know where to find me,' she said.

'Wait,' he said.

'No,' she responded. 'I'm sick of being palmed off with hints of things to come. I don't want to waste my time on the night shift any longer. I bought myself a computer and I can work at home, freelance, if I don't have what it takes to be a reporter at this paper. You're the deputy editor, for God's sake – you should be able to take a stand.'

She closed the door behind her as she left.

Schyman watched her go, saw her pass through the newsroom without talking to anyone, not even to say hello. She was an oddball, a loner, and she meant business. She had what it took to be a reporter, but the paper had a recruitment freeze. Still, it would be stupid to let her go. To top it off, compared to the other reporters her salary was peanuts.

He picked up the phone and dialled the direct line of the front desk. Since this obviously was his lucky day, Tore Brand was on duty.

'Annika Bengtzon is on her way down,' he said. 'Could you catch her for me?'

'Do I look like a fisherman?' Brand grumbled.

'It's important,' Schyman emphasized.

'You're all so damn important upstairs, aren't you . . .'

Schyman sat there, the phone in his hand and his mind reeling. The Yugo story was up in the air, but it was damn good stuff. The police tie-in was controversial, but it was the quickest and most reliable way to verify the facts. The approach would certainly be challenged, but that was no problem. He relished the thought of going to *Publicist-klubben*, the National Press Club of Sweden, to defend the paper and the freedom of the press. It was time to take his place in the public eye.

Sink or swim, it's time to test the waters, Anders Schyman decided.

'Bengtzon, you're wanted on the phone.'

There was a lot of scraping and rustling as Tore Brand handed the phone to Annika Bengtzon through the front-desk window.

'What is it?' Annika said.

'As of 1 January, you will be a reporter,' Anders Schyman said. 'You can choose your beat, the one p.m. report, night coverage, crime, or whatever.'

Apart from the mutterings of Tore Brand the line was silent.

'Hello?' Schyman said.

'Crime,' Annika said. 'I want to work the crime beat.'

THEY HAVE CONFRONTED ME.

*T*hey've caught up with me. Together, they dictate the charges, the verdict against me, my punishment.

Violence, guilt and shame. My comrades-in-arms, my driving forces, my guiding lights.

Welcome!

Violence, you were the first, you shaped my destiny, I took you to heart and made you my own.

That spring day it had rained all morning, it was grey and wet. It cleared up in the afternoon, a show of feeble sunshine.

I ran to the square to do some shopping, the vegetables were sorry-looking, I took my time.

I saw the men in between the houses: black outfits, black berets.

I didn't know that you had arrived. Didn't recognize the face of violence.

I was standing outside Stoyilikovic's café when the man, Ratko, dragged my father from his bakery. I saw him point his gun at my father's temple and pull the trigger. I saw Papi collapse on the street, I heard my mother's screams. Another man in black shot my mother in the chest. My sister-in-law, my *brother's wife Miriam, was only a year older than me: they shot her in the stomach, repeatedly. She was pregnant.*

Then they brought out my brother Petar, my baby brother, my sunshine, only nine years old. He screamed, oh, how he screamed, and he caught sight of me over by Stoyilikovic's café and broke loose. He ran, screaming: 'Aida, Aida, help me, Aida!' His outstretched arms, his boundless terror.

And I hid.

I curled up behind the fence by Stoyilikovic's café, and saw through the chinks how Ratko raised his gun. I saw him take aim and fire.

My Petar, my baby brother, how will I ever be absolved?

You were lying there in the mud, calling out my name: 'Aida, Aida, help me, dear Aida!' And I didn't dare go to you, I didn't have the guts, I cried behind the fence there by Stoyilikovic's café and saw Ratko approach you, saw you turn your face towards him, saw the man take aim and fire.

Forgive me, Petar, forgive me.

You should never have had to die alone.

Forgive me for failing you: welcome, guilt; welcome, shame. It was your turn to take over.

And I used violence to keep you at bay.

I cured my guilt with death, the right kind of death, the death of Serbs. It didn't help. Each death gave birth to even more guilt, more hatred, brought shame to others who had failed their loved ones.

My shame was eternal, it lived in my every breath, pervading every moment of my life, because my shame was due to my being alive.

Then I heard that Ratko, the leader of the Panthers, was in Sweden. When I was wounded, the time had come.

I had to be strong to wield violence against its very source, the man who had planted its seeds in my heart. I infiltrated his circle, slept with his men, slept with him, but death was not enough, he would have to experience guilt and shame too, as I brought about the downfall of his operations, crushed his life.

I feel sorry for the young men from Kosovo, the poor fools I tricked into joining me. All they were supposed to do was drive off with the trailer and I would take care of everything else, and then they went and stole the wrong vehicle. The trailer loaded with cigarettes is still parked at the free port in Stockholm — now, isn't that ironic?

But violence failed me, it wouldn't comply.

It all started with the storm, so punishing, whipping at buildings and people alike.

I had to be so very careful, climbing the roof and opening my bag.

The stock and the action were one section. The other section contained the barrel, the telescopic sight, the muzzle bell and the rifle bolt. I screwed the barrel on to the stock. Attached the base plate and a chin rest for the scope. Then I screwed on the muzzle bell. At this close range, a stand wouldn't be necessary.

I steadied myself by holding on to the ridge of the roof and angled the rifle, a Remington Sniper with a carbon-fibre stock.

They came into sight: there were three of them, standing out black against the golden light, Ratko trailing slightly behind the others as they struggled against the ocean winds. I picked off the first one with a clean shot to the head, the entry wound high on one side. A second later and the next one fell. Another second and Ratko had disappeared, swallowed up by the storm.

I slithered down the rooftop, my rifle stuffed in my bag, and hurried to avoid getting trapped.

But violence failed me. I had to run. Illness drained me.

When I had bided my time long enough to get on my feet again, I contacted him. Made a date.

Knowing he would come.

But violence failed me.

The square was full of people. The location I'd singled out on the roof of the culture centre was useless.

I had to get him on the ground.

When he shoved the muzzle against my neck, I knew I had won, no matter what happened.

'Game over,' he whispered. 'You lose.'

He was wrong. He hissed something else, something pathetic.

'Bijelina,' he whispered, 'do you remember Bijelina?'

I broke free and whipped out my gun but a baby buggy got in the way and I dropped my gun when he hit me. It skittered out of reach on the pavement. I saw my chance evaporate, felt the hard cold metal at the base of my neck.

Spelling out my verdict, the wages of violence, guilt and shame.

'You won't win,' I whispered. 'I've destroyed your life.'

Out of the corner of my eye, I could see him.

And I smiled.

Indictment, judgement, punishment.

Absolution.

EPILOGUE

Once more, snow had begun to fall, soft fluffy flakes that drifted slowly down onto the asphalt below. Annika walked towards Rålambhovsvägen, calm and heavy; she had been eating all day long. Her lower back hurt and she felt slightly nauseated – it was the baby's doing: her son, the fair-haired boy. She went to the taxi stand by the hot-dog place, got in the back seat and told the driver to take her to Vaxholm.

'We'll be headed for gridlock,' he said.

'It doesn't matter,' Annika said. 'I have all the time in the world.'

It took them forty minutes to get out of town. Annika sat in the warm back seat; the radio was on low, playing old Madonna hits, the storefronts with their Christmas shopping displays slipped past, excited children pointed enthusiastically at mechanical figures of Santa Claus and his elves and plastic toys. She tried to look up at the sky, but it was obscured by the falling snow and the strings of coloured lights.

I wonder if they celebrate something like Christmas on other planets.

Once they reached the highway, traffic thinned out. Route 274 to the coast was practically empty. The fields were white, lighting up the dark afternoon, and the trees were wrapped in heavy skirts of snow that weighed their branches down.

'Where can I drop you?'

'Östra Ekuddsgatan,' she said. 'Could you drive past it first? I want to see if there's anyone home.'

Annika showed the driver where to turn off. When the cab turned right and started climbing uphill, her nerves started to act up. Her mouth went dry, her palms went damp and her heart started pounding. She craned her neck to see where she was: which house was it?

That one. She saw it. White brick – his green Toyota was parked out front. The lights were on, so someone was home.

'Like me to pull up here?' the driver asked.

'No!' she exclaimed. 'Keep driving!'

She flung herself back in the seat and looked away when they passed the house, trying to make herself invisible.

The street came to an end. They were back on the main thoroughfare again.

'So,' the driver said. 'Are we heading back to Stockholm, or what?'

Annika closed her eyes, holding her tightly clenched fists over her mouth. Her pulse was roaring and she was completely out of breath.

'No,' she said. 'Drive past the house again.'

The taxi driver sighed and glanced at the metre. Well, it wasn't his money.

They drove past the house again. Annika studied it closely – it was ugly. Sure, the garden went down to the waterfront, but the house was boxy, so 1960s.

'Pull over at the next corner,' she said. The ride had been expensive and she paid with a credit card. She remained at the side of the road while the cab disappeared into the darkness as the snow fell; the brake lights lit up and the indicators flashed, showing that the driver was heading back to Stockholm. Annika took a deep breath to get her breathing and her heart rate under control, to no avail. She jammed her hands, slick with nervous sweat, deep into her pockets. Headed for the house, slowly. The residence of Thomas and his wife, Östra Ekuddsgatan, in the fancy part of town.

The front door was brown and well oiled, bordered on both sides with coloured stained-glass panels. A buzzer with a name on it: Samuelsson.

Hardly able to breathe, Annika closed her eyes, suddenly on the verge of tears.

A silly melody chimed inside the house.

Nothing happened.

She pressed the buzzer again: tinkle, tinkle.

Thomas came to the door; his hair was a mess, his shirt unbuttoned, no shoes, only socks and there was a pen in his mouth.

She forced air down into her lungs. The tears were threatening to spill over.

'Hi,' she whispered.

Thomas stared at her; he had gone all pale and he took the pen out of his mouth.

'I'm not a ghost,' she said, the tears falling now.

He stepped back and held the door open.

'Come in,' he said.

She went inside and realized how cold she was.

He closed the door and cleared his throat.

'What's the matter?' he asked softly. 'What's happened?'

'I'm sorry,' she said in a throaty voice. 'I'm sorry, I didn't intend to start bawling.'

She shot him a quick glance. *Damn it* – she was so ugly when she cried.

'Do you need help?' Thomas said.

Annika swallowed.

'Is she . . . here?'

'Eleonor? No, she's still at the bank.'

Annika took off her jacket and kicked off her shoes. Thomas disappeared off to the right, so she stood in the hall and checked out the surroundings. Furniture from an upscale store, R.O.O.M., some heirlooms, ugly paintings. A staircase leading downstairs.

'May I come in?'

She didn't wait for an answer, just followed him into the kitchen. Thomas was at the counter, pouring coffee.

'Would you like some?' he asked.

She nodded and sat down.

'Why aren't you at work?'

He set down two mugs on the kitchen table.

'I'm working,' he said. 'Only today I've been working at home. I'm conducting an investigation for the Association of Local Authorities, so I'll be doing some of it at home and some in town.'

Annika hid her hands under the table and tried to make them stop shaking.

'Is there something wrong?' Thomas asked, sitting down and looking at her.

She gazed into his eyes and took a few breaths, not knowing what reaction to expect from him – she didn't have a clue.

'I'm pregnant,' she said.

He blinked, but otherwise his expression was unchanged.

'What?'

She cleared her throat and clenched her fists under the table, still maintaining eye contact.

'You're the father. There's no doubt about it. I haven't been with anyone since . . . Sven died.'

She looked down at the table top, felt him look at her.

'You're pregnant?' he said. 'And the baby is mine?'

Annika nodded, the tears stinging in her eyes again.

'I want to keep the baby,' she said.

At that very moment the front door opened, and she felt Thomas freeze while her heart started racing.

'Hello? Honey?'

Everyday sounds came from the hall as Eleonor wiped her feet, brushed her coat off and closed the front door behind her.

'Thomas?'

Annika looked at Thomas. He looked back, speechless, his face drained of all colour.

'I'm in the kitchen,' he said, and got up and went into the hall.

'What awful weather,' Eleonor said. Annika could hear her kiss her husband on the cheek. 'Have you started making dinner yet?'

He murmured some kind of reply and, feeling unable to move, Annika stared out the window. Reflected in the window, she could see Eleonor enter the kitchen and stop short.

'This is Annika Bengtzon,' Thomas said, his voice unsteady, 'the journalist who wrote those articles about the Paradise Foundation.'

Annika drew a deep breath and looked at Eleonor.

Thomas's wife, wearing a moss-green suit without lapels, and a thin gold chain around her neck.

'What a pleasure,' his wife said as she smiled and extended her hand. 'Did you know that your article gave Thomas's career quite a boost?'

Annika shook Eleonor's hand. Her own hand was cold and damp and her mouth was as dry as dust.

'Thomas and I are going to have a baby,' she said.

The other woman continued to smile for several seconds. Thomas blanched where he was standing, behind his wife's back, before flinching and covering his face with his hands.

'What?' Eleonor said, still smiling.

Annika let go of the woman's hand and looked down at the table.

'I'm pregnant. We're going to have a baby.'

Eleonor stopped smiling and turned to face Thomas.

'Is this some kind of joke?' she said.

Thomas didn't reply. He raked back his hair and closed his eyes.

'The baby's due at the end of July,' Annika said. 'I think it's a boy.'

Eleonor whirled back around and stared at Annika. The colour left her face, her eyes narrowed and the whites acquired a reddish tinge.

'What have you done?' Eleonor hissed. Annika got up and backed away, Eleonor spun around to face Thomas again.

'What have you done? Did you sleep with that piece of trash?'

Thomas's wife walked up to him. He didn't back away, but his gaze was fixed on the floor.

'Damn you!' the woman said in a strangulated voice. 'Bringing home God knows what kind of diseases, risking my health!'

Thomas met his wife's gaze.

'Eleonor, it was . . . it just happened.'

'Just happened? And why is that, Thomas? What were you thinking with?'

He rubbed his forehead. Annika felt her brain

imploding: *I'm going to die*, she thought as she held on to the kitchen table to keep from falling.

'Do you realize what this means?' Eleonor said, trying to pull herself together. 'You'll have to pay for your mistake for eighteen years; as long as he's a minor, you'll be financially accountable for this kid. Was it worth it? Was it?'

Thomas stared at his wife as if she was a stranger.

'You're unbelievable,' he said.

Eleonor tried to laugh.

'*I'm* unbelievable?' she said. 'Have I done something wrong? You cheated on me and now you present me with a bastard child. Do you expect me to just accept something like that?'

Suddenly, Annika couldn't breathe: there was no air left in this house, she had to get out, go home. So she forced herself into action and started moving in the direction of the hall and the front door, her knees shaking. Eleonor noticed that she was moving and whirled round to confront her, a resentful expression on her face.

'Get out of my house!' she shouted.

Annika stopped, allowing the woman's hatred to hit her, and managed to catch Thomas's eye.

'Are you coming?' she asked. Thomas stared at her.

'Get out, you whore!'

The woman walked towards her with a menacing air. Annika didn't budge.

'Thomas,' Annika said, 'come with me.'

Thomas moved. He headed for the hall and got his coat and Annika's jacket.

'What are you doing?' Eleonor said in a confused voice. 'What do you think you're doing?'

He went over to his wife, put on his coat and slipped into his shoes.

'We have a few things to discuss,' Thomas said. 'I'll call you.'

His wife gasped and she grabbed him by the lapels of his coat.

'If you leave,' she said, 'if you walk out through that door, you're not coming back.'

Thomas sighed.

'Eleonor,' he said, 'don't be so—'

'You deceived me!' she screamed. 'If you walk out, you're not coming back. That's final!'

Annika stood by the front door, her hand resting on the door handle. She saw the man's back, the hair that spilled over his collar, that shiny, strong hair. She saw him reach for his wife's hands.

Oh no, he's going to stay, the bond between them is too strong, he can't break it.

'I'll be in touch,' he said.

Thomas turned around, his eyes fixed on the floor, his lips compressed into a line.

Then he looked up at Annika. His eyes were clear and friendly.

'Let's go,' he said.

Bulletin from the Swedish News Agency Tidningarnas
Telegrambyrå
Date: 13 March
Dept: Swedish National Affairs

Woman Accused of Fraud Comes Forward

STOCKHOLM (TT) For the first time, the 31-year-old
director of the Paradise Foundation comes forward.

On Monday the court will return its verdict on the
highly publicized case where charges include conspiracy
to murder.

'It was a witch hunt', the woman claims. 'The tabloid
Kvällspressen has destroyed my life.'

Last December *Kvällspressen* published a series of articles
about the Paradise Foundation and its operations. The
director of Paradise, a 31-year-old woman, was accused
by the paper of crimes such as attempted fraud, unlawful
threat, assault and conspiracy to murder.

'I never received the opportunity to defend myself,'
the woman tells TT. 'The articles appeared in the paper
before I had a chance to sort things out. The entire
business is due to a misunderstanding. Given the chance,
I could have explained everything.'

*The paper featured several women who claimed to have been
misled by you.*

'You must keep in mind that these people are in poor
shape. They aren't always aware of their best interests.

We were well on our way to helping one of these families when they decided to run away.'

In addition to this, several local authorities claimed to have been the subject of attempted fraud.

'Our foundation was new. It's true that our procedures had a few minor discrepancies. But our intention was to offer people protection. It wasn't a part of the public health-care services. The whole point was to maintain the integrity of the clients. This was unacceptable to some factions within Social Services.'

The charges against you include breach of trust, false accounting, several counts of tax fraud, and attempts to obstruct tax supervision.

'I've tried to do business in this country, to create jobs. At times I've worked with people who have failed me, tricked me. But I've never tried to trick anyone out of money – not the government, the local authorities or any individuals. It's true that I've had certain financial difficulties, but most of my debts have been written off.'

The Prosecution claims you ordered the murder of Aida Begovic that took place at Sergelstorg last November.

'That's the worst charge of them all,' the woman says, having difficulties keeping her voice steady. 'I don't know why anyone would be so cruel as to accuse me of such a thing. I did everything I could for Aida, but she was much too traumatized by her wartime experiences to benefit from any measures.'

You are also accused of complicity in an assault case and unlawful abduction with regard to Thomas Samuelsson of the Vaxholm Social Services.

'He committed a crime. He forced his way on to the premises and threatened us. My brother and I were merely defending ourselves, but we were too rough, and I regret that.'

Are you worried about what the verdict will be?

'Not really: I have faith in the justice system. But I do feel violated. Misunderstood. Crushed. It took me three years to lay the groundwork for Paradise, that's why my finances were strained. But I put everything I had on the line, and my only intent was to help other people. A society that would treat me like this is unworthy of being called civilized.'

(nnnn)

Copyright: Tidningarnas Telegrambyrå

Bulletin from the Associated Press
Date: 18 April
Dept: News

War Criminal Starts Private Army

South Africa (AP) The Serbian war criminal Ratko, suspected of involvement in the massacres at Vokuvar and Bijelina at the beginning of the war in Bosnia, is presently commanding a private army of mercenaries in South Africa. This was reported by sources in Cape Town today.

The army operates all over the central and southern regions of Africa, and is commissioned by governments and international corporate groups.

Ratko purportedly financed his army with funds from Serbian cigarette smuggling operations in Scandinavia along with loans from the Russian Mafia.

(nnnn)

Copyright: Associated Press

London: 4 July

Dear Annika,

I hope you've had a great Midsummer.

My family and I celebrated the weekend in traditional fashion at the cottage we rented when we left Paradise. We're all doing well.

I'm writing you from Gatwick Airport on the outskirts of London. We have a few hours to kill before we continue our journey.

The formalities have been wrapped up, and we have received residence permits. This is our last stop before we reach our new home. It was hard to leave Sweden, but everything will be better over there, especially for the kids.

All the best,

Mia Eriksson

Dept: Swedish National Affairs
Author: Sjölander
Date: 10 August
Page: 1 (of 2)

The Russians Are Taking Over

The peace was short-lived.
The crime rate is back to where it was before the police
clean-up of the Yugoslav Mafia.
'The Russians have taken over,' a police source informs
Kvällspressen.

Last year, during the Lucia Day celebrations on 13 December, *Kvällspressen* published an exposé of Yugoslav Mafia operations in Sweden. This series of articles brought about the largest coordinated police sweep of organized crime in history. More than thirty-five buildings, cars, boats and trailers were searched or impounded during the raids that took place for twenty-four hours straight. Significant quantities of arms, narcotics, illegal alcohol and cigarettes were confiscated. Some fifty illegal immigrants have been deported so far.

Interrogations have been conducted all summer long, but much still remains to be done before charges can be brought against all those arrested at the time.

According to a police source: 'The investigation is hampered by the fact that each suspect denies all charges.'

'We are unable to press charges before we have obtained a total picture of the operations.'

Russians take over

The reduction in the crime rate that could be observed directly following the raids is no longer in effect, according to the police.

'Our conclusion is that the void left by the Yugoslavs has been filled sooner than we expected,' the police inform us.

'The Russian Mafia has simply moved in and taken over.'

So all those arrests turned out to be in vain?

'You can't see it in those terms. Every criminal brought to justice is a victory for society.'

(Cont. p 2)

Bundsförvanten, Issue No. 9: 21 September
The Swedish Association of Local Authorities
House Publication

Page 13

New Faces:
Thomas Samuelsson, the project manager of the recently concluded investigation regarding the quality management of welfare payments, has joined the Delegation for Negotiations.

Prior to his employment here, Thomas Samuelsson worked for the City of Vaxholm for four years, in the capacity of Chief Accountant. He lives on Kungsholmen in Stockholm along with his fiancée and their newborn son.

ACKNOWLEDGEMENTS

This is a work of fiction. All the characters originated in the mind of the author, with one exception: Maria Eriksson. Mia exists: her story is described in the non-fiction book *Gömda*. Mia has read and approved the sections inspired by her in this novel.

Apart from this, any similarities to any real individuals are sheer coincidence. The newspaper *Kvällspressen* does not exist, and neither does the Paradise Foundation. They were inspired by a number of existing organizations, but the configuration they have in this book is a product of the author's imagination.

The description of Serbian crime syndicates, both in what was formerly the Yugoslav Republic and in Sweden, is based on conclusions made by the author, and is her creation.

The information about other criminal groups and their sphere of operations is based on previously published facts, mainly from the Swedish newspaper *Aftonbladet*.

On a number of occasions I have exercised my right as an author to tailor the details of locations and floor plans of actual places and buildings, as well as routes to and from them, to suit my purposes.

I would like to thank all the people who have been kind enough to answer my occasionally odd questions. They are:

Johanne Hildebrandt, a war correspondent, a TV producer and my close friend, for her extensive and thorough expertise with regard to the war and the situation in the Balkan states.

Shquiptar Oseku, the spokesperson for the Kosovo Information Office of Scandinavia, for insights and information about the way different groups operate in the Balkans.

Peter Rönnerfalk, physician and medical adviser, for expert help in a medical capacity.

Ann-Sofie Mårtensson, the Chief of Information at the Stockholm Harbour, for information and a tour of the free port and its facilities, buildings, history, offices and procedures.

Rolf Holmgren, a Customs officer with the Coastal Defence Unit in Stockholm, for information on freight-transportation procedures, as well as for expert help and a demonstration of the ingenuity of cigarette smugglers and how they are discovered.

Hasse Ek, a bank manager, and Petra Nordin, a banker, for their time and knowledge.

Jonas Gummesson, the head of the National Affairs Department for Sweden's Channel TV4 news team, for assistance with facts concerning Social Democratic policy.

Lotta Snickare, the Head of Development at Föreningssparbanken, for information about banking and the management procedures of the local authorities.

Thomas Snickare, project manager at Telia, for his insights into the inner workings of a social-welfare board.

Pär Westin, Regional Manager of the Cemetery Management Administration of Stockholm, and his staff, for details of funeral ceremonies and interments.

Birgitta Elvås, for her advice on matters concerning the management and administration of local authorities.

Catarina Nitz, a reporter at *Katrineholms-Kuriren*, for details about the province of Sörmland.

Linus Feldt of Bajoum Interaktiv AB, a brilliant prize-winning computer programmer, who always seems to be saving me from digital meltdowns.

Jan Guillou, an author and a journalist, who has helped me with details concerning weapons and ammunition, and their effects on the human body.

Kaj and Maria Hällstrm for more details about the province of Sörmland.

Ann-Marie Skarp, Jessica Örner and Elisabeth Bredberg, my friends and colleagues over at my Swedish publishing company, Pirat.

Karin Kihlberg, who makes everything work.

Sigge Sigfridsson, my phenomenal publisher who made it all possible.

And, last but foremost, my brilliant editor: the dramatist Tove Alsterdal.

Thank you one and all.

And, finally, any errors in this book are mine exclusively.